Jackie Seal

W9-DHX-177

FIREWEED

A WOMAN'S SAGA IN GOLD RUSH AMERICA

CAROLYN EVANS
CAMPBELL

FIREWEED

A Woman's Saga in Gold Rush America

*On the westward trail the wild fireweed
is the first plant to appear after a fire
or other disaster.*

*Fireweed is a metaphor for women who
survive and flourish under adversity.*

*This novel is dedicated to those courageous
women who took part in the opening
of the American west.*

Carolyn Evans Campbell

Georgetown Editions

FIREWEED
A WOMAN'S SAGA IN GOLD RUSH AMERICA

Published by
GEORGETOWN EDITIONS
Evergreen, Colorado

Library of Congress Control Number 2003090912
ISBN 0-9631703-7-6

First Edition
Printed in the United States of America
Copyright ©2003 by Carolyn Evans Campbell

All rights reserved. No part of this book may be reproduced
or utilized in any form or by any means, electronic or mechanical,
including photocopying, recording, or by any information storage
and retrieval system, without permission in writing from the
publisher, except for brief quotations in a review.

Inquiries should be addressed to Georgetown Editions,
31012 Clubhouse Lane, Evergreen, Colorado 80439

With the exception of fictionalized historical personages, the
characters are entirely the product of the author's imagination
and have no implied relation to any person in real life.

ALSO BY CAROLYN EVANS CAMPBELL

A Fish Nobody Knew
Reflections of a White Bear
Soiled Doves of Colorado
Tattooed Woman
Waiting for the Condor

For my husband and two sons

"What is, is. The road lies ahead, my girl, not behind.
That's why you stay strong.
You keep a-goin' no matter what happens.
You just keep a-goin' like a wagon wheel."

ONE

J ENNA DAGGETT LAY AWAKE under a mountain of quilts listening
to the hushed voices and soft shuffling feet of people moving about the
camp. When she heard her mother slip out of the tent, Jenna raised up
on her elbows and peered out into the dim light of a drizzling dawn. She
watched her mother throw a black wool shawl over her head and shoulders
and walk toward the meadow until she disappeared in the gloom.

One by one, a man or woman emerged from a tent or wagon and joined
a shadowy procession through the wet grass to the gravesite. A few carried
lanterns or candles spinning circles of light in the fading darkness. They
were attending the burial service of Mr. Iverson, who had died the evening
before.

Hardly anyone had known he was sick. He'd been traveling alone in
a small wagon with only one yoke of oxen, had kept to himself, rarely
speaking to anyone. "An odd sort," Jenna's papa had said. Still, it was the
passing of a life into another realm, and the emigrants felt it their Christian
duty to give the man a proper burial and pay their respects by singing a few
hymns and saying the Lord's Prayer over his coffin.

Jenna wrapped a blanket over her nightdress. She scurried in bare feet
over the wet ground and crouched under a wagon where it was dry. From

there she could watch the somber funeral proceedings and listen to the murmur of *amens* following the preacher's mournful words. The lantern light carved strange, deep shadows in the preacher's distorted face and when he sang, his mouth opened and closed on his hinged jaw like a coffin lid.

She hugged her knees and listened to the familiar hymns, wondering if anyone would ever find Mr. Iverson's body in such a lonely spot on the prairie. She wondered if the wolves that howled nightly from the row of trees along the riverbank would catch the odor of a fresh grave.

When Jenna heard the scrape of a shovel and the earth being thrown into the open hole, she ran back to the tent and waited for her mama and papa to return.

Burial days or the Sabbath broke the routine of the wagon train moving forever west, one step at a time across the endless prairie heading for Oregon or California. Today was one of those interruptions. After the company buried Mr. Iverson, they voted to hold an auction to dispose of his oxen, wagon, supplies, and personal belongings.

Everyone said Mr. Iverson died of "a stomach ailment." They did not say "cholera" for fear the breath used to utter the word would start a wildfire contagion throughout their eighteen wagons. Cholera hovered like a specter over the shoulders of every man, woman, and child and struck with such fury one could take ill in the morning and die before the next sunrise. All one could do was pray to God, keep heading west, and hope to move beyond the power of the disease.

The children, careful to avoid the new pile of gravestones, played together all morning, running and tumbling in a sea of prairie wildflowers like young colts. It felt good to stretch their legs after riding mile after mile over grasslands and roads full of ruts. On this particular May morning somewhere in Kansas Territory, they had the luxury of being children, carefree and full of springtime.

The adults, too, were grateful for a break in the routine. After breakfast, everyone had something extra to do before packing up the wagons. The blacksmith worked at the makeshift forge making repairs and helping the men fasten chains to lock the wagon wheels. The women washed clothes down by the creek, aired blankets, coats, and bedding, and spread damp clothes on the ground to dry in the warm sun. Some of the men left the encampment to cut strong limbs for extra axles and tongues.

With their full-bellied oxen leisurely grazing on sweet grass, and with ample supplies to last six months, the emigrants felt optimistic in the morning's warmth. The cloudless sky and delicate, nodding golden buttercups stretching across the blooming prairie gave them a sense of well-being. No one was in a hurry to leave.

Emily Polley, round as risen yeast bread, smiled broadly as the men unloaded her precious cook stove onto the grass. Everyone thought she was foolish to haul such a weighty object all the way to Oregon, but whenever extra time allowed it, the women gathered around the stove like honeybees and baked loaves of bread, cakes, and pies as special treats for their hungry families. Mrs. Polley, a good-hearted soul who always smelled a bit like cinnamon, enjoyed the companionship of the "bake-up," as she called it.

"We'll be having fresh bread for supper, gentlemen, for all your trouble," she said. "The ladies is mighty obliged. Mrs. Daggett, Mrs. Butler, and I are baking sugar rolls and soda bread this morning since we ain't fix'n to leave till this afternoon. If you're lookin' for the other ladies, they're doin' the wash or a-settin' up the auction to sell off Mr. Iverson's things, bless his soul."

Mrs. Polley had brought her old, crippled mother along to share the wonders of the Far West. Mother Boyles, dry and brittle as a weed, deaf and silent from a stroke, sat in a wooden chair in the wagon looking straight ahead. No one was certain she knew where she was, but she never complained and was docile as a newborn lamb. The men lifted Mother Boyles, still sitting in her chair, onto the grass to enjoy the sunshine and smell of fresh bread.

Jenna, dressed in a faded blue calico frock and a flour sack apron she had made herself, helped her mother, Martha Jane, with the baking. She thought it might please her mother to see her learn the skills of a good homemaker. And Martha Jane responded by showing her how to do her work properly.

"Listen well, Jenna," she once said, "for I won't be troubled to repeat what I tell you. After this you can help me with the baking and lighten up some of the burden I carry."

When Jenna finished her work, she begged Mrs. Butler to let her braid her daughter Nettie's long, silky hair.

"Nettie's got lice, you know," Mrs. Butler said. "If you want to be a help to me, you can rub in some kerosene and pull out them little white eggs. They're hard to see in the tyke's blonde head.

"Careful not to burn her scalp, now. Just run your fingers along a few strands at a time and pull 'em off at the ends. Then you can soap her up in the creek and braid her hair.

"I'd be obliged if you'd help. All my youngsters have lice, I guess. I could do with an older daughter the likes of you to help me with my children on the crossing. Maybe you could help me keep their heads clean. You're not very big yet, Jenna, but you're like me—tough as wire."

"Yes ma'am," Jenna said. She felt very adult about taking care of Nettie, who was a beautiful and dainty child. Jenna thought Nettie was like a doll with a white china face. Her thin, fair skin showed small blue veins at the temples. Her eyes, wide open with curiosity, didn't reveal the slight naughtiness in her spirit. Jenna adored her little friend.

Of course, she loved her own brother, Solomon, too, who was a year older than Nettie, but not as much fun. He was a crybaby and his nose always ran. She got tired trying to teach him his letters and numbers, reading to him and watching so he wouldn't wander to the river or fall off the wagon.

Jenna knew she was smarter than her brother. She had taught herself to read by the time she was his age and could read parts of the Bible aloud to her mother. She was good with numbers and penmanship as well, for she had gone to school as far as the third grade.

She and Nettie sat on the grass in the sunshine while Jenna combed and parted the silky hair into three strands and wove them into thin braids.

"What's in that blue bag hanging over yonder?" Nettie asked her.

"I don't know. It's your mama's medicine bag, I think. Stay out of it,

Nettie. When I finish your hair, we'll play in the grass, maybe blind man's bluff with Solomon and some of the other children. If Hannah has finished her chores, she'll come, too."

"Is Hannah your big sister, Jenna?"

"You know she's not. She's Mrs. Polley's daughter. Hannah is my best friend, though—at least since we left Missouri."

"Does Hannah have lice?" Nettie tossed Jenna an impish smile.

"No, silly girl—not yet anyway." Jenna gave Nettie a playful squeeze. "There! You're finished." She poked a purple wildflower above Nettie's ear as a finishing touch. "You look real pretty, Nettie. Now wait here by your mama's wagon and I'll get Solomon and Hannah. Promise you won't wander off."

"I promise," Nettie said and crossed her heart.

Jenna returned a few minutes later, but the little girl was nowhere in sight. "Nettie? Nettie, where are you? Don't hide from me. You know that's naughty."

She rushed through the tall grass turning in time to see Nettie climbing out the back of the Butler's wagon. "You gave me a fright, Nettie. I told you not to move and you broke your promise. You know you're not supposed to go inside the wagon by yourself. If no one can find you, they'll think an Indian stole you away."

"I wanted Dollie. She's sick. Her stuffing is coming out." She showed Jenna a rip in the doll's arm.

"I'll sew it for you after we play. Come on, now. And put on your bonnet. We can play for awhile before they load the wagons. We won't be leaving much before three o'clock on account of the auction," Jenna said.

"Stay close to camp where we can all see you," Martha Jane called after the children as they ran toward the endless expanse of prairie.

"You don't want any Indians a-carryin' you off," Mrs. Butler shouted, placing a loaf of soda bread in the oven. She said it playfully, but the women glanced at each other knowing that within a week the wagon train would be moving slowly along the Platte River through Sioux and Pawnee territory.

So far they'd had no trouble with unfriendly Indians. Sometimes, straggly bands of Fox or Sacs, curious about the white-skinned emigrants, followed the wagon train. They kept their distance, showing no interest in harming anyone, but slipped into camp at night to steal food, an iron pot, or even a blanket off a sleeping emigrant. Still, the women had heard stories of the Plains Indians stealing children and horses, and they hid their fear behind the deep shadows of their sunbonnets.

"I'll want you back soon to help me, Hannah," Mrs. Polley added.

"You too, Jenna. I'll be needing you to fold up the bedding," Martha Jane hollered.

Mrs. Butler turned to Emily Polley. "My, my, I do believe your Hannah is becoming a young lady right before my eyes, Emily. A pretty one, I might add. That smile will win her many a beau in Oregon. Isn't that right, Mrs. Daggett?"

"Yes, indeed. Hannah is a pretty girl," Martha Jane answered without enthusiasm.

"It's not to say your Jenna ain't pretty, too, you understand. Most all youngsters her age is plain and kind of skinny. She's just not growed up yet." Mrs. Butler somehow felt she had offended Martha Jane and feared the troubled woman might retreat into one of her dark moods.

Emily Polley quickly changed the subject. "Hannah's got Dr. Polley's mother's dark brown eyes and thick black hair. They say she was French, but I always wondered if there wasn't some Pocahontas in her somewhere. Something about that dusky look around her eyes, that olive complexion, and high cheekbones. She don't favor my side of the family at all. And she's got worrisome ways that I just don't understand."

The other two women didn't comment. It was common knowledge that Hannah was mature for her thirteen years and far too interested in the young men in the company.

Before long, Jenna returned holding Nettie's small hand. "She doesn't want to play anymore," Jenna said. "She says she's sleepy and wants to nap."

"Well, sometimes she takes a nap midmorning, and after a hard nineteen miles yesterday, the little tyke is probably plumb wore out." Mrs. Butler picked up Nettie and felt her forehead to be sure there was no fever. "Here, child, lie down on your warm quilt that auntie made, right close to your mother."

Nettie quickly slumped on her mother's shoulder.

"She's got no fever. God forbid she's coming down with something. We've hardly started our crossing. It's five days before we reach Fort Kearney and so far we've been pretty lucky. 'Cept for Mr. Woolsey, of course." Mrs. Butler shook her head. "Such a sad thing. Who'd have thought he'd get kicked in the head like that?. I've always said it was a blessing he died on the spot the way he did. Probably didn't feel a thing, poor man."

"And don't forget the Johnson's boy who drowned," Martha Jane added.

"And now Mr. Iverson with an ailing stomach, a runaway physic, God rest his soul," Mrs. Polley said.

The women were silent for a moment. Each wondered if the man indeed had died of cholera.

Martha Jane broke the silence. "In my opinion, he had a poorly done mess, not right provisions, and no one to administer him proper or he might have lived."

"Why Martha Jane, how can you say that?" Emily said. "You know Dr. Polley tended him all through the night, giving him opium and mustard plasters on his bowels. He was called in too late to do anything for him except ease his pain. That man was as weak as a kitten."

"I wasn't meaning your husband not a-carin' for him properly, Mrs. Polley," Martha Jane said. "I was saying he didn't have no wife with him. He left her back in Illinois 'til he got himself some good Oregon farmland. No harm was intended. We are grateful to have Dr. Polley in our company. Why, he's a godsend."

Mrs. Butler watched Emily turn her back on Martha Jane to hide her irritation. "Leave it be, Emily," she whispered. "Martha Jane didn't mean nothing. You know how she is. She don't ever say anything right."

The women continued to chat as they finished baking and washing the tins. The children still played tag and keep-away. No one noticed how deeply Nettie slept.

It wasn't until time to roll up the bedding and clothes that Mrs. Butler tried to wake Nettie, gently at first. The small figure curled in the folds of many colors looked oddly still, and when Mrs. Butler turned her over and saw the thin blue-white skin, transparent as shell, she knew, as only a mother knows, that her Nettie was slipping away.

"I can't wake her!" she shouted. "Someone get Dr. Polley, quick! Nettie, sweet baby girl, wake up! Wake up! Sweet Jesus, wake up my baby!"

Jenna lay awake through the night listening to the footsteps and low, murmuring voices of people passing her wagon to visit the Butlers. The arc of their swinging lanterns threw a march of strange shadows into the wagon, a parade of misshapen silhouettes moving on, leaving her in fearful darkness.

Jenna sobbed into her blankets. She never should have left Nettie alone. Mrs. Butler had said it wasn't her fault that Nettie had climbed into the wagon to look for Dollie, and that what had followed next was the devil's temptation.

"The little tyke saw that mysterious blue bag a-hangin' on a nail out of reach and curiosity got the better of her. I'd told her many a time to stay away from it, but I figure with her head all clean and full of sunshine, she felt growed up.

"She overturned the bucket so she could stand on it to reach the bag. I'm a-guessin' she opened it up and saw all them pretty colored bottles. Lord Almighty, she drank a whole bottle of laudanum. It's kind of bitter sweet, you know. She probably thought it was something real special."

Nettie did not wake up. She died by four o'clock the next morning. Nothing could counteract the effects of an overdose of opium.

The women dressed the tiny body in her Sunday smock, washed her small white face, feet and hands, and placed her in a quickly made pine box fashioned from extra wagon siding brought for just such a purpose. They left her hair as it was, braided with the crumpled purple flower stuck above her ear and wrapped her in her auntie's quilt within which she had

had her final sleep. Mrs. Butler placed her own mother's heart-shaped mother-of-pearl locket around Nettie's pale neck and kissed her beloved child goodbye.

In a lonely, nowhere spot—flat, windswept, and three hundred miles from the only home the Butlers had ever known—they placed the small casket in the ground.

The Reverend Faithful Squibb performed the service and, with his wife, Cora, sang "God Has Called Up His Newest Angel." Mrs. Butler moaned into her apron. The women cried and hugged their own children.

Jenna stood alone, without her mother's comforting arms, and stared at Nettie's coffin being lowered into the ground.

Israel Daggett, Jenna's papa, carved a wooden slat that simply read:

Nettie Butler
A Lamb of God
B. 1844—D. 1848

Although the women gave Jenna sympathetic smiles from time to time, they fell silent when she walked by. Mrs. Butler had told them it was her own fault for not placing the medicine bag out of reach; nevertheless, their fingers pointed at Jenna for leaving Nettie alone. Jenna's guilt sank like a stone inside of her and began to erode that special beauty and sweet innocence that belongs to childhood.

🕊 🕊 🕊

The wagon train moved across the wide expanse of land like a slow white snake. Some days it seemed the sun would never set as it hung relentlessly like a fiery ball blazing into the faces of the travelers.

Jenna liked the night best of all—partly because Martha Jane seemed more pleasant, not so irritable and complaining, and partly because she and her best friend, Hannah, were free to be together without Solomon or Hanna's twin brothers tagging along. For a brief period after the evening meal, when the dishes had been put away, the emigrants enjoyed a bit of socializing and friendly conversation, and the older children called on each other throughout the encampment hoping to get better acquainted or to send a special smile to someone of the opposite sex. Hannah smiled at many young men and even at some older ones as well. And the men smiled back.

But still, what Jenna treasured most was sitting close to her papa around the campfire and watching the stars pop out one by one until the heavens filled with twinkling lights.

Jenna thought the stars were brighter on the prairie than back in Sapling Grove, Missouri—so bright and sparkling they almost made noise. On such nights, sitting next to Israel, she felt his warmth and breathed in the delicious manly smell of his leather coat and the wood smoke in his hair.

All through the encampment, small fires illuminated the night and silhouetted figures moving about in their shadow play. From time to time, someone from another wagon stopped by to chat about the weather and to guess what lay just up ahead. The company officers conferred on the day's progress with Blue, the wagon master, or they discussed plans, problems, and the needs of the wagon train as a whole. The women cradled the toddlers in their laps by the fire or attended the ailing in other wagons, offering the comfort of biscuits and milk gravy or the encouragement of hopeful words.

Jenna liked the evening gathering to hear Dr. Polley tell wondrous stories and yarns or to hear her papa play the harmonica with Blue and his fiddle. The two men played together like old friends, sometimes familiar melodies so melancholy that the emigrants cried inward tears remembering the homes and families they had just left; but mostly they played sprightly tunes, faster and faster into a frenzy of sound that ended in an explosion of laughter. Mrs. Polley, who could never resist a happy tune, usually started everyone clapping hands or grabbing a partner to do a jig or schottische. Jenna always danced with Hannah, who tossed her dark hair from side to side and smiled over her shoulder at the young men lining the circle of firelight.

Martha Jane didn't talk much in the evenings, but gazed into the fire with a faraway look in her eye. When Israel talked about the new land they were going to, the new farm they would carve from the Willamette Valley in Oregon, she would turn her head and look at her husband with little expression. When he talked about the house they would build just like the one they left back home in Sapling Grove, she would smile only slightly. It was a sad smile, a smile of remembering something gone forever.

Sitting in this dry, treeless land with an endless horizon, Martha Jane longed for her white farmhouse surrounded by intense green, lush trees, flowers, and soft hills of rolling pasture. It had been a home that made sense, a place Martha Jane understood. She had expected to be buried next to her parents in the lot cleared by her father, not in some foreign land. She would never forgive Israel for taking her away from her home.

Jenna often looked at her mother's thin face and couldn't decide if she was pretty or not. Surely she had been so once. But now her thin mouth and set jaw seemed to clamp down on any laughter or joy. Her face revealed no gratitude, no pleasure in the little things of life, and a permanent frown had carved a deep line between her eyes.

Sometimes at bedtime, as Martha Jane turned out the lantern, Jenna would peek from under her comforter to look at her mother. It was the only time Martha Jane's luxuriant hair was free from the tight bun at the back of her head. In the spill of the lantern light, her locks fell below her shoulders in soft auburn waves, and Jenna thought her mother looked like an angel. She longed to reach up and touch her mother's hair. Then Martha Jane would turn, the light catching the shadow of her deep-lined frown. Jenna's angel had turned into someone cold and frightening.

🌿 🌿 🌿

In nearly one and a half months of travel, there had been very little rain. The dust kicked up off the prairie floor by plodding oxen and blew into the faces of the emigrants, into their eyes and mouths, and into every crack and crevice of the wagons. It settled in the creases of skin and the folds of clothes and bedding.

While Martha Jane drove the wagon with the children sitting next to her, Israel walked beside them leading Honey, a pony they had bought in Independence when they outfitted their party for the journey.

"This dust is going to choke the oxen to death and kill Israel for certain before we get to his precious land of milk and honey," Martha Jane said aloud. She needlessly snapped the reins of the oxen, as if to hurry the poor beasts along. "Israel! I say, Mr. Daggett!" Martha Jane shouted to her husband. "Cover your face with your handkerchief. Do you hear? You can't be a-breathin' this dust and expect me to nurse you a-wheezin' all night long. I got enough to worry about as it is!"

"A little dust won't hurt us, Mrs. Daggett. Don't forget we're made out of the dust of the earth. The Lord created dust, He did. It can't be all that bad." Israel turned his face to hide a small smile.

"Well, He didn't mean for us to eat it," Martha Jane shouted back.

"Better not to open your mouth then, Mrs. Daggett." Israel refused to let his nagging wife spoil the wonderful adventure of moving west. She could complain all she wanted. Moving to Oregon was a dream come true—free land to farm and the best soil in the world.

He'd read *The Emigrant's Guide to Oregon* and all the reports of the magnificence of the Willamette Valley. It was his duty to his family to take this opportunity. Besides, the "bad air" of the Mississippi Valley made it hard for him to breathe. The air in the Far West was pure and good for the health of men. Martha Jane would see the decision was the right one as soon as she got over feeling homesick for her sister.

Israel broke into a song just to show his indifference to her bossiness.

Jenna smothered a laugh behind her hand. She thought her papa was the best in the world, always her comfort and joy. Whenever papa was around, there was sure to be fun.

Walking with Israel, her hand small and safe in his large rough hand always made Jenna feel that everything was happy in the world. He'd often squeeze her hand as if to secretly say, "I understand, I love you," or "everything is all right." Whenever she looked up at his strong, friendly face shaded by a weather-worn hat, she hoped to catch a wink or that very special smile that belonged to her alone.

Although she preferred to be with Israel, or to sit on Honey's back while he held the halter, she spent most of her time riding in the wagon with her mother and little brother. On dusty days, she had to keep Solomon's handkerchief from slipping off his face. On muggy days, she had to keep him free from mosquitoes. Martha Jane constantly reminded her, "Tend to your brother! Can't you see he's ailing? I've got my hands full, child. I can't be everywhere at once!"

🌿 🌿 🌿

As the emigrants approached Fort Kearney, the first real stop to get supplies, they began to see an increase in the number of graves along the way. The women always counted the graves, noting which ones looked small or fresh and which ones were marked with wooden crosses or headboards. They read the names to see if, by some chance, they belonged to families they knew and commented to each other about the belongings that were left nearby—clothing, a trunk, even an occasional mattress. As the women rolled past the lonely graves, they remembered the tree-shaded cemeteries "back home," the pretty little spots where one could rest in peace, and they said their private prayers for the dead.

Jenna counted the graves with Martha Jane, who seemed preoccupied with every one they passed. She thought it would please her mother, that it would bond them in some peculiar way. But, in fact, each grave made Jenna's personal loss seem greater. Under the mounds piled with stones, Jenna visualized Nettie, either pale and still or wide-eyed and crying out for the wagons to wait. Jenna would shut her eyes to keep the tears from spilling. She especially did not want Martha Jane see her cry.

Her mother repeatedly brought up the tragedy of Nettie's untimely death and the poor Butler family, and how Jenna should have kept watch over the little girl. It seemed to Jenna that her mother's sideways glances were to see if Jenna was about to cry or to break out into red splotches.

"I suspect Nettie's grave has been tore open by wolves by now. What do you think, Jenna?" Martha Jane said as they passed an open grave, obviously mutilated either by wolves or Indians.

Jenna couldn't answer but felt her face flush hot and her eyes begin to burn with tears. Jenna couldn't understand her mother's deliberate cruelty. Martha Jane seemed to enjoy hurting or embarrassing Jenna, though never in front of Israel. When he was around, she might be irritable and complaining, but she did not go out of her way to make Jenna feel so worthless, so heartsick.

What confused Jenna most was that sometimes her mother was pleasant and even smiled. When she did, she looked pretty and young.

Israel was the only one who could make her smile at all. Usually she wore the deep frown and scowled about her lot in life. "A woman's life is full of pain and suffering, Jenna. You'll see. Mark my words," Martha Jane said over and over. "And children, nothing but trouble!"

There was a time before Solomon was born when Jenna had felt her mother truly loved her. She had made her a rag doll with a dress just like Jenna's from leftover white-and-green-striped cotton. And even now, whenever Jenna read the Bible to her mother, she thought Martha Jane softened toward her.

Once she said, "Jenna, you're a good girl, a good daughter. Too bad you was born a girl, but I do believe Jesus favors you anyways," and she drew Jenna close to her and held her for a moment. Her body was lean and full of knots, not warm and comforting like Israel's, but Jenna always remembered that moment and longed for her mother's touch.

Blue gave the signal to break for the noon meal. The emigrants pulled into a circle, grateful to stop for food and a chance to settle the dust, shake out bonnets and shirts, wash out mouths and eyes, and clean up the little ones who had messed themselves.

The children spilled out of their wagons and scattered like puppies into the center of the grassy encampment. The women, already efficient in their makeshift kitchens, began to unload the food for the noon meal. The older children, happy to be away from the eyes of their parents, sauntered in pairs onto the prairie to scavenge dry buffalo chips, the main fuel of the cooking fires. In a short time, the sweet smoky aroma of the chips and sizzling antelope steaks filled the air.

Harke Polley, whose family traveled in front of the Daggetts, helped unload Mother Boyles and place her in the thin shadow by the side of the wagon. Harke, the oldest of the Polley children, was a strong fifteen-year-old boy, long and lean with large hands and feet he had not quite grown into. Without his hat, a long shock of wheat-blond hair fell over his forehead, and he had acquired a habit of tossing his head or sweeping the hair off his face with his hand. His eyelashes and eyebrows, bleached nearly white from the sun, made his blue eyes, already serious with responsibility, stand out like a cloudless sky.

Jenna noticed Harke watching her as she spread an oil cloth on the ground and set around tin plates and eating utensils. She thought he wanted to say hello, but changed his mind and turned to the task of watering the horses. In fact, there were other times the young boy with the tousled hair and friendly grin had approached her, only to turn away and pretend to be busy. Sometimes, she thought he showed off for her benefit. But she liked Harke, the gentle way he talked to the oxen and gave others a helping hand. Jenna wished she had a big brother just like him. Hannah didn't know how lucky she was.

Jenna heard Mrs. Polley talking loudly to Mother Boyles.

"Open your mouth, mother. This here is pudding for you. It's nice. You'll like it. Open your mouth, dear. Don't make me fret now. I know you hear me." Mrs. Polley stood up and sighed. "Lordy, I can't get her to eat today. She's stubborn as a mule. She don't like pudding and she don't have but one tooth in her whole head to do much chewing."

Martha Jane handed Jenna a plate of rhubarb cobbler glistening with thick, pink syrup. "Take this over to the Polleys to see if Mother Boyles will eat it," she said without smiling. "Don't drop it now. That rhubarb took more than its share of sugar. You won't be eatin' the likes of it 'til you reach Oregon."

"What a nice thing for you to do, Jenna," Mrs. Polley said. "Now Mother Boyles just might like this cobbler. It's sweet and moist and not much chewing. She always did have a hunger for rhubarb. Maybe you'd feed her for me while I fix up some beans. I don't know where Hannah has run off to. She's never around when you need her—always parading around somewhere when it's time to help me."

Jenna approached the old woman sitting in her chair staring out from under the roof of her stiff bonnet. Her small face gathered into wrinkles like a drawstring pouch pulled tight around the mouth. She had no lips, only a thin line that flew open when someone gently pushed a spoon into the crack. Sometimes her eyes followed the children running past the tunnel opening of her bonnet.

"Put a little of the sweetness on her tongue and see if that don't open her mouth, Jenna," Mrs. Polley said. "She's just being ornery this afternoon."

Jenna was a bit nervous about feeding the old woman, but she approached her slowly, bent down, and stared into the watery eyes. "Hello, Mother Boyles. I've brought you some rhubarb cobbler," she said softly.

Mother Boyles didn't respond, only looked at Jenna like a silent animal in a cage.

"Go ahead, Jenna. Once she tastes that rhubarb, she'll open her mouth and start chewing. Don't be shy now, girl."

Jenna cautiously placed the tip of the spoon on the old woman's thin lips and pushed the thickened juice into her mouth. Suddenly, Mother Boyle's mouth flew open like a hinge and she clamped down over the spoon like a vice. Jenna tried to pull the spoon out, but Mother Boyles held fast.

Oh dear. Now what shall I do?

Jenna could feel the red splotches breaking out on her skin. She tugged at the spoon, but Mother Boyles would not yield. The two of them looked at each other, and Jenna thought she saw a flicker of awareness in her eyes. Jenna was certain the old woman knew exactly what she was doing and felt there was a small, invisible battle going on between them.

Jenna tightened her mouth with determination and tugged at the spoon a little harder. She didn't want to hurt Mother Boyles or pull out her only tooth. She was too embarrassed to call attention to the situation, and she wasn't going to give up. She could be just as stubborn as this small, shriveled enemy. It was a wordless war with Jenna tugging and Mother Boyles holding firm.

Harke Polley had been watching the contest while he watered the oxen, grinning the whole time. He often watched Jenna. There was something about her that made him want to smile, a happy feeling he couldn't understand himself. She was still a little girl and he was nearly a man, but to him Jenna was special. Even though she did all the girlish things she was supposed to do to please the ladies, Harke knew there was something else in Jenna—a rebellion, a determination that set her aside from other girls her age.

And she was nothing like his younger sister, Hannah, who was always fussing with her appearance, sneaking precious buttermilk to whiten her skin. Jenna played keep-away like a boy, and whenever she played tag, she would throw off her bonnet, letting the wind blow her straight brown hair in all directions, and would pull up her skirts to run as fast as possible. If she took a tumble, she always laughed, and her eyes sparkled with fun, her cheeks grew red as raspberries, and laughter bubbled out of her throat.

Harke walked over to her. "Maybe I can help you, Jenna. She's a might stubborn sometimes. I think she's trying to get attention and this is her way of being funny."

He leaned his face into Mother Boyle's bonnet. "Look a-here, grandma, if you open your mouth, I'll give you a big kiss." Harke untied her bonnet and let it slip behind her neck. "Come on, now, don't be a mule. We know you're just a-teasin' us and you want this rhubarb cobbler bad as anything." Harke kissed his grandmother on the cheek.

Mother Boyles unhinged her mouth. The spoon fell out and she began to smack her lips.

"There, you see, Jenna? She'll eat now." Harke laughed. "What she don't eat, I will."

"Thank you for helping me, Harke. I'll save you some of my cobbler."

After lunch, Martha Jane laid a blanket on the ground and stretched out in the shade close to the wagon. She said she'd been feeling poorly all day and needed a bit of rest.

"You just rest comfortable, Martha Jane," Israel said. "Jenna, Solomon, and I are taking Honey and a-ridin' over to the banks of the Blue River. It will be the last time we ever see it. We might just stick our feet in for a moment since we seem to be ready to move on before everyone else. We'll head out over that rise and see what's yonder—maybe a jackrabbit or two, or an antelope if I'm lucky. You're lookin' a bit pale of late."

Israel hoisted Solomon onto Honey's back while Jenna walked along holding Israel's hand. Martha Jane and the other ladies considered it indecent for a young girl to straddle a horse. "It just ain't fittin'," her mother had said. But when they were out of sight of the camp, Israel lifted Jenna onto Honey's back; she threw her leg over his neck, her bare legs firm against the pony's body. Israel smiled and said nothing.

A warm afternoon breeze blew old tumbleweeds across their path. Occasional puffs of dirt spiraled into the air whenever a prairie dog darted into his hole. As soon as their three-some passed, the prairie dogs' courage returned and they stood up straight as soldiers, scolding and barking at the intruders.

While Solomon and Israel chatted about the noisy little animals, Jenna breathed in the endless land all around her—the grass that rippled like water and the brilliant-colored wildflowers that carpeted the earth. Jenna loved the Indian paintbrush poking through the grass in clusters of red and orange, the clumps of red maids, and the graceful shooting stars dangling from their long, graceful stems. The prairie was alive and moving, full of color and sweet air, a delicious feeling that she'd never had before. In the very emptiness of the place, she felt small on the one hand and powerful on the other.

The land excited her. The wind billowed her blouse, whipped her stringy, straight hair into her mouth, then blew it away from her forehead like an impatient mother brushing her hair. Jenna laughed for no reason. She thought she could never be happier than that very moment, being with her papa and Solomon riding through such a glorious patch of yellow goldenrod.

"Papa, I love the prairie. I didn't think I would, but I do! I don't even miss the big trees anymore," Jenna said.

"Ah, Jenn, my girl. I'm glad to hear you're happy, too. I reckon we're alike, you and me. I'll never get enough of this land. It is my strength, kind of like they talk about in the Bible. Sometimes I feel something rush through the bottoms of my feet right through the soles of my boots and into my very heart and hands. You ever feel like shouting, Jenn, for no reason?"

"I do, Papa!"

"That's how I feel right now. Let's shout!"

Jenna, Solomon, and Israel let out a series of whoops that made them all laugh and the prairie dogs flash into their holes.

They walked along in silence. Then Israel started talking, as if he was thinking out loud.

"If the Indians was organized, they could turn this land into wheat country. Those few Indian farmers outside of Independence might catch on being farmers in time, but they're happier a-roamin' rather than a-settlin' down. It's their way, you know. And they is always fighting amongst theirselves. This land here is mostly Pawnee and Sioux, and they just can't get along, leastways not long enough to farm wheat."

Israel stopped walking, took off his leather hat, and ran his fingers through his thick brown hair. He squinted into the sun, scanning the horizon. "This land has to be irrigated. Soil's good, though. They say the soil in Oregon is so rich it's black. And there is plenty of water and sunshine to grow great crops."

"And pigs, too," Solomon added.

The children had heard Israel's story about "the pigs" over and over, and they always laughed.

Israel's eyes twinkled. "There's folks that say in Oregon the pigs run about under the acorn trees a-gruntin' and a-squealin', fat and round and already cooked with knives and forks stuck in their sides."

"A-hollerin', 'Eat me! Eat me!'" Solomon laughed at his own addition to the story.

"Tell us about Oregon being Paradise, Papa," Jenna said.

"They say it's God's country, all right. Ain't ever any sickness out there—no ague or fever. You see, there ain't bad air out there in the Far West. I'm already breathing better since we left the Missouri Valley." Israel took a deep, unobstructed breath. "We've done the right thing a-movin' west. You'll see. I'm goin' to get me a square mile of land and a quarter section for you and Solomon."

"And a house for mama," Jenna said.

"That's right. A big one with lots of space and glass windows to see our crops a-growin' and the trees a-bloomin,'" Israel said.

"And you said we're goin' to drink lots of milk and honey." Solomon added.

Israel laughed. "That's right, I did." He broke into a faster walk. "Hang on, children. We're goin' to run up this rise and see what's on the other side. Who knows, maybe the river is already overflowin' with milk and honey."

Israel led the pony into an easy trot up a gentle slope. He stopped abruptly. "Lord God!" Israel gasped. "Don't move, children. Hush now. Quiet, quiet! Take a look at that! That's buffalo, children! Ain't seen one before, except in pictures. I count nine of them, including the little one. My God, they're huge! Bigger than I thought. Fierce-lookin' beasts, ain't they?"

The land stretched out before them, sliced only by the Little Blue River moving slowly along. Nine shaggy, brown buffalo grazed on the tender grass by the banks. Their enormous heads looked too large for their bodies. Clumps of thick fur hung from their massive shoulders like loose rags.

The animals, not noticing Israel and the children, continued grazing and switching their tails. Solomon began to whimper.

"Be still, Solomon. I don't know much about these animals' ways. I know I don't want to scare 'em. They stampede easy if they're spooked," Israel said.

"Papa, where are the rest of the buffalo?" Jenna asked.

"I don't know, Jenn, but I ain't stayin' to find out. I'm a-goin' back to camp and get some of the men and powder and we're goin' to eat buffalo steaks for a good long time. No one in the company has ever shot a buffalo that I know of, except Blue."

"Don't kill that baby one, Papa," Jenna said.

Israel didn't answer. He pulled Honey around and, half-running, headed back to the encampment.

Solomon began shouting as soon as he neared the family wagon. "We seen buffalo, mama! I'm goin' to shoot 'em!" Solomon hopped up and down nervously. "I mean, Papa's goin' to kill a buffalo!"

The emigrants, hoping to get a glimpse of the huge, wild beasts, rushed outside of the encampment, excited to see the cloud of dust over the horizon. They had heard of the great herds that roamed the prairies, so vast in numbers they looked like moving rivers of black water.

Several men grabbed their rifles and mounted ponies and horses and rode off in a wild gallop, shouting like Indians. A few unhappy men stayed in camp with ready shots just in case the buffalo should turn and run toward the wagons.

Some of the women gathered in groups and talked about the little they knew about buffalo. Others took advantage of extra time to mend rips and tears or to work on a calico shirt. Now that the weather was warmer, the men preferred cotton to their wool clothing. It seemed the women never had enough time for sewing.

Martha Jane didn't feel like socializing or working. She was tired, and the noon meal left her feeling nauseated. She preferred to be alone.

"Are you feeling poorly, Mrs. Daggett?" Emily Polley asked. "I'm making mother some nice chamomile tea and taking some over to Mrs. Butler, poor soul—still a-sufferin' bad over Nettie. Let me pour a cup for you, too. It might be good for what ails you." Emily looked at Martha Jane as if she already knew she was more than two months along.

Martha Jane had suspected she was pregnant the day the company rolled out of Independence. She had been having morning sickness, and as the wagons had moved farther away from the sight of civilization, the neat farms, and the familiar landscape, a dark foreboding had hovered around and hung over her shoulders like a shawl. She couldn't shake it. Almost immediately she had begun retching over the side of the wagon seat. Israel hadn't noticed. His face was burned into the west, and his eyes blazed with the light of a zealot.

"That would be fine, Mrs. Polley," Martha Jane said, taking the cup of tea, "but if you don't mind, I'll drink it in the wagon. I have some straightening up to do." Martha Jane smiled, but she didn't feel friendly. She thanked Mrs. Polley and carried the hot tin cup into the wagon.

In her privacy, she opened the wooden medicine chest stashed at the rear of the wagon and took out a bottle of turpentine used for cuts and bruises. She poured some into her tea, let the cup cool, and drank down the ghastly liquid as fast as possible.

For a moment, she couldn't get her breath. Her mouth and throat became a fiery cavern with flames reaching into her nostrils and setting her eyes on fire. She slumped to the floor and coiled into a tight, painful knot trying not to vomit.

Too much. I've taken too much!

She had to be careful—subtle—for to lose a baby by her own hand was unthinkable. Still, a sickening combination might not offend God and just might burn her insides enough to make the new life let go of its determined hold inside of her. She took another swallow straight from the bottle before corking the top.

Martha Jane leaned against the canvas wall of the wagon, an oiled membrane between herself and endless loneliness. She shut her eyes to make the world around her disappear and pretended she was back home in Missouri leaning against the cherry tree by the side of the house. In the daydream, she placed her dear sister, Lizzie, next to her when they were mere girls wearing fresh dresses and starched aprons, embroidering dreams of marriage and a farm of their own. Lizzie was the cheery one, round and rosy as a plum; Martha Jane was the pretty one but, lean, awkward, and unsure.

She remembered Israel then—handsome, hard working, with a brightness in his eye. Everyone in Sapling Grove had figured he and Lizzie would marry. He was a terrible tease and made Lizzie laugh out loud like no lady should. But Lizzie was claimed by a man twice her age. No one figured it, especially Israel. Even after Martha Jane and Israel married, he still teased Lizzie from time to time just to make her laugh and to see her eyes dance.

Her dream drifted forward and she remembered that cricket-singing night Israel told her they were moving to the Far West. It was summer, and the farm was swollen with corn, ripening pumpkins, squash, apples, and cherries; it burst with the fragrance of clover, herbs, and sweet grasses; blue-eyed mother goats were content with their full, swinging udders. Martha Jane was happy then, cultivating her beautiful farm, so abundant and safe.

But everything changed that night when Israel climbed into bed next to her, slipped her nightdress up to her waist, and rolled over on her, coughing and wheezing.

It was not lovemaking, but a release from the tension and toil of farm life. Martha Jane seldom resisted, for a good wife never did. When he lay back on the pillow, coughing, trying to free his clogged air passages, she slipped out of bed into the kitchen. In dim candlelight, she carefully removed a vinegar-soaked sponge that she wore during ovulation. Israel never knew about it—never would have believed she'd taken God's matters into her own hands.

Dear Lizzie, able to share intimate information with other women, had found out how to protect herself from an unwanted pregnancy. Some women used strong tea instead of vinegar, and others claimed they cooked lard mixed with boric acid, cooled it, and cut it into suppositories. Martha Jane never dared try anything that modern. Vinegar and soapsuds worked well for her, at least for the six years between Solomon and Jenna and four years after that. She had been lucky.

When she returned to bedroom, she expected to find Israel asleep; instead, he lay on his back, coughing spasmodically. The candlelight caught deep ridges in his contorted face. She climbed in next to him. *A good wife ought to say something comforting.* But she preferred to say nothing and blew out the light before it aroused the pesky miller moths from their dark corners.

Lying together in the darkness, Martha Jane had an unexpected sense of foreboding, as if someone dear to her heart was preparing to meet his Maker—surely not Israel.

"Martha Jane," he said softly. "I'm a-sellin' the farm. Now don't say nothin' 'til you hear me out."

Martha Jane held her breath. He couldn't be serious.

"I've been a-thinkin' on it a long time. I'm emigrating my family to the Far West—to Oregon Territory. A lot of men are a-thinkin' same as me. It's opportunity, land, good air."

She lay stunned, clutching the sheet in her fists, unable to gather a single sound in her throat or utter a word of protest. If she spoke, she'd scream.

"It's no use figuring to talk me out of this decision. I done too much prayin' on it and the Lord is guiding my path. It's His will, and that's the way it is. We'll be a-leavin' in the near bye and bye—in the spring." Israel's spasmodic cough shook the bed and disturbed a community of moths that flew to the window and battered their wings frantically against the pane.

They were silent for a long time.

Finally, she said in a voice so tight it was barely audible, "You'd leave a first-born child alone back yonder in his grave tended by strangers? How could you!" She turned her back on Israel and let angry tears run down her nose. It was the first of many nights when she never closed her eyes.

Whenever Israel said anything was the will of the Lord, Martha Jane did as she was told. After all, her only way to the Lord was through her husband, the Christ head, and she obeyed.

There was no comfort for Martha Jane that night, or the many days and nights that followed. She retreated into a cold silence that froze him throughout the winter months. One night, she was aware Israel was watching her as she sat spinning in the hearth light.

"I like to watch the flames from the hearth flicker in your loose hair," Israel had said, and reached out to touch her face with his dry, cracked hand, hoping to comfort her, to break the silence. She inwardly shuddered and turned away. His hand had become her enemy.

Many women had talked leaving their farms, friends, and beloved families, of settling in unknown land. Some women, young and strong, were eager to have an adventure and to dream along with their husbands. Martha Jane felt certain Lizzie would have loved to go; ironically, her husband said he was too old to start over.

"Just think, Martha Jane," Lizzie had said, "our own ma and pa settled this very valley here in Sapling Grove when we were mere youngsters. This won't be the first time for you to settle land. In no time at all, you'll have blackberry bushes so high you can't see over, a-standin' on tippy toe."

Martha Jane resigned herself to the fact that emigrating was not a choice and like other women leaving Sapling Grove in the spring, she began the arduous preparation for the journey—knitting socks and sweaters; making the double canvas cover for the wagon and sacks to hold coffee, flour, salt, and cornmeal. She sewed clothes for all of the family, pickled beef, dried apples and peaches, made pockets for inside the wagon, and organized the kitchen and medicine box. She set her lips into a grim line and sold or gave away precious items and household treasures she could not take with her. In a few short weeks, Martha Jane tore her life into bits and pieces small enough to pack into tight spaces.

The wagon shuddered again with a gust of wind. She heard Jenna calling her. For one brief moment, Martha Jane allowed herself to remember her last tearful embrace with Lizzie and to see her dear sister smile bravely through a river of sadness.

Jenna popped her head into the wagon. "Mama? Are you sick?" she asked.

Martha Jane wheeled around. "No, I ain't sick! And stop sneaking around a-spyin' on me. Can't I ever have no privacy? Where's Solomon?" she snapped.

Jenna watched her mother close the medicine chest and fasten it with a leather strap. She kept her back to Jenna and said nothing more.

"Solomon is playing in a water hole he found yonder. He calls it his 'drinky hole'." Jenna laughed slightly, hoping to steer Martha Jane away from a possible scolding for not being with him.

"Israel didn't dig a seep hole today on account of we have settled water from the river. It must be a hole dug just recent by someone a-travelin' ahead of us. You'd better go get Solomon before he gets full of mud."

Jenna jumped from the wagon just as Solomon walked up carrying his stubby, wrinkled boots. He was wearing a wide-brimmed hat that sat down over his whole forehead, nearly covering his eyes. He tilted his head back and peered under the brim, grinning. "I found a drinky hole, Mama. And I found a hat, too . . . and other stuff. You want to come see it?"

"You're filthy, Solomon!" Martha Jane grabbed his arm impatiently and marched him to the other side of the wagon to the water barrel. "Take off that hat," she said, pulling it off his head and throwing it under the wagon. "We can't leave with you lookin' like one of them savages." She filled a wash pan half full of water and scrubbed Solomon's small hands and feet.

"Now go towel off and then lie down, and don't you move from that spot until your papa comes back from hunting. Do you hear me, Solomon?"

Solomon did as he was told but whimpered purposely for attention. After awhile, he gave up and turned his attention to a bug wandering through its grass jungle oblivious to its fate by a pudgy hand hovering overhead.

"Jenna, you come and write a letter for me to your Aunt Elizabeth. We'll post it at Fort Kearney . . . God knows if we ever get there."

Jenna loved to write for her mother, but she had never written a letter before. She'd never needed to. Everyone she cared about, all of the Daggetts and Conveys—her mother's people—lived in the same settlement in Sapling Grove, Missouri and attended the same church.

Jenna missed her cousins and aunts and uncles just as Martha Jane did, but unlike her mother, she was excited about the crossing on the Overland Trail to Oregon and felt the adventure, like her papa.

"I'm a good farmer," Israel had said. "I'm strong and I have a good wife and family to help me. I can't pass up a chance to get so much land. All I have to do is improve it, clear some trees, build a fine house, and it's ours forever. I think I might just die knowing there's paradise somewhere in the far western shores and I can scarcely breathe here in Sapling Grove. I *must* go! I talked to Jesus over and over and he told me to go west with my family. Don't argue, Martha Jane. It's a calling of sorts, and you're obliged to do Jesus' bidding along with me."

"How should I start the letter to Aunt Lizzie, Mama?" Jenna asked.

The two of them sat on a blanket in the warm sun without their bonnets. Strands of Martha Jane's auburn hair loosened from her bun and blew around her face.

"Begin with . . .

Indian Territory, June 7, 1848. Dearest Sister Lizzie,

I'm sorry I ain't written for so long. There is little time to rest on our journey what with all the cooking and washing and labor. I collect buffalo chips for fuel, and I'm always packing and unpacking and drying out clothes or shaking the dust out of them. I work like a hired hand. It is a worrisome journey. A lot of people get sick. Three people have died. The Johnsons from our church lost their boy, Seth, to the river soon after we started our journey. He called out, "Big brother, save me!" and then he was gone. We looked downstream all the next day and found his body hooked on a log. We buried him right that evening, and poor Mrs. Johnson wailed and wrung her hands. Our company is pretty healthy so far and we only have minor problems. A dose of calomel every day does the trick for most our complaints, like fever and flux and ague, and we all take a dose of citric acid every day so as not to get the scurvy. The mosquitoes is bad right now. The only Indians we seen don't bother us none. In fact, some are right helpful on river crossings. We bought some coffee from an Indian farmer. I can't figure where he got the coffee first. Oh, sister, I grieve for you. I fear I shall never see home again or your face. I am so fatigued and suffer daily. I'm afraid I ain't adequate to the task. You must be a-picking a lot of strawberries by now. Eat some for me.

Your Loving Sister, Martha Jane"

Jenna looked up from her letter and caught a deep sadness in Martha Jane's face she'd never noticed before. Suddenly, the muscles in her face dropped and sagged over the bones like melting beeswax. There seemed to be no life force to hold up the tissue. "You sign your own name, Mama."

Martha Jane's face changed back into her normal frown. She sighed loudly, took the pen, and carefully wrote her signature. "There. I'll post it in Fort Kearney."

Just then, Mrs. Polley walked over to Martha Jane and Jenna. "We've got company," she said quietly.

A small, motley group of Indians had wandered into the encampment. There were six of them—four men and two women. They had no horses with them, which possibly meant they intended to ride away with some. At this moment, however, every available horse was pursuing buffalo. With no men in camp, the women felt vulnerable. They immediately called their children to their sides and clustered in small groups close to their wagons.

These Indians were different from the ones they had seen earlier. They were especially ominous since they were wearing white men's clothes, soiled and stained. Two of the men wore felt hats and cotton shirts; a nearly naked man had hung doe skin in front of his groin from an emigrant's belt and had attached a pair of suspenders to his pants. A third man with very bad skin wearing a brown wool coat with no buttons stood silent.

One of the women, a very fat one with wild, greasy hair, wore a black silk dress that gaped in the back. The sleeves were ripped open along the seam to accommodate her fleshy arms. Next to her, a younger woman with a flat, moon face peered solemnly out of a sunbonnet; an emigrant's green-checked apron covered her filthy doe-skin dress, and she wore a pair of men's heavy boots on the wrong feet. The Indians looked mawkish, childish, even comical . . . but not harmless.

Mrs. Butler quickly hustled her brood of children to where Emily Polley stood with her twins. Martha Jane and Jenna moved closer together.

Emily, who always saw the best in every situation, still had a practical, cautious side. "Now you fetch Solomon, Mrs. Daggett, and bring him here with us and act friendly. You ain't seen Hannah, have you Jenna?"

"No. She might be inside your wagon rolling her hair in rags," Jenna replied.

"Them Indians is a curious bunch—not like the others we've seen. I can't tell what tribe they come from all dressed up in white men's clothes," Mrs. Butler said.

"They're probably scavengers," Mrs. Polley said. Turning to Martha Jane and Jenna, she added under her breath, "or grave robbers."

"What do they want, do you suppose? They don't have anything to trade unless maybe that buffalo robe one of them is carrying over his shoulder. They don't have horses. Where do you figure they come from?" Martha Jane said. "It's like they appeared out of nowhere."

"They're probably camped in them sparse trees in the islands in the middle of the river. They've been a-watchin' us to be sure. Now they're checkin' out what they can take. You can bet they know the men is gone from camp," Mrs. Polley said.

The Indians took their time walking from group to group, peering into wagons, lifting up a soup kettle, touching a skillet, a cup, or whatever piqued their curiosity. One of the men bent over and peered into Mother Boyles' bonnet and then spoke to her. The woman with the black silk dress peered into the bonnet as well. Mother Boyles did not respond.

Mrs. Polley walked over to them, smiling. "This is my mother—my *mother*," she shouted. Then, through gestures of pointing and rocking an imaginary baby, they understood and smiled back. The fat woman had a handsome, caramel moon face and a broad nose with wide nostrils. She gave a toothless smile and patted Mother Boyles' freckled hand. Then she lifted the old woman's skirt to see what she wore on her feet. When she discovered leather boots, she pointed to her companion's acquired boots and spoke her lilting native words as if trying to find a common meeting ground. Mother Boyles remained staring straight ahead while the fat woman began unlacing Mother Boyles' boots, apparently intending to take them for herself.

Emily stepped forward. "No, you can't take my mother's boots," she said firmly.

The woman paid no attention.

"I said, *no*! Do you understand me? These boots belong to her," Emily said, gently moving the woman's hands away and lacing up the boots.

Mrs. Butler stepped forward. "Here, Mrs. Polley, give her my button box."

The Indians gathered around inspecting the different shapes and colors of buttons and bits of corded trim. The fat Indian woman smiled, satisfied at the present. The tension eased, and soon the emigrant and Indian women began a primitive but friendly conversation, pointing out an object and speaking the word for it—baby, mother, pot, sugar, apron.

The women were doing well, communicating and enjoying their visitors until Reverend Faithful Squibb—carrying a black Bible—and his wife, Cora, marched into the circle, accompanied by the other men in the camp. He wore his black preacher's suit and a frayed black silk hat for the occasion.

As missionaries headed for the Pacific coast, they were armed with righteousness to convert all heathens to the Christian ways. Squibb felt certain Destiny had brought the Indians to him for his first opportunity to save their dark souls.

"Good afternoon, friends," he said.

The Indian in the brown coat returned the greeting for the rest of them. The two women said something to each other and stifled a bit of laughter.

"Welcome to a Christian community." He smiled at the women around him and continued. "I will trade this Holy Bible for your buffalo robe."

He extended the book and gestured for the robe. The Indian took the book, flipped the pages, handed it back, and pointed to the reverend's watch fob.

"No! The Bible or nothing, my good man. A watch won't get you to heaven." Again, he smiled at the women, revealing a mouthful of stained teeth, and then looked sternly at the Indian. Cora nodded approval at everything her husband said.

Mrs. Polley interrupted. "They can't read, Mr. Squibb. It don't do 'em no good."

"Ownership is a beginning, madam. They will have the mustard seed of Christian consciousness in their possession. They will learn. More of my fellow missionaries will follow along with the ABCs." The reverend continued bargaining until the two Indian women got bored and wandered over to peek into the Polley's wagon.

"Let us sing a lively hymn of praise, Cora. Ladies, join us.

Yes, we'll gather at the river,
The beautiful, the beautiful river . . ."

Suddenly, a scream erupted from inside the Polley's wagon, and Hannah jumped out with her hair in rags and ran to her mother. The Indian women broke into loud, playful laughter, not only at the funny sight of the frightened girl with rags in her hair, but at their own surprise. They laughed hard until silenced by the leader of their group.

No bargain was struck. The reverend and his wife bid good day after advising the women to keep a watchful eye out for theft. They turned and left the campsite, Bible in hand.

The fat woman walked into the meadow a short way off and returned with a handful of plants she'd pulled up by the roots. She placed them on Mother Boyles' lap and gestured to Mrs. Polley that they were to be brewed for the old woman. Emily thanked the Indians, apparently believing the gesture was to help her mother, that the plants had a tonic or medicinal effect.

Meanwhile, Jenna watched her mother make a trade that surprised her. She gave their small stew pot to them in exchange for something.

"What did you trade, Mama?" Jenna asked.

"Hush now! Never you mind! I swear you got eyes in the back of your head, child!"

Mrs. Polley traded a calico shirt for the buffalo robe. Satisfied, the Indians wandered away from the encampment. "A warm buffalo robe is a mighty nice thing to have," she said.

The men of the wagon train returned victorious, with strips of bloody red meat draped over the ponies' rumps or wrapped in oil cloth. They had carried away the hump, tongue and upper hind quarters, the choicest parts of the beast and left the rest of the carcass to rot on the plains. It had taken all of the men to kill only one beast by firing thirty shots into its head. The rest of the animals, crippled or wounded, would later die of infection or starvation.

As the men divided the meat and fastened the strips to the sides of their wagons to dry and cure, they told and retold their adventure, recounted near misses or direct shots, and congratulated each other for a successful first buffalo hunt.

One of the hunters proudly displayed two bloody buffalo horns. The horns reminded Jenna of the oxen pulling such heavy loads across the plains, their horned heads bobbing up and down with each step, the dust and flies clinging to their eyes. *The poor, faithful beasts. If they die, we could die, as well*, Jenna thought.

Killing animals so brutally or pushing them beyond their strength seemed unfair to her. She whispered in Israel's ear, "Papa, did you kill the baby buffalo?"

Israel frowned. "How many times have I told you, Jenna, to stop a-thinkin' about such things. You're a farm girl. You ain't a frail female with a dainty disposition. Now help me salt down some of this meat and stop a-frettin' over that baby buffalo. When we bake up some delicious marrow from this leg bone you'll forget all about that little critter."

Jenna did as she was told.

The emigrants did not break camp until four o'clock in the afternoon. The unexpected visit from the Indians and the buffalo hunt had caused a great deal of excitement and an exchange of stories. So much had happened they scarcely remembered what they'd eaten for lunch.

It was not until late that night when Martha Jane and Jenna were away from the circle of wagons looking for a place of privacy to take care of bodily functions that Martha Jane confided in Jenna.

She put the lantern in the grass and the light spilled around them, enclosing the two of them and creating an illusion of a haven from the darkness. For Jenna, in that moment, there seemed to be no one else alive on the earth except her and her mother.

"Jenna, I'm a-trustin' you, girl, to understand what I done in a trade with the Indians." She opened her palm and in it lay Nettie's heart-shaped mother-of-pearl locket.

Jenna gasped, "Nettie's locket! Oh, Mama, how come?" Her eyes smarted, holding back the tears.

"I just caught a glimpse of it with the corner of my eye. One of the Indians was a-wearin' it around his neck. His shirt fell open and I seen it plain as can be. Those Indians dug up Nettie to be sure and robbed her of her only earthly tie to her mama. I couldn't bear to have Mrs. Butler know the fate of her little Nettie. So I traded quick to keep her from a-knowin'. It would be sorely painful for any mother to know her child's grave was desecrated and her poor dead child's body discarded like rubbish in some God-forsaken place. It's beyond bearing." Martha Jane dabbed her eyes with her apron. "Now, you take this locket, Jenna. It's yours. Something made me think it was important for you to keep. Hide it and don't show it to no one—especially to Hannah. It's our secret."

Jenna held the locket in her hand and closed her fist tightly around it. She put her arms around her mother and pressed herself close into her body. Martha Jane folded her arms around Jenna for only a moment and seemed to soften to the touch.

Jenna closed her eyes and let the feeling of warmth and closeness flow through her. She knew she would keep the locket forever. It was not her bond to Nettie, but to her own mother. "Our secret," Jenna said softly.

TWO

E VER SINCE THE TRAGIC ASSASSINATION of the missionaries, Narcissa Whitman and her husband, in the Oregon Territory, travelers and settlers were more concerned for their own safety. No one quite understood the behavior of the different Indian tribes. Some were peaceful—helpful even. Others were hostile. As more and more emigrants traveled across the plains, their stories of hardship and encounters with Indians filtered back to the states.

Accounts of harassment, robbery, rape, and the kidnapping of women and children as they trekked westward made it clear that the emigrants needed the protection of the U.S. Army and safe escort through territories where Indians were openly hostile. Fort Kearney was a safe haven for the travelers.

Situated where two major trails converged, the Fort was the first significant stopover on the two-thousand-mile journey west, the place where, for the first time, the emigrants met the Platte River—Old Muddy- a slow, murky river, shallow and wide—their highway across the Great Plains.

The Fort was not exactly what the emigrants had imagined, for it was still being built by the United States Army. It looked like a busy town. Rows of white tents, a confusion of wagons, teams of mules and oxen, livestock, corrals of horses, barking dogs, and building materials surrounded the low, wooden structures.

Fort Kearney was a "place" in the vast plains, a center, an ark in the ocean of grasslands, and the travelers were grateful to stop here for longer than an overnight. The women rearranged their wagons and the mixed-up boxes and supplies, cleaned out the dust, and placed necessities in handy pockets in the sides of the canvas walls. The men repaired harnesses and wheel rims, shoed the animals, and re-tarred the bottom of wagons so they could float across rivers.

Even though the fort was not yet well supplied, there were plenty of potatoes, kerosene, matches, molasses, rum, sugar, candles, soap, more beans, dried apples, and a few other items left by emigrants who needed to lighten their loads.

"I'd surely like to have that lovely old rocker," Martha Jane said to Israel as they walked between the items thrown casually in the weeds. Kettles and cook stoves, sacks of flour and sides of bacon, picks and heavy tools lay moldering or rusting with neglect. "Imagine someone bringing that heavy mirror this far and then a-throwin' it away. It was probably the missus' precious family tie. And now it's all broke up a-lyin' in the grass. Maybe the missus died. Maybe one of them fresh graves we passed was hers." Martha Jane sighed heavily.

"We all have to part with a few precious items, Martha Jane," Israel said, "or them poor beasts will give out before we get where we're a-goin'. Them women was warned at the start not to be bringin' extras."

"The women had no choice in a-goin' west! They was dragged away from their friends and kin with precious few comforts," Martha Jane snapped.

"That's enough, woman! I don't hear no other woman a-fussin' all the time. Be glad we're without troubles. Thank the Lord we're healthy."

"Well, we ain't all fine! Solomon is a-sufferin' from the summer complaint. He's feverish and restless. I think he's got the bloody flux, Israel. I can't keep him clean and he's beginning to weary me. He frets all the time and nothing seems to stop his upset bowels. He's plumb wore out from the constant jostling of the wagon. Solomon needs rest."

Israel quickly set up the tent and gently laid Solomon on his bedding. "He's weak as can be, Martha Jane. If he don't show any improvement, I best get Dr. Polley to look him over. We ain't in any hurry to clean out the wagon. We'll just do what's necessary and go over supplies. You look like you need rest, too."

Martha Jane sat at the opening of the tent and watched a group of women pick their way through the discards in the grass.

"Look at that lovely old rocker," she heard one of them say. "What was they a-thinkin' bringing that rocker clear out here?" They walked past without noticing her.

Jenna and Hannah ran up to Martha Jane. Their excitement sparkled in their eyes. "Mama," Jenna said in a rush, "can I go to the river with Hannah to take a bath? *Please*, Mama, please. You ought to see the river, Mama. It's huge! The biggest I ever saw—you can hardly see to the other side! There's a big sandbar that's cut off a nice pool. The river is calm and shallow, no current at all, and there are bushes to hide behind. Some of the other women are doing the same thing and rinsing out clothes. *Please*, Mama. We won't go all the way in, just up to our knees."

"There are too many menfolk and soldiers ambling about. Ain't fittin'," Martha Jane said, eyeing the bustling fort. Another wagon train of migrating Mormon families, who had come in from Council Bluffs on the Mormon Trail north of the Platte, were preparing to move on.

"And I seen a couple of Indians poking around. Besides, that Platte River water is dirtier than you are."

"One of the women is taking her little ones down to wash their bottoms and rinse diapers. She'll be right close by," Hannah said.

"All right, then *go*! It don't matter to you that your little brother is feverish and I'm wore out tending him. You just think life is a cherry tart."

Jenna's exuberance died quickly. "I'll stay with Solomon, Mama, if you want. You go on, Hannah."

"No! Go on! I don't want you around. I'm too tired to put up with your nonsense. It don't matter to you that I'm sickly and haggard. Do what you want to, *but leave me in peace*. And take a bar of soap and wash your apron while you're at it." Martha Jane waved the girls away and slumped into an abandoned chair.

As soon as the girls were well out of sight, Martha Jane climbed into the wagon, opened the wooden medicine box, and gulped a large swallow of turpentine. The burn in her throat gagged her, but she had discovered that by quickly drinking whiskey afterwards, the taste of turpentine vanished immediately and the after belches were not as sickening.

The whiskey eased her exhaustion and calmed the tightness in her chest. She managed to open the large bottle daily—sometimes several times on bad days. All of the emigrants kept whiskey on hand for medicinal purposes—coughs, headaches, insect bites, cuts, the ague. Martha Jane rationalized that what she was doing was of a medicinal nature. Still, she hid her actions, never told Israel, and wondered what she would do when the bottle of whiskey was empty.

🌱 🌱 🌱

The girls walked away, the fun momentarily dampened by Martha Jane's sharp tongue. "Don't pay her no mind, Jenn. She's probably in her woman time. That always makes them cross," Hannah said.

"What do you mean, woman time?"

"I mean, she's sick, like every month. Don't you know about bein' sick every month?"

"Of course I know. I just didn't know it made you irritable," Jenn said.

"Well, I know all about it. You can ask me anything you need to know. Come on, let's go to the river."

The two girls ran toward the wide, muddy Platte, their skirts catching around their ankles, making them lurch and stumble. With their bonnets in hand, they raced to the freedom of air and cool water and to a moment of independence.

Hannah and Jenna found a private spot by the river's edge. The large sandbar isolated a pool only a couple of feet deep at the center. The musky water flowed silently past the other side of the bar, leaving the pool slightly clearer. A few leafy bushes held the bank's sandy lip in place, and a scant grove of young cottonwoods provided shade.

The girls removed their heavy, dusty boots, aprons, and smocks, stood in their long summer underwear, and squealed with delight from being free of so many layers of clothes, feeling the air touch their chests and shoulders.

Jenna stepped into the pool and watched the sparkling silt float to the surface as the soft ooze slipped through her toes. Hannah stepped into the pool with her.

"Let's take all our clothes off, Jenna," Hannah said.

Jenna sucked in her breath. "Oh no, never Hannah! That would be a sin."

"No it wouldn't. That's silly. God made us naked first. I'm going to do it, Jenna . . . if you turn around and don't watch me. Promise you won't tell."

"I won't. But please, Hannah, don't do this. What if someone sees you?"

"So what if they do? It ain't none of their business."

Jenna turned her back and listened to the rustle of under garments sliding down Hannah's young thighs into the grass. She heard Hannah hang the clothes on some tender willow branches and step into the water. She held her breath. Going naked was a daring thing to do.

"You may turn around, now. I'm under water," Hannah said. Jenna turned. Hannah was sitting in the water visible from the waist up.

Jenna gasped. Hannah had breasts! She stared and said nothing but felt the red splotches bloom on her face and neck.

"Quit staring," Hannah said. "I'm nearly fourteen after all. Take off your clothes, Jenna. I've taken *all* of mine off. I'm as naked as a baby."

"Oh, Hannah. What if someone sees you?"

"I don't care if someone does."

Jenna Take off your undershirt. It feels wonderful. No one will see you and I won't tell. Hurry up!"

Jenna deliberated the right and wrong of the situation, then impulsively took off her camisole and sat in the pool. The girls laughed and splashed until all self-consciousness left and Jenna thought nothing of the two small bumps barely forming on her own boyish body.

The sun filtered through the rustling leaves of the cottonwoods, making eyelet shadows on the girls' wet skin. Suddenly, Hannah stopped playing. "Hush, Jenna!" she said in a whisper. "Someone is standing behind that bush yonder a-watchin' us. I saw a figure . . . a man!"

"Is it an Indian?" Jenna asked, her heart beating fast in her throat.

"I don't know. Pretend we didn't see who it is and just turn your back. I'll dash out and get our towels."

But before Hanna could leave the pool, the figure eased away from the bush and backed into the trees.

"I think I saw who it was, Jenna."

"Who? Tell me!"

"I could be wrong. It would be awful to be wrong. Oh, Jenna, maybe we done a bad thing being naked."

"Who was it?" Jenna whispered.

"It looked like Reverend Squibb!"

🍃 🍃 🍃

That evening, the emigrants and soldiers held a dance. Fiddles, harmonicas, and a lonely flute joined in such gay music and irresistible rhythms that the curious Indian on-lookers, whose bodies glowed outside the ring of blazing fires, bounced on their heels and tapped their toes. The white man's actions amused them, the shouting, whooping, and stomping their feet, and the dancing—men and women together. They were, however, less amused at the increased numbers of wagons crossing through their buffalo lands. For the time being, they would tolerate the emigrants and get the best trade for money or goods. The white people did not know how to bargain, and they were gullible. The men were poor shots and the women quite homely and lacking knowledge to survive. They were not a threat.

Harke Polley had slicked back his unruly, blond hair and changed into a fresh shirt for the dance. In spite of his shyness, he felt comfortable dancing. He didn't have to talk much, and he knew he was as good as any of the men keeping the beat of the music.

He and Jenna danced the Virginia Reel together, his favorite dance. Afterward, while Jenna watched the laughing, swirling dancers, Harke stared at the little flames from the campfire reflecting in Jenna's blue eyes.

The firelight shimmered in her hair and shone through the light brown tufts around her forehead like a halo.

He watched her intense face break into smiles of pleasure. Sometimes, when she stretched her skirt over her knees and the toes of her boots, or clapped her hands, Harke thought she looked like a child, but then when she stopped smiling, he'd catch a look of wisdom and intelligence that belonged to an adult. Sitting around the campfire on this particular night, Harke said to himself, "I love you, little Jenna Daggett."

Hannah, without doubt, was the prettiest girl at the dance, though Harke barely noticed his sister. If he had taken his eyes off Jenna, he would have noticed his sister's appealing dress and flirtatious behavior. He would have seen the eager stares of the young men, and the side glances of the married ones. She wore a white, full-sleeved muslin blouse with a ruffled high collar and a bit of red ribbon at the neck. Her full, dark blue skirt patterned with small white flowers, red dot centers, and light blue leaves flounced playfully as she danced, and a flirty red petticoat peaked just below the hem.

Instead of letting her hair fall free and wild, Hannah had pulled back part of the top and sides and tied the strands with a large white bow. The rest of her black hair, shiny from numerous brushings, hung down her back and bounced fetchingly to the music as she pranced with the young soldiers.

One young man, Colonel Brian LaGrange, kept his eager eyes on her most of the evening. She seemed to know she had his admiration, as well as the other men's, and sent him sideways glances and strutted ever so prettily around the circle.

While the music played, the emigrants danced, and the crackling fires sent red sparks into the starry night, Martha Jane, Israel, and Dr. Polley sat with Solomon.

"It ain't good, Mr. and Mrs. Daggett," Dr. Polley said. "It's got all the looks of cholera. I'd bet my last dollar that's what it is—cholera. And damn me, I don't know what to do about it, except bed rest and keeping him away from other folks. He's a mighty sick little boy. I'm sorry."

Israel put his arm around his wife while she sobbed softly into his chest.

"Oh, Israel, I just won't be able to bear it if we lose our Solomon." She raised her head and looked icily into Israel's face. "This cursed trip! If he dies, it's *your* fault! *Your* fault! Oh, God!" She cried hard and held tightly to Israel.

The words "your fault" hit Israel like a hammer. He loved his son, his wife, and Jenna. No, his journey west was for them—for opportunity and health. Solomon would be better by morning. He was a strong little boy. The strong live and the weak die. The Daggetts were always a strong people. Solomon Daggett was like himself and all his people—strong. Besides, there had been no cases of cholera reported. This couldn't be cholera—maybe the bloody flux. "I'll call Jenn to bed in a bit," Israel said. "She can sleep in the wagon with you and I'll sleep with Solomon so you can rest. I'll call you if he needs tendin.' "

🌿 🌿 🌿

The next morning the sky was full of dark clouds. The wind flapped the canvas doorways, whipped the women's skirts and aprons into a frenzy, and scattered laundry around the campsite. The wagon train's elected officers had called a general meeting to air grievances, discuss new rules, reaffirm regulations and inform the people about the progress of the trip. Blue stood before them and with his quiet, reassuring voice told the emigrants what to expect on the next leg of the journey.

"What you been a-doin' the past few weeks is a Sunday picnic, folks. We're now in Sioux country until Fort Laramie. Now, the Sioux is a fine, handsome-lookin' people, but not so friendly as the Pawnee. We might be lucky, and we might not. Sometimes they bargain and sometimes they don't. Some days they is friendly and right helpful, and then some days they is ornery as rattlesnakes and stubborn as mules and you got to pay money to pass by their camps or ford a river. They is always hungry for white man's food, especially hard bread and sugar. It's best to have a few shirts or buttons on hand for trade.

"From now on, we'll double our men on night watch. We might surprise you with an Indian drill to see just how fast you can grab your firearms or protect yourself. Ladies and children, when I shout, 'Indians!', why you drop your doin's and get in that wagon fast and lie down.

"We're goin' to do a bit of practice shootin' on the way, so as the men can take down a buffalo or antelope or a hostile if need be. Noon stops are goin' to be shorter—cold coffee and cold meat—no fires, unless the oxen need more time to graze or need extra rest.

"We'll rest ten minutes every hour, more if necessary, and let them poor beasts stop their pullin'. We'll stop sooner for our evening camp 'cause we might have to walk farther for good grass. Good food for the livestock is harder to come by being as the grass is burning out now. The oxen is pullin' mighty big loads and they're tired. Ladies, dump things you don't need *now*. You'll be glad you done it when you start a-seein' abandoned wagons and bones of dead oxen bleachin' in the dust.

"One last thing. We're losin' two wagons. Two of our good families is a-goin' back. They ain't happy with how things is. Since they have two milk cows betwixt them, they is kindly leavin' behind one of them which the Daggetts bought and is happy to share her milk for a few pennies.

"But we're pickin' up two families come in from Council Bluffs on the Mormon Trail. They come in last night late and are joinin' our company. Both these families got too far behind their own companies.

"The Edwards family has eight children, but they ain't Mormon. The Doneleys got no youngsters on account of their only one died on the way from an infected foot. These wagons lagged behind because of sickness and a broken axle. When you lag too far behind, you can't always catch up. It's dangerous to be by yourself in the wilderness."

Blue took a deep breath. Too much talking all at once sometimes wore him out, but he never missed an opportunity to expound a bit.

The emigrants never minded hearing Blue's advice. He was a good wagon master who understood the trail. No one knew much about him and it was not proper to pry into a man's past. In spite of his easy manner and playful conversation, he carried an air of private sadness, a sorrow that floated behind his kind brown eyes.

Jenna especially liked Blue, probably because he and her papa had developed a strong friendship. When the two men played their music or joked together, Jenna felt warm and safe.

"Colonel Brian LaGrange is haulin' goods and his own mess in a two-yoke spring wagon to Fort Laramie," Blue continued. "He says he's a lousy cook and is mighty obliged to pay someone for his meals who's willin' to endure him. He's bringin' a nice shepherd dog with him. Her name is Belle and she's a honey. She don't bite and loves children. Welcome aboard all you new folks."

The emigrants clapped and nodded a welcome.

"That's all I have to say, except you ladies were mighty fine dancers last night and the fiddlin' is still playin' in my ears. Oh, yes. Dr. Polley has a few words."

Dr. Polley's normally jolly face was serious. Instead of engaging in some friendly or humorous remarks that made him beloved by the emigrants, he got right to the point. "The train before us reported back two deaths from cholera. We don't know the cause."

"It's them Mormons what carries the disease," Mr. Edwards shouted from the crowd. "There's hundreds up ahead of us—smitten with sin . . . like the lepers. Ain't that right, Reverend Squibb?"

"Indeed the plagues strike the souls of the wicked, Mr. Edwards," Faithful replied.

The emigrants nodded. "Amen," someone said.

"This is no time for debate," Dr. Polley said. "The Mormons were plenty sick last winter from chills and the like, but no cholera that I heard of. The fact is we don't know how you get the disease. It's been pretty calm since the thirties epidemic, but we never know when it's going to reappear.

"Some folks say the body don't have sufficient electricity in it. That's why some folks get it and others don't. I don't know. I sometimes think it's passed along through water . . . maybe them water holes dug up by emigrants, but I doubt it. And I'm not accusing any one religion or race. My only advice is precautionary.

"From now on, I want everyone to take a spoonful of pepper sauce daily and put a bit of it in any water you drink. Keep drinking the citric acid and sugar daily. It's good for scurvy and maybe other sicknesses. A bit of lemon extract and you can pretend you're on the porch swing back home—sipping lemonade and listening to the crickets. Keep dry and call me any time, day or night, if you feel sick. God forbid, cholera is back after these past good years. We've been a pretty healthy company so far. Let's keep it that way."

The wagons moved out by eight o'clock in the morning, a late start with ominous clouds darkening by the moment. In the wagon, Solomon jostled like a milk pail and did not open his eyes. Martha Jane and Jenna sat staring at the pale child.

🌱 🌱 🌱

Before the first rest stop, Martha Jane watched the change from life to death pass over the young boy's face. It was as silent as blowing out a candle, almost imperceptible to anyone but a mother. Something about the eyes falling deeper into the sockets, the dry lips parting, the immediate waxen skin, the stillness, told Martha Jane that Solomon was dead—gone from his little body. She did not signal Jenna, nor say a word, but listened to the endless creaking of the wagon, the turning of the wheels, the drops of rain pelting the canvas top, and the wind blowing about the crevices like greedy fingers probing to come in.

After awhile, Jenna seemed to feel the stillness, too. "Mama?" she said, searching Martha Jane's face.

"Hush, Jenna. Don't wake your brother from his sleep. Let him rest."

Martha Jane wanted to return to Fort Kearney to bury Solomon so that he could be with people, not in the lone, wild prairie so cold and harsh. It meant, however, lagging behind, away from the comfort of friends. Israel convinced her it was best not to go back and promised the wagons would roll over and over the grave to pack the earth tightly. They would leave it unmarked so that it would never be discovered by Indians.

Martha Jane clipped some fingernails and a few snips of Solomon's hair and placed them in her only treasure from home—a small shell box her sister had given her. This would have to serve as Solomon's grave and headstone—his only remaining place of memory.

The women helped Martha Jane dress the boy and place him in a wooden packing crate and the men lowered him into a deep grave in the middle of the trail. Once again, the Reverend Faithful Squibb gave the sermon and

Cora led the emigrants in singing "Nearer My God To Thee." The rain dripped off the wilting brims of the pasteboard bonnets like tears, while the ladies cried and held their wet aprons to their eyes. No one said Solomon had died of cholera, but they knew it in their deepest fears and waited for it to claim its next victim.

Martha Jane did not hear the words of the sermon, only the wind far out on the prairie, calling to her to join in a spinning death dance, become a whirlwind racing headlong across the land destroying everything in its path, until somewhere on the other side of the horizon, it would blow itself into light.

🌱 🌱 🌱

Farther down the trail, Jenna watched Israel throw out Solomon's bedding, his baby comforter, his clumsy, small boots, and all his meager earthly belongings, and she wondered what wickedness could possibly be inside her baby brother.

Solomon's death left a terrible silence in the Daggett family, and an even deeper silence in Martha Jane. Mile after mile, the oxen pulled the heavy wagons, moaning under the weight of the yoke and the constant rubbing on their necks. Jenna rocked in the seat beside her mother. She wanted to say something comforting, but Martha Jane's face was drawn tight, closed shut like an iron door through which no one—not Israel, not friends, or Jenna—could enter.

Even Israel didn't talk much lately. He kept his face straight ahead, always squinting into the western sun as if he were trying to see beyond it.

Jenna thought her father looked different, his face dry as hide, cracked and brown as the buffalo meat that swung on the wagon sides. He did not speak about Solomon, except once when he said to Jenna, "What is, *is*. The road lies ahead, my girl, not behind. Your brother is where God wants him. You never know when the Almighty will call a weak or lost sheep up yonder. That's why you stay strong. You keep a-goin' no matter what happens. That's what you do, Jenn. Remember that. You pay no mind to discomfort. You just keep a-goin' like a wagon wheel. Moanin' don't do no good at all. Just like that old bossy cow tied up behind our wagon. She can moan for her calf, but it don't do her no good."

Blue had advised the emigrants to spare the animals' load by walking whenever possible. Jenna's light body hardly made a difference, but she found companionship walking with Hannah or some of the older children. Jenna found relief from the heavy-heartedness of her parents by trailing after the women and listening to them talk of home and family, ideas on health remedies, and knitting patterns. Some of the women knitted or tatted while they walked or stopped to pick wild onion and garlic, or to marvel at patches of dainty pink mimosa, prairie geranium, or Indian paintbrush. She found special comfort walking with Mrs. Polley, who smiled down at her from time to time.

"Look here, Jenna," Emily Polley said, pointing to a field of reddish-purple flowers—tall, proud stalks with blossoms trumpeting off the spine. "These here are fireweeds—ain't they grand? There must have been a grass fire here. These are the first flowers to poke up through the charred ground. How they survive their calamity is a marvel . . . but they do . . . somehow. God must take care of them." She picked a stalk and handed it to Jenna. "We all got to be like the fireweed."

🐦 🐦 🐦

The company had set up a constitution with articles of agreement on the conduct of the passage west. So far, there had been little trouble and few fights. One such agreement reflected their decision not to travel on the Sabbath. Time was precious and any stop should be used to make repairs. The needs of the teams took precedence over the strict Sabbath observances they would have followed back home.

On this particular Sabbath morning, the early sun predicted an especially hot day. The emigrants had stopped in a place near Ash Hollow where there was still good grass, even though it was parched and turning to straw. The cattle, oxen, horses, and milk cows grazed leisurely, their noses inching along the ground with their velvet lips moving slowly as they chewed the tender grass.

Before the Sunday service, Martha Jane and Jenna made a special breakfast of dried applesauce, boiled beef and bacon, biscuits, and real butter churned in the milk can by the constant motion of the wagon. At 8:00 a.m., Reverend Faithful Squibb walked to the center of the circle of wagons, stood on a wooden crate, and banged a bucket with a spoon to get the attention of the people. He wore his preaching outfit—the long, black coat and frayed, collapsible silk opera hat. Cora stood close by holding a hymnal and wearing a dressy bonnet of crushed purple velvet trimmed in black ribbons and a deep lavender silk shawl.

"Sinners!" he shouted, banging the bucket. "Listen to the words of the Lord that you may be saved from your evil ways. Can't you stop your doin's and repent your sins for one hour on this glorious Sabbath? Look at you all. This is the Lord's Day, a day of rest, and you're a-workin' like it was any old funeral! You'll be sorry on the Judgment Day, you will—all of you!" Faithful's face was flushed with emotion. He pointed a finger at Doctor Polley. "You there, Doctor, can't you get your hair cut on any other day besides the Holy Day?"

"No, Reverend, I can't. The sick and needy don't wait for the Sabbath or any other day to need my services. I take a shave and haircut when I can and the missus has time to lather me up. I reckon the Lord will be well pleased to call up a clean-faced and trimmed sinner instead of a scruffy old goat."

A few of the men chuckled softly.

"Silence! Remember, you are in church—God's lofty sky is our dome, the wagons our walls."

The emigrants went about their business. The women sewed patches on ripped and worn out clothes. Everyone—women, bachelors and children – worked at the endless chore of darning socks. God's day or not, this was the time for soaking beans, washing clothes and young children's diapers in tubs of boiling water, writing letters, keeping diaries, oiling harnesses, and repairing wagons. But the Edwards and their eight scrubbed youngsters, who had recently joined the company at Fort Kearney, marched grandly into the center of the circle to hear the preaching.

Jenna thought they all looked alike with their thin, straight noses, tight lips, and eyes set close together. In fact, she thought they looked a bit like

Faithful and Cora. She wondered if these were Bird People who simply pecked at life's small things or if they were indeed God's holy people who knew all about Hell and the way to Heaven.

Israel and Harke moved Mother Boyles in her chair closer to Reverend Squibb so she could hear and see better. She remained stiff and passive, looking out through her bonnet at the reverend. Her hands nested in her apron like two severed chicken feet.

"You have two choices, sinners!" Faithful Squibb shouted. "To suffer and die without pardon for multiplied transgressions, or to find peace through atonement and penance, admitting you have sinned against God and are unworthy in His sight."

"Amen!" mumbled the Edwards family as they looked around at the busy sinners.

The reverend's voice rang into the clear, blue sky, intensifying to a crashing crescendo at important points. Suddenly, he pointed a finger directly at the only person who appeared to be in rapt attention—expressionless Mother Boyles.

"It is you, sinner, who remains in a state of doom—wrath, indignation, tribulation, and anguish are upon your soul which doeth evil. You are sinful of the flesh! You are full of lust and evil thoughts! You . . ."

Quite suddenly, Mother Boyles' face split into a mass of new wrinkles. Her eyes squeezed into a web of many lines reaching to her ears. Her mouth cracked open into a wide, toothless smile and out tumbled a dry, unearthly cackle and an unmanageable tongue that didn't know where it belonged.

Everyone stopped what they were doing, startled at the old woman's sudden sounds.

"Mother?" Emily Polley rushed over to her.

But Mother Boyles had retreated behind her face once again, and all that remained of her outburst was a single line of drool on her puckered chin.

🌿 🌿 🌿

Late in the afternoon, while Jenna was looking for Hannah, she was stopped by Reverend Squibb.

"Miss Daggett, I would like a word with you, my child. Let us sit together on this fine Sabbath day and get better acquainted."

Jenna did not want to sit with the reverend, but he was, after all, a church father.

"Since your dear brother departed so tragically, I thought you might need to talk to a friend. You see, Jenna, how quickly the Almighty calls you up . . . and you mightn't be prepared. I'm here to help you find your way to Heaven. It's my job." Reverend Squibb smiled benignly at Jenna.

"Thank you, Reverend Squibb." Jenna kept her head down and her hands folded in her lap.

"Look up, child. Look at me." He took Jenna's chin and raised her face. "Don't look away. It ain't polite when I'm talking to you."

Jenna looked into the sharp face shadowed by his hat brim. He smiled again, showing badly formed, stained teeth. "Do you know what sin is child?" he asked.

"I'm not sure. I know everybody talks about it."

Faithful Squibb took off his hat, pulled a soiled handkerchief from his pocket, and wiped his sweaty face and neck and the thin charcoal hairs on the top of his head. "Was you baptized proper?"

"Yes, Sir," Jenna answered.

"And Solomon?"

"Yes, Sir."

"Well, leastways Solomon is probably in Heaven on account of he didn't have much time to get himself saved the regular way. But *you* . . I can tell already you ain't no lamb of God. I can help you if you put your trust in me." He touched her cheek with his sweaty fingers and ran his cold thumb across her lips.

Just then, Harke walked over to them. "Hello," he said.

"Harke!" Jenna said, jumping to her feet. She was grateful that Harke had interrupted her talk with the reverend.

"We've been having a soul talk, Harke, but I guess we're finished . . . for now." He smiled down at Jenna and patted her head. "Remember what I said, now. Say your prayers nightly, and keep a-readin' your Bible," he said, placing his hat back on his head.

The two of them watched the tall, lean figure walk away—a slow, ambling gait, a rocking sway like someone quite sure of himself.

"What was old Faithless a-sayin'? That you was a sinner?" Harke asked.

"I don't feel I'm bad or done evil things, Harke. Solomon either. I'm scared I'm not going to know in time all the right things to meet my Maker. That's what Reverend Squibb says. Why Harke, we could die any moment . . . right here, today . . . just like Solomon and Nettie."

"You ain't goin' to die and you ain't doin' nothing wrong. Forget what that old buzzard says." Harke playfully pulled Jenna's hair. "By the way, you ain't seen Hannah, have you?"

"She hangs around Colonel LaGrange like he was her beau. I was looking for her to gather buffalo chips."

"You go ahead, Jenna. I'll find her and we'll all go a-huntin' for 'em together. There's millions of real dried ones over yonder by the bluffs. We'll meet you by the humpback one," Harke said, pointing to a bluff. "That's where everyone is a-gatherin' the chips."

Harke watched Jenna run off, his smile fading in the wake of his concern. He started off toward Colonel LaGrange's tent. As he passed by a cluster of tents, haloed with clouds of blue tobacco smoke, he overheard some young men laughing and talking in low voices.

"That dark one . . . Hannah. She's the one I want to get in the grass," one man said.

"You wouldn't be the first."

The men laughed.

"They say she's got an enormous, curly muff beyond her years and black as an Indian's . . . a perfect triangle."

"And a fanny as soft as a calf's nose."

Harke stood still, nauseated at the trashy talk about his sister. How dare they say such vulgar lies! He could stand it no longer. Without hesitating, he burst into the group of three young men. They jumped to their feet.

"Don't get touchy, Harke," one said, backing away.

But before he could say more, Harke lunged for him, fists flying. The other two men grabbed Harke from behind and held him fast.

"You want your dirty mouth shut, permanent?" Harke struggled to free himself.

"Look, Harke, we ain't done nothin' to your sister," one of the men said. "You can't blame us for talkin' about her. All the fellas do. You ain't blind. She's been a-throwin' her little ass around since we left Missouri."

"Damn your hide! Shut your mouth!" Harke shouted, straining against the men's firm grip. "If any of you violated my sister, I'll kill you . . . *I will!*"

Harke sounded brave, but the fight in him was overshadowed by a terrible doubt about Hannah. He, too, had watched his younger sister flaunt her good looks and use her body in suggestive ways. He couldn't deny it. "Who's been talkin' about her? Tell me!"

"We ain't sayin', Harke. You just keep your eyes beholdin' her ways. You'll find out yourself," one of the men said, loosening his grip on Harke.

"You keep your damn mouths shut! Do you hear?" Harke picked up his hat, slapped the dust off it, and walked away, trembling with anger. He wondered when that moment had come when Hannah's blooming body had become a lure to men, when the sweetness of her face, the innocence of her ways had changed into a game, a bait, a seed of wickedness.

🌿 🌿 🌿

Martha Jane gradually began talking to the other women. Still, it was apparent she felt ill. Her face was as gray as sage, and her dark eyes sunk deep in their sockets. She had an unkempt appearance and a soiled apron that was not her ordinary dress at all. Martha Jane had always been meticulous about her starched, white apron and a clean bonnet.

There were days when she was so exhausted, she lay in the wagon until noon and then only did the minimum food preparation. Jenna and Israel worked well together when she couldn't get up at all. Jenna tried to keep up her mother's strength by preparing soft, digestible foods—a sweet pudding or clear broth—but Martha Jane would turn her head away, saying, "Take that food away. It ain't fit for a dog. You expect me to eat that? Who told you you could cook, child?"

The other women, sympathetic with the Daggett's situation, sent over little extra treats, but Martha Jane usually pushed them away and refused to eat.

Martha Jane walked over to the Edward's encampment carrying an earthen jug. She had already borrowed from the Butlers, the Polleys, and the Doneleys. The Edwards children stopped their bickering and watched Martha Jane's approach. They weren't used to friendly visits.

"Mrs. Edwards, I don't suppose you have any spare whiskey or rum? I guess ours spilled out back a ways, tipped over in the wagon, and must have leaked all the way from Fort Kearney. Now, I believe I got a touch of the ague, feverish, you know, and I thought a bit of whiskey might fix me right up," Martha Jane said.

"We got sufficient. How much do you need?" Mrs. Edwards inquired, wiping her hands on her apron.

"Whatever you can spare," Martha Jane said shyly. "I'll have Mr. Daggett replenish our supply in Fort Laramie and pay you back."

Mrs. Edwards, unsmiling, took the jug and climbed into the wagon. Martha Jane waited self-consciously while the Edwards children stared at her like a brood of baby prairie hens.

🐦 🐦 🐦

Jenna worried about her mother and tried to do special favors or extra chores to please her. Once, when Martha Jane lay resting in the wagon, Jenna brought her a clover chain of large purple balls she had woven that morning. "I made it just for you, Mama," she said, placing it around her mother's neck.

"You think you got time to waste on little pretties. There's work to do, Jenna," she said, ripping off the flowers and crumpling them in her hands. "Now go tend your little brother. He's a-sufferin' with mosquito bites and scratchin' them to pus. I can't do everything."

Jenna stared at her mother in disbelief, trying to understand the dark, distant look in her eyes. "Mama?" she asked tentatively. "Are you feelin' poorly? You want me to call Dr. Polley?"

"I want you to tend to Solomon! Now, *get out!*"

Martha Jane began to sing in a thin high voice,

" . . . Baby, my dolly, oh, he never cries!
Lie still, my darlin' and close little eyes
Mother must go, dear, and look for the others.
All the dear sisters and all the dear brothers."

Jenna did not want to tell anyone about Martha Jane's strange behavior. She thought it might pass when she stopped grieving or when she finally reached the Promised Land of Oregon.

But Martha Jane did not stop her odd behavior. She often spent long hours in silence or sang tuneless nursery rhymes over and over—

"We're all in the dumps,
For diamonds and trumps,
The kitten's are gone to St. Pauls.
The babies are bit,
The moon's in a fit,
And houses are built without walls . . ."

🐦 🐦 🐦

The landscape had changed just as Blue had predicted. The wagon train now ran south of the North Platte River through a lovely expanse of prairie and open sky, dry swells, golden bluffs, escarpments, and islands of trees in the middle of the wide Platte.

The pull of the beasts was increasingly tiring, and often they lay down at noon instead of grazing. Some were sick, bloated, infected, or suffering from sprained legs and were unable to work.

The affected beasts died or were shot or left on the prairie to live or die as fate would have it. As the wagon train passed bleached bones and decaying carcasses, the emigrants tossed their barrels and heavier articles to further lighten the loads.

Chimney Rock, jutting into the sky like a church spire, was an exciting landmark for the emigrants.

The travelers had been watching it grow from a tiny point on the nearly flat horizon to a looming stone tower. The guidebooks described this dramatic sandstone formation sculptured by relentless wind, as about one-third of the way on their westward trek. Like many of the other wagon trains before them, the pioneers journeyed a short distance off the main road to camp in its grand shadow. They felt proud of their achievement to have traveled so far, and for a brief moment, they relished the smell of sage, mustard, and yarrow, and saw the dome of blue sky as God's handiwork.

Like the earlier emigrants, some of the daring men tried to climb the steep walls of Chimney Rock to scratch their name higher than the last one. Others were content to carve their names at the base.

Hannah, Jenna, and a couple of other young girls scrambled up the cone-shaped slopes to the base of the cliff to watch the young men climb the rocks. They held their breath as Colonel LaGrange inched his way to the highest point anyone had gone so far on Chimney Rock. As he climbed, the wind gusted sheets of sand and dirt across the floor of the prairie before dissipating into the air, or spun little dusty whirlwinds of ballerinas on the horizon's stage. The Colonel's dog, Belle, ran back and forth barking and whining nervously at his master.

"Write *my* name," Hannah shouted. "Write *Hannah*!"

She jumped up and down and waved a wide-brimmed straw hat. Then she saucily put in on her head, tied it under her chin with a wide, blue ribbon, and looked at the other girls in their awkward sunbonnets.

"Where did you get that straw hat, Hannah?" Jenna asked admiringly.

"Somebody," she answered coyly.

"Who, Hannah? Tell us," Jenna begged.

"Up there," she said, pointing to the rock. "Colonel LaGrange. He give it to me."

The girls gasped in surprise. A gift from a man!

"Is he your beau?" one of them asked.

"Maybe so . . . maybe not. Anyways, it belonged to a lady friend of his in California. He says I'm too pretty for a sunbonnet and he wants me to have it."

"Well, you better wear it all the time," another girl said coldly, "cause you're brown as a darkie."

"And pinching your cheeks won't do no good, won't show up rosy on brown skin like yours," another girl said.

"I don't pinch my cheeks!" Hannah answered, but the girls, except for Jenna, didn't hear her. They had already turned their backs and were walking back to the wagons.

Blue and Israel rode up on horses. "Time to move on, folks," Blue shouted. "It ain't respectable, but you girls can carve your own names up ahead at Independence Rock, if you insist. Now go on back and help your families."

He turned to Israel. "I'll wait for that darn fool hangin' up there on the rock. He may need help gettin' down. They can always go up, but can't get down . . . get froze, I guess. Who is that, anyways? Colonel LaGrange? He should know better showin' off like that. Well, you all head back, now, and I'll be along shortly."

"I'm a-waitin' for Colonel LaGrange to take me back, if you don't mind, Mr. . . . Blue," Hannah said.

Blue nodded and rode off.

Israel helped Jenna up on the horse behind him. "Your mama ain't doin' too good today, Jenn." He sounded tired.

"What's the matter with her, Papa?" Jenna desperately wanted to talk to him about her mama's strangeness, her singing, and sometimes talking as if Solomon were still alive, but seeing Israel's worried face, she held her tongue.

"Can't figure her. She's talkin' crazy, lately. You been readin' the Bible to her regular?"

"Yes, Sir. Whenever she asks. Sometimes when she looks sad, I just start reading, hoping to make her feel better. She hasn't asked for some time now, leastways not since Solomon died. And when I try to read to her, she falls asleep," Jenna said, resting her cheek on Israel's warm back.

"Well, maybe I'll have the good Reverend Squibb talk with Martha Jane. He's a kindly man and knows the right words to say to the sufferin'."

Jenna didn't answer. There was something about Faithful Squibb that made her feel uneasy, probably because she truly was some kind of a sinner, like he said. She didn't want to think about that just now, but only to enjoy the special ride with her papa back to camp. She pressed in close to him, shut her eyes, and breathed in the glorious prairie air and the oily odor of Israel's leather coat.

The wagon train slowly rolled away from the landmark, leaving behind names and messages scratched into the cliffs for friends or family members following on other emigrant trains. Hour by hour, day by day, Chimney Rock grew smaller and fainter. Ahead loomed a series of oddly shaped bluffs, too stubborn to dissolve in the harsh land. The guidebook called them Scotts Bluff, and the emigrants fixed their eyes on the landmark to relieve the sameness of the landscape.

Without warning, the wagons stopped, and a flutter of hooded vultures with bloody beaks and talons flew awkwardly up into the air and scattered some distance away. Clearly, something had occurred up ahead. The emigrants hurried on foot to the front of the train to see what caused the delay. A crowd of men gathered in the middle of the road while the women stood back in shocked silence, holding their children and covering their mouths with their aprons.

Jenna pushed her way through to see. At first she wasn't certain what it was she saw lying in the road, and then it became clear. It was the partially eaten, decomposing body of a naked woman. Her arms and hands were tied above her head with leather thongs. She had been scalped. A partial auburn plait, once neatly pinned across the top of her head, now lay coiled in the dust like a prairie rattler.

Blue stood up slowly. "The woman has been violated and tortured, tied to a horse, and dragged back and forth across the ruts by the Indians— probably the Sioux—and left here to frighten us. The poor soul. God curse these savages! No man or beast deserves to die like this! It ain't even human." Blue turned to the stunned onlookers. "Men, keep your guns loaded. Ladies and children, no more walkin'. No one is to lag behind. Now let's get this miserable lady buried proper."

Martha Jane hung back from the crowd, listening. She watched the men lift the bruised body covered with dirt and dried, black blood onto a rubber poncho and carry it away from the road. Then she returned to the wagon and quickly found the whiskey bottle. She didn't cry but began to laugh quietly. "Ain't it ridiculous to bury a body with no name," she mumbled. "No one will ever know she is gone. No body, no name, no kin who knows nothing," she chuckled, "and no breasts . . . clean cut off."

Martha Jane lay down in the wagon. She wanted to sleep in order to forget where she was. In spite of the warm day, she pulled a blanket around her and tucked it under her chin. Gradually she felt a detachment, a vacuum, what she guessed it would be like inside a soap bubble. The voices and Belle's shrill bark began drifting away. She was floating, not sleeping, but gently lifting and swaying until suddenly a tiny feeling rippled in her stomach. Martha Jane opened her eyes, held her breath, and concentrated. Ever so slightly, the movement within her began again, like a tiny root wiggling through the soil, a soft touching against her inner walls, a tapping. The seed within her had quickened. There was no mistaking it. A new life was growing inside her.

🍃 🍃 🍃

The large black wing of night finally spread over the solemn encampment. The moon rose on the horizon like a vulture's golden eye watching for helpless movement on the prairie.

Jenna awakened several times during the bright night and looked out at the small city of canvas tents and the coiled caterpillar of wagon tops glowing eerily in the moonlight. The full moon flooded the sky, splashing its queer light over the backs of lowing oxen and onto Jenna's nightgown. The pale squares in her quilt, Martha Jane's white apron, and a ghostly dish towel hung over the wagon tongue and looked oddly luminous. This was not a night to sleep, but to spy on fairies hiding under the milkweed or dancing on the tops of the bluffs.

Jenna wanted to find Israel, who was on watch, and to talk to him about the night and all the secrets of the big sky, but she knew she must not wander about. And so she lay half-asleep, listening to the silver coyotes howl to each other through the moonlight.

The sun, still sleepy on the other side of the world, yawned its coral tint across the horizon. Jenna awakened suddenly and looked out of the wagon at the full moon, still white and shiny as a bone china plate, hanging on the other side of the sky. This time, she heard voices and saw a lantern light coming from inside her parent's tent. Mrs. Polley opened the tent flap and hurried to her wagon. The emergency in her step made Jenna shiver. Something was wrong. Emily Polley rushed back to the tent carrying flannel sheets.

Jenna climbed from the wagon and stood on the dewy grass, the hem of her nightie a wick to the wetness, and listened to the voices—Israel, Emily, and Doctor Polley.

"God help me, I didn't know she was in a family way," Israel said, his voice tight and harsh. "Martha Jane, why didn't you tell me? It weren't a shame, woman. Now you've gone and committed the mightiest mortal sin against the Lord. Can you hear me, Martha Jane? Are you talkin' to the Lord this minute, beggin' forgiveness?"

"None of us knew for certain, you know, Mr. Daggett," Mrs. Polley said sympathetically. "We'd have helped her some. Poor soul. She's had a terrible sufferin' journey—feelin' so poorly, losin' a child and all. Bless her miserable heart."

"Open your eyes, Martha Jane. You can't hide from your sin behind closed eyes. Cryin' don't do no good," Israel said.

"She wasn't right in the head lately. It was clear. I should have paid closer attention to her," Mrs. Polley sighed. "The Lord will take into account all her sufferin' and confusion. Let her rest."

"I just hope I can stop this hemorrhaging," Dr. Polley said gravely. "She's a-bleedin' way too much. Now just maybe the medicine will stop this flow. Emily, you steep some strong shepherd's purse tea. Use the flowers, too, and as soon as she can take something down, keep her drinking it. I got to stop this bleedin' somehow."

Jenna moved in closer to hear better. Her whole body shook with fear.

"Now we ain't sayin' one word about this—not a word. She's simply had a miscarriage. That's all," Dr. Polley said firmly. "And Emily, get rid of that knitting needle."

"How could she do this to herself?" Israel cried out.

"I'll take her bedding and nightclothes down to the river and wash 'em up good before the camp is awake. I can't let the blood set. That fine river sand will be a good scrubber. I'll get it clean. Now give me that knitting needle and I'll throw it in the river."

Jenna hid behind the tent as Mrs. Polley, carrying a bundle of bloody flannel, headed for the river. Jenna stared at Martha Jane's nightdress soaked bright red, trailing on the ground, and tried to comprehend what was happening. She knew her mother had lost a baby, but she didn't understand the amount of blood, the secrecy, or the anger in Israel's voice.

Back in the wagon, Jenna looked at the cold, white eye of the fading moon and the blood-red gash along the skyline that split open the morning.

🌱 🌱 🌱

The emigrants packed up and pulled out of camp by 7:00. They were only eight miles from Fort Laramie, the second major stopover for the travelers. Martha Jane lay in the wagon with Mrs. Polley by her side. The wet sheets washed in the river hung discreetly inside the wagon. Jenna rode Honey while Israel walked silently beside them.

"Is Mama going to die?" she asked quietly.

"I don't know, Jenn. If the Good Lord wants her, He'll call her up. Nothin' we can do about it. You can't beg God. He already knows what He's a-doin'."

"Are we going to stop a couple of days at Fort Laramie so as Mama can rest?"

"If the company says so, we will. Otherwise, we won't."

"Could we stop now for a bit? She seems awful sick," Jenna pleaded.

"She's restin' fine in the wagon."

"But it's rocking and jiggling so bad it chatters your teeth."

"We can't stop here, Jenn. We've got to keep a-movin', you know that. Martha Jane is goin' to be fine."

But that was not the case. Martha Jane bled to death before they reached Fort Laramie.

It was Emily Polley who comforted Jenna. More than once, she cradled Jenna in her fleshy arms, rocked her like a small child, and let her sob herself to sleep.

For Jenna, Mrs. Polley was life. She rested her head on Emily's soft, pillowy breasts and listened to the great heart beating, the lungs breathing—a steady, unending rhythm, a logical, certain motion. Her arms, large and strong, warmed Jenna, while the child's own inner fire gave no heat at all.

Mrs. Polley had time for all creatures that hurt—a blackbird with a tumbleweed stick caught in its wing, an ox with an abscess on its neck, or a cow with a sliver in its udder. At night, after she put the twins to bed and had attended to Mother Boyles, Emily would hold Jenna on her lap around the campfire while the families talked, sang, or told stories. Whenever Emily laughed, Jenna's head jiggled on her chest and gave her a sense of well-being. Many nights, after Israel had tucked Jenna in bed and said the Lord's Prayer with her, Emily Polley would sit on the wagon seat where Jenna could see her, looking up at the stars, saying nothing, just being close until Jenna fell asleep.

Israel was grateful for Emily's compassion as well. Something in him had coagulated into such a hard, cold anger he was incapable of giving his daughter the tenderness and reassurance she so desperately needed. He struggled with Martha Jane's deed, sometimes wandering alone at night into the dark prairie, pounding his temples with his fists and crying out his anguish to the empty space.

Emily must have recognized his torment, because she patted his stooped shoulders and said in her kindly way, "Cast your burden on the Lord, Mr. Daggett. His burden is light. He'll ease your pain, Sir. Indeed, He will. He'll be your strength—Jenna's, too. He'll uphold you with His righteousness, He will. You just hang on now, Mr. Daggett. He says, 'Lean not to thine own understanding.' That's what He says. It's the best way."

Israel made a decision after they buried Martha Jane at Fort Laramie. "I'm sending you back to Sapling Grove to your Aunt Elizabeth, Jenn. She'll care for you and raise you proper."

"No, Papa, no! I won't go! You're all I got in this world! I'll cook and learn all the ways to take care of us. I can farm. I'm growing up fast . . .

nearly twelve. Papa, *please* don't send me back. I'm a survivor, strong, just like you and Grandpa Daggett," she said clinging to Israel's waist.

He picked her up and hugged her tightly.

Jenna held his cheeks in her hands and looked at him with her blue, intense eyes. Israel thought she no longer seemed a child.

"You can teach me how to hitch the wagon and drive the team. I can do it, Papa. I'll help you farm in Oregon—milk the cow, bake, wash, churn butter, feed the animals. I know how. You need me, Papa. Please."

"I'll think on it, Jenn," Israel said. Then, without hesitation, he said, "I don't need to think. The Lord will show us the way. You're a-stayin' with me, Jenn . . . and that's that."

Before leaving Fort Laramie, once again Israel threw away personal belongings—this time, his wife's. He left behind her trunk of clothes and more cooking pots. The other emigrants joined him, dumping items they once believed they could never abandon.

Emily admitted it was time to say goodbye to her precious cook stove. Hannah said a tearful goodbye to Colonel LaGrange and his dog, Belle. Jenna and Israel took one last look at the fresh grave covered with bouquets of yellow goldenrod and marked with a crudely carved wooden cross, and said goodbye to Martha Jane.

Jenna kept her mother's small, hinged shell box that held Solomon's hair and fingernails. She added Nettie's mother-of-pearl locket, closed the lid, and tucked it deep in the bottom of her chest of belongings. In that small box was all the incompleteness of her life with Nettie, Solomon, and Martha Jane. It now contained overwhelming sadness, something unfulfilled, unfinished in her life. Its symbol of mother love was fleeting and uncertain.

THREE

B EYOND FORT LARAMIE, for the next hundred miles, the emigrants gazed at the Black Hills and snow-covered Laramie Peak in the distance. After the flat, dry plains, they were refreshed by pines and juniper, clear springs, and tributaries that ran into the North Platte some distance from the trail. From now on, they would be pulling up gradually to a higher altitude.

They were to encounter other changes as well, at least until they left the big river altogether—timber and abandoned wagons providing fuel instead of buffalo chips, less danger from the Great Plains Indians, and less fear of cholera, which was reported to disappear west of Fort Laramie. The abundance of clear streams and good grass meant health for the oxen as long as their masters provided rest and care and understood that the animals faced a greater uphill pull and the pain of cut hooves on the rugged, rocky trail.

The wagon train crossed several major streams—Horseshoe Creek, La Bonte, La Perle, Box Elder—until it once again met the wide, rushing muddy Platte. At this point, the travelers had to ferry across. Some of the emigrants removed the wagon's wheels and floated across on tar-caulked wagon beds. Others paid a group of enterprising young Mormons to ferry them across on a platform fastened to eight canoes. The animals, frightened and confused, churned the water and tried to turn back to land.

On the river crossings, the Polleys learned to secure Mother Boyles by tying her into her chair and lashing the chair to the inside wagon ribs. Crossing La Perle, she had tipped over, chair and all, and lain on her side for at least an hour before being discovered. When they tipped her right-side up, her eyes were sharp as broken glass, her quivering cheeks filled with air behind her closed lips, and she blurted out, "Peaches!"

"Peaches, Grandma?" Harke asked, straightening her crooked bonnet. Than he remembered. He, Hannah, and Dr. Polley had selfishly eaten all the stewed peaches at the noon stop—a special treat, sweet and delicious—and had left none for Emily and Mother Boyles—not even a spoonful.

Harke patted her hand and kissed her old spotted forehead. "I'm sorry, Grandma. Next time we have peaches, you can have all of mine. How about some applesauce?" Harke laughed and left Mother Boyles sulking and doing her best to pout.

Jenna learned to drive the wagon, at first in easy places, then on more difficult terrain—rocks, sand, steeper hills, slippery clay banks. Israel sat with her, teaching her how to have authority over the animals.

"You do right fine, Jenn," he said. "You got to be firm, but always remember that these old beasts have their limits. Don't ever push an animal to exhaustion. Check their hooves for cracks and sores. A lame ox is not good for pullin' and it's needless to make any creature suffer. It just ain't right." Israel slapped a mosquito on his cheek.

"We got to boil up some tar and resin and patch our team's hooves before they get pebbles in the cracks and get crippled. Blue says we ought to bind leather on their feet—make a kind of shoe. Says it helps some. He's got buffalo hide we can use."

"We'll have to repair the wagon tongue at the next ferry crossing. There's a settlement there of some thirty Mormons, hard-workin' folks who have supplies and a blacksmith shop, and Blue says they'll ferry us across the Platte. Of course, it'll cost us a-plenty—three dollars a wagon and one dollar for each of us, but leastways we won't have to make a raft and take a chance of losin' everything we own like some folks."

Jenna was glad Israel was talking again. She knew he had grieved over Martha Jane's death, sometimes walking alone far out into the parched land, never wanting to talk about her mother. For many days, he had retreated into a private world and spoke little. But lately, he acted more like her beloved papa.

"Hannah says that nobody likes the Mormons."

"Oh? Why not?"

"Because they kidnap little girls and make them wives. One man can have a hundred wives if he wants."

"Well, that's not true, Jenn. None of it. There are some mighty fine Mormon people. The only problem folks have is that the Mormons have more than one wife and they all live as a family. It's their ways, their religion. We don't take kindly to the idea of a bunch of wives—most men can hardly handle one—but they do it because to them it's kind of like a sacred duty. Anyways, they couldn't get along back in the states. Had a lot of folks pesterin' them and so they moved clear out here to live in peace. They don't bother no one and they help a lot of people a-movin' west. They're smart folks, I hear. Call theirselves the Saints, the Latter Day Saints, I believe. I suspect there are some ornery ones, a few cheaters and fuss budgets just like in our own company here. One thing for certain, they're mighty strict, got lots of rules."

Jenna looked at Israel. "They don't smile much. I saw a lot of them at Fort Kearney just pulling out when we arrived. None of the ladies or children said anything."

"They probably don't feel real easy with strangers around. I imagine they're different with their own kind."

"Are they going to Oregon, too?" Jenna asked.

"They're a-goin' to a place called Salt Lake, a real desert not far from here—to the south. They say near two thousand left just before we did, and even more is a-followin' us. Can't farm there. It's all alkali—poor soil, cold, hot, dry, windy. Can't imagine they'll survive. But, they're a hard-workin', God-fearin' people. If the Lord wants 'em to settle there, He'll find a way. Not me. I'm a-goin' where it's already green."

🌱 🌱 🌱

Since leaving Fort Laramie, the wagon train had suffered only mishap. One of the Edwards' children had jumped onto the tongue of the wagon before it had come to a full stop. He had tumbled into the dirt. Luckily, he was neither trampled nor crushed by the heavy wheels. Still, his arms and legs had been badly scraped, his face raw and bruised, and the main bone in his arm had poked through the skin like a broken spoke. The accident had frightened the mothers, who had become lax with the children's safety.

The wagon train stopped for the night by the Mormon settlement and the ferry that would carry them across the North Platte River. The Mormon's camp consisted of tents and a few wooden shacks scattered about. The hanging laundry, tubs of boiling clothes, penned livestock, good cooking smells, and a handful of shy, barefoot children who eyed the emigrants suspiciously signified the presence of women.

It was clear the Mormons were in the process of building a more substantial community, and the families were doing quite well in business.

That evening, while the women cleaned up the cooking pots, the men spoke with the Mormons about the challenges that lay ahead. Beyond the Upper Mormon Ferry, the wagon train would periodically lose the protection of the North Platte and face countless miles of alkaline desert and saline lakes filled with poisonous water unfit to drink. The emigrants feared for their animals, knowing many would die, their stomachs burned clear through. Their death meant the travelers might never reach their destination. If left stranded with a sick team, a family could face disaster or die.

The men sought to minimize these problems as much as possible and turned to the Mormons' and their *Latter Day Saints Emigrant Guide* for assistance. Inside this tome was priceless information about springs, edible grass, antelope, how to doctor a poisoned ox by giving it pork fat to "soap" its insides. The men also discussed a very narrow canyon called Devil's Gate and, just beyond, a unique place in the desert where, curiously, ice lay a foot below the surface. They talked about the Sweetwater River and South Pass, their halfway point to Paradise.

The company settled to bed early that night. They planned to get an early start the next day. It would take the better part of the morning to ferry all the wagons across the river.

The next morning the usual confusion of the crossing began and unhappy cattle were driven into the water. The bellowing animals and cursing men charged the air.

Jenna stood a safe distance away from the animals, her heart pounding with excitement at the power of the moment. Suddenly, she saw a confused calf, who had become separated from its mother, standing in the midst of the moving animals, bawling loudly. Against her better judgment, she headed for the calf to pull it to safety. It could never swim the deep water without its mother to call it forward, to help it along. She moved in dangerously close to the frantic animals.

"Get back, Jenna Daggett!" Blue shouted to her. "Don't you have no sense? Leave that little critter be!" He picked Jenna up and stood her firmly on safe ground.

"But the little calf!" Jenna cried.

"You watch now. That little one has a strong will to keep a-goin'. He's stronger than you think."

Jenna was relieved to watch the calf swim instinctively. "Will he make it to the other side, Blue?"

"You can bet your boots, Jenna. He's old enough now. We'd ferry a newborn." Blue's kind smile reassured Jenna. Behind his dust-covered lashes, Blue's brown eyes looked as soft as the oxen's.

He would never let an animal die or suffer, Jenna thought.

The Polleys tied Mother Boyles into her chair and she set sail. The family, except for Harke, crossed with the other emigrants, separate from the wagons.

Inside the wagon, Mother Boyles had been placed away from the opening so she would not be frightened by rushing water spilling on the platform. Suddenly, a head popped up from behind a pile of rolled bedding. A pair of eyes, wide as a white teacup, looked with surprise at Mother Boyles. The young woman clearly had not expected to find anyone inside the wagon.

"Don't you say a word, old woman! Do you hear me? Don't you say a word!" The woman said in a frightened whisper. "May the Heavenly Father strike you dead if you tell on me!" The young woman sank below the piles of bedding, leaving Mother Boyles staring silently at the place of disappearance.

Harke peered in the wagon. "Grandma, you doin' all right in there? We're a-crossin' the river now. Don't be afraid. I'm right here with you."

By noon, a hot sun beat down on the wagon train as it continued west like a heavy chain dragging across the sand. Mother Boyles kept her eyes on the horizon of the bedding. After a while, the woman raised up. "Missus, thanks for not sayin' nothin'. I'm obliged. Do you have some clear water? I'm mighty thirsty," she whispered.

Mother Boyles did not change her expression.

"You ain't a-goin' to help me, are you?" She slipped down below the bedding once more.

It was not until bedtime that the strange woman was discovered. Hannah went to the back of the wagon with her lantern and began pulling out the bedclothes to arrange for the night. First, she saw a pair of knobby boots sticking out from under a bundle of bedding . . . and then a pair of thin legs. Hannah let out a frightened squeal and the young woman sat up quickly.

"Don't say nothin', *please . . . please!*" she said, her voice full of panic. "I'm not a-goin' to do nothin'. I'm just scared. Help me, please. Oh, God, *help me*, but don't give me away!" The woman broke into such tears of anguish that Hannah climbed into the wagon and turned the lantern light down low.

"Who are you? Where did you come from?"

The young woman grabbed Hannah's arm. "I'm a-runnin' away. I *got* to get away. Please, don't tell on me."

Hannah raised the lantern up to the intruder's face and turned up the light. She saw a very young woman, a girl, really, not much older than herself—possibly sixteen or seventeen. It was hard to tell behind the swollen tissue, the bruises, the cut eye, and the dried scabs around her puffy mouth and nose.

Hannah sucked in her breath. "Who beat you up? Good Lord, you've been beaten bad! Do you hurt awful?"

The girl's tears washed white streaks through the trail dust covering her contorted face and she fell into deep, silent crying. "I hurt everywhere, Miss," she said, her cheeks and lips trembling as she spoke. "He beats me regular and hurts me . . . you know . . . down here . . . at night he has his way with me and does terrible things. He even makes me carry round stones inside . . . there . . . so's I won't be tempted by the Devil. Please don't tell anybody I'm runnin'. They'll all be a-comin' lookin' for me. You've got to help me, Miss."

Hannah stared at the shaking girl, so frightened and distraught she seemed almost mad. Never before had Hannah been required to be the strength for someone else, nor had she carried the weight of someone's secret pain. No one had ever asked Hannah for help. Her mother, Emily, always took care of such matters. For the first time in her life, Hannah felt a kind of responsibility, an involvement.

"You can't stay here. They'll find you. The twins and me sleep in this here wagon with my grandma. There ain't no room. I'll hide you in Jenna's wagon. Jenna won't tell. She's my friend."

"Please, Miss, I need water so bad."

"I'll bring you some food, too. Here, take my shawl and come with me. You can move about in the dark outside the wagons away from the campfire. I always do. No one will pay no mind. What's your name?"

"Zelda."

"Are you one of them Mormons?"

"Yes."

"Was you kidnapped to be a slave or a wife?"

"No. I was orphaned and the church gave me to Luke Willis. He agreed to take me as his second wife and to care for me. But he don't care for me . . . he hurts me. And Eula—that's his first wife—well, she don't like me. She knows what he's a-doin' and don't say anything. I think she's afraid of being turned out. I got to get away!"

"Come on, Zelda. I'll hide you."

The two girls slipped out of the wagon. Zelda disappeared into the dark and relieved the pain of a full bladder and climbed into the back of Jenna's wagon unseen. Hannah, with some hard bread and cold rabbit meat wrapped in a towel, found Jenna and whispered, "Come quick. Follow me. I got something to show you."

Jenna could not believe her eyes seeing Zelda hiding in her wagon. The girl's story made Jenna cry, for she had never heard of any man hurting a woman—a wife, daughter, child. Certainly, no one in Sapling Grove would do such a thing! Like Hannah, she was committed to hiding Zelda, even excited about the intrigue of it all. She felt a sense of independence and adulthood and wanted to play out her role as caretaker rather than tell Emily Polley or Israel.

Jenna and Hannah moved a wooden storage box and a chest to create a crawl space for Zelda.

"You can hide here when someone comes. At night you can sleep with me after everyone has gone to bed, and while we're traveling, you can sit up at the back behind the bedding. I'll keep the canvas drawn tight so no one can see you from the back," Jenna said.

"And when you *must* leave the wagon, we'll watch out for you," Hannah added.

"Are you hurting real bad?" Jenna asked, looking at the swollen, puffy lip and the deep cut over the eye.

"I'm real tired and awful scared," she answered. "I'm shakin' so bad I don't know if I can sleep."

"Mama has some special tea she gives to nervous folks. The kettle still has hot water. I'll get some for you when everybody's busy doin' something," promised Hannah.

Jenna gave Zelda a blanket. "Do you mind sitting in the dark, alone?" Jenna asked.

"No. I like it. I wish it was a small hole in the earth . . . and I could crawl into it and cover myself up with the cool soil. I'd like that." Zelda shut her eyes.

Even before sunup, as the women were making fires and brewing the first coffee, a group of men on horses thundered into the encampment, their horses sweaty from the run. One man with a heavy black beard and ice blue eyes spoke for the rest.

"We're looking for a young woman—short, plump, dark hair, brown eyes. She's a bit tetched and we're afraid she either drowned or wandered off," the bearded man said.

Blue approached the group. "You say one of your women is lost . . . out here?"

"I did. We come a good many miles yesterday—that is, after searching up and down the river—and didn't see no one."

Blue put his hands in his pockets and rocked on his heels. "In this heat and with no water, I doubt a woman could get this far." Blue did not appear friendly.

"Mind if we look around?" the man said, reining in his nervous horse too tightly.

"Well, Sir, I don't know. It's up to the different families. If they say so, go ahead. Some folks is still sleepin' or dressin'."

"Much obliged," the man said. "It's possible she's amongst you . . . thinkin' this was her people a-goin' to Salt Lake."

The men peered into each wagon. Jenna's heart beat fast when they came to her wagon and pretended to be confused with sleep.

The Saints assembled and galloped away in clouds of dust. Zelda remained undetected.

For the few days, Jenna and Hannah, delighted with their secret, managed to keep Zelda hidden. The wagons rolled slowly through the heat of the day past the stench of decaying carcasses. This stretch of land was bone dry, and the oxen's saliva hung in strings from their parched mouths. The emigrants carried water in every available container and waited for the luxury of flowing water.

The low sun of late afternoon stretched long shadows across the plains. The women, tired from squinting into the relentless sun, were anxious to stop for the night, to wash their papery faces and heal the cracked skin with lard or lanolin. There was no special place to rest in the arid land—no landmark, spring, or tributary—so Blue simply gave the signal that the day's journey was over. As the emigrants unloaded wagons and set up tents, a shaggy, gray man rattled into camp in a dilapidated wagon pulled by two bony mules. His face was covered with chalk dust except in the creases around his eyes.

"Good evenin' to you all. I see the Heavenly Father is guiding you safely through the desert and providing an abundance of blessings around your stew kettles. My name is Harley B. Tucker. The B is for Bean, my dear, departed mother's name. I'm a-lookin' for discarded metal of any kind all along the trail and taking it back to Salt Lake. The Saints are forging it into plows and picks, shovels, hammers—things we need to do God's blessed work. I'm also picking up old stoves, trunks, saddles, and things that bring in a few pennies."

"You're welcome here, friend," Israel said, standing with Jenna by the Polley wagon.

"Thank you kindly, Sir. You mind if I join you for a nice bit of home-cooked stew or beans maybe? I ain't fussy and I'll pay with work—sharpen knives, fix a harness, you name it. The Heavenly Father made me a jack-of-all trades, 'cept He left out cookin'."

"You're welcome to eat with us, Mr. Harley B. Tucker, that is, if you like rice pudding, salt pork, and biscuits with gooseberry jam," Mrs. Polley said, smiling.

"Indeed I do, Madam," he said, tipping his hat.

"You'll have to wash up first sparin' the precious little water we have, and when you finish, you can milk the cow and help Harke water the oxen. Now be sparin', because Blue says we have a ways to go before we meet the Sweetwater." Mrs. Polley turned her back and went about her business.

When night closed around the lighted ring of wagons, Hannah and Jenna helped Zelda out of the wagon into the privacy of cool darkness. From where the three girls stood looking at camp, the community seemed carved out of nowhere, clustered into knots of little people around pinpoints of fire, looked insignificant and fragile under the big sky.

"I know that old man, Mr. Tucker. He comes to our settlement every now and then on his collectin' trips. He'll recognize me if he sees me," Zelda said.

"He won't see you," Hannah said, "We'll keep you hid."

"This hiding ain't goin' to do. I'm a-dying in that wagon, it's so hot. And the mosquitoes is eatin' me alive. I can't stand it. We've got to roll up the sides and back flaps or I'll perish in there. I got to have more water. I'm not goin' to make it. Oh, God! I think He's forsaken me. He wants me to burn up," Zelda's tears ran down her dirty face. "I hurt everywhere . . . all over . . . inside my heart."

Jenna and Hanna did not know what to say or how to comfort the poor girl, and so they remained silent and listened to her sobs. Jenna wondered what her own mother, Martha Jane, would have done in this situation. She did not recall her ever consoling anyone, or offering comfort or advice.

"You go on and let me rest here in the cool. I'll sneak into your wagon when I can."

The two girls walked back into the camp. Jenna looked for Israel. She wanted to sit next to him by the fire, lean into his shoulder, and feel his reassurance. She liked to hear what the men had to say. They spoke of important things—always about mileage, good feed and water, risks, hunting and farming, getting to Oregon, testing new trails and routes through the mountains. They told stories of dropping an elk with one shot, of possible Indian trouble, and how they would face the steep, rugged Rockies and hoist wagons up and down cliffs with ropes.

This time, however, all the attention was on Mr. Tucker.

"Well, as I say, I don't know much more than I just told you. A couple of months back, some of the Saints was workin' up in the hills building a sawmill for that Sutter fella, some sixty miles from his place, and they found gold in the river. I'm tellin' you the truth, they got pieces the size of your eyeball to prove it. The place is so full of gold, all you got to do is bend over and pick it up. Oh, you might have to scuff up a few stones in the shallows, but it's all over the place—like pickin' up eggs from under a good layin' hen and just fillin' a basket. Folks is gettin' mighty excited."

"If it's true," Blue said doubtfully. "You hear all kinds of crazy rumors out here in the wilderness—like my friend, Grizzly, who claims he found a cave with purple crystals hangin' from the ceiling—he says . . ."

"Mister, it's true, all right," Mr. Tucker interrupted. "My people don't lie. One of our flock rode clear back from California to Salt Lake to tell

Brigham Young, president of the Council of Twelve apostles, the head of
the true church, that he seen gold with his own eyes—that folks are already
leavin' San Francisco with picks and shovels and eyes as big as fryin' pans,
to see for theirselves."

"How come them Mexicans never found gold if it's a-lyin around plain
as can be?" Harke said.

"Now you're a smart fella. I figure they wasn't amongst the Chosen
Ones . . . bein' Catholic and all. *He* don't want the Mexicans in charge of
the gold. That's why they lost the war. Our Lord wants the right folks to
find the gold."

"Makes sense to me," one young man said.

"Papa," Jenna whispered to Israel, "is that old man crazy?"

"Maybe he is . . . and then again, maybe he ain't." Israel looked intently
at the old man. "If he ain't, maybe we're amongst the Chosen Ones way out
here in the wilderness."

Jenna looked at Israel. His eyes had that familiar dreamy look, bright as
a faraway star.

                              🍃 🍃 🍃

Jenna and Hannah managed to execute their plan hiding Zelda during
the day and supplying her with food and water, but under Emily Polley's
sharp eye, their plan quickly fell apart.

Emily walked over to Jenna's wagon and startled Jenna and Hannah
unwrapping a large square of gingerbread. "Well, I guess you girls have got
some company hiding in that wagon."

The girls looked blankly at Mrs. Polley and said nothing.

"It's no use pretending. I've been a-watchin' you and your suspicious
ways of late. That Mormon woman is a-hidin' in there, ain't she? That
is, unless you've got a jackrabbit for a pet." Emily threw back the closed
canvas.

"Please, Mama, don't say anything. She's hurtin' so bad. She's sick
and feverish and, well, we were about to call on you and Papa. She's been
beaten, Mama—real bad," Hannah said in a rush.

Emily's face darkened. "Let me take a look at her." She climbed into the wagon. "You girls know this is big trouble . . . big trouble. All right, young lady, come out and show yourself. Hurry up, now. Let me see your face and hear your explanation."

Zelda crawled out from her cramped space and began to sob.

"Land-o-Goshen, child! You've been sorely beaten! Why, that eye is festerin'." She reached over and felt her forehead. "And you've got fever. Jenna, go fetch me a bucket of water and a towel and some soap. Hannah, fetch me some lard and that bottle of camphor. Then go your way and leave me with this poor girl." When they had gone, Emily turned to Zelda and said, "Now I want to hear this story—the whole of it—and find out just what's a-goin' on here."

"Don't send me back, Missus. Lord in Heaven, be merciful! I'll die if I go back. Luke will kill me. I know it."

Emily gathered the trembling girl in her arms. "There, there, child. No one's a-goin' to hurt you now. We'll help you the best we can."

When she heard Zelda's story, anger swept over Emily. "We're near fifty miles from the ferry. They won't come after you now. As soon as you're fit, you're free to wander in this camp. The womenfolk will see to your care and you'll be in my charge. The company will decide what's best for you. For now, it looks like you're a-goin' to Oregon. There's Mormons up there, too, I suspect—unless you want to go to Salt Lake."

"The Mormons will send me back to Luke. I'm his wife. They won't allow me to leave him. Never! It's the will of God that I'm his wife," Zelda said through her sobs.

"Nonsense!" Mrs. Polley said emphatically. "What this husband, as you call him, done to you is against the laws of God!" Emily gently bathed Zelda in warm water, then rubbed camphor and lard on bruises that covered her entire body, arms, legs, and inner thighs.

"We needn't speak of these injuries to the menfolk. It ain't fittin' talk. And they needn't know that you've run away. I may have to tell a white lie or two, but the Lord will forgive me because He knows all anyways. Maybe I will tell Dr. Polley. Lord knows, he's seen some strange things in his ministering to the ailing."

Emily helped Zelda to dress. "Now you rest, child. I'm going to brew up some nerve tonic to calm you down."

Outside the wagon, Emily discovered Harley B. Tucker helping himself to the Daggett's water barrel. How long he had been standing there eavesdropping, Emily could not say, but it was clear he had heard an earful. Emily glared at him.

"I'll just be on my way now, Madam. I needed a bit of water to wash down that heaven-made gingerbread. I thank you for your kindness and pray the Lord will save you from any temptations and protect you on your journey." He smiled slyly, climbed into his wagon, and rattled down the trail singing,

> *"She gnawed her tongue before she died,*
> *She rolled, she groaned, she screamed and cried,*
> *'O must I burn for evermore*
> *Till thousand, thousand years are o'er?*
>
> *Young people, lest this be your case,*
> *O turn to God and trust His grace,*
> *Down on your knees for mercies cry,*
> *Lest you in sin, like Polly die."*

The next morning, Mrs. Polley quietly escorted Zelda around the camp, introducing her as the "lost" Mormon girl who, a few miles back, had wandered into their wagon train exhausted and fallen asleep in the Daggett's wagon. Emily mused what a shame it was to have missed the visit of "her people" who had come looking for her.

"Zelda would be obliged if we'd assist her to Oregon. She can't pay, but will cook and work for her food," Emily said to a group of emigrants packing up from the noon rest stop.

"She don't seem tetched to me," Israel said. "She's mighty banged up and pretty scared of something, though. Probably afraid of anyone outside her faith."

"Please, Papa, let her come with us," Jenna pleaded. "She can share my bed."

"Well, I guess. She's no bother. She can sleep in our wagon."

The company accepted Zelda, even without knowing the full story, and acted kindly toward her. Still, they talked in small groups about the bruises on her face and the infected eye and lip.

"I'd say she looks like she fell out of a tree or off a cliff if there was any about in these parts," Mrs. Butler said to Emily and some of the other women. The exchange of looks between the women spoke for them. They'd seen the signs of a hard-handed master somewhere before.

Mother Boyles, who sat nearby in her chair, made some unintelligible sounds that tangled up in her tongue. She clawed the air excitedly, trying to say something.

"Emily, I do believe your mother is improving. She's trying to tell us something, bless her old heart. I bet she wants more applesauce," Mrs. Butler said. "And look at the way she's waving her hands. She couldn't do that back in Kansas Territory. More applesauce, Mother Boyles?"

Mother Boyles stopped trying to speak and glared at Mrs. Butler.

The company officers met briefly to discuss Zelda's fate.

"Don't you worry, little lady," Blue said. "We'll get you back with your people as soon as possible. The Mormon Trail Cut-off is just beyond South Pass not many days from here. We aren't far behind that large company of Mormons that pulled out of Fort Kearney just before us. Maybe some pokey ones are laggin' behind or they're fixin' a broke wheel or the like, and we'll catch up with them at the pass. I'm just mighty sorry we didn't know your whereabouts when your people come lookin' for you and that Mr. Harley B. Tucker left not knowing one of his flock had befell a misfortune." Blue seemed pleased with his touch of eloquence.

Zelda lowered her eyes and said softly, "Thank you, you're most kind."

The next morning, before the emigrants had hitched up their wagons, a group of a dozen hard-riding men galloped into camp.

"Which one of you Missourians is in charge here?" the leader snarled. He was the same heavy-handed man who had come looking for the young girl. Both he and the horse were perspiring and covered with dust. The horse's mouth bubbled with blood and foamy saliva.

"I'm captain," Blue said, stepping forward.

"I'm Luke Willis, and I've come to take my wife home. Where is she?"

"There's no need to be testy about this, Mister," Blue said, his friendly expression vanishing quickly.

Luke Willis pulled the reins on the horse's mouth so tightly the horse reared, scattering the emigrants into a wider circle. "Zelda!" He shouted. "I know you're hiding. It won't do you no good. You're coming back to the settlement before you're corrupted by these Missourians."

"Now hold on here just a minute, Mister Willis," Blue said, grabbing the horse's bridle to keep him in control.

The emigrants fell silent. The men moved in closer.

"If you're hiding my wife, Mister, we're prepared to rip apart every wagon you've got to find her. I know she's here somewhere. Mr. Tucker seen her with his own eyes. He met up with us and said you were harboring my wife."

"Hold on, my friend. We've got no intention of keeping you from your wife. Somebody go inform Zelda her people are here to take her home," Blue said.

Mrs. Polley stepped forward carrying a heavy frying pan. "She don't want to go back to the settlement on account of this man beats her. You all seen her. Dr. Polley can vouch for me. He tended her festerin' lip."

Dr. Polley spoke up. "That's right. She says she was beaten by her husband here . . ."

Luke's horse reared again, the bit cutting farther into his tender mouth. "Zelda is *my* wife! She's an uncooperative member of the flock, a rebellious wife, and she's got sinful ways. I'm taking care of her and teaching her the ways of God and our faith. I never laid a hand on her. My men here can stand behind me on that. It's my duty to keep her in line."

"It's unlawful to beat your spouse," Dr. Polley said angrily.

"Whose law?" snapped Luke. "Your United States law? Well, I ain't in the United States. I left your law when I left Navoo. There ain't no law here except my law and Mormon law . . . and the Almighty's law! Your laws don't count out here, Mister. Search the wagons, men!"

The horses scattered in different directions. Zelda threw back the canvas flap of the Daggett's wagon.

"I ain't goin' back," she said, trying to show courage. She jumped down from the wagon.

"Get on the horse. Now!" Luke shouted, riding over to her. "God is going to punish you for this, Zelda. I'm only trying to protect you from yourself. Do as I say!"

"I ain't goin'!" Zelda cried. "Please, don't let them take me back. I'm beggin' you all," Zelda pleaded to the emigrants.

Mrs. Polley went over to Zelda and stood between her and Luke. When she heard Zelda's story, her face flushed with anger and her eyes, usually so loving to the world, narrowed into points of fire.

One by one, the women of the company surrounded Zelda and faced her husband.

Blue tried to cool down the tense situation. "We don't want trouble or to get mixed up in a family squabble. We're Christian folks windin' our way to the Pacific, but if you insist on makin' everybody mad, I expect we're up to the task of settling this here problem in a variety of ways." He turned to the men of the company. "Are we fixin' for a fight here, men, or not? I put it to you."

"She's his wife. He's come to take her back home. I can't see why we're stopping him from doing his job taking care of her," someone said.

The men nodded.

"It's their ways," another said.

"What's she going to do in Oregon, or California, or Salt Lake City?" Mr. Butler asked.

"She's his property. You can't argue with that," Mr. Edwards said.

"A woman alone ain't fit to take care of herself. She can't make decisions or work a farm. She just ain't strong enough. This poor girl needs her people," Mr. Doneley said.

Again the men nodded in agreement.

"Step aside," Luke said harshly. "Zelda, I'm taking you home. Now get on this horse!" The look in his eyes made the ladies shrink away. Zelda hung her head and sobbed in defeat.

"Did you tell them, little wife, you left your own son, Benjamin? He's been crying for his mother for ten days. Get up on this horse."

The women, suddenly disarmed by the new information, looked at Zelda blankly and shook their heads.

"You abandoned your own youngster?" Mrs. Butler asked, stepping aside.

The women parted.

Luke got off his horse and lifted Zelda onto the saddle. There was no fight in her. She slumped forward and covered her face in her hands. Luke dug his heels into the horse's flanks and rode quickly out of the camp.

Jenna and Hannah ran over to Mrs. Polley. The three of them huddled together and watched the riders' dust rise in the air and blow away in the morning breeze.

As the men started back to work, Faithful Squibb raised his Bible in the air. "There is no room in God's kingdom for an unfaithful wife and an unfit mother. Read your Bible, friends. It's all in the book . . . all in the Holy Scriptures. A woman's place is by her husband's side. 'Whither thou goest, I will go, and where you lodge, I will lodge; your people shall be my people, and your God my God'—Ruth, chapter one, verse sixteen. Are you listening, sinners?"

"Amen to that, Reverend," Mrs. Edwards shouted. "If you ask me, the problems with families is *bad bread*. A wife who don't care about her bread, don't care about her husband and children. It's *good* bread what keeps a husband out of the grog shop. Bread is the glue of the family. This little missy don't care about bread. She deserves a good thrashin'."

"Amen, Sister Edwards," Faithful said and continued to shout until Blue gave the signal to move out. Jenna and Hannah held each other and cried.

"It ain't fair!" Hannah sobbed, her pretty face contorted with anger.

"Oh, Hannah, I know that man is going to keep hurting her until she throws herself in the river."

"If it was me, I'd fell him with a hammer, or poke a pitchfork in his eyes!"

"Her poor baby! Do you think it's true she left him?" Jenna asked.

"What if it is! She knew she'd die if she stayed there. Someone else would care for her baby."

"But . . . *her own baby*? She must have been grieving awful for him. I don't know if I could ever leave my baby unless I was crazy with fear."

"Well, I could—if I had to," Hannah said, climbing into the wagon. "Come on, Jenna, ride with me and we'll make up some clover wreaths for our hair."

🌢 🌢 🌢

For days the emigrants suffered high winds and dust storms that tore all but the sturdiest canvas coverings off the wagons. Several men lost their good hats to the gusts. Mrs. Edward wailed when her black, silk bonnet, so carefully packed for church and funerals for the Far West, lifted out of the wagon into the air and flapped away like a buzzard.

At last, the company entered the Sweetwater Valley, a benign stretch of land renewing their flagging spirits despite its continual strong wind. With delight, the travelers met the Valley's clear, shallow river.

"The dearest little river I ever seen," Mrs. Butler exclaimed.

The grassy banks, warm in the sunshine, invited the emigrants to take off their heavy boots and wade in the cool, sandy bottom. "Seems like paradise," Mrs. Polley said as she eased her calloused feet into the water.

For some time the company had watched the outline of slate blue distant hills, elephant gray bluffs, and the large outcropping known as Independence Rock, so named by earlier fur traders who had celebrated their stopover on Independence Day. Like so many before them, they now stopped to set up camp and to scratch their names on the broad granite rock that loomed up from the prairie floor. They hoped it would record forever their frail existence, their moment on this earth.

Harke, Jenna, and Hannah climbed to the top of the broad expanse of rock and picked out a spot where they could carve their names together.

The day had begun with a cloudless sky, and they were so occupied in their task, they did not notice the dark storm clouds gathering in the west. The wind picked up and blew an army of tumbleweeds across the flat land. Prairie dogs hopped into their holes whenever a cloud cast a shadow and popped out again when the sunshine lighted their doorways. They seemed to know a shadow meant danger. Not so, the youngsters. When a crack of lightning flashed in the bruised underbelly of the clouds, Hannah shouted above the wind, "I'm going back! There's going to be a bad storm."

"Come on, Jenna. Hannah is right. Let's make a run for it," Harke said.

"Wait, Harke, I want to carve Solomon's and Mama's name next to mine."

"There ain't enough time. It will take too long, Jenna."

"Please, Harke; they almost made it this far."

"That storm is movin' too fast. We've got to go, Jenna." Harke's blond hair blew wildly across his face.

When Jenna looked at him with her penetrating blue eyes, he knew he would do as she asked. "All right, but let's just carve their initials—MJD '48 and SD '48. The clouds is a gatherin' into a funny shape, and I don't like the way the wind is behavin'."

"Put them right below mine, Harke . . . and maybe draw a heart, too."

The sky began to take on a yellowish hue; the air turned cold and the wind splattered large raindrops against the rock.

Harked worked as fast as he could.

"How come all the names are men? There aren't any girls' names except for Hannah's and mine," Jenna said.

"I don't know. The women were too busy cookin', I guess. Maybe it ain't fittin' for women to write their names in a showy way . . . kind of indecent. Anyways, it's kind of a man's thing to do. He puts his name there for the whole family," Harke explained.

Jenna looked puzzled. "What if you haven't got a family? What if you got just yourself and you're a girl?"

Harke ignored her questions and kept working. "There—it ain't carved very good, but we've got to get out off the top of this rock and return to camp. That lightning over yonder might just seek us out and fry us on the spot. *Now*, what are you scratchin' out?"

Jenna stood back and looked at her handiwork—a 'Z' for Zelda and an 'N' for Nettie.

Their job completed, Harke and Jenna ran toward the wagons, which were now drawn into a circle with their ponies and livestock inside.

The rain hurtled down in large drops as the emigrants grabbed food and blankets and shoved them under the wagons or carried valued items inside with them inside. There wasn't enough room for everyone. Some unfortunate souls had to find refuge where they could. All of them looked at the swollen clouds hoping a tornado wouldn't suddenly drop down and race toward their encampment.

Blue galloped into the circle shouting, "This looks like a twister, folks! Fasten down what you can, and if you see that old funnel drop, lie flat under your wagon, hang onto the wheels, and say your prayers. Somebody help Dr. Polley lift Mother Boyles out of the wagon. There's some funny clouds over yonder ready to spiral down. The sky is yeller, so we're goin' to get hail for sure."

Just then a crack of lightning ripped straight down to the ground, making everyone's skin tingle and the livestock bunch together, bellowing their displeasure. The men in India rubber coats and oilcloth ponchos quickly tied the wagon flaps and secured what they could from the wind.

Suddenly, the rain turned to balls of hail the size of walnuts hitting the ground in thunderous fury. It pelted the metal buckets and iron pots and ripped holes in the wagon tops. The frightened animals reared and screamed above the deafening roar and ran frantically inside the enclosure of wagons, looking for an escape from the painful balls hitting their backs and heads, searing their flesh, and tearing at their eyeballs.

Israel shouted to Blue, "Those animals are going to make a break for it . . . right through one of our wagons!

No sooner had he spoken than two beasts headed right for the Doneleys' wagon. Israel waved his hat and tried to shout the animals back. Their eyes white with terror, the oxen threw their horned heads into the air and circled Israel. He felt the blow of one beast with its iron muscles and staggered backward.

Lightning split the sky and the pair of animals stampeded through the circle of wagons, turning the Doneleys' wagon on its side and crushing the wagon tongue into splinters of wood.

The animals charged into the storm, running wildly until, somehow, they understood there was no escape, no safety, and stopped in sight of the wagons. They hung their heads as the storm beat them like a cruel master.

Blue and some of the other men rushed to the overturned wagon. The Doneleys weren't hurt, only frightened. Mrs. Doneley wailed and shouted through her tears, "Mr. Doneley, I'm sick to death of this venture! It's taken my only child and it's going to kill us both. This is the Devil's land!" She stood in the open, her once-starched bonnet flapping against her cheeks like wet leaves, and cried, "God, take me home!" The hail raised welts on her upturned face as she wept openly.

Israel put his coat over Mrs. Doneley's shoulders. "Come now, Ma'am, let me help you back into your wagon. It's upright now and things just got tumbled around a bit. You're all right, that's what's important. This storm won't keep up much longer and it looks like it's a-movin' east, twister and all. These summer storms pass right over in no time at all."

Mrs. Doneley looked up. "Why, Mr. Daggett, you're drenched in blood! Look at your jacket. You've been cut bad somewhere. There! On your neck . . . it's pumpin' blood! You better get out of the storm and sit down . . . and stop that bleeding."

Israel wadded up his handkerchief and pressed it to his neck. "One of them oxen tossed his head when he charged and caught me right under my jaw with the point of his horn. I'll get Dr. Polley to stop the bleedin' and fix me up."

While the emigrants waited out the storm, Israel went to Dr. Polley's wagon.

"It's deep, Israel. That horn caught you in a bad place—right in the neck and up under the jaw. It's a miracle it didn't fracture the bone or pierce the jugular. I'm not worried about the bleeding as much as infection settin' in. We're going to have to keep the swelling down so's is won't close up your throat. You best lie flat for the next couple of days. We'll douse it real good now with brandy and lime water, then Mrs. Polley will help me put a hot pitch and turpentine compress on it. Then we'll just have to keep an eye on it. The rest is up to the healing ways of the body and to God."

Israel showed little concern for himself but worried about all the work with the animals and the successful crossing of the Continental Divide at South Pass. "Jenn can do the driving until it gets too rough," he said. "She's pretty confident."

"I'll drive," Harke said.

"Your pa needs you to drive your own wagon, Harke. I'm much obliged, though."

"Emily handles a team as good as I do," Dr. Polley said. "Harke is right to be your driver. Now that's settled. You take care of yourself and try not to tax your jaw by chewing. Eat soft food—oatmeal, rhubarb, mashed potatoes, milk pudding, and the like."

When Israel left, Dr. Polley looked at Emily. "I don't like the looks of the hole . . . no sir, not one bit."

FOUR

THE COMPANY ENCAMPED in a green valley by the Sweetwater River. The emigrants had heard the large outcropping, Devil's Gate, would protect them from the endless wind; but no one had warned them about the mosquitoes.

The Indians believed a hideous horned beast had crashed through the wall of rocks, leaving a narrow passageway for the meandering river. For them it was a place of superstition and fear; for the emigrants it was an oasis—a gentle, shallow, clear stream so inviting they decided to remain for a few days.

The oxen could fatten on the lush grass which lay close to the river banks; the men could soak their wagon wheels and swell them to fit the metal rims that had loosened in the dry air; and they could cut and bind the grass to stockpile for the dreaded, barren cutoff to the Green River. The women could wash in clean water.

Everyone wanted to bathe. The relentless wind across the Great Plains had blown dirt and dust deep into the pores of their skin and scalp. It would take many scrubbings to bring the flesh back to its normal pinkness.

Emily Polley went from wagon to wagon. "Ladies and children, we're all a-goin' to bathe in the river. Dr. Polley says it's good for the body and soul and advises us to drop our shyness and go as a group. The sun is warm and the rocks is perfect shelter from the wind. First, we women are a-bathin', and then the menfolk. While they bathe, we can fix a meal they won't forget. We've got two antelope to carve and a mess of chokecherries to make up jam for a lardy cake. We won't have much luxury after leaving Devil's Gate. Better clean up now."

The idea of really bathing, soaping up, and washing the hair appealed to everyone. The delighted children shouted and clapped their hands. In no time, the women gathered at a lovely spot where the water was slow, the riverbed shallow and sandy, and the grass warm and full of dainty wildflowers.

They laughed and chatted as they undressed by the river's edge. They overcame their shyness at being nearly naked and vulnerable and squealed happily at the first shock of cold water on their sore feet. The children, unafraid to submerge their whole bodies, rolled and splashed as naturally as baby cubs, kicking, jumping, and dunking each other. Even the ladies briefly joined in the games, then waded into deeper water to soak tired muscles and inflamed insect bites.

Jenna thought Mrs. Edwards, usually so stiff and stern, had become rather sociable and had changed her frown to a slight smile. Only Cora Squibb refused to bathe with the women, claiming it was a disgrace to be without clothes—indecent, "ungodly, the indulgence of heathens," she had said.

Mother Boyles sat in her chair staring at the undressed women and children playing in the water.

"Maybe Grandma would like to bathe, too?" Hannah teased.

"That's a splendid idea!" Emily exclaimed.

Hannah and Jenna broke into giggles imagining Mother Boyles with her boots off and her white, naked feet dangling in the water. Mother Boyles' eyes were wide with fear as the women carried her to the water's edge and began unlacing her heavy boots. She waved her arms and clearly formed the word "No!"

"We ain't a-goin' to throw you in the water, Mother. Relax. You'll enjoy the foot bath . . . just like at home." The ladies removed her boots and let the cold water play with her feet. She looked terrified.

"She thinks we're goin' to drown her." Hannah laughed, deliberately dripping water drops off her fingertips down her grandmother's nose. "Doesn't that feel good, Grandma?" she teased.

"That's enough, Hannah. You can see she's plumb scared. We got to be gentle with the poor old thing," Emily said, dabbing her mother's wet face.

"Come on, Jenna. I'll soap your back, then you can soap mine. Then, let's wash our hair and fix it up real pretty." Hannah leaned close to Jenna and whispered, "Mr. LaGrange says he likes my curls. When no one's a-lookin', he nuzzles his nose right into them like a hungry pup."

The ladies began soaping themselves and the children using the soft sand or a smooth stone as a gentle scrubber. Soon the shivering children glowed anew like pink salamanders. The mothers dried them with towels and dressed them in clean clothes while their soiled ones lay soaking. Mother Boyles finally cracked a smile when Emily slipped clean wool socks over her bony feet.

The emigrants had a renewed sense of well-being. Their high spirits and happiness lasted well into the night with singing, dancing, and storytelling.

Israel sat near the campfire unable to play his harmonica. His swollen neck and jaw were wrapped in a clumsy compress. Still, he enjoyed Blue's fiddle playing and watched his little girl, Jenna, delight in the dancing and merrymaking. For the first time in a long while, he indulged in thinking of Solomon and Martha Jane . . . of all the loss, all the pain of the passage west. He fought the idea that their deaths somehow might have been his fault. Maybe he'd been too insensitive to see that Martha Jane was not strong enough to take on such a journey, not steady, not able to leave her kin.

He looked at Jenna dancing a do-si-do with Harke.

She don't look anything like Martha Jane. She's going to be tall and proud like my own mother, and she's got those large, clear, blue eyes wide apart and a high, fine brow like my Norwegian grandmother. One day she'll be a handsome, strong woman with wide shoulders, a stout bust, and a slim frame. She'll be handsome, all right.

Israel suddenly felt tired and slipped away into his tent. Lying in his bed, he felt his heart throbbing in his neck and clamped his teeth tightly to shift the pain. It was getting hard to swallow, even the soft food.

🌱 🌱 🌱

The trail to South Pass was a corridor of sadness: abandoned wagons, broken wheels and axles, animal skeletons, and gas-bloated beasts decomposing belly-up, their legs sticking strangely in the air. The stench was so strong, the emigrants covered their noses when they passed the decaying animals.

The landscape would have been completely tedious except for low-lying mountains rising in the distance. The surrounding land provided no relief from relentless wind—strong gusts that carried the emigrant's voices from their mouths, making conversation seem futile. The oxen, too exhausted to bellow, pulled steadily upward across the barren landscape. South Pass lay in the distance, a broad expanse marking the halfway point of the journey.

Israel lay in the wagon with his eyes closed, his body moving to the rhythmic trod of the animals. Harke sat next to Jenna as she drove the wagon. Together they watched the landscape change from what Jenna thought looked like headless camels lying down, to melting brown sugar lumps. To pass the time, they played the cloud game—figuring out shapes of animals, ships, birds, stampeding buffalo, Indians with feathers. They watched a bumpy, bearded old man cloud until his nose split away, then changed him into a parrot smoking a pipe. Always, legless sheep scampered across the wide, blue sky.

"I think we've reached the summit, Jenna," Harke said excitedly. "Wake your papa! He'll want to see the top."

The wagons stopped. The emigrants shaded their eyes to look down into the most barren land they had ever seen—a brown desert where nothing seemed to grow but scarce clumps of sagebrush.

"Jenn, my girl, we're almost there. We've made it to the other side of the world. Just think of it!" Israel whispered in a hoarse voice. Jenna could tell it was too hard for him to talk, but not just because of his injury. His emotions seemed to choke him. She watched his eyes fill with tears and his lips mutter a silent thought before he returned to the wagon to rest.

"We're takin' Sublettes Cutoff, bypassin' Fort Bridger as we agreed when we started this here journey." Blue shouted above the wind. "Now, friends, this next fifty miles will be torture for everyone—man and beast. It's what I expect Hell is all about—fire and brimstone creepin' up through the ground, searin' your feet, scaldin' your eyeballs, burnin' your lungs, and heat devils dancin' all around. Take note, Reverend Squibb. It might give you some ideas. There's no mercy for a man alone.

The vultures will follow us, circling overhead just waiting for an ox to stumble. There's no water, only what we carry, and no river until we meet the Green. Use it sparin'. We'll save ourselves a week by the cutoff. Many folks have already took it before us . . . but no foolin' around." Blue paused for effect. "When we meet the glory of the Green, we'll follow it north, pick up Fontanelle Creek, the Bear, and then on into Fort Hall, where as you all know, I'll be a-partin' company with you. You'll be taken on to Oregon by a fur trapper friend of mine, Mr. Henri Marchand. We call him 'Ornery' 'cause that's the way he says his name. The fact is, he's a fine fella and a good scout and will carry you safely to your destination. I'm a-goin' to California with whoever is a-waitin' us there."

The wind blew away his words.

The emigrants climbed back into their wagons anxious to start the arduous crossing.

On the third morning, Jenna awakened before Israel and walked a short distance from the encircled wagons. The air was dry and cold, the sky crispy clear. She breathed in the whole of this new world and felt a joy, a newness she couldn't explain. She wondered if this was how the Israelites felt in their desert, waiting for Moses. She wondered if the dry cells that sloughed off her skin were like little seeds that would someday grow in this waterless country. She was sure they would sprout living things, because she loved the land. To Jenna, it was not Hell, but Heaven.

When Israel awakened, he could barely speak. His face was badly swollen and a deep red color reached to his temples. Infection had developed in spite of careful attention and daily compresses.

"Jenn, come here, girl," he whispered. "I got to tell you something. Last night I woke up hearin' someone a-callin' to me. I thought it was you, so I sat up. Outside, way off yonder, I seen Solomon and Martha Jane as clear as can be . . . standin' right there."

Jenna gasped. "Mama? Solomon? Oh, Papa!"

"I can't explain it, girl, but they were there . . . a-callin' for me, kind of blowin' in the wind and reachin' out. Martha Jane's beautiful, long, auburn hair was a-blowin' every which way, wild like and free. And Jenn, she was smilin' like when she was young and not troubled."

"And what about Solomon? What was he doing, papa? Was he walking around in your big boots making us all laugh?"

"He was laughin', clownin'. He was real happy. I think they need me with them, Jenn."

Jenna threw herself down on Israel's chest. "No, you're not leaving me, Papa! You can't. I need you, too—more than anyone. We've got to go to the Far West, Papa, to Oregon to farm. You *can't* go. *Please* . . . Oh, please, Papa."

Israel patted Jenna's shoulder. "If I do go, Jenn, you'll find your own way. You've got a road to follow. You're proud and strong like my people. We never give up . . . never, no matter how tough it gets. There's always an answer, always a way. You gotta ask the Lord what to do, then listen. The problem with most folks is they don't listen."

Israel died before nightfall. Many had expected his death and whispered about it. Whenever they gathered in small groups, they spoke of the terrible sadness in the Daggett family. Now that their worst fears were realized, the women rushed to Jenna, crying openly into their aprons, taking turns holding her, rocking her, and trying to fill the horrible moments of suffering with mother love and deep caring.

Everyone gave what comfort he could. All were so deeply grieved that a gloom pervaded the wagon train. Israel's passing was like a personal death to everyone. To Jenna, it seemed as if her joy had died with Israel. She wondered if she would ever be happy again.

She sat with the women, unable to cry more, to eat, sleep, or comprehend the reality of Israel's death. She sipped skullcap tea to calm her shaking and quiet her shattered spirit.

"Poor little orphan. That's what you are now, Jenna," Mrs. Edwards said. "Imagine me fearin' one of my eight youngsters could meet our Maker any day . . . and we seem to have nothing but good fortune. The Daggetts have had the worst possible luck."

"I grieve for my Nettie . . . my lamb. I know the sting of death, but still we're all a family. Still together. Poor Jenna, poor, lone child—she's got no one," Mrs. Butler said, starting to cry all over again.

Emily placed her fleshy arm around Jenna's shoulders.

"Your papa has crossed over to the other side of the veil. He ain't far off. I suspect he's close enough to know what's a-goin' on right now, feelin' mighty good, maybe a-playin' a harmonica for some of God's angels. The Lord has somethin' special for Israel to do, that's certain. He knows what He's a-doin'."

"That's rubbish, Mrs. Polley. It ain't our privilege to know when or why the Lord decides to call up a sinner," Cora Squibb said.

Jenna wanted to argue that her papa was not a sinner, but said nothing and sipped her tea. She preferred to think about the word "orphan" for that was what she was. Who would take care of her now? What would happen to her? Would they send her back to Aunt Lizzie in Sapling Grove? She was too exhausted to think further and fell asleep with her head on Emily Polley's lap.

The ladies dressed Israel's body in his Sunday clothes, but when Jenna looked at him, she asked if he could be buried in his leather coat. "He doesn't look quite right. He'd be more comfortable in his leather coat," she said, remembering her papa looking strained sitting on hard, wooden pews on hot, summer Sundays.

"The black suit is more . . . formal—more like a regular corpse," Mrs. Butler said.

"Leave it be, Jenna. We'll lay the coat over him if you like," Mrs. Polley said, putting her arm around her shoulders.

"Can I keep his leather hat?" Jenna asked, hugging it to her chest.

"Of course, child. Now come with me and show me the spot where you want the grave. The men are a-waitin' to start digging."

Blue approached. "Miss Daggett, I'm sorely sorry about Israel. He was a good friend, a fine man. I wish we could linger and pay more respects, but we have to move out soon as possible. Time is an enemy out here . . . the water and all. You understand, don't you?"

"Yes, Sir," Jenna said softly.

"You're a brave girl. We won't let you down. The company has had a meetin' and we've figured out a good plan for you. I'll talk to you after the burial."

Jenna picked a spot close to a large clump of late-blooming sage, the only flowers around. "It smells nice here. Papa always liked sage tea and Mama used it in sachets sometimes," Jenna said. "Please, Blue, dig it deep." Jenna turned away quickly.

"Okay, men, you heard the little lady. Go to work."

After the ceremony, Blue called a meeting of the entire wagon train. He outlined Jenna's fate. They would hold an auction of the Daggett's belongings—from soup kettles to clothes, hammers, shovels, Israel's rifle, and food, such as flour and a side of bacon and what coffee was left. They would auction off two oxen teams. Jenna could keep Honey, her pony, a small trunk of clothing, and her own bedding. What didn't sell would remain on the dry plains along with the Daggett's wagon. "No sense makin' the poor animals pull a useless item. We'll need spare ox teams to make the crossing," Blue said.

Blue turned to Jenna. "Now, the company here decided you should be under the guardianship of the good Reverend Faithful Squibb and his wife Cora. They're a childless couple longing to help a poor, misfortunate orphan. The Reverend hisself volunteered the idea, sayin' he'd treat you as his very own daughter, seein' you get safely to Oregon and then back to your people in Missouri. All they want is a few dollars for your board and to take the milk cow for their labor." Blue turned to the Squibbs. "We thank you, Reverend, for your good works."

The emigrants clapped and nodded approval.

Jenna gasped. "No! No! I'm going with the Polleys." She ran over to Emily, who looked stricken.

Emily embraced Jenna. "Dr. Polley and I been arguin' for you, Jenna, but the company says we're too crowded, too overloaded as it is. They voted us down and as you know, when we left Missouri, we agreed to abide by the company's decision. I'm heartsick, child. Nothing seems fair. But the Squibbs is good people and will look out for you." She hugged Jenna with her fleshy arms and they cried together.

Harke took Jenna's hand. "It won't be forever, Jenna. Once we get to Oregon, I'll take care of you myself. I promise. You can live with us. For the rest of the journey, I'll ride with you as much as I can. It won't be so bad." Harke gently wiped Jenna's tears with his soiled hands. He looked deep into her eyes, then quite unexpectedly put his hands around her small face and kissed her on the forehead. The emigrants said their final goodbyes to Israel Daggett and climbed into their wagons.

It was a somber group rolling westward. Blue helped Jenna into the Squibbs' wagon, loaded her trunk, and tied Honey to the back. Jenna held the last of her family on her lap, all that she held dear—Martha Jane's shell box with Solomon's hair and fingernails, Nettie's locket, and now, Israel's leather hat and harmonica. She placed the cold metal to her cheek and stared out the back of the wagon at the lonely grave, a mound of stones barely a bump in the landscape. Soon it disappeared completely. After a time, Jenna turned to look at the strange backs of Reverend and Cora Squibb—two strangers hunched together like black vultures . . . waiting. Faithful Squibb began to recite . . .

"'Verily I say unto you, except ye be converted, and become as a little child, ye shall not enter into the Kingdom of Heaven . . . and whosoever shall receive one such little child in my name receiveth me. But whoso shall offend one of these little ones which believe in me, it were better for him that a millstone were hanged about his neck, and that he were drowned in the depth of the sea . . . if thy hand or thy foot offend thee, cut them off . . . if thine eye offend thee, pluck it out . . . it is better for thee to enter into life with one eye, rather than having two eyes to be cast into hell fire.' Matthew eighteen."

"Amen," Cora added.

Jenna felt a peculiar coldness tightening around her body like icy bands. She shivered and shivered and wondered if she'd ever be warm again.

🍃 🍃 🍃

The emigrants were overjoyed to look down from the high plateau at the Green River, a winding, silver ribbon.

"A grand sight," Emily said.

"God's deliverance," Faithful shouted.

A few covered wagons, some hand carts, and a cluster of Indian tepees dotted the grassy banks. "Shoshone," Blue said. "They is friendly enough so far, but don't turn your back."

Blue advised everyone to unhitch their teams quickly, for the suffering animals soon would smell water and were certain to stampede down the steep slopes, overturning wagons and overrunning anything in their way.

All the animals ran to the river, some stumbling down the deep, sandy slopes. The emigrants waited while the animals cooled their painful hooves and quenched their thirst in the river before yoking them back up to carry them and the wagons down to the water. They had lost a number of animals in the last fifty miles. One family had lost two mules from exhaustion and a pony from a lightening strike. It was time to think more considerately about the endurance of the animals.

For the remainder of the trip, the trail would be steep and even more difficult than before. Only the toughest and most seasoned travelers would arrive at their destination. The weak, both man and beast, would not survive, and their bones would mark the way west.

Jenna did not like traveling with the Squibbs and chose to ride Honey or walk rather than listen to Faithful recite scripture or sing hymns off-key.

Cora had insisted on hiring one of the young men traveling in the company to load and unload the wagons, feed the stock, hitch the oxen, do repairs, fetch water, and do part of the cooking. Still, she found plenty for Jenna to do to earn her way, including setting up their sleeping tent, cooking, cleaning, washing clothes, and gathering fuel—wood, shrubs, or dried dung.

Faithful and Cora spent their time earnestly trying to convert the loose bands of Shoshone Indians who wandered into their camps to trade fresh fish for bread, calico, crackers, sugar, or tobacco. While some Indians distracted the bargainers, others stole a hammer, a spoon, a mirror, a comb—whatever they could find. One Warrior, who wore a lady's discarded hoop skirt, stole a bolt of calico and Cora's prized bees wax candles.

Although Jenna ate her portion of food, the Squibbs denied her extras, such as a wedge of cheese, a piece of pie, or a mug of hot coffee with milk and sugar. Coffee was precious and had to last another thousand miles.

One morning, in the valley of the Bear River, where an abundance of large trout shimmered in the clear stream, Faithful approached Jenna to go fishing with him.

"We need never barter with heathens, Jenna. It's like paying the Devil. We'll catch our own fish."

"I can't go fishing with you, Reverend Squibb." Jenna turned away as if to leave.

"Come back here this instant!" Cora demanded. "The Reverend is a-speakin' to you. Didn't your mother teach you manners? You think you can just turn your back on a man of God?"

Jenna's face burned red with anger. How dare Cora Squibb speak to her of her mother! Martha Jane had taught her manners if nothing else.

"I promised Hannah I'd help her mend the holes in the Polley's wagon top," Jenna said.

"Do as I say, Little Miss Prideful. And don't think you can talk back in this wagon," Cora said with a scowl.

"Come along, Jenna. Follow me." Faithful Squibb nodded to Cora, and together they smiled at their ability to manage one of their flock.

Jenna hated their smugness and constant self-congratulation at their ability to manage an undisciplined child.

"We'll walk along the river until I find the right fishing hole. I've brought some cheese and our daily bread for our lunch, a nice repast and a little time with the Lord. Come, girl, and quit looking so solemn. Ain't we been friends, you and me?"

Jenna sighed and followed Faithful down to the river and along the banks so thick with dogwood and willows they nearly hid the river. He took her a long distance from the wagon train.

As they walked, Faithful said, "The Lord provides for us, Jenna . . . our needs, our bounty. Do you thank the Lord every day for His blessings, Jenna?"

"I try, Sir."

"Do you sing praises to the Lord and ask that He grant pleasures through uprightness?"

"Yes Sir . . . I think so."

"Speak up! I can't hear your answers. Do you thank God for His temple?"

"Yes, Sir," Jenna answered loudly.

"Do you know what His temple is? No, you don't. It is your body . . . my body . . . Christ's body . . . a holy thing . . . a temple."

Jenna didn't answer. She didn't understand.

"Do you know what plagues a woman's body? I'm askin' you, Jenna, and you ain't a-listen'! You ain't listenin'. What did I just say to you?"

"I don't know. I guess I wasn't paying no mind, Sir," Jenna stammered.

Faithful pulled aside some thick bushes and led Jenna to an enclosed grassy slope by the river. He laid down his pole and the lunch sack and took off his hat and coat. "Do you read your Bible regular, girl?"

"Yes, Sir—that is, when I can. I try, but sometimes I can't get to it. I will, though, once I get to Oregon. And I pray everyday . . . for Mama and Papa and Solomon . . . and Nettie." Jenna squatted by the river and cupped the cool water in her palms.

"Prayin' ain't enough. You got to show the Lord that you mean it. You got to do righteous things to *show* God you're good. Now you're growing up fast, Jenna. Soon you'll be off marryin' some wicked boy. God or the Devil will follow you all the days of your life."

Jenna said nothing. She picked up a handful of small rounded stones and let the water slip through her fingers.

"Do you know what an issue of blood is?"

Jenna did not like the conversation, but she felt she had to answer the Reverend's questions.

"Yes, Sir. I think so."

"It is a plague, because of the evil ways of women. Didn't your mother teach you nothing?"

Jenna didn't answer.

"I'm talking to you," he said, raising his voice. "Have you had an issue of blood?"

Jenna flushed. "No, Sir."

Faithful smiled. "Then it ain't too late to rid yourself of the sin of it. You remember in the Bible how the woman came to Jesus with an issue of blood for twelve years? She was full of sin and God punished her with the plague of it for twelve long years," he said, taking off his sour-smelling shirt and laying it carefully on the grass beside him.

Jenna kept her eyes down and pretended to be interested only in the rocks. She was embarrassed at seeing his loose, white flesh and hairy nipples. Surely it was wrong to look at a preacher's nakedness.

"I'm going to help you rid yourself of the evil of that plague before it starts. The woman touched Jesus' hem and she was cured of sin. I'm going to let you touch my shirt. Go on, don't be afraid. I'm a holy man, too. I got the power."

"I don't want to. I want to go back to camp now."

Faithful took her forcefully by the wrist. "I'm going to show you the power of God. You're going to know my power, feel my power, taste my power."

With his other hand, he pulled his erection from his trousers. "See here, Jenna." His eyes blazed. "This here is the holy power of God . . . before you. Kneel down."

Jenna tried to pull away. "No! You let go of me!"

Faithful grabbed a handful of hair at the back of her head and began forcing her face down on him.

Suddenly, Jenna and Faithful heard a muffled chorus of laughter coming from behind the bushes. He let go of her and quickly covered himself.

Whoever was on the other side of the bushes remained silent, but the branches quivered and twigs crackled underfoot. The giggles began again. Faithful appeared to be too stunned to move.

They heard more whispering and then the bushes parted. Four Indian women carrying leaves and willow branches emerged. Jenna didn't know how long they had been watching, but it was clear they understood Faithful's intent, along with Jenna's struggle and her helplessness.

Three of the women surrounded Faithful, talking and giggling among themselves. The fourth woman, who carried a papoose, came over to Jenna and said something in a low, soft voice. Her eyes were deep and sad, her movements slow and graceful. While the other women looked at Faithful and touched his white skin, the other one laid down her bundle of willow and sumac branches and began touching Jenna's bonnet that was tied around her neck. Still talking softly, she removed the bonnet. It now belonged to her. The other women, still laughing playfully, picked up Faithful's shirt, sniffed it, made terrible faces, and placed it in the water to wash it out. It now belonged to them.

Jenna turned and ran back to camp, leaving the cowering Faithful to his own fate and with the problem of explaining to Cora how he had lost his shirt on a morning of fishing.

When Jenna caught sight of the wagons, she stopped to catch her breath and tried to comprehend what had just happened to her. She knew she had been vulgarly approached by the Reverend Faithful Squibb, that what he had done and what he was trying to do before he had been interrupted by the Indian women was against every law she had ever been taught. She felt sick and dirty. Surely she was so full of sin, herself, she had caused this horror.

She wondered if maybe Faithful was really trying to show a way to God through Jesus. After all, he couldn't possibly say all those things about God and love and heaven without believing. Maybe all women went through a similar introduction to conversion, to adulthood. She would have to think about it. She knew one thing for certain. She would never be alone with him and would never tell anyone—ever—about the shameful experience. She knew she carried the burden of a terrible secret about Faithful Squibb, whom everyone seemed to trust. When she finally composed herself, she sought Emily Polley and hovered around her until bedtime.

Before the emigrants left the next morning, the soft-spoken Indian woman who had taken Jenna's bonnet came shyly up to her in the camp. They stood looking at each other for a moment. The woman spoke to her in a quiet, lilting way and smiled slightly. There was something gentle and comforting about this woman, a depth in her black eyes that dwelt in a place of understanding. For a fleeting moment, Jenna felt a strange bond with her, an unexplained love, a gratitude. She knew Jenna's terrible secret, but her beautiful eyes showed no judgment.

The woman, dressed in soft doeskin designed in bright bead florets, radiated the warmth of sunlight, as if she had absorbed the very sun itself. The air around her gave off an aroma of smoke, wet woods, juniper, and sage. Jenna wondered if this woman was not an angel, someone "sent" to ease her pain, to cleanse her.

The woman took Jenna's hand and gave her a small leather pouch covered with bright beads. She smiled and walked toward the river. Jenna knew she had received a special gift, something she could hang on to. She put it among her treasures in Martha Jane's shell box.

Jenna had been saved once, but not for good. The next night, and for several nights thereafter, the Reverend Faithful Squibb climbed into the wagon where Jenna slept and thrust his swollen anger into her. He covered her mouth to silence her and moved on her with such violence that she lay awake for hours trembling and hearing his words over and over: "You are a fornicator, a blasphemer against God, full of wicked imaginings. If you bear false witness that speaketh lies and soweth discord among the brethren . . . thy tongue shall be cut out, thy eyeballs plucked from thy face and sucked on by Satan. They that hate me . . . love death."

Jenna had never heard the word rape. In the darkness of the wagon, helpless under the weight of a man, she tried to detach herself, to float away somewhere else, pretend she was a cloud or the river. She could not move and was too afraid to resist. His large rough hand over her mouth, pressing her head awkwardly into the mattress, felt like a giant spider trying to suffocate her. She would squeeze her eyes tightly, hold her breath, and endure the painful humiliation until Faithful's grunting and rutting subsided. The putrid smell of rotting teeth and soiled underwear and sweat lingered in the wagon long after Faithful left, as did his warning—"Say one word about this, and I'll wring your neck. No one is going to believe a slut like you anyways."

Jenna would lie awake for a long time sobbing and waiting for the painful sensation between her legs to ease. The air around her still carried Faithful's weight; it loomed over her like a hideous monster. Sometimes she pretended it was only a dream, something to be forgotten by morning, a night terror that would vanish with the light, the new day, the sun and familiarity. She could look again at her own hands and feet, feel her own cheeks and lips, see her familiar dusty boots. This was her reality, not the night. And, too, there was an angel—she had seen her—a lovely Indian woman full of light who knew her pain and told her with her eyes that she was still a beloved child of God, a day child that could never be destroyed.

Jenna knew the women dismissed her paleness, saying it was due to her great loss of family. She overheard Mrs. Polley say, "Of course the poor thing can't eat. She's a-sufferin' more than any child should," Mrs. Polley said. "I'll fix her up a vinegar and sugar tea to kind of spruce up her appetite. She don't eat as much as a sparrow. I hate to see her so withdrawn. It will take a long time to heal that little soul."

Jenna rode Honey into Fort Hall alongside Blue. The next day he would take the California Trail to Sutter's Fort, and she would probably never see him again. He had been a good friend, very kind to her, especially since Israel's death.

"I wish you weren't leaving us, Blue . . . going to California and all," Jenna said.

"Old Ornery will take care of you, Miss Daggett," Blue said, smiling at the compliment.

"Can I go with you, Blue? I won't be any trouble. I can cook and drive a team. I can do your washing and mending. I'll even teach you how to read."

Blue threw back his head and laughed, then spit a cheekful of black tobacco juice from his mouth. "I don't need no learnin' at my age, but thank you for your kind offer just the same." He chuckled again.

They rode awhile in silence until Jenna looked earnestly at him and said,

"Why can't I go with you? I don't want to go to Oregon. I've got no people, except Aunt Lizzie. You can send me back to Sapling Grove just as easy as Reverend Squibb."

"There's nothing there at Sutter's Fort for little girls. Hardly any females, and those that is ain't fit company. And besides, the road to California is just too durn tough. I ain't equipped to take a child. You know why they call me Blue?"

"No, how come?"

"Cause one trip back in '45 I started too late on crossing them treacherous mountains and I got caught in the Sierras in a snowstorm, a mighty blizzard that folks still talk about. I nearly froze to death, right in my saddle. When some trappers come upon my body sittin' upright stiff as a starched porcupine, I was the color blue. Well, they thawed me out, fed me hot coffee and the like . . . and called me Blue. It stuck."

Jenna laughed. "What's your *real* name?"

Blue's expression changed. "It ain't important; Blue does me fine." He spat again.

"The point is, them Sierras is a rough go. Some people just can't make it. I don't want to bury no little girl up there in the snow . . . a little girl what ain't kin. You just can't go, Jenna. It ain't fittin'."

"Please, Blue," Jenna begged.

"No, girl. I'm sorry. I owe it to your papa to do what's right. It ain't right you goin' to California with me. There's no use talkin' further on it."

🍃 🍃 🍃

"Hannah, I want to tell you a secret," Jenna said the last evening before the company split into two wagon trains. "Come with me."

The two girls slipped away from the campfire and the singing, into the shadows.

"I'm not going to Oregon, Hannah. You mustn't tell. I'm running away. I can't stay with the Squibbs any longer. I just can't," Jenna said.

"He sure got dirty teeth," Hannah said. "But you ain't really goin', are you?"

"I'm going to follow Blue tomorrow morning; I'll ride Honey just out of sight. No one will miss me until the rest stop in late morning. When they discover I'm gone, you can tell them it won't do any good comin' to get me. I won't go back . . . not for anything. Tell your family goodbye and that they've been real good people. I'll never forget them—never."

Hannah started to cry. "I'll tell them I saw you fall in the river and drown . . . or that some Indians kidnaped you."

"No, just tell them the truth. I'm not goin' to go to Oregon with the Squibbs. I'll die first." She reached over and hugged Hannah.

"Since you're a-leavin', I'll tell you *my* secret. No one knows, not even Mama. I'm a-carryin' a baby inside, eight or nine weeks now I figure. It's Brian LaGrange's baby. He says he's a-comin' to Oregon to marry me." Hannah coyly pulled her loose, black curls to one side of her head and twisted the ends in her fingers.

A baby! Jenna could not believe her ears. How could Hannah have willingly allowed a man to enter her, to do to her what Faithful had forced upon Jenna? It was impossible. She could not find words to say anything.

"Of course, he don't know anything about a baby. He wants me. But things happen. Sometimes babies drown in the river or suffocate. I even heard of one drowning in a bucket of dirty wash water. I might never even deliver this baby. Who knows? But I wanted to tell you my secret, since I might never see you again." Hannah hugged Jenna again. "I won't tell on you if you won't tell on me."

"Goodbye, Hannah. I pray we will meet again someday and you will always think of me as your best friend." Jenna ran back to the circle of campfire light, a light that had comforted her so often in the darkness.

The next morning, amid the bellows of animals, the shouts and curses of the men, and the last farewells, the wagons parted—most heading north to Oregon and only six wagons heading south to California. As planned, Jenna started on the Oregon Trail riding Honey, but lagged farther and farther behind until she could safely turn around, retrace her steps, and pick up a hidden bundle containing a blanket, a coat, Israel's harmonica, the precious shell box, and some crackers. She tied Israel's leather hat on her head, then galloped up the wagon road to catch up with Blue and the others.

When at last she saw the rear wagon, Jenna again lagged safely behind, hoping not to be discovered too soon. If she could keep hidden until the next morning, she would be a safe distance from Faithful Squibb. Blue could not possibly send her back.

That night, Jenna, wrapped in her coat and blanket, could not sleep. The evenings were cool in the mountains, the woods damp and breathing like something alive. She stayed as close to the glow of the campfires as she dared, close enough to hear the muffled voices or an outbreak of laughter.

When the sun burned high overhead, Jenna caught up with Blue. She trotted alongside and said, "I'm going with you, Blue. I'm not going to Oregon." Blue looked at her without saying a word. He spit some tobacco juice and looked straight ahead. Jenna felt uncomfortable.

Finally he said, "You put me in a bad spot, Jenna. I've been a-thinkin' on it. It's no good turnin' around and tryin' to catch up with Ornery's group . . . 'course you already figured that. So I'm a-guessin' you planned this whole thing a ways back. Somethin' wasn't right in the company's decision or you'd have abided by the rules. Am I a-figurin' it right so far?" Blue looked at Jenna without revealing how he felt about the situation.

"Yes, Sir," Jenna said, searching his face for a reaction.

"The Squibbs is goin' to think you're lost."

"I told Hannah to explain to everyone I was going to California—with you."

"I guess then we'll just have to work out the wrinkles with the other folks."

"I haven't got any money. Reverend Squibb kept it locked up in a box. I can work for my food."

"You left all your worldly goods, Jenna. I don't know how I'm goin' to get you back to your family now. You put me in a tough spot."

"I'm sorry," she said softly, and then in a burst of determination, "but I'm *not sorry to leave the Squibbs. I hate them!*"

Blue looked at the strain on Jenna's face. He thought how much she had changed since the trip started. The eager little girl that once played ring-around-the-roses and picked spring bouquets back in Kansas Territory now seemed older, sadder, in some ways as hardened as the women at Sutter's Fort.

"What happened to you, girl?"

Jenna lowered her head. "He hurt me."

Blue's expression changed from concern to rage. He clenched his teeth to hold in his frustration of not being able to strike. They rode for awhile in silence until he said through is teeth, "Don't worry, girl, if I ever see that son-of-bitch, I swear on my mother's grave, *I'll kill him!*"

FIVE

AS LONG AS THE EMIGRANTS followed the proven trail to California along the rivers—the Humboldt and the Truckee—they were able to wind their way successfully across desert, steep rocky mountains, through extremes of climate and unpredictable weather to their destination—California, paradise, the land of milk and honey.

After tortuous desert and the High Sierras, Jenna thought the sight of the Sacramento Valley, so green and pastoral, was surely what Heaven must look like—everything soft and lovely, with rolling buff-colored hills dipping gently into a lush valley. Clear streams and brilliant flowers, the air, sweet with the green and bloom of every kind of vegetation made Jenna's heart light and her young spirit happy as a song. It was a contented earth.

Jenna stood on a high hill and looked down at the pastures surrounding Sutter's Fort. They were filled with the fattest cows and sheep she had ever seen.

Oh, how I wish Mama and Papa and Solomon could be with me now, standing right here in this very spot.

Honey pulled at the reins as if she, too, knew the journey was over . . .

that there was sweet grass and sweet water waiting below.

Jenna was too tired to think long about her family. She had thought of them every step of the way to California, often lying awake at night, imagining they were in the dark comforting her, telling her not to give up. As she and Blue rode into the fort, she clutched her shell box and Israel's harmonica.

The last week had been one of courage for all of them in the small wagon train. The food was nearly gone and their spirits spent, but Captain Sutter kept a lookout for travelers and met many wagon trains with fresh food and water to help them make the last leg of the journey. In many cases it was a mission that saved the lives and strength of the exhausted emigrants. Blue's small group was no exception.

Sutter's Fort was a welcome sight to all travelers. Not only did it signal the end of the journey, but it radiated a special spirit of comfort, safety, well-being, and joy. The fort reflected Captain Sutter himself, a man known for his good-heartedness and generosity—a vigorous man of vision who had come to California in the thirties and loved it so intensely that he wanted everyone to love it with him. Sutter's Fort, in a land Sutter named New Helvetia, was a good place to begin building a dream in an enchanted land.

"Welcome, welcome, welcome, my friends," Captain Sutter said, rushing out to greet Blue and the wagons. He was a giant thunderstorm of a man, with bellyfuls of laughs and lightning in his eyes. He grabbed Blue's hand and shook it heartily. "My old friend, how good it is to see you again! You look well after your long journey." He quickly gave orders to some Indians who had gathered around to unhitch the wagons and to feed and water the animals without delay. He greeted the women with a broad, warm smile, assisted them from the wagons, shook hands with the men, and welcomed everyone in a personal way.

"There's fresh-squeezed orange juice in the dining room. It's a special tonic to put some sunshine in your soul and a smile on your face. We've got Chinese beer and English brandy for those who have aches in their bones . . . and our own whiskey made here at the fort if you got the stomach for it. We always have a feast of food for hungry folks. Now go on in and get some cold beef and cheese, bread, hot lamb stew with biscuits, and there might be some turkey left over, some corn pudding and hot coffee . . . oh yes, and lemon cake. That's our cook's specialty." He ushered the ladies into the dining room. "We got plenty of food here, so eat all you want whenever you want, and make yourselves at home as long as you like. No charge. We're all family in New Helvetia." Sutter continued shaking hands, pumping the men's arms enthusiastically.

The emigrants couldn't help smiling back at this man. He was as refreshing as a cool drink of water. His energy and friendship spilled into every corner of the fort.

"Now you folks find a place to sleep. There are rooms in the center of the courtyard and some along the north side. You may have to bunch up—men together and women and small fries together, but there's a place for everyone and plenty of blankets, washtubs, and bathtubs. You name it, we got it." Captain Sutter laughed heartily; his eyes twinkled with good humor. He slapped Blue on the back again just for friendship.

"By the way, these Kanaka Indians camped around are my best friends. They have their own ways of eating and sleeping, so they won't bother you. In fact, they'll help whenever they can—good folks, these Kanakas. We're all a family here and that includes them and you all." He turned to Blue. "Who is this youngster, Blue—one of your own? It could be a laddie under that hat, but I guess more than likely it's a lassie in that dress. Whoever you are," he said to Jenna, "I'll call you Bright Eyes." He laughed loudly and slapped Jenna a little too roughly on the back.

"I'm Jenna Daggett, Captain Sutter," Jenna said, removing Israel's soiled leather hat. Her light brown hair stuck to her head with dirt and sweat.

"So you are, young lady. But you're Bright Eyes to me."

"She lost her family on the crossing, Captain. She's an orphan and needs some proper attention," Blue said.

Jenna suddenly felt uncomfortable, like someone out of a storybook—a waif, a pitiful creature whose fate was being discussed. She straightened up as tall as possible and said in a strong voice, "I'm Israel Daggett's daughter and I've come to make my way in California. I can take care of myself. I can work for you, Captain Sutter."

The captain smiled. "Well, maybe you can at that. A lot of my help has suddenly disappeared up the American River, taking all my wash pans with them—gold panning."

Jenna overheard Blue say under his breath, "So it is the American River. I'll keep that in mind."

"Well, come along now and meet Darcey Higgins and her daughter, Dumplin. I call her Dumplin, but her name is Pearle. Darcey does laundry for me and for some of the men and weary folks like yourselves and people on the way to the diggins. She's kind of an orphan, too, Bright Eyes. Lost her husband and son on the crossing in a bad accident. It's a shame. They were one of the first families to emigrate here on the California Trail. They almost made it, but, son-of-a-gun, if one giant boulder didn't tear loose and crush the two men. It tumbled the two teams and the wagon down a cliff.

"They lost everything, including the animals. They had to shoot them they were so broken up—necks, legs, shoulders, backs. By God's mercy, Darcey and Dumplin were riding a horse a ways back and were spared. The horse threw them off. Darcey knocked out her front tooth, but poor Dumplin broke a leg that never mended right. She walks with a limp, poor little tyke—leg shortened up, you know. But she's got a lot of spunk—like her mother."

Jenna and Blue followed Captain Sutter across the courtyard to the far side of the fort.

"I think there's room to stay with Darcey and her daughter. You can help Darcey make soap and do the wash and the like. She'd like that, I'll bet," the captain said as he escorted the pair to the laundry room.

As they walked, he pointed out that the single long adobe building held a variety of rooms for provisions, a blacksmith shop, a small two-bed infirmary, a still, a kitchen, and a bathhouse with large tubs. The fully-stocked fort could meet all the needs of its community.

The inhabitants ground their own wheat and corn, made tallow candles and furniture, grew grapes for wine, and had ample herds of sheep, goats, lambs and lush pastures to feed them, as well as countless pigs, poultry, and strong work horses. Indeed, they could do about everything from amputating a leg to assaying gold. A mile from the fort, their boats carried supplies down the river to San Francisco Bay.

The laundry room was at one end of the long adobe building. Outside, clothes and towels hung on lines and draped over railings and a few scant bushes. Large tubs boiled and bubbled in the open air. Under a canvas tent were barrels of soft soap, tables, and baskets of clothes and bedding—some clean, some dirty, some folded neatly, with the soiled ones heaped high in piles.

Darcey put down a large wooden paddle with which she rotated and lifted the dirty clothes in boiling water, and came over to greet her visitors. She was a handsome woman with a glowing, round face, broad and freckled. Her green eyes sparkled with joy and humor. Thick red hair, tough like springy wires, bounced out from under a faded pink scarf tied neatly around her head. Jenna thought she looked like a giant oak tree bursting with autumn colors.

"Hello, Captain," she said in a hearty, loud voice. She wiped her hands on her apron and extended her hand. "New arrivals? Hello, I'm Darcey Higgins," she said with her large, throaty voice. She took a long look at Blue and shook his hand vigorously. Her smile stretched clear across a face as welcoming as warm buttered bread on a chilly morning. The fact that she was missing a front tooth didn't detract from her robust good looks.

Blue grinned. "Hello, Mrs. Higgins. Pleased to make your acquaintance."

"Likewise, I'm sure," she said, tucking a wet wiry strand of red hair under the scarf.

"This here is Jenna Daggett," Blue said.

"Hello," Jenna said shyly.

She was surprised at the feeling of friendship sweeping over her as she met this stranger. Jenna wanted to reach out and put her arms around Darcey's ample waist, as if she were greeting an old aunt or dear neighbor—even Emily Polley. But Darcey looked younger than the women on the wagon train—much younger than her own mother.

Darcey immediately hugged Jenna, yielding to her own instinct of embracing the children, the tired, or the sick who had survived the arduous journey. Everyone fit inside the circle of her arms. She seemed to know instinctively that Jenna was alone in this world, that she had suffered a terrible ordeal. Jenna's losses showed on her young face, and the "bright eyes" that Captain Sutter saw were unnatural against the weariness and pale skin—like the eyes of a feverish child.

"Jenna, I do believe you win the prize for the dirtiest emigrant to pass by here in a long time. And maybe the skinniest. Now you men excuse us while we go to the bathhouse and get started bringing Jenna back to her real self. We'll meet you gentlemen later for supper after you've tidied up and trimmed your beard," Darcey said, smiling directly at Blue.

She turned to go. "Come on, Jenna. I want you to meet my baby, Pearle—not a baby, really. She's five years old. Poor child, she's out back shivering in the sun . . . just getting over a bad bout with ague. She'll be happy to meet a young person. How old are you?"

"I'm twelve. I turned twelve on the crossing somewhere around the Humboldt Sink. I forgot my birthday until just a few days ago."

As they walked away, Blue noted Darcey's roundness moving softly under her dress. *Not that's what I call a rare woman*, he said to himself. He turned to Captain Sutter. "Guess I'd better find a tub and someone to trim my beard." He winked at the captain, who chuckled and nodded his head with approval.

"This evening I'm entertaining two officers of the Mexican army—still old friends in spite of the war. Why don't you join us in my quarters? I'll send word to Darcey to be my guest as well. We'll have a chance to get better acquainted around here." Captain Sutter threw back his head and laughed playfully.

Jenna was amazed to meet Pearl, a small, blond child, dainty and frail, who somehow reminded her of Nettie. Maybe it was the transparency of the thin skin, the delicacy of her slender hands that recalled her little friend and drew her to the shivering child. Pearle had a mountain of matted, kinky hair, all wires like her mother's. So much hair made her thin face look even thinner and her serious, brown eyes even larger.

Pearle looked up and smiled timidly, but didn't get up. Jenna noticed how she trembled slightly as she held onto her rag doll. Dark circles under her eyes clouded her sweet face.

Jenna knelt down beside her. "Is this your dolly?"

Pearle nodded.

"What's her name?"

"Annie." For a moment Pearle's shaking eased.

"May I hold her?"

Pearle nodded and handed her the doll.

"She's a nice dolly, Maybe I can teach her numbers and letters. We can play school. Would you like that?"

Pearle smiled slightly and nodded shyly, then reached for her doll.

"She don't have anyone to play with," Darcey said. "The emigrants come and go so fast. She'll enjoy you, Jenna. Let me show you where you can sleep with us. It's just a cot with a straw mattress, but the pillow and comforter is duck down and feathers. We'll share a wash basin. There's room for two others if they care to join us." She put her arm around Jenna's shoulder. "We're going to be friends, Jenna. I just know it."

Darcey smiled broadly, the black space prominent in her mouth. "The first thing we're going to do is get you a soapy bath in a tub. Then we're going to wash that tattered dress. There's not much to save—the hem is just strings. But we can save the top and cut if off to make a shirtwaist, piece the skirt into an apron and a matching sunbonnet . . ."

"No, please, no sunbonnet," Jenna interrupted. "I'm never going to wear one again! I've got my papa's hat."

Darcey laughed. "I hate sunbonnets, too. I'll never wear one again either!" She hugged Jenna. "We'll braid us a fancy straw. I know how. And when winter comes, we'll skin us a wolf for a fur hat. But no more sunbonnets!"

"What dress can I wear?" Jenna asked.

"I've got a faded gingham skirt that don't fit me anymore and I can cut it down for you and still have material left over for a smock for Pearle."

Jenna liked Darcey, Pearle, Captain Sutter, the fort, and California. She had the feeling of belonging somewhere at last. Suddenly, she was so tired she wanted to sleep and sleep. After her bath, Jenna curled up in the comforter and sank into the feather pillow. Her last words before she slept were, "Could you please be sure Honey has feed and water. She's so tired . . . so tired."

Darcey fed Pearle early and put her to bed next to Jenna. She took off her work dress, then washed and rubbed her arms and chest and heavy breasts with rose water. She added a few drops of ammonia to fresh rinse water and wiped away any lingering perspiration odor, a trick she learned from a doctor's wife when she was becoming a young lady.

Without the scarf, her long, red hair spiraled out uncontrollably, but after a good brushing, it shined like polished copper, and Darcey pulled it back and pinned it attractively into a luxurious French knot. She liked to dress up for supper in case there was a single man among the new arrivals who might catch her eye. Tonight's dinner with Captain Sutter and the officers might prove to be interesting.

She already knew she pleased Blue. In spite of his awkward shyness, she read the brightness in his eyes, the side glances, the unmistakable interest. He was a manly sort, nice-looking in a rough way, she thought. He could even be kind of handsome—cleaned and trimmed—and his mannerisms were warm and genial. Yes, Blue wasn't too bad—a little old, perhaps, but worth the trouble of fashioning a front tooth out of candle wax for the evening. It meant, of course, she wouldn't be able to eat, but at least she could sip some brandy and carry on bright conversation with the gentlemen.

Darcey looked in the mirror and was pleased with her appearance. Her buxom shape pressed against the hand-sewn seams of a recently made gingham, a deep red color trimmed in rose ribbons. She placed a stock of blue lupine in her bun and smiled in the mirror. "That hideous empty space!" she said aloud. How would she ever catch a decent man looking like an old farmhand?

One day she was going to have a gold tooth, or at least some kind of a tooth, to fill that space. One day she would get to a dentist to fit her a proper tooth; meanwhile, she would have to put up with a temporary invention of her own—one that only made a good first impression. You never knew when a good man might come courting. As for supper, well, she could fix a plate and eat it later in her room.

Darcey was the last to arrive at Captain Sutter's quarters. She planned it that way. It was better to enter a room already warm with brandy and conviviality among the men when one was smiling only halfway to keep a false tooth in place. Her entrance was a success. Darcey had the same magnetic attraction as the captain—an energy, a vibrancy that flirted all around her. The men found her pleasing to the eye, not glamorous or refined, but tempting, like a crisp red apple or hot berry pie covered with thick cream.

Clearly, Blue was smitten with her and hoped his trimmed beard and clean, slicked-back hair would catch her attention. He knew he reeked of more than a manly odor when they met, more like a sweaty horse . . . which wasn't too bad in his opinion, but he wasn't a lady. Ladies liked soapy smells.

"Good evening, gentlemen," Darcey said demurely, keeping her lips as close to her teeth as possible.

Captain Sutter noticed the change in her countenance immediately. He was used to her raucous laugh, open smile, throaty greeting, and bubbly wit. Who was this new creature? The captain leaned forward to see why she held her mouth so oddly. So did Blue.

The atmosphere in the room quickly turned into strained cordiality, with Blue silently staring at Darcey's mouth, the captain attempting to be humorous and courteous to his Mexican guests, and Darcey speaking unnaturally through inflexible lips.

The Mexicans, dressed in black velvet jackets with gold braid and silver buttons, looked imposing and austere. They showed little appreciation for the captain's humor, for they had business on their minds and resented the *Anglos*.

The tension in the room stemmed from the fact that Mexico had lost the war and California now belonged to the Americans. It was humiliating to the Mexicans that their beloved capital fell so quickly to the Americans only a year ago.

A host of issues followed the Mexican defeat and establishment of the state of California. Primary among these was a tangle of contradictory land claims that would have to be sorted out. Sutter, himself, had single-handedly contributed to this chaos. The Captain, a Mexican citizen, had given away land grants to Americans like passing out flags at a Fourth of July parade. In his wake, he'd left confusion over land titles. The Mexicans' official visit to the fort was their attempt to address this problem.

More was at stake in this post-war era than land deeds and claims, however. The very lifestyle of the Californios, those respected Mexican families who had settled on land now comprising much of the new state, was about to be challenged. Their days filled with fine fiestas in Monterey and the tranquil luxury of their vast haciendas was about to become part of the past. With the discovery of gold, these changes would happen sooner than anyone had suspected, as Californios found their beautiful land invaded by a continuous wave of riffraff.

"Señora?" One of the Mexican officers offered his arm to escort Darcey to the table.

"Pleased, I'm sure," she said.

Blue felt slightly threatened and stared at the Mexican captain, so polished and handsome.

The table was set in fine china and silver on a lovely Damask cloth from Europe. Blanca, Captain Sutter's middle-aged Mexican helper, poured deep red wine into the goblets and served bowls of clear consommé.

So far, so good, Darcey thought. She was hungry and wanted to bite into a crisp French roll smothered with sweet butter, but knew that chewing of any kind was out of the question. She felt her deception was working well and congratulated herself on her own cleverness.

Captain Sutter raised his glass to toast his guests. "To my friends, Captain Sanchez, Lieutenant Escobar, Señora Higgins and Señor . . ." He stopped the toast midway. "My dear friend, Blue, forgive me, I have forgotten your name."

"Blue is good enough, Captain," Blue said, looking down at his soup.

"No, tell us your name," Darcey said, trying to flirt with him a bit. "No one ever introduced us proper."

"It ain't important," Blue said. It was clear he didn't like to be the center of attention.

"Come now, Blue, you aren't one of them desperados, are you? Tell us your name," Darcey insisted.

Everyone looked at Blue and waited, their glasses raised in an incomplete toast. Blue cleared his throat. "Quigley Gump," he said, his voice a little louder than he intended.

"To my friends and Señor Gump," the captain said.

Everyone took a silent swallow except for Darcey, who tried to stifle a laugh and only succeeded in snorting a spray of red wine into her nose. She wiped her face and raised her glass again. "To my kindly host and his guests, and to Mr. Quigley Gump." This time she opened her mouth into a very wide smile that crinkled her eyes. Then, unable to hold back her reaction to Blue's name, she let out a whoop of laughter. Suddenly, the wax tooth fell out of her mouth landing with a splash in the cooling consommé. She grabbed her napkin to her mouth, and the contagious laugh, already in progress, now rolled louder than ever into the party and startled the guests, even Captain Sutter.

Darcey was uncontrollable, her fleshy face squeezed into a million lines, her eyes lost somewhere behind a rise of freckled cheeks. Her whole body shook with laughter against the table, and everyone hung on to the jiggling wine glasses.

The captain and Blue tried to contain their laughter to be polite, but it was a hopeless attempt. However, the Mexican officials, accustomed to refined ladies, clearly found the entire episode crude, distasteful and humorless, which made the *Anglos* laugh even harder.

Darcey at last got control of herself, fished the tooth from the soup with another burst of giggles, and said, "Well, now I can enjoy dinner. Pass a roll, Señor Gump."

Blue smiled, happy to have the return of this delightful, buxom redhead with a toothless . . . and a large appetite.

He watched Darcey enjoy hearty mouthfuls of spicy pork followed by large swallows of ruby red wine. Mostly he enjoyed the playfulness in her candle-lit eyes over the goblet's rim when she looked at him. The skin on her upper arms, which rarely saw the harsh sun, looked as creamy as vanilla pudding, tasty and delicious. She smacked her lips, cooed like a pigeon at each sumptuous course, and smiled broadly throughout the meal. When she finished the last forkful of her second helping of rhubarb pie, she sat back in her chair, satisfied and bursting inside her dress. The men had waited for her to finish, all of them watching with admiration her seemingly bottomless capacity for food.

Darcey excused herself early after dinner so the men could talk and smoke their cigars. Blue escorted her back to her room.

The two walked slowly, enjoying of privacy together. Even in the night shadows, Blue thought Darcey shone like a full moon. He liked walking next to her, being in her atmosphere. Her fun-loving manner put him at ease, erased his shyness, made him feel younger, happier.

They laughed again about the tooth in the soup. "I thought you was carryin' a mouthful of cherry pits in your cheeks," Blue teased.

"Well, that fool tooth idea worked before . . . for a short while. But, mark my words, I'm getting a tooth somehow—a gold one!"

"I'll tell you what, Darcey. I'll *make* you a tooth myself before I leave for San Francisco. I'm no dentist, but I bet I can carve one out of wood, or maybe horn or bone. I'm a good carver . . . helped my old man make furniture and cabinets. I'll shape and file you a tooth and glue the durned thing in, afix it snug betwixt the other two!"

Darcey's eyes lighted. "Do you think it would work?" she asked, grabbing his shoulders.

"Why not?"

"Let's try! Tomorrow?" she inquired eagerly, beginning to bounce on her toes.

"I'll give it a go . . . no promises. And when I come back from San Francisco, I'm thinkin' on goin' to the American River with a wash pan and pickin' up those gold nuggets everyone is talkin' about. By golly, I'll bring you a gold nugget and hammer it into the best durn tooth you ever saw!"

Darcey threw her arms around Blue and kissed him so hard on the cheek his jaw shifted. "Tomorrow, then. Goodnight, Quigley," she said playfully. Then she ran inside the room.

Blue could still hear her laughing and singing on the other side of the door.

🌿 🌿 🌿

By the time Blue and Jenna had arrived at the fort, the discovery of gold at Sutter's sawmill had not only leaked out, it had started a wild brush fire of gold seekers into the region—a conflagration that could not be stopped. They called it gold fever. Men stopped whatever they were doing and grabbed a wash pan. The baker left his bread to mold; the farmer, his crops to wither; the sailor, his ship to flounder in the harbor. The idea of picking up gold nuggets just lying in a shallow river or washing out gold dust simply by swirling a pan full of river sand was too hard to resist. A man could become wealthy in a month's time making as much as one hundred dollars a day by doing practically nothing.

One old man on his way to the diggings told a group of spellbound travelers at the fort, "I heard thirty wild Indians helped some gents from Monterey pan gold on the Feather River, and I swear on my mother's grave, in only seven weeks they panned $77,000!"

Everywhere, the electrifying news charged the air: Gold! Gold! Gold on the American River! Gold on the Feather River! Gold in the gulches! The word spread north to Oregon and Canada, south to Monterey, Los Angeles, Baja, and Mexico. The news traveled around the tip of South America, across Panama, over the ocean to Hawaii, China, and Japan, and to all of Europe.

San Francisco exploded like a Roman candle. Men dropped their shovels. The saloons and banks, boardinghouses, and bordellos emptied and turned silent. Mothers and children were left to fend for themselves. Even livestock was left unfed and unattended. Ships rocked idly in the harbor, unmanned. Captains and generals found themselves struggling without servants, trying to cook a simple herring for breakfast.

Within a few months of 1849, the gold seekers, called the Forty Niners, would spread out across the prairie like a fast-moving storm and jam the Oregon Trail singing:

> *"O Susanna, oh don't you cry for me,*
> *For I'm off to Californy*
> *with a wash pan on my knee."*

California would fill up. Every gully and gulch, every river, stream, and rivulet would soon be crowded with hopeful miners greedy for gold. In the fiery time, not a single stone would be left unturned in or around the riverbeds. Wild tent towns would spring up over night. The fancy women would don bright feathers and red stockings and drag the hems of their silk dresses across muddy roads into hastily-made saloons. Piano tunes would fill the air and rattle the news that life, after all, was a great party, with a never-ending supply of gold as the main attraction.

Captain Sutter had hoped to keep the gold discovery a secret, at least long enough to get a sawmill built, but like everyone else, his workers left the fort for the rivers. Sutter's Fort served as a rest stop or supply station for people going to the diggings. They came daily—some on horseback, leading mules, others pushing hand carts. Some even arrived sick, old, or on crutches. The excitement became a kind of madness that blasted into normal domestic arrangements, turning the head to the tail and the tail to the head.

🌱 🌱 🌱

Darcey pushed her way through a crowd gathered around a man who had just returned form the North Fork. His eyes blazed as he boasted about his $5,356 after working only fifty-seven days.

"Them little bright yellow scales are just winkin' at you from the riverbed," he said, passing around nuggets for the people to examine.

Darcey took one bright nugget and held it beside her gold wedding band. It looked like gold all right.

The people in the crowd, anxious to rush to the diggings and already imagining nuggets bulging in their pockets, scattered to their horses like a swarm of fireflies.

As Darcey watched them come and go, she'd slip her tongue into the empty space between her teeth and imagine it filled with shiny gold. She wished she were a man . . . or had a man, for that matter. A man could go to the diggings, do whatever he liked, pan the gold, become rich, own land, travel the world.

It seemed she always had both arms crooked around something—a load of laundry on one side and Pearle on the other. How could she ever free her arms and hands to find a future for herself?

Surely, one day soon, the gold would be gone. She had heard of the fights among the rough characters that were pouring into the mountains every day. The Mexicans, still angry over their losses, and a raggle-taggle army of one-time soldiers and adventurers clashed and cursed each other and found any excuse to brawl. The men were rowdy and red-faced, full of vulgarities.

It was no place for a woman. Darcey thought that if she were a man, she'd have already been to the river and made her fortune.

Sighing, Darcey plunged her strong, tanned arms into the soapsuds, lifting out the men's overalls and long underwear again and again. She wrung the heavy clothes between her large hands, squeezed out the last drops, and hung the clothes on the line. The underwear and men's pants hanging lifeless on the line became the men in her life. On lonely days, she imagined them full of flesh.

During the next few days, Blue was true to his word. He carefully filed and sanded a cow's tooth into a fine tooth for Darcey. He was embarrassed moving in close to her, bending over her, but couldn't help enjoying the soapy smell of clean that clung to her.

After fitting the tooth between the other two front teeth, Blue tapped it into place with a small tack hammer. He measured and filed the tooth many times to get a snug fit, all the while repressing an urge to kiss Darcey squarely on her plump lips. He covered up his desire by playing the role of dentist, doctor, and surgeon, talking with authority on medical matters.

Darcey sat open-mouthed, unable to talk, and looked up at Blue's intense face, his stallion eyes, and grizzly chin full of grey and black whiskers. Her eyes followed his and when, by accident, they met in one powerful moment, each one looked away, pretending there was nothing there but the job at hand.

Blue's hands, so large and rough, held the tooth gracefully, and at last he glued it into her mouth, a perfect fit. "Let her dry, now," he said. "I'm goin' to prop your jaws open with a couple of acorns for awhile. You just set there in the sun." Blue bent over her one last time and lingered just a bit longer than necessary.

Jenna, who had been entertaining Pearle, walked over to Darcey. She lifted Pearle so she could peer into her mother's mouth.

"That's a nice tooth, Mama. Can you eat apples now?"

Blue laughed. "She'll have to be careful, I suspect . . . eat only sliced apples and pull the meat off the bones first. Maybe not. If the glue holds, she can eat about anything but my biscuits."

Blue had finished his business at the fort. He had brought the wagon train safely to California; he'd made a fine woman a perfect tooth and had hoped to be quickly on his way. But now there was this matter of Jenna, his charge. He knew he couldn't take her with him. He was single, free—no obligations, no ties to the past or the present. It was his duty to find the right place for her where she could get a proper start in life. He knew Jenna didn't want to return to Sapling Grove; she'd said so many times. Besides, there was no telling when someone reliable could take her back East.

He'd have to find a temporary situation for Jenna. He owed that to Israel. Sutter's Fort was as good a place as any for now. Captain Sutter and Darcey had kindly agreed to look out for Jenna for a few weeks while he went about his business in San Francisco and decided just how to handle the situation.

Now, however, the idea of getting some gold in his pockets was becoming an obsession. He'd never had money and had worked hard for every penny. Once, long ago, he'd had a start—a nice farm in Illinois, a pretty wife blooming with his child. Sometimes on lonely nights, he'd allow her sweet vision to float into his thoughts, see her scattering feed for the chickens, carrying a pail of milk back from the barn. Life was good then, full of dreams—not big dreams—only ones to protect his family, improve his farm, work from sunup to sundown with the rich land, and raise a brood of healthy children. Things change. That was long ago and no use dwelling on the past. He had to think about what to do with Jenna.

Blue began rolling up his clean change of clothes inside his bedding. He thought about the child he never had. Was it a boy or girl? It would be about Jenna's age by now, if it had lived; if it had not burned up with fever inside a dying woman.

But what if it had lived—without a pretty mother with curly brown hair spread out on a pillow, wet with perspiration, gnarled from rollin' back and forth, back and forth? What if he, himself, had caught smallpox? His babe would be an orphan like Jenna.

There wasn't any fittin' place for an orphan out in the undeveloped West, except maybe the goodwill of folks. Back East, the churches sometimes took care of poor little souls and found homes for them. He thought maybe he'd stop by the mission in San Jose and talk to the old priest there, Father Ortega, who'd been there when the mission was run by the Spanish. He was a nice old man who knew everyone—all the Californios, the rich folks in Monterey, the high gentlemen in the presidio in Monterey, the people who had already settled in the valley to farm. Father Ortega would know of someone willing to take in a child.

A lot of riffraff was moving into the mountains: foreigners, Chinese Devils, drunks and sailors, and painted women. He needed to find a proper place immediately to shield Jenna from bad influences. This wasn't a place to raise a little girl who was showing she wasn't so little anymore.

California was changing. It was going to become a state with lots of important people, and Monterey was going to be the capital for certain. And didn't President Polk say there was gold all over California? Surely, someone would want a little girl like Jenna, a kind of pretty girl all cleaned up and washed, and stubborn, too—not the worst quality. Jenna certainly was a tough one, headstrong—a survivor. No man could have handled the rough times on the crossing any better than she did. She never complained once. She worked hard and never cried when times was tough. No, Jenna was a survivor, all right. There had to be a place for her somewhere.

🌱 🌱 🌱

Darcey, Pearle, and Jenna stood close to Blue as he tied his bedroll in back of his saddle, the final packing before leaving for San Francisco.

Blue's leaving was another loss for Jenna, but he'd promised that he'd return soon. She wanted to trust him, just as she had Israel. On the other hand, she was cautious about entrusting her fate to him or any other adult. After all, hadn't he gone along with the others in the company in placing her with Faithful and Cora Squibb?

Jenna had become accustomed to departures and farewells; it was a part of life, something she had to accept and move on without fretting. She learned to keep her sad thoughts to herself, shut up tight like Martha Jane's shell box; there was no need to burden anyone else. She realized that whoever made the crossing no doubt suffered as she had. All women without husbands, fathers, or brothers had to keep going—had to use whatever it took to survive.

For Darcey, Blue's leaving was part of the mystery of men and women playing out the game of attraction. She liked Blue; she knew he liked her. She filled the long-johns hanging on the line with his body and imagined herself lying next to him on a cold night under a mountain of down comforters. Blue would return, and if he didn't . . . well, someone else would eventually fill the underwear and overalls.

Darcey, Jenna and Pearle watched Blue fasten his bedroll onto his horse. Darcey put her arm around Jenna.

"You're coming back, aren't you, Blue?" Jenna asked, rubbing the velvet nose of Blue's horse.

Darcey knew Jenna was holding back her tears for fear Blue would know how much she'd miss him.

"I can't promise when," Blue said, "but I'll be back, you can reckon on it. Right now, I got matters to attend to."

"Are you going to the diggins?" Darcey asked.

"Maybe I am and maybe I ain't," Blue said.

He sounded indifferent, but Darcey he knew he had to go. The excitement was too much for any man to resist.

"I promised you a gold tooth, didn't I?" he said, mounting his horse.

Darcey picked up Pearle in her arms. "Goodbye, Quigley. Take care of yourself. You did a good job on my tooth. No dentist could have done it better." She reached up to shake his hand.

"Bye, Darcey," he said, shaking her hand like it was a man's. "Don't eat no taffy now. Bye, Pearle . . . Jenna. It won't be long before you hear from your Aunt Lizzie, your own kin."

"Will you be back by Christmas, Blue?" Jenna asked.

"Can't say that for sure, girl," Blue said. He turned his horse away and road quickly out of the fort.

"Come on, children," Darcey said, "I have a mountain of laundry to hand up on the line."

🍃 🍃 🍃

In the weeks that followed, Jenna began to change. The strain of the crossing that settled in her wide blue eyes and tightened her mouth turned quietly into a new face. The plump bud of childish innocence was opening into a young girl with a haunting beauty, a classical oval face with high cheekbones and a tapered jaw. As new skin, smooth as cream, replaced the pealing onion skin of her journey, an aristocratic beauty surfaced. There was nothing soft about her like a new tumbling puppy. Jenna was tall for her age, slim, long-legged, and graceful, more like a wild bird that sits in hidden lagoons and lifts into the air slowly when startled by an interloper.

She was not someone who was easy to approach or tease. Her manner, though friendly, was curiously aloof and thoughtful. She carried an air of strength, a resistance that one might mistake for a streak of coldness. She could be as stubborn as a stone lodged in a stream of flowing water, but gentle and yielding when it came to the approach of an animal . . . or Pearle. The warm and caring side of Jenna was reserved for any creature that was helpless—a bird with a broken wing, a lame horse, a dog with a burr in its ear or a thorn in its paw. A suffering animal tore at her heart, crumbling any inner walls she had built in her young life.

Jenna spent hours playing with Pearle. Gradually, the frail child recovered from the shaking brought on by malaria. Jenna loved to watch the little girl smile and laugh at her storytelling and knew she relished their walks in the meadows and woods outside the fort.

Jenna created fantasy worlds that delighted Pearle and never tired of watching her tuck her short legs under her as she fantasized pebbles and sticks into people, families, Indians, princesses, brides. Pearle told her she knew how to shrink into a miniature world where tall grass became a jungle to a tiny eye, and how she made beautiful ladies in satin gowns by turning hollyhock blossoms upside-down and attaching the bud for a head, a leaf for a plumed hat. She showed Jenna how she drew roads in the dirt with her finger and made hills and rivers, covering them with stick bridges and adding a community of tents and tepees made from scraps of material.

Jenna was amazed how quickly Pearle, eager for reading, learned her letters simply by drawing them in the dirt with a stick. She learned to sound out words so easily that Jenna wrote down simple nursery rhymes to teach her how to read. Captain Sutter, seeing the young schoolteacher and her pupil, brought them a book of *Aesop's Fables* and the *New England Primer* when he returned from a trip to San Francisco. After that, Pearle was seldom seen without her books in her hands.

"There's something very smart about her, Darcey," Jenna said. "I learned to read when I was young, too, but she's faster than I was . . . faster than others her age. She can even read parts of the Bible and she's only six years old!"

Darcey smiled, "Takes after her mother, I guess."

Jenna loved Pearle like a little sister. She and Darcey were a family to her. Darcey was not quite like a mother—certainly nothing like Martha Jane—more like a dear aunt or older sister who made her laugh or comforted her. Sometimes at night, as they all lay in the darkness, Darcey would sing lullabies and melancholy songs of Ireland until the sweet ease of sleep erased Jenna's longing for family, the arms of Israel . . . the time when she lived on the other side of the world.

Jenna often hugged Darcey for no other reason than to feel her fleshy arms fold around her reassuringly. Darcey was about the only one who could break down Jenna's developing aloofness. Her easy manner, throaty laugh, playfulness, and ability to touch and hug without self-consciousness gave Jenna a sense of safety, of belonging to someone. Unlike other adults, Darcey always broke the rules just a little to make life more fun—like sneaking a loaf of fresh-baked bread and a jar of precious honey under her apron for the three of them to eat before bedtime. Jenna adored Darcey for breaking the rules.

Before blowing out the candle, the girls would lie in their beds watching the lights and shadows flicker on the wall and wait for Darcey to tuck them in and kiss them each goodnight. In the darkness, they always said their prayers together, then Darcey would sing songs in a low voice. Jenna often thought of the lonely cows lowing for their young back in Sapling Grove . . . a sweet memory, a sleepy memory.

One night, Darcey darted across the room to the dresser completely naked, her body white and fleshy, jiggly as cooked oatmeal. She bent over and plowed through folded clothes in a bottom drawer of the chest. The girls held their comforters to their noses and giggled.

"I can't find my nightshirt! Shut your eyes and quit your peeking."

The girls giggled all the louder. Pearle laughed because her mother looked funny naked. Jenna laughed from embarrassment. It wasn't normal for her to see anyone undressed all the way. She had never even seen her own mother completely naked. It was not proper. The body was a thing of shame, and to exhibit it was the work of the Devil.

In fascination, Jenna watched Darcey wash herself every morning, a ritual of carefully pouring the cold water into the wash pan, soaping a wash rag, washing her face and neck, dipping her forearms into the bowl, washing her breasts, holding up one, then the other. Then she would wash under her petticoat, rinse the rag, throw soapy water out the door, and fill the bowl with clear water to rinse. All the while, Darcey's large breasts would heave from side to side.

"Wash every morning and every night, Jenna. Most folks don't wash enough and they smell bad. And don't forget the little drops of ammonia in the rinse water now that you're growing up . . . and keep your hair shiny and clean. Your hair is lovely and straight and takes the shine. Wash it often, at least once a week, and if there is lemon about, rinse it with the juice and those little dancing red and yellow lights will fire up your head like you're wearing a crown."

Darcey tiptoed across the cold floor to her trunk. In the shadowy room,

Jenna imagined Darcey's pearly body moving like a large fish in the sea and her red hair rippling in all directions like seaweed.

"Where's that fool nightshirt? I must have left it in the laundry tent. I'll just have to wear my petticoat and blouse to bed," she said.

Jenna watched her slip into her clothes. She waited for the special goodnight kiss, the closure of the day. She watched Darcey climb into bed and blow out the candle. Jenna often tried to turn Darcey into Martha Jane, into a mother, but something was missing. Maybe mothers were too busy, too distant. She felt closer to Darcey than she ever did to her own mother.

"All right, girls. Let's say our prayers. Father, we thank thee for the heavenly darkness so that we may rest and dream. We thank Thee for shelter and health. We place ourselves and our loved ones in Your perfect care, and know You are looking out for them as You do for us. Anything you want to add girls? And, Lord, thank Thee that my tooth is holding just fine. Amen."

"Amen," the girls said together.

Darcey began to sing a slow, melancholy tune softly:

Mother, I would marry and I would be a bride.
And I would have a young man forever at my side.
Or if I had a young man, O how happy I would be,
For I am tired and O so weary of my virginity.

Whistle, daughter, whistle, you shall have a sheep.
I cannot whistle, mother, I can only weep.
For if I had a young man, O how happy I would be,
For I am tired and so weary of my singularity.

When Darcey stopped singing, Jenna waited to hear the low purr of first sleep, the deep, steady breathing that said all was well. In the darkness, Jenna shyly touched her own forming breasts and nipples, soft as a baby kitten's nose. She wondered if they would ever be as large as Darcey's—such heavy, useless things. Poor Darcey. She must be tired hauling those large breasts around all day. Jenna turned over on her stomach and soon fell asleep.

Darcey lay awake thinking, first about Blue, then about the diggings. She thought more and more that what she wanted was not at the fort, but by the rivers—a man and gold. Lately, a terrible urge, a ridiculous idea, had been taking shape in her private thoughts.

A soft rain began to tap, tap, tap on the roof. Winter was setting in, a relentless pounding like her own restless heart. What was to become of her? How could she raise Pearle in a fort? Was her destiny to be a laundress for the rest of her life? If she had money of her own, enough money, she could open a boardinghouse, maybe in San Francisco or near the diggings. Why not? She could charge good money. Maybe in time, she and Pearle could homestead, "prove up" the land somewhere. Why not? She was strong and could work as hard as any man. On the other hand, maybe she could find a rich man to marry, someone with gold in his pocket, someone who also wanted land of his own.

Darcey's thoughts drifted in and out of sleep. She wondered how the men at the rivers could keep digging in the icy water. Where did they sleep in the rain? Why didn't they stop and rest? Did gold drive men into a madness where nothing else mattered, not even human life? There were so many rumors about the lawlessness in the camps, along the sandbars, wherever men gathered—hangings, beatings, stabbings, fighting, cursing, drunkenness. Was it the gold that turned good men into fools, gentle men into savages? Come spring, when the weather turned warmer and the rivers were not so cold, she might have to go and see for herself.

SIX

ON CHRISTMAS DAY, Jenna secretly waited for Blue's return. Many times throughout the day, she squinted down the road leading to the fort for any sign of a single man on horseback. Although many guests came for the day's festivities—the feast, and the evening dance, Blue was not among them.

The week of activities leading up to Christmas had kept Jenna from dwelling on Christmases past. She helped string pine garlands and bright ribbon on the heavy door of the fort. She helped Blanca make pies and learned to make Mexican lanterns from Blanca's husband by hammering nail-hole designs into tin cans. They looked festive lining the courtyard and provided a path to the fort to welcome the guests.

On the day of the party, Jenna placed pine boughs on long tables set up in the courtyard. She thought the clumps of red pomegranates and yellow, ripe persimmons, nuts, and cranberries resting on the boughs looked even more beautiful than tables set at home with fine chinaware and silver candlesticks.

About fifty people from nearby ranches, farms, and shanties along the Sacramento River came for the generous party and for a mass and Holy Communion service performed by a young Catholic priest traveling to the

Santa Clara Mission.

While a pig turned on a spit in the courtyard, spattering fat into the fire and sending smoke into the air, the women placed piles of baked sweet potatoes and jellies, breads, and custards on the tables. Nearby, the Kanaka Indians, still suspicious of white man's food, sat on the ground around a wooden trough filled with *atole*, a corn mush, which they ate with their hands. They could not be persuaded to try the delicious pumpkin pie, but they chewed bits of honeycomb instead, and smiled with pleasure.

Jenna and Pearle wore their new blue plaid gingham dresses Darcey and Blanca had made in secret to surprise the girls on Christmas morning. They did not have to wear their aprons at all on Christmas day.

Jenna made a Christmas present for Pearle—a reading book with a story about a chipmunk and a field mouse who married and lived under the roots of an old oak tree. She made a sweet sage and wild rose sachet for Darcey from a bit of leftover lace Blanca had given her, and with Darcey's help, she hemmed a new neck scarf for Blue.

In the evening, everyone danced to a fiery fiddler. In the middle of a circle of guests, Blanca and her husband performed the fandango, an exotic dance accompanied by a Spanish guitar, wild shouts, clapping, and stomping feet. Jenna had never seen such a haughty dance. Blanca, usually so quiet and slow moving, turned into a woman of sensuality, power, and pride, moving her wide hips in ways Jenna thought impossible. She arched her back, casting a daring glance at her partner—never smiling. The excitement tingled the air like static from an electrical storm. The Mexicans clapped a new rhythm and let out high-pitched cries and yips that sounded like coyote pups on the plains. Jenna's excitement made her break into red splotches. She wished she could dance like Blanca.

This Christmas was not like any celebration in Sapling Grove. Back home, Jenna would silently leave the candlelit church and listen to the murmurs of the congregation, a somber greeting of "Merry Christmas," or "Bless you, brother." There would be pious nods and religious smiles saved up for Sundays.

She loved this new life, so strange and full of energy. She loved singing the carols under the stars with these strangers with whom she shared a common understanding . . . *Silent night, Holy night . . . All is calm, all is bright* . . . Jenna held hands with Darcey and Pearle and looked at the stars. She thought of her family, Sapling Grove, Emily Polley, Hannah, Harke, Mother Boyles . . . Nettie. Maybe stars are souls winking down on us, she thought. Her eye caught the brightest star in the sky. "Is that you, Papa?"

Silent night, Holy night . . . All is calm, all is bright . . .
Sleep in Heavenly peace . . . Sleep in Heavenly peace.

That night, Jenna held Martha Jane's shell box and Israel's harmonica under the covers close to her heart.

🌱 🌱 🌱

Over the next few months, rains puddled the courtyard and dripped from the eaves. Fog rolled over the hills and breathed into the fort, obscuring faces and forms. Bundled figures darted from one door to another with their shoulders hunched and their eyes to the ground. They hardly noticed the acres of Captain Sutter's budding rose bushes outside the fort perfuming the air, nor the brown hills quietly turning into tender green.

The puddles began to dry and the air sparkled with a fresh beginning—a new rosy blush. California was emerging from its cocoon of winter, opening like butterfly wings.

Throughout the winter, shanties, tents, and canvas houses had sprung up along the river filled with restless miners. The harbor, once serving only Sutter's Fort and a few scattered small ranchos, now became a place with a name—Sacramento—a town laid out by Sutter himself.

Building had never stopped—a boardinghouse here, a saloon there, a trading post, a bordello, a gambling house, a jail, and always another saloon. The eager miners had tumbled off the ships that had come up from San Francisco and had created a shanty town where they waited for a break in the weather; for the swollen winter rivers to subside and the thick mud to dry. They grew impatient, brawled and staggered with drunkenness, cursed each other, kicked the dogs, whipped the mules, and reminded themselves their own savagery was only temporary.

They retold stories of men who dug out gold nuggets from the bedrock weighing fourteen pounds, and how one miner found an eight pound nugget and enough dust in a single pan to yield five thousand dollars. Their eyes shone, their voices rose, their arms waved in the air like tree branches in a high wind.

Their obsession for gold turned them into mad men whose wives or children, or mothers would not recognize. But they were convinced they would make their money quickly and return home to friends and family, heroes with heavy buckskin pouches.

As the sky turned blue once again, the miners would head up the valleys to the mountains.

Darcey talked to everyone coming or going to the American River or Feather River trying to gather information.

"They're a-comin', thousands of folks," one man said to Darcey as he loaded more supplies onto an already overloaded donkey. "Rumor has hit, over five thousand emigrants have already assembled and formed into companies and have started west like a swarm of crazy bees, a-racin' each other to be first at the ferry. They're a-cuttin' a road a mile wide in places just so as they won't trample each other to death. I'm gettin' gold while the gettin's good."

"Where are you going, Mister?" Darcey asked.

"Up the American River, Ma'am—Hattie's Bar—'bout three miles beyond Red Man's Bar. Been a rich find up there, so bountiful, people are a-pourin' into the area. One fella told me he scratched enough gold out of a rock crevice usin' only his pocket knife, and filled hisself a hatful of gold flakes.

"They say Hattie brung 'em all good luck. Wasn't much up there till a bunch of old Bear Flag soldiers brung her up there to cook and . . . keep the men fit. Them Bear Flaggers a rough bunch, still wanting to fight their own war with the Mexicans. I wouldn't want to be no Mexican around Hattie's Bar."

"Is this woman, this Hattie, still there?"

"Still there? Hell, she runs the place! The men built her a two-room wooden slat cabin. Toted the slats and a brass bed up the mountains just to please her. I ain't seen her, but I heard tell she's bigger than three men put together, fat as a dumplin', an' heavier than twenty sacks of flour. They toted her as far as they could in a wagon, then carried her the rest of the way on a kind of Indian-style litter, sort of dragged her on a bed of canvas stretched between two long poles. No horse could bear up under her weight without expiring. She's there all right, a mighty obligin' woman. I aim to see her."

"Do you think the gold will still be there by summer?" Darcey tried not to sound too eager for information.

"I reckon so, but it won't last forever. A bunch of men already got a new system—a kind of cradle that can wash near a dozen buckets of pay dirt at one time. Folks is gettin' smart, figurin' ways to get the gold faster. They dam up the rivers to make shallow water, and one smart fella I hear is diggin' a hole in the side of the mountain and washin' dirt down to the river, pickin' up more gold than he can carry away.

"One old slave and his master found twenty thousand dollars just makin' a hole for a cabin, and another fella found two thousand dollars of pay dirt under his doorstep. Hattie's Bar is payin', so I'm headin' there before the swarm of emigrants come a-buzzin' in there."

The old man spit, just to emphasize his point.

"Where did you come from, Mister?"

"Oregon. I come last year up to Oregon to farm, but when I heard of the gold, I come south along with others from Willamette a-seekin' the riches. I'm stakin' a claim before they get to it first."

"How do you stake a claim?" Darcey asked.

"Hell, woman . . . excuse me—Madam—you throw a blanket down or hammer a stake in the ground. That's your claim. You pitch a tent along the river or on the flat land nearby—that's what's called a 'bar.' There's no rules . . . just a gentleman's understanding of space what's reasonable.

"If someone crowds you too close, you stand up and say, 'Look, fella, that there's far enough. This here is mine!' If he don't pay no mind, you let the word out and he'll be run off down river like a dirty cur . . .leastways that's what I hear. There's kind of a code among the men along the river and the sandbars. The miners make their own rules, and if you want to keep from being flogged or hung from a tree, you abide.

"You do your work, keep your mouth shut, don't keep company with Mexicans or Chinee, stay out of other folks' way. That's what I aim to do." The old man slapped the donkey on the rear to get him moving. "I got four youngsters and a wife in Oregon to feed. I'm a-headin' home when my pockets is full. Did I tell you about the fella who found near eight thousand dollars of gold nuggets clingin' to the roots of a dead manzanita?"

The old man walked away shaking his head and muttering to himself.

"Good luck, Mister," Darcey watched the old man ride out of the fort, then turned away thoughtfully. "It's time to talk to the girls," she said, untying the scarf around her head and letting her red hair spring out in all directions.

That night, as Darcey, Pearle, and Jenna sat on Darcey's bed spooning bread pudding and thick cream into their mouths and enjoying the wickedness of sneaking it out of the kitchen under the cook's nose, Darcey thought it the best time to tell the girls her plan.

"Can you keep a secret? I'm going to the diggings, girls . . . and you're coming with me. I can't leave you here and I need you, Jenn, to help pan gold and watch out for Pearle while I'm wading in the river. Now don't say 'no' 'till you hear me out. You're going to have to put up with some inconvenience for a short while—long enough to get some gold. You're going with me and that's that. I got the gold fever . . . been sick with it all winter long."

"Oh, Mama! Oh! Oh!" Pearle put her hands to her mouth, and a worried frown crumpled her delicate face. "Can you die from gold fever?"

"Pearle, my silly girlie, I ain't dyin'. It ain't even my fault I'm hungerin' after the gold." Darcey put her arm around Pearle and pulled her close. "You see, once upon a time this land was ruled by Califia, the Black Amazon Queen. All the women here were large, black women, so beautiful a man could scarcely breathe around them. But they were bigger than the men, so big they could squash 'em like bugs. These women didn't want any men around, if you can imagine that! Their arms and faces were covered with gold. They wore gold earrings and headdresses, and gold cups over their enormous breasts."

"Like yours, mama."

"Yes, like mine, Pearle. These women loved gold more than men, if you can imagine that! They fevered after gold. But the men wanted the gold, too. They gathered together an army and killed the great Amazon women. The point is, if a woman don't have a man, she fevers after gold. In this land named California, that gold left by the Amazon women is still tucked away in the mountains and streams, and we're goin' to get us some!"

Jenna, reddened with a rush of excitement. "When, Darcey, when?" she cried.

Pearle caught the excitement. Her worry vanished, and together, the girls pounced on Darcey like two baby cubs.

"When, Darcey? Tomorrow?" Jenna asked again.

"A couple of days, I imagine. You'll have to keep another secret. Poor old Captain Sutter is in a bit of trouble, I guess. He owes a lot of money. All that land he sold between here and the harbor on the river is paying off some of his debts, but he still owes the Russians at Fort Ross. He's leaving for Europe right away and hasn't said when he's coming back. The fort seems to be dying. No one comes here now. Instead they go to Sacramento City. He ain't been himself lately—so sad in his eyes. I think he wants to see his people in Europe. Anyway, I don't want him to leave without clean shirts. You must not say a word."

"Poor Captain Sutter," Jenna said.

"No man, not even Captain Sutter, would allow us to go to the diggings. It ain't proper—immoral, you might say."

"Then how can we go?" Jenna asked.

"We ain't going as females. We're going disguised as men . . . or boys in your case. I'll be your papa and you two will be my sons. We'll say your mother died of food poisoning or consumption," Darcey said with a sly grin.

"You mean we're going to dress up like . . . *men?*" Jenna's eyes shone with excitement.

"Yes!" Darcey threw herself back on the pillow, laughing heartily. The girls tumbled with her, laughing and giggling to Darcey's jiggles. The whole idea was incredulous!

Jenna sat up. "Dare we do this? What if we are discovered?"

"We'll leave immediately and come right back to the fort. We won't be gone long—two or three weeks at the most. It will be a good caper, don't you think?"

"I guess so," Jenna said thoughtfully.

"What's the matter, Jenn? Ain't you excited to be rich, or do you want to be a poor farmer's wife happy to scratch a few yams or turnips from the dirt?"

"I was thinking about mama and papa. They wouldn't like me cutting my hair and lying to folks. I think we're committing a sin, ain't we?"

"Sometimes our lives take strange turns, Jenn. We're goin' along on our road happy as a June bug, then all of a sudden we come to a fork and have to choose which way to go. Our situation changes right then and there. Who'd have thought I was goin' to be widowed and you orphaned, and poor Pearle always a shakin' with bouts of malaria? Who'd have thought there was gold all over these hills, just a-waitin for us to find? Now cheer up, and put your head to our caper. It ain't no sin tryin' our hand at gold diggin'. It's goin' to be grand."

"Mama's going to wear gold cups over her bosoms," Pearle said, giggling behind her hand.

"And we'll be very rich and wear the latest French fashions," Darcey said, strutting around the room like a fine lady.

"And look like princesses with a golden coach and footmen . . . and glass slippers, not ugly boots that make you limp," Pearle said, hobbling after her mother.

Darcey opened the dresser drawer and pulled out a pair of scissors. "The time has come, girls. If I don't do it now, I'll lose my courage." She grabbed a thick clump of hair below her ears.

"No, Mama! Don't cut your hair!" Pearle shrieked.

"No, Darcey. Don't do it!" Jenna cried.

But it was too late. In one quick snip, a handful of red hair lay in her hand. The room fell silent. Even Darcey looked shocked, as if she had received the news of a sudden death. The girls bent over and looked at the hair like it was a corpse. Pearle began to cry softly, touching the lifeless red springs.

"Goodbye, hair," Pearle whimpered.

"Good riddance, hair," Darcey said, gathering her composure and slowly cutting the rest of her hair, clump by clump. "How do I look?"

"You look like a lady who's growing out her hair after a fever," Jenna said.

Darcey grabbed a fistful of hair and laid it under her nose as a bushy mustache. "*Now*, how do I look?"

The girls howled. "You look like Captain Sutter," Jenna said.

Darcey held more hair up to her chin. "How's this? A beard *and* a mustache."

"You *do* look like a man," Jenna said.

"Then this is how I'll look. I'll glue it on, even if it don't stick for long. I'll keep it on long enough for an impression, long enough to stake a claim. I'll first glue a full beard to a strip of material and then to my face. Same with the mustache. I'll take my extra hair and a jar of glue with me. It'll work; I'm certain of it." Darcey gathered the hair and carefully wrapped it in a silk scarf.

"What about us?" Jenna asked. "Do you think I should cut my hair, too?"

"It's your choice, Jenna. Your hair is fine enough to braid and tuck up under your papa's leather hat."

Jenna jumped up and impulsively shouted, "Do it! Cut it now!" Their arms and faces were covered with gold.

"You'll have to hide it under a scarf till we leave."

"I don't care! I want to go to the gold diggings with you! I want to be a boy, too!"

In three quick snips, the silky hair fell on the floor. Jenna reached up and touched the blunt ends. Her eyes widened with surprise. She walked over to the mirror and looked curiously at herself. Once again, no one spoke.

"You could pass for a laddie," Darcey said.

"Yes, I could. I look like my cousin James in Missouri." Jenna touched her stubby hair. "It feels funny without my long hair, like a billy goat's beard."

"Now me," Pearle said. "Cut my hair, too. I want to be a boy."

"I'll cut just a little—just enough to make you look like a boy who needs a haircut," Darcey said, snipping the ends of Pearle's hair.

The three of them stood looking in the mirror at the new images before them. Darcey began to laugh. "Hello, fellas," she said. In a rush, they put their arms around each other, forming a knot of friendship, squeezing tightly, pressing cheeks hard to bind their secret.

It was done. That night, in the flickering lantern light of their room, Darcey showed the girls how to make doeskin pouches to hold their gold nuggets, flakes or dust. Two days later, Darcey gambled that the captain would not miss one of his mules and loaded it with supplies she had stealthily set aside: a tent, blankets, beans, flour, salty ham, coffee, a lantern, pick axe, cooking pots and wash pans.

They slit the toes of Pearle's cramped, gnarled boots to ease the pain of her growing feet, and rubbed beeswax into the seams of their own boots to keep out water. The trio outfitted themselves in men's shirts and pants they'd hidden in the laundry. Darcey wore a workman's coat from the stable. When the time was right, they "borrowed" a horse for Darcey and Pearle, and Jenna rounded up Honey.

Under a shining moon almost ready to give way to the glow of a new day, the three females quietly led the animals out of the fort and headed west under the fading stars.

In the early morning hours, Darcey and the girls were not alone on the road to the American River. Pack mules and miners, mule trains, clusters of men on horseback, and men alone carrying bundles on their shoulders, pots and tin cups dangling from their belts—all made a steady parade alongside the river. There was an urgency in their stride, an impatience in their voices, a constant cursing at the slowness of the mules.

Jenna, Darcey, and Pearle stepped aside when miners passed them. They tried to be as inconspicuous as possible. No one paid much attention to them except for an occasional, "Comin' through," or a "Hello thar, whar you folks headin'?"

Darcey's usual response was, "Upriver", or, "To the diggings, same as everyone," thinking that sounded manly enough to pass for a miner.

No one seemed curious about Pearle, the only small child heading for a mining camp.

"I guess we'll just keep following everyone else until we come to the south fork," Darcey said. "It seems a lot of these miners are going to Red Man's Bar or Hattie's Bar."

By noon, Darcey, Jenna, and Pearle stopped to rest and eat a lunch of cheese and bread. While they were sitting on a grassy riverbank, feeling quite proud of themselves, a party of Indians—three women, two men, and two children—walked silently on the other side of the river, gentle and graceful as deer in the forest. Their nearly naked bodies blended with the brown earth, but their satin smoothness was strangely out of place—not textured like tree bark, fur, or feathers. They carried large, cone-shaped baskets on their strong backs, secured with a wide strap across their foreheads. The Indians walked past without looking at them.

But in a few minutes, Darcey became aware of the same Indians standing behind them. They had crossed the river and had moved quietly through the trees until they stood only a few feet away. The two men carried machetes in their hands. Unlike the Indian women who gathered food on the plains, these Indians did not smile, had no expression, and gave no clues to their intentions.

Darcey stood up and faced them. "Stand by the horses, Jenna. Get behind me, Pearle. I don't know what they want, but I have a funny feeling about them."

The Indian men, without speaking, moved in closer. They held their machetes up by their chests. One man started forward toward Darcey and Pearle, the other toward Jenna. The women and children stood silently back by the trees. Darcey could see the fear in Jenna's face as the Indian man approached her. Though he tried to appear friendly, his half-opened eyes and the turn of his mouth were menacing. Darcey felt certain this man was about to harm her.

"What do you want?" Jenna shouted.

The Indian stopped. At that moment, a shot split the air. The horses tossed their heads and pulled at their reins. Pearle began whimpering quietly. The women and children ran into the trees. The men followed.

Out from behind a clump of thick bushes stepped an old man whose face was nearly covered by a matted, white beard, mustache, and mantle of white eyebrows. "I figured you fellas got caught up short without your rifles and needed a hand. I saw them critters cross the river like they was up to no good, kind of sneakin' they was, and so I figured they was about to steal a miner's pack or hell, maybe slit his throat."

"Thanks," Darcey said, pressing her red mustache against her lip to see if her beard was still in place. "We're mighty obliged you came along when you did."

"I'm Ebenezer Cootz here, number-one mule packer, trader, and supplier, up and down the American. I'll bring you anything you need except a whore. She's mine." He laughed at his own humor, his eyes nearly disappearing behind the eyebrows.

"How about bringing me a wife?" Darcey asked, just to see if wives were on the supply list in the camps.

"Sure . . . if you're fool enough to want one. I aim to please. I can bring a couple of ugly women up from Sacramento City right now, just waitin' to crawl into someone's underwear."

He laughed again good-naturedly, then blew his nose in his hand and wiped it on his horse. "Who are you folks?" he asked, smiling.

Darcey hesitated. "Cole . . . uh . . . William Cole and my young son, Benjamin, and his older brother, Charlie," she said, pointing to Jenna. She had already thought up the names but didn't know she'd need to use them so soon.

"You headed up the south fork, are you?" he asked.

"Yep. Past Red Man's Bar a few miles," Darcey said.

The old man nodded approval. "Up to Hattie's Bar. A good choice. They're findin' plenty of gold up there. But a word of advice. There's some real sinners up the south fork. Them Indians just now have been known to isolate lone miners and murder them—no reason, except revenge. About a month back, the men at Red Bar dragged a couple of naked Indians into camp, took turns whippin' 'em, then hung 'em for no reason 'cept they was tired of the mud and bored waitin' to get to the gold."

"Thanks for the warning," Darcey said.

"Yes, sir, a bunch of crazy Irishmen up there," Ebenezer Cootz said, shaking his hairy, white head. "Well, my mules is waitin' around the bend. I'm headin' back to Sacramento City to pick up supplies—whiskey, canvas, flour, axes, canned oysters—you name it. Might even go to San Francisco this trip and get supplies off the dock. Lot of ships is just sittin' in the water with no crew to unload goods from the foreign ports and the East Coast. Somebody could make a lot of money just gettin' supplies off the ships and to the miners." He pulled a plug of chewing tobacco from his pocket and tucked it inside his lower lip. "If I had more time, I'd tell you my adventures on the sea in the otter trade back in the thirties, but I bet you're scratchin' to get to the gold . . and I better be on my way. I make my rounds to the bars. Too old and too smart to beat my brains out gamblin' on the yellow. If you boys is up Hattie's way, I expect I'll see you again."

Darcey nodded, hoping to get the talkative old man on his way.

Ebenezer Cootz started to leave, then stopped and looked at Jenna. "A little hard work will put some meat on your bones and give you some muscles, boy."

He leaned forward and looked closely at Darcey. "I didn't see no rifles. None of my business, but takin' youngsters up past Red Bar ain't the usual. I'd have my rifle handy, if I was you."

When he was gone, Darcey said, "Do you think we fooled him?"

"I don't know," Jenna said, scrutinizing Darcey's disguise. "He was a smart old man."

Darcey worried that Jenna had doubts about going to the diggings dressed as males.

"I'm scared, Mama," Pearle said. "Let's go back home."

Darcey picked Pearle up in her arms and hugged her. She realized that lately she'd been so caught up in gold fever she'd neglected her little girl. The past few months her world had been crowded with gold-hungry miners and talk of Sutter's Fort losing its place of importance, giving way to boom towns sprouting up everywhere. If the fort folded up, or was sold to pay Sutter's debts, where then would she and Pearle live? Darcey convinced herself that going to the diggings was her best way to survive. She repressed the thought that she was obsessed, that she tasted gold in her soul . . . that is was all that mattered.

"Listen, Pearle. This caper won't last long. Give me a week or so to pan. That's all. If we can't find any gold, we'll go back. I promise. Let me at least find enough gold to make a tooth. Be my big girl." She kissed Pearle's cheek. "Come here, Jenna." Darcey hugged Jenna as well. "Are we still together in this venture? If you want to go back, we will—right now—but think about it first. Gold will change our lives."

Jenna looked at Darcey's serious face. She saw a different Darcey, not the safe shelter, not the rock to lean on that she had seen before.

"I'll go with you, Mama," Pearle said. She smiled happily and held Darcey's face in her hands.

Jenna looked at Pearle's pale, sensitive face. *What if something happened to her? To Darcey? They're my only family now.* "I'll stay with you Darcey, and help you find a gold tooth," she said.

Darcey squeezed Jenna. "After that we'll go back. I promise."

🌱 🌱 🌱

In four days of riding over a narrow, rugged mountain path, Darcey and the girls descended into Red Man's Bar, a shamble of tents and crude structures, even primitive huts made of pine boughs and covered with scraps of calico, a lady's apron, a few towels. Around the camp lay discarded barrels, tins, whiskey bottles, garbage, bones of deer and elk, a jumble of items tossed indifferently here and there, slices of red meat hanging on tree branches and tent poles, which, along with unwashed cooking pots and piles of dung, attracted swarms of flies. Mud-caked mules and flea-infested mutts ambled about. Jenna thought this was not a civilized place, not nearly as orderly or clean as the difficult conditions on the Oregon Trail, and there were no women around to clean the messes!

No one paid much attention to the threesome as they rode through the camp. The tired miners in camp, taking a break from the arduous labor, lay exhausted under a tree or against a stump, wet and gaunt and unsmiling.

The girls rode quickly through Red Man's Bar and followed the river toward Hattie's Bar. All along the way were tents and muddy holes where miners had staked and worked their claims. They saw miners knee-deep in the water, some working the banks, piling stones to dam the water, some using picks and shovels on the mountainsides, some felling trees, shoveling, panning, building cradles, working in teams to get to the bedrock, and some staggering under the weight of buckets of dirt to be washed.

It was not what Darcey had expected. She did not see any gold nuggets lying on the ground. She saw only back-breaking work and exhausted men and wondered how long her high hopes would last.

By late afternoon, Darcey and the girls had descended a steep precipice into a narrow canyon flanked by high rock walls. They looked down on about two hundred tents and lean-tos and a couple of hastily made shanties placed on the widest part of the canyon floor. The structures, arranged haphazardly, on either side of a narrow road, were reminiscent of a main street. Smoke rose from small cooking fires throughout the bar and hung in the shadows.

As they rode down into the canyon, leaving only the tops of the mountains to enjoy the sun, Darcey wondered if warmth and light would ever find their way into this cold place called Hattie's Bar.

A crudely made wooden structure with a canvas roof and only one window dominated the camp. A sign, painted with the words, "Hattie's Place," hung over the canvas-curtained doorway. Various papers and boards were tacked to the walls announcing claims, along with items for sale or trade.

Darcey remembered the old miner at Sutter's Fort had said. Hattie's was the center of the mining camp, the main place to find an outdated newspaper to read, to buy a few supplies and groceries, a drink, a cup of coffee, or bowl of stew when Hattie felt like cooking.

As they rode past her establishment, Jenna stared at the curtained window.

"What are you doing?' asked Darcey.

"I . . . I just wanted to see the woman . . . Hattie."

"Don't look in there!" Darcey snapped. "Keep your eyes straight ahead. Act like we know what we're doing and don't say a word. Just keep riding through the camp and up the river until we're out of sight of the men. When we're by ourselves, we'll make our claim."

"How do we do that, Darcey?" Jenna asked.

"I don't know. Pitch our tent, I guess, or hammer a stake in the ground with a rock and then start panning. If it ain't right, I imagine we'll be told."

Jenna was anxious to stop. She was as tired and hungry as on the Oregon Trail—"bone tired" Mrs. Polley used to say. As they rode through the camp, Jenna heard something behind her that made the back of her neck prickle.

It was a voice, familiar, haunting, a suffocating sound like a cry corked inside a bottle.

A pulsating fear crept over her face, covered her nose and mouth, pressed her eyes shut, squeezed her temples like a vice. She strained to hear . . .

"Sinners—ye who seek only gold and riches. I say, lay not up for yourselves treasures upon the earth. You're not a-listenin', sinners. It's in this here good book. I say, lay not up for yourselves treasures upon the earth where moth and rust and gold doth corrupt and where thieves break through and steal."

Jenna shuddered. Could it be? Did that voice belong to the man she had thought lay entombed in the darkest places of her heart, a man she'd carefully buried in her mind and believed she'd never see again? She held her breath and felt her heart jump inside her chest and pulsate in her neck.

"But lay up for yourselves treasures in heaven, brothers, treasures in heaven," the voice said.

No, it could not possibly be Faithful Squibb. He was in Oregon. Yes . . . yes . . . This was just another preacher of the Gospel. She was safe, far away from him. Still, her heart beat loudly. She shook Honey's reins to move faster away from the chilling voice.

Darcey picked out a flat area with gentle banks set back from a shallow place in the river. The water moved slowly and she could see the colorful rolled rocks on the bottom. They would not have to wade deeper than below their calves in any one spot. Farther upstream across the river, another miner had pitched a tent.

Darcey figured she could watch him to see exactly how panning for gold was done, how to rotate the wash pan while tipping the lighter sand and dirt over the edge and letting the heavier gold collect at the bottom. It looked easy.

They unloaded the weary animals and tied them to a tree, then pitched a primitive tent by hammering two posts into the ground, laying the canvas over the top and staking the sides. It would have to do, even though it sank in the middle like a sway-backed horse.

Pearle looked up at their makeshift home, then turned to Darcey with a broad smile. "Isn't our little home wonderful?" Still smiling, she began limping back and forth from the supply mule to a far corner of the tent carving out a special, protected place for herself in an unfamiliar world."

While Jenna gathered wood to make a warm meal, Darcey went to the river's edge to try her hand at panning before it grew too dark. She was certain a nugget, unseen for eons, lay in the dirt at her feet. With little light, she could not see any bright flecks at all and decided to wait until morning. Tomorrow she would begin amassing a fortune, filling dreams, but tonight, she would remove her makeshift beard and mustache, which were losing hair and badly irritating her skin; she would heat some water for them all to bathe under cover of darkness. After a hot meal of beans and pork, coffee, and an apple, she and the girls would say their prayers and ask God to help them find a nugget as big as a peach pit. It was going to be lovely.

Darcey was up early the next morning, careful not to disturb the girls as they slept. She gently covered Pearle curled up like a tiny mouse in nests of blankets, and quickly brewed coffee before plunging into the ankle-deep water. Around her, the air in the canyon was cool and smoky and breathed a fragrance of pungent pine. The river bubbled quietly and birds flew high above the rosy, sun-tipped mountaintops.

She began to squat over her wash pan as she'd seen the miners do the day before, but her large frame made this position uncomfortable. Instead, she kneeled on one knee in the cold water and braced her frame over the other knee.

Darcey heard movement behind her and turned to see Jenna run to the river and flop down onto the grassy bank near her, pulling on her boots.

'Have you found any gold, yet?' Darcey could hear excitement in the girl's voice.

"Look here, Jenna," Darcey said, pointing to some tiny flakes in the bottom of the pan. "This is gold . . . but so small! It will take a lifetime to get an ounce."

"I've seen it much bigger. Maybe you're in the wrong spot."

"We've got to move these millions of stones to get to the dirt underneath. I heard it's in the blackish sand down a-ways. We'll have to shovel away the stones." She stood up, her pant leg dripping, her shoes soaked. "This is going to be harder than I thought . . . but I've got to try."

Darcey caught Jenna staring at her and realized she'd allowed her irritation and anger to show. She quickly smiled.

"This will be fun. Come on, Jenna. Remember, we split everything fifty-fifty."

Throughout the day, they overturned large rocks, shoveled the riverbed, swirled the pans. Pearle worked in the soft sand at the river's edge with a spoon until she lost interest, then made a village of stones, sticks, and weeds for trees. By the end of the day, the two women had a small amount of gold flecks, enough to fill two thimbles, which they knotted in a bandanna. They were exhausted and wet.

"We probably have a half ounce, enough to buy some fresh food. Let's go to Hattie's Place to weigh it and stock up on stores. I'm sick of beans and pork. We'll buy some eggs and milk and fruit and cheese," Darcey said. "I'll glue my beard on. Remember, no talking to anyone. We'll go about our business and leave."

As they rode into Hattie's Bar, there seemed to be a flurry of excitement—not jubilant as in gold discovery, but angry with shouts and cursing. Two men were squaring off for a fight, and the miners from up and down the river were running toward the crowd.

Darcey noticed Jenna looking around uneasily as if searching for someone, but was too concerned with the activity swirling around her to question the girl.

"Good. No one will bother us," Darcey said, as they got off their horses and walked cautiously into the dark shanty known as 'Hatties Place'.

The interior smelled strange and vulgar. A drooping, red calico curtain sectioned off one end of the room. The other end, partitioned by stacked boxes and barrels, served as a store. A crude table and long benches sat in the middle of the room. Along one wall stretched a wooden shelf where gold was weighed; on the other side of the room stood a stove and a wall of pots and motley cooking utensils hanging on nails. A pie tin of half-eaten biscuits dotted with flies, along side a forlorn, rusty tea kettle, rattled on the stove with the slightest vibration. Another pie pan of gleaming gold, perched proudly on the table, was the only brightness in the room.

No one was about. The brewing fistfight had pulled everyone to the jostling crowd outside.

"Hello? Anybody here?" Darcey called out.

There was no answer, but someone stirred behind the red calico curtain. It sounded like a person laboriously turning over in a bed.

"It must be Hattie," Jenna whispered.

The person coughed—a low, hollow, congested sound. "What do you want?" a hoarse female voice said. "Ain't Samuel out there to weigh your dirt?"

"No one's here," Darcey said.

There was a moment's hesitation. "You new here? I don't recognize your voice."

"Yes," Darcey said.

"Then identify yourself and state your business."

"I'm William Cole with my two sons, Charlie and Benjamin. We're working up the river a short ways. We come to weigh our gold and to buy some supplies."

"Well, you'll have to weigh your own gold and get your own food."

"Are you Hattie?" Darcey asked, walking over to the closed curtain. She could smell strong camphor medicine.

"Some call me that," she said through a fit of coughing.

"We've got a little over a half ounce," Darcey said, weighing out the gold in a brass balance scale.

"Clean, or mixed with sand?"

"Clean. We'd like to buy some eggs and fruit, some meat and . . ."

"You got about seven or eight dollars, I'm guessin', enough for a half-dozen eggs. Help yourself. They's in a barrel what looks filled with hay and sawdust."

"Only a *half dozen*?" Darcey gasped, thinking how outrageous it was. She could buy a whole dozen for forty cents. "That's a ridiculous price!" she snapped.

"You'll pay double that in a week's time. Eggs is as precious as gold. Take it or leave it," Hattie said, coughing again. "Some meat is hanging' in the shed out back. Deer or elk, I don't know which. If you want meat instead of eggs, you'll have to cut off a half pound or so."

The noise outside got louder.

"Jenna, you get the eggs while I check the horses and see how you make a claim. Come with me, Pearle," Darcey whispered.

Jenna cautiously peered and poked in different barrels until she found the eggs. She carefully counted out six eggs, wrapped them in a tattered newspaper, put them in her big pockets, and was about to leave when Hattie shouted. "You, there! Come in here for a minute. I need a favor."

Jenna stopped but didn't answer. She felt her face redden with splotches.

"I'm askin' you a favor. The men around here don't say 'no' to a favor for Hattie. You'll find out I'm as precious as them eggs. Pull back the curtain so I can see you. I won't bite . . . at least for now."

Jenna slowly drew aside the red fabric. In the brass bed, supported by pine logs, lay an enormous woman, so large she seemed inhuman. Her face sat in a puddle of flesh that drained into her shoulders, swallowing up her neck. The weight of fat on her face sagged her eyes, pulled the loose lower lip down to her whiskered chin, and folded over her throat. Pillows propped up her weighty torso; fat breasts lay on the horizon of her rounded belly. Her long brown hair, stuck together with greasy liniments, spread out on the pillow like Medusa's snakes. She smelled peculiar, like something fermenting. She breathed with noisy labored rasps.

Jenna could not believe that anyone as fat and grotesque as Hattie could be alive, let alone be carted up the mountains to cook for the miners. She could barely move her cumbersome, elephant body.

"Come here, boy. Let me look at you." She reached out and touched Jenna's arm. "Give me your hand."

Jenna, repulsed, extended her hand and stared at the toadish woman.

Hattie smiled shyly. "You ain't a boy at all. I know boys. You ain't a boy, are you?"

Jenna didn't answer.

"No need to worry. I won't tell on you. I'm full of secrets. That's why I'm so fat."

"I'm Charlie Cole."

"No you ain't. You ain't a boy with that pretty slim face of yours and the person with you ain't a man. I ain't very smart, except when it comes to knowing what's a man and what ain't . . . and you ain't."

Jenna didn't answer.

"All right, Charlie Cole. I won't spill your beans, but I know what I know. I just don't know the why of it, but it ain't important. Kind of amuses me knowing there's another female here foolin' the gents. I'd like to talk to a female for a change." Hattie went into such a terrible coughing spasm it turned her face purple. Jenna thought she was going to have a heart attack.

"Can I get you something?" Suddenly, that place in Jenna that grieved for trapped and injured animals took over. She looked into the large, sad eyes of a woman with a body trapped inside an unwieldy casing. She saw in her brown eyes unspeakable suffering and loneliness, a history of untold pain. "Are you all right?" Jenna said softly.

"No, Charlie, I ain't. I'm dying . . . soon. I feel it. Something different every day. The light in the corner of the room, the air around me. Sometimes, I wake up and think people are standing at the foot of the bed—lots of people—but then I see they really aren't there at all. They vanish." Hattie sighed. "I've wanted to tell somebody about that."

"Have you seen a doctor?"

"There ain't no doctors about and them that says they is, ain't doctors at all. Most is barbers and actors full of demon rum, misfits. I take laudanum and sip sarsaparilla tea. Maybe you could get me a cup of tea. The kettle should be hot on the stove. Samuel usually keeps it going for me. I don't know where he's gone to."

"I'll get you some tea. Anything else, Hattie?" It felt strange saying the woman's name.

"No, just your company for a minute more. Can you stay and chat awhile?"

"I'll come back tomorrow. But I have to go now."

"Do you promise?" Hattie asked, trying to sit up.

"I promise."

"That would be fine." She lay back on the pillows and shut her eyes, breathing with a noisy rasp. Jenna had seen pneumonia before. Hattie was very sick. She placed the cup of tea by Hattie's bed and slipped out of the room.

Riding back to their camp, she told Darcey all about Hattie. "She figured us as females, but she won't say anything to anyone. I didn't tell her about us at all. I'm going back to see her tomorrow. I promised."

🌿 🌿 🌿

The next two days were eventful. Darcey and Jenna gradually worked upstream, increasing their yield with each panful. Between the two of them, they panned one and one-half ounces of larger flakes the second day, and on the third day, they uncovered several small nuggets that totaled two ounces.

Their good fortune was increasing. At about fifteen dollars an ounce, a good day brought in thirty dollars. If they could continue this lucky streak, their hard work would be rewarded. Unfortunately, they had to buy food—any food—even dried jerky from another miner. Nothing was left after they paid the inflated prices of the mining camp. Eggs cost a dollar a piece, a half pound of cheese cost three dollars, bread, two dollars, and canned goods were an impossible price. Only the lucky fellow who struck it rich could afford sixteen dollars for a tin of sardines or a bottle of ale, or, like one digger, buy a jar of brandied peaches to share with his pet pig.

Each day, Jenna brought Hattie a cup of tea and chatted awhile. Darcey preferred to stay at the claim panning while Jenna bought food at Hattie's Place. Besides, it was tedious gluing on the ratty beard, which had become hard and scratchy from the old, dried glue. It didn't stay on well and needed to be made all over again. Darcey didn't want to take the time. When miners rode past, she kept her head down or darted into the tent.

She was unaware of Jenna's cold fear that somewhere nearby was a man wearing a black frock, tipping his black silk hat and smiling with yellow teeth.

Hattie was getting worse. For the next couple of days, Jenna's visits grew longer. Occasionally, a grizzled man would step into the cabin and shout, "How you doin' Hattie?" or "Where's Samuel?" and "Don't bother to get up, I just come for some flour." Miners came and went, always trusted to buy their goods, weigh their dust, and pour the required amount into the wash pan of gold.

"I like you, Charlie," Hattie said weakly. "I'm sorry you lost your family on the crossing. I'm an orphan, too, you know, only my mother and father are on the bottom of the sea somewhere around the Horn in South America. They both got sick on the ship—food poisoning, I guess. I didn't eat the canned salmon, not being agreeable to it.

"On the other hand, they both ate the large sea turtle caught off the coast of the Galapagos Islands. Everyone was excited catching that poor creature trapped in his own shell, his old wrinkled eyes full of fear and confusion. I couldn't bring myself to eat the critter. No, not me, hungry as I was.

"It was a miserable, long voyage that took three-hundred and nine days, longer than promised. We ran out of decent food. The water turned stinking and foul in the barrels, and the only way you could drink it was if it was loaded with sugar and molasses. Maybe they both died from the bad water. I never was certain."

Hattie took a swallow of tea and sighed. "They parted from life on the same day. They was good people.

"The funny thing is, they come west for *my* health. Ain't that the limit? I was pretty fat back in New York . . . fatter than most. My father thought comin' to California might improve my health—maybe give me half a chance to get married and have a family. But when I stepped off the ship in Yerba Buena, goin' on six years back now, I didn't have no place to go. And I was sick, real sick, way down deep in my heart.

"I worked in a saloon 'til my legs give out. Then I stayed most of the time in bed in a back room, eatin' everything that come my way, including the men." Hattie started to laugh, but it turned into a cough. "I gained over one hundred and fifty pounds in just three years. The men was real nice to me, though. They said that sleepin' between my legs was like bein' wrapped in a silk comforter." She tried to laugh again.

"Some of the soldiers, friends of mine, brought me here. Yerba Buena, what you call San Francisco, was gettin' too big anyhow. I thought the change might do me some good then damned if I didn't get a bad winter cold in my chest."

All the talking seemed to tire her. She shut her eyes. "You and me, Charlie, are orphans. I only hope you do better than I did."

Jenna watched Hattie's eyeballs move behind the waxy lids like small trapped animals. She listened to the raspy breathing, the struggle for oxygen, and the unearthly moan that parted Hattie's lips. Jenna got up to leave; Hattie's eyes sprang open.

"Don't leave me, Charlie."

Jenna sat back down.

"Tell me your name."

"It's Jenna. Jenna Daggett."

"You got family up yonder—in Heaven?" She had forgotten she'd asked the question before.

"Yes, my mama and papa and baby brother," Jenna said softly.

"I'll tell 'em hello for you when I get there." She coughed. "And don't think I ain't going there, Jenna. I've made an army of gentlemen happy every day. Men like more than a release, honey. They like *lovin'*; some of them are just like little boys. Have you had a man yet?"

"No, Ma'am."

"Well, when you do, don't hold back nothing. What you do with a man betwixt the two of you is your own kind of ceremony, you might say. They is always mighty grateful, and some of 'em cry like babies." She shut her eyes. "I should have had a baby. I always wanted children."

Jenna left Hattie's Bar feeling sad.

Poor Hattie, poor trapped beast.

The next day when she came to visit Hattie, she found a crowd of men hanging around outside. Hattie was dead. She had died in her sleep. She was finally free from her cage of flesh.

The men talked about building her a fine casket and burying her upriver away from the bar—"Up on the mountain a ways so as not to interfere with the digging." The men from the Bear Flag Army would be the pallbearers, and Samuel would fiddle a dirge if he could slow down the bowstring. "She was a good one, old Hattie, as long as she didn't roll over on you. Warm as a baked yam, and just as tasty."

Jenna sat on her horse, Honey, listening to the men talk about the good old days with Hattie. She was about to leave when she saw a familiar figure riding into camp. This time she was positive. It *was* Faithful Squibb. She turned her horse around just as he rode up to Hattie's Place.

"I'm told there's a burial and you need a preacher to say the right words. Friends, I'm happy to send this sinner to the Lord. It will cost you five ounces. That includes a solo of 'Nearer My God to Thee.'"

Jenna mounted Honey and rode away from Hattie's place as fast as possible. She was certain he had not recognized her or Honey—not yet, anyway.

Jenna returned to her own camp to tell Darcey about Hattie's death. By late afternoon, a party of men carrying shovels rode past on horseback looking for the right spot to dig a grave. A short distance beyond their camp, the men scrambled up the side of a crumbly mountain to a level place. Tomorrow, in the early morning, they would lower Hattie into her final resting place.

At daybreak, Jenna and Darcey watched the procession of men carrying on oversized casket. Jenna ducked into her tent when Faithful passed. Standing in the trees, she watched the men place the casket on the ground. It was a somber affair. The men removed their hats and lowered their heads when Faithful began his sermon.

"Brothers, we are gathered here this morning to say a final farewell to

Miss Hattie—what's her last name?" No one knew it. "Hattie, a woman of substantial goodwill. Now friends, the Lord giveth and the Lord taketh away."

Suddenly, someone interrupted the preacher.

"Glory be to God, look what's lyin' at my feet!" The man picked up a gold nugget the size of a pea. "We've hit gold! I'll bet this is the Mother Lode! It's pay dirt! Hattie, you done it again!"

Pandemonium broke out as the men plunged into the dirt, raking their hands through it as quickly as they could to find more. Hattie's casket lay neglected on the ground. Some men filled their hats with dirt and ran to the river to wash it. Others jumped into the grave hole to scrape the sides for nuggets. Excitement charged the air as the men broke tree limbs and plunged them into the earth and topped them with a hat or scarf to stake a claim. Hattie would have to wait.

She would not be buried until the next day, after the men made a law that no man from the Bear Flag Revolt, who had carried Hattie to the sierras, could stake an individual claim. They would divide the take equally—fair and square. After all, they had all shared Hattie's favors while she was alive. She would have wanted it that way.

SEVEN

THROUGHOUT THE NIGHT, miners flocked to the area around the grave site and staked new claims along the river. As they passed by, the arc of lantern light splashed strange shadow patterns inside the tent where Darcey lay awake thinking.

All night Darcey contemplated their situation at the camp. When the clip-clop of horses, rattling tools and the men's loud curses awakened Jenna the next morning, Darcey still struggled with her thoughts.

"We're being squeezed out, Jenna. Most of the gold is higher up the river. We're too low. All the miners are going to take the bulk of the surface gold. Some are already forming groups to build that new contraption, the Long Tom, that will help them move tons of dirt. We haven't been too lucky." Darcey shook out a dirty sock and slipped it on her foot.

"What are we going to do?" Jenna's eyes searched Darcey's face.

The older woman knew her face reflected her disappointment. "I don't know. Maybe it's time to go home. We need a lucky break. We haven't taken out enough gold to keep us struggling here like darkies.

"Just look at my hands! The dirt has bored clean into the cracks and split my fingernails. Your face, Jenna, is full of sun scabs and mosquito bites, and you look like a runaway. Poor Pearle, her nose ain't stopped running since we been here."

Darcey sighed. "Maybe it's time to go. I'll think about it." She pulled on her boots, crawled out of the tent, and walked slowly to the river to fill the coffee pot and splash cold water on her face. She ran her wet hands like a comb through her wiry red hair. As she was setting the pot to boil, Jenna looked at her curiously.

"Darcey, your tooth is gone!"

"What?"

"Your tooth! Your tooth!"

Darcey slipped her tongue through the empty space. "Oh, Lord, it is!"

"Maybe it's in the river where you washed," Jenna rushed to the water's edge.

They squinted into the water but could not see the tooth.

"I'll look in the bed covers. It might have fallen out in your sleep. You might have swallowed it."

"What's the matter?" Pearle said, sitting up sleepily.

"Your mama lost her tooth."

"Oh, no!" Pearle said with a worried look. "Mama loved that tooth."

Darcey returned wearing a toothless smile. "I didn't find my tooth, but I found a small nugget. There's still some gold on our claim. Give me one more day. What we find today, if anything, will be the last. We'll go home and figure what to do next."

By late afternoon, Jenna and Darcey had collected about an ounce of gold.

"I'm going to Hattie's Place to get some supplies for our journey back to Fort Sutter," Darcey said.

"Can we go, too, Mama?"

"Not this time, Pearle. I've got thinking to do. You two stay close to the tent. Jenna can tell you a story or you can practice reading from your primer. I'll be back shortly. Maybe we'll splurge and buy some elk steak if there's any good meat hanging in Hattie's storage shed. Then tomorrow, we'll go home."

"Hooray!" Pearle shouted, clapping her hands and hopping up and down awkwardly on her mismatched legs.

Hattie's Bar was nearly empty since so many men had moved up river to make new claims. Darcey entered Hattie's Place, strangely silent, still smelling of camphor and death. The bed was left as she died—pillows and sheets rumpled and stained. A half-empty tin mug of tea sat on an upside-down barrel by the bed. Hattie's boots crouched in the corner, and a huge dress and straw hat hung like a lifeless ghost on a nail.

They had buried her in her nightdress without preparing the body, dressing it, or washing it. That was women's work. The men had simply rolled her in a wool army blanket and placed her in a pine box made from old wagon slats. No one had bothered to pack her meager items in her trunk.

Darcey walked about the room fingering the dress, touching the brass bed. She felt uneasy, like she was intruding in space still reserved for the departed. It was as if the final sigh of breath still lingered in the room . . . a living, watching thing.

She moved toward the trunk, and in spite of thinking it was sacrilegious to open it, she yielded to the temptation and lifted the lid. On top, a red Chinese silk scarf fringed in black lay neatly folded. Underneath lay a fan of brilliant blue peacock feathers, a carved silver hair brush, and a faded photograph of a man and woman on their wedding day. They were dressed simply, people of little means. Though they stood together in the new union, they looked straight ahead with wide, brown, expressionless eyes like strangers. She thought she saw a trace of fear in the young bride's face, the look of a frightened fawn. She could not have been more than fourteen.

Darcey ran her fingers over the images and thought of her own parents, also farmers, humble, always struggling with the land until they died.

Suddenly, the reverie was broken by loud voices as a group of men stomped into the shack. Darcey turned quickly, embarrassed to be caught looking into the trunk.

"Where's Hattie?" a gruff voice asked. The man steadied and walked over to Darcey. "Where's the fat lady?"

Darcey could see the men were drunk. "She died the day before yesterday. I'm packing up her things," she lied.

"Damn my hide! What luck! I been wanting to see this lassie for two weeks. Any other females about?" He staggered to the bed and flopped down.

"No, no women anywhere." Darcey was thankful she was still in her male disguise.

"Too bad, friends. We're out of Irish luck. No beavers. No furry little beavers for miles and miles." He peered at Darcey through red eyes. "How about whiskey? You got whiskey?"

"Yes—over there, behind the boxes," Darcey said nervously.

"Bring us a bottle of good whiskey!"

"You run this place?" another man asked.

"I—I help out. That is, yes I do. I run this place."

"What's for supper? We're hungry as boars and we'll pay with gold." The man pulled out a leather pouch that looked full. "Can you feed the four of us?"

"Why, sure I can. Let's see, we've got some elk steaks or maybe ham." She could always count on there being smoked ham somewhere.

"What else?"

"Let's see. Fried potatoes. Creamed onions? Biscuits? Canned pears and coffee."

"Then start cooking and bring us a bottle. How much is whiskey here?"

She had no idea but blurted out, "One ounce."

"How much for a plate of food?" Again, she merely guessed. "Three dollars," she said emphatically. It was an outrageous price, but she thought it might discourage them and they'd leave.

They didn't argue the price. "We'll be outside playing cards. Holler when it's ready."

The men staggered out the door, and Darcey suddenly found herself obliged to cook dinner for four hungry miners. If she could pull this off, she'd make twelve dollars with a lot less effort than panning for gold . . . and in no time at all!

Darcey quickly went to work. In the shed behind the shack hung smoked hams and strips of red meat. She waved the flies away from a strip of aging flesh and cut it into steaks. After she fired up the stove, she rummaged around for potatoes, onions, canned fruit, and set the water to boil for coffee. She would pay for the supplies she used and still come out ahead.

Before she finished rolling out the biscuit dough, four more men came into Hattie's Place.

"Hear you're servin' up supper. We'll be joining you if it ain't too late."

Twenty-four dollars! Why, that is more than I usually make in a whole day at the river! I could get rich doing this. Darcey's excitement grew as she flew around the room fixing the meal.

I could make this a place for me and the girls. Fix it up nice, with another window and curtains, maybe a grass mat rug, some pictures, a cupboard. When I make enough profit, I could add rooms, make it a boardinghouse or a respectable eating establishment—clean, respectable—no spittoons, cursing, or ungentlemanly behavior.

Before she finished peeling potatoes and onions, another man, full of mud, stepped into the shack. "The men say you're servin' supper."

"That's right," Darcey said confidently. "Bring your own plate, cup, and utensils—and wash up."

The man looked surprised at the order. Darcey caught herself and said, "Wash up your own dirty dishes afterwards." She then plopped the onions in a boiling pot.

Dinner was a success. Nine jovial men sat at the table red-faced from whiskey and hearty laughing. They listened to a man who told one story after another, each one funnier than the last.

Darcey also listened as she cleared away greasy platters, and served strong black coffee, boiled and strained through a piece of old flannel.

She heard him say, "This gentleman from the England was a real dandy. Mind you, he brought five dressy white muslin shirts, seven fine long coats, and five waistcoats to the hills. By God, he even brought evening clothes and dancing slippers! He never figured he might have to dance with one of us ugly Irish boys since there aren't any ladies for partners.

"He lost interest mighty fast when one of our smelly boys from Limerick with bosoms made from wool socks, asked him to dance on the Fourth of

July. It wasn't long before he was sloggin' in river clay in his fine duds along with the rest of us."

The men hollered, grew crimson in the face, and gulped more whiskey. Although all of the men told a story, one voice in particular with a thick Irish brogue made them explode with the heartiest guffaws, foot stomping, and back slapping.

"Tell us another one, Danny McDaniels, you crazy Celt."

"I met an old geezer up river peddling a curative elixir called *Dyno Might*. 'I tell you, mister, It's a miracle cure and I know the inventor,' he says. 'My friend from Angel's Camp consumes a hefty pinch of gunpowder in his ale every day. Been a'doin' it since he left New York to work the river in California. He swears it prevents cholera, malaria, consumption, hemorrhoids, scurvy, eczema and the cancer. Only problem is, you can't smoke. One fella did and we're still panning him out of the American.'"

The red-faced men laughed and pounded the table. "What happened then, McDaniels? Did you buy a bottle?"

"Hell, yes. I bought *two* bottles. *Dyno Might* is made up of two-thirds fire water and one-third cheap brandy. And by damn, that gun powder tastes great when there's no woman around to take its place!"

Darcey, curious about the story teller, singled out the man at the head of the table. She caught herself staring at the most handsome man she had ever laid eyes on: a dark, curly-haired Irishman with aquamarine eyes, exciting as a crashing blue sea. His rugged face and an impertinent smile made her heart pound.

He was as cocky as a schoolboy, full of impudence and rebellion. In every bite of food or swig of whiskey, an animal hunger lurked about his mouth. Darcey sensed a wildness, an untamedness in him like a storm. Even when her back was turned to him as she scraped the dirty plates, she felt his energy tingle up and down her spine.

This man has ruined lots of young lassies, she thought.

It was nearly dark when Darcey rode into camp. The fire blazed inside its ring of stones, and the inevitable beans and pork bubbled in the black kettle.

"Mama! Where have you been?" Pearle demanded. "I've been so scared you was killed by an Indian or a grizzly bear." Pearle threw her arms around Darcey's stomach.

"I'm so sorry, my little dear. So sorry I'm late and worried you. But I can explain. Something exciting has happened. You'll never believe it." Darcey stopped talking as a man stood up by the fire. She gasped.

"Hello, Darcey."

"Blue!"

"He found us, Mama!" Pearle said, dancing around excitedly. "Ain't that grand?"

Darcey was struck dumb. At another time, she might have rushed to hug him. But now, she felt caught like a naughty child.

Blue was not smiling. His expression was as cold and hard as granite. He remained silent, obviously waiting for her to speak.

"Blue . . . I know you're wondering about all this." Darcey fumbled her words, hoping to explain her actions. She felt especially ridiculous in her red beard. Still, Blue didn't speak glaring at her as though he was thoroughly disgusted.

Jenna stepped forward. "I already told him about what we were doing, at least some of it." Darcey knew Jenna was hoping to ease the tension between Darcey and Blue.

"Say something, Blue. I feel foolish," Darcey said.

"You *look* foolish."

"I can explain."

"No, you can't. You done an irresponsible thing. I can't believe what you done, a-totin' these here children into this place . . . full of every kind of danger . . . and dressed up uncivilized!"

"Blue, please. I can't be scolded now. You'd never understand, never. I've got to depend on myself and to care for Pearle. I wasn't going to stay, but I had to try."

"You ain't a man. This here is men's work. It ain't fittin' and proper for a female to be here. You know what I'm a-sayin'. You plain got gold fever and yielded to it. That's called temptation, woman. I thought you had more moral character than that. I read you wrong." Blue shook his head and looked away. "Worse yet, I trusted you."

"Blue, I'm sorry." Darcey was crushed.

"Sorry won't do—not now. I'm takin' Jenna out of here first light. I'd take Pearle, too, if she was mine."

Darcey glanced at Jenna, who was staring at Blue. She followed the girl's gaze, noticing how Blue's playful, brown eyes were now hard as river stones. They held a look Darcey had never seen before.

"Can't we talk together after Pearle and Jenna are in bed? I need to explain, Blue. Please." Darcey thought at least she could ease his anger, but she wasn't sure she could convince him that her caper was harmless. In fact, she suddenly felt jolted out of her temporary madness over gold and realized Blue was right. She had been irresponsible and selfish—totally selfish and absorbed in finding wealth in the diggings.

Standing there facing him in her muddy clothes, her oversized coat, a shapeless felt hat, and a ratty beard, she had no strength. Her true power lay in the truth of her own self. She was a woman, a good woman who had survived hardship and tragedy and remained strong and proud. This foolish disguise made her suddenly feel weak and vulnerable. Any power she had, especially with Blue, was as a woman, not as a man.

"Jenna, please help Pearle to bed, and tell her a long story while I talk to Blue down by the river. I have no more secrets. And I swear, I never will again."

Blue and Darcey sat by the river with only the glow of the fire to outline each other. Darcey could not clearly see his eyes, but she still felt his anger. "How did you find us?" she asked, hoping to change Blue's dark mood.

"I talked to Blanca and her husband. She said you kept a-talkin' about gold on the American River. When I seen the horses was gone, I figured you went a-seekin' gold. I headed upriver to the diggins and met an old man who called hisself Ebenezer Cootz. He remembered he seen a *man* with a red beard a-totin' two children up to Hattie's Gulch. I guessed it was you, then I kept arguin' with myself, tellin' myself it couldn't be. I didn't figure on you bein' so bull-headed and crazy you'd disguise yourself and the girls as males!" He sounded disgusted.

"Pretty clever, don't you think?" Darcey laughed nervously.

In spite of Blue's irritation, she still felt her adventure was an exciting caper. Wasn't a woman entitled to pursue a dream, take a chance, be independent?

"I don't admire what you done. Anything could have happened to you or the girls. But you done it, and now it's time to go home."

"I had been planning on leaving tomorrow myself, Blue—honestly. I even told the girls it was time to go home."

"I know. It don't matter to me one way or the other. What matters is my trustin' a woman what chose to be a man and shirked her duty and acted . . . just crazy. I can't abide any of it no matter what you say."

"Then I won't try to explain myself further. Blue, we failed at panning gold. I admit that. But I have another idea, and this time it ain't foolish. I can make a lot of money—fast."

Blue didn't look up or answer. He picked up some pebbles and tossed them into the dark water.

"I'm going to open a boarding house—take over Hattie's Place. Tonight, I fed nine men for three dollars a piece. Are you listening to me? That's twenty-seven dollars!"

"That's robbery."

"No one thought it was. They paid and when they walked out the door, they said they'd be back for breakfast and the noon meal! I put a sign out in front already. I'm charging a dollar a meal, and three dollars for supper. When the word is out, I can serve twenty men at a time! Think about it, Blue!"

Blue sighed. "I see you lost your tooth."

Darcey heard disappointment in his voice. The anger was gone. But there was something more, not just in his tone, but in the way his shoulders sagged.

"I thought maybe you'd come back down to the valley and stay a while longer . . . get better acquainted and all. I made you another tooth like I promised—a gold one." He took a piece of shaped gold from his pocket and handed it to Darcey. "Here, you'd better keep it. No tellin' when I'll see you again."

This time Darcey was sure. What she had heard underneath the anger was hurt. She had hurt Blue's feelings. She knew Blue liked her, but now she was certain Blue had other thoughts about her. She was struck with the irony of the situation; that he would enter her life just as she was about to launch a venture giving her the security she'd always craved. Then again, she couldn't presume Blue had any more interest in her than friendship. Maybe he just wanted a companion.

"Stay here, Blue. Stay with me and the girls! You could pan, or join a group of miners while I cook. It could work!" Darcey grabbed his hand. "Think on it, Blue."

"I'm finished with the life of a gold miner. It's a terrible life. I got what I wanted. Made some money and now I want something more solid in my life. Placer minin' is no way to live. As for Jenna, well, I promised her papa, Israel, that I'd see she got the right kind of life and upbringin". I had a couple of plans in case one or the other didn't work out. Now I know what I'm goin' to do. Jenna and me will be leavin' in the morning for San Jose. I got a nice place for her to live with a respectable woman, a Californio."

"I can't let you take Jenna away. It will kill Pearle!"

"Then leave with me . . . tomorrow," Blue said, taking Darcey by the shoulders and looking intently at her.

She hesitated. "I got breakfast to cook tomorrow."

"I see. Well, then that's that." He slowly rose to his feet.

"Blue, could you ask Blanca to pack my things for me? I'll arrange to have them sent here by pack train."

"I'll do that for you. There was hardly anyone at the fort except Blanca and her husband lookin' after things and carin' for the animals. Blanca will take care of it." He turned to leave.

"I'll see you in the morning, Blue."

"Maybe, maybe not. I plan to get an early start." Blue walked away without saying goodnight.

🌿 🌿 🌿

Early the next morning, before the sun reached the tops of the high mountain walls, Blue saddled the horses and placed a halter around the donkey. His demeanor had not changed and he refused to look in Darcey's eyes. As he rolled a few belongings into a rubber poncho, he turned his back on Pearle's broken-hearted sobs and Jenna's angry glare.

Darcey could no longer hold in her temper. She marched over to Blue, planted her feet, and shook her fist at him. "How can you do this to the children? To me? What kind of self-righteous, bullheaded man are you? I picked you wrong, too! You're not the man I thought you were. You're just like all the rest of them—what you say, goes. It don't matter about feelings or trying hard. You can't see anything beyond the end of your nose!" Darcey raised her fist to pound Blue on the chest.

He caught her wrist in midair. "I tried to talk sense into you, woman. But you're more stubborn than that donkey—willful and full of female nonsense. I gave you a chance to be together. You, me, the girls. You're still a-thinkin' of yourself alone—not Pearle, not Jenna. You give me no choice."

Blue let go of Darcey. She suddenly felt weak. Was she doing the wrong thing not going back with Blue? The two of them stared at each other. Darcey wanted to say, "Let me try for a week, a few days. Give me one small chance to see if I can make it on my own. I have dreams . . ." But she said nothing, only locked her eyes on his until they watered with frustration. Blue turned to Jenna. The moment was lost.

"I explained this to you, Jenna. You needn't turn to stone on me. You ain't growed up yet. And anyways I promised your papa. I ain't a-goin' back on my word. You need responsible care and education, no more grubbin' around in places what ain't fit for women and children."

"I'm not going. I'm staying with Darcey and Pearle! You can't make me go!"

"You're a-talkin' foolish. If I have to, I'll hog-tie you to Honey's back. Listen here, girl, I got you a fine place to live with a goodly woman. Doña Maria Juana de Archuleta, one of them rich Spanish ladies what agrees to take you in and educate you like a lady. I know her kin—a fine old family, the Archuletas. I worked for them when I first come to California. They have a rancho what takes up thousands of acres of grassland, and so many cattle you can't count 'em all."

"I don't care!" Jenna retorted sourly.

"You're an orphan, Jenna, and you should be mighty grateful to old Padre Ortega at the San Jose Mission for workin' out this here arrangement. I met with the woman. She's a fine, respectable lady of breeding, and I seen the rancho. It's called Rancho San Gabriel, a mighty pretty place with orchards and willow trees and a fine stream running near the house. There's even a small lake full of wild ducks and pet geese.

"Doña Juana served me the best coffee I ever tasted and hot tortillas rolled around some kind of spicy meat. There are lots of people around, Indians and guests . . .people a-singin' and laughin', and lively fiestas all the time lasting for days. And there are rich folks, too, all dressed up in fine silk dresses callin' on the doña. And the adobe house is a grand sight to see.

"You wait and see for yourself. You think sloppin' around in this mud with a bearded lady is right for you? Think on it, Jenna, then get on that horse."

"But they're Mexican, Blue. I won't be able to understand a word."

"Well, that's part of the bargain. The Doña Maria Juana don't speak English too good, and she don't read or write it neither. She wants you to teach her, be her companion. She says now that the war is over, she's a-goin' to deal with the Americans on her own terms. She says she's never goin' to give up her land, and she ain't a-goin' to be cheated out of it. Smart lady." He looked at Darcey. "Yep, a smart, refined, worthy lady, the doña is," he repeated. Darcey glared back at Blue.

"I know I won't like her. I'll hate her!"

"The doña is reasonable and kindly, unless you talk about the Americans takin' over California. Then she's cold as a frozen boot. I don't know much about the Catholics, but I know she's God-fearin' and carries herself with a straight back and don't look hither and yon when she's a-talkin' to you . . and she don't wear no beard," Blue said, looking sideways at Darcey.

Jenna, her jaw clamped tight, glowered at Blue with indignation.

"You don't have no choice in the matter, girl, so get on your horse."

"I never have a choice, do I?" Jenna said with angry tears. She stomped into the tent to get her rolled blankets.

Blue turned to Darcey. "You see there what you done? She's a-talkin' back already like a cussed child . . . lost her manners and her respect."

Darcey threw back her shoulders, swelled her chest like a ruffled robin, and squared her jaw. "Well, Sir, she don't act disrespectful to *me*. Respect is something you *earn*."

The two of them stared at each other until Blue said, "We're set to leave now, Jenna. You best say your goodbyes."

Darcey's eyes flooded with emotion—partly anger and partly grief over Jenna's leaving.

She and Pearle hugged Jenna tightly.

"I'll come and get you, Jenn, when I get rich. One day I'll own a fine house in San Francisco and you can live with Pearle and me. Or maybe we'll buy land, a homestead. I promise you."

The women cried and held each other. Jenna had said goodbye to so many people on her road of life that she wondered if this farewell was forever, too.

In spite of her love for Darcey and Pearle, she felt that something was not altogether right about staying with Darcey. She feared for them, especially for little Pearle, so shy, and small as a woodland animal. Jenna felt responsible for Pearle in ways she couldn't explain. She only knew that if her new life worked out well, she might be in a stronger position to care for her . . . maybe talk Darcey into letting Pearle live with her at Rancho San Gabriel.

Jenna knelt down and cupped Pearle's pale, tear-streaked face in her hands. "We're forever friends, you know. You must practice your reading and writing and send me a letter or even a story. I'll write you, too."

Pearle sniffed. "You won't forget me, will you? Because I'm your best friend, ain't I?"

"Yes, my best friend."

Pearle stopped crying. "What can I give you so's you won't forget? I know—I'll give you Miss Little from my Pebble Family. She needs extra care because sometimes she feels scared and lonely. And it's hard for her to do things. She can't run and play like other youngins. You'll take good care of her, won't you?"

Pearle unwrapped a scarf that held a few round, polished river stones, each one marked with a smiling face. The smallest stone was smooth and white with large, round eyes and a crooked smile.

"I'll keep it always, in my little shell box with my most precious treasures," Jenna said and quickly mounted Honey. She did not look back at her friends but heard their muffled sobs behind her.

Jenna rode in silence past Hattie's Place and through the cluster of tents and pack mules crowding the small community.

Blue tried to make general conversation to no avail.

As they rode into Red Man's Bar farther down the river, they saw a crowd of angry miners gathered in the center of the camp.

"Hang 'em!" people in the crowd shouted. "Hang the Mexicans! Hang the thieves, the dirty dogs!"

"Wait here, Jenn. Stay clear of these ornery men. You can never trust a crowd what thinks like a mother grizzly."

Blue rode in closer to see what the problem was.

From where she waited, Jenna could easily see what was happening. A swarthy man lay on the ground stripped to the waist, with his hands tied behind his back. Another man snapped and cracked a leather whip in the air while some other men slipped a rope, which was tied to a post, off the captive's neck. Someone rolled the flogged man out of the way with the heal of his boot.

"Bring the other Mexican dog! We'll teach 'em about stealin'!"

Jenna's heart beat fast. She'd never seen a man flogged or heard such a savage crowd.

A fat man on a small horse rode up next to her. "Think we should hang them two Mexicans, boy, or just beat 'em to death?"

Jenna shrank inside her oversized coat hoping, as always, not to be discovered as a girl. "What did they do?"

"Stole another man's gold, boy, that's what they done. Worse yet, they stole from some Irish and that don't settle well. You don't mess with an Irish, boy. Anyways, they caught 'em four mile downriver with a bunch of pouches. They don't know the American ways. They're the lowest kind of skunks and ought to be hanged from their pissers."

Just then, the voices rose higher as two men dragged the second Mexican into the crowd, forced him to his knees, and slipped the rope around his neck. The Mexican snarled, spit, and shouted curses in Spanish.

"That's a wild dog. I met him before—smelled him first. He stunk so bad the lice fell off stone dead on everybody in the saloon," the fat man said.

"Strip his shirt off!" the man with the whip shouted.

Suddenly, there was total silence. The men backed away from the tied Mexican exposed from the waist up, revealing two hanging breasts.

"By God . . . it's a *woman!*" The fat man jumped off his horse and ran to the crowd.

The men were incredulous. A female, a woman disguised as a man, stunned them into silence.

"I ain't whippin' no female,' the flogger said, throwing down his whip and stepping back.

The Mexican woman threw back her head and laughed viciously. She hissed and spit at the crowd and shook her breasts. "You're all stupid pigs . . . *cochinos! cochinos!* I hope you die! *Vive la República de México!* May your mother burn in hell and vultures eat your *coños!*"

The men untied her.

"What do you want to do, McDaniels? It was your men's gold," someone said.

A man with black, curly hair stepped forward. He pulled off the woman's hat and grabbed a fistful of greasy black hair.

"Take your boyfriend and get out of here. Go back to Mexico. If we catch you anywhere on the American River, we'll hang your ass! Now get out of here!"

The crowd dispersed with shouts and curses and talk of forming a vigilante committee to take care of matters.

Blue rode back to Jenna. "Well, you and Darcey ain't the only liars. You see what can happen? Now I ain't sayin' women ain't welcome around here. We could use some civilizin'. Women is bound to be a-comin' to the camps, joinin' their husbands. But they'd do better a-comin' as womenfolk!

"The men will always respect a decent woman, no matter what she's a-doin' to make an honest livin'. A boardin' house ain't a bad thing, as long as a decent female is in charge—one that's *dressed* like a woman and smells like soap instead of a plow horse."

Blue said nothing more, but he knew he would return to Hattie's Gulch as soon as he'd settled Jenna. He would bring Darcey's belongings, including her female wardrobe, to her himself, and maybe stick around long enough to see her ample figure walk away form him swinging gently underneath a soft skirt.

"Well, well, well . . . if it ain't our esteemed wagon master, brother Blue," a familiar voice said. "It is, indeed, and I do believe I'm looking into the eyes of Miss Jenna Daggett! Ain't that right, sister? Two transgressors. I see you've been led into the ways of the wicked. Faithful Squibb here, your humble servant." He removed his threadbare hat and smiled with yellow rat teeth.

Jenna, too scared to speak, stared at Faithful. The familiarity of his eyes made her feel like a trapped animal—a tortured, helpless thing that could run to all four corners of a cage and find nothing to hide under.

"Hello, Faithful," Blue said coldly.

"You two don't act heartily glad to see me. It seems the sinners shall be together, and they that forsake the Lord shall be consumed together. Ye shall be confounded for the gardens ye have chosen. I believe you have taken over my duties as guardian of this here child."

"That's right," Blue said, looking straight into Faithful's eyes. "But I do have some unfinished business to discuss with you."

"This little seraphim broke Mrs. Squibb's heart. She cried herself into her grave . . . God rest her soul. After all our kindness to this ungrateful child, this young heathen rewarded us by running away. It's in her nature to do evil. She don't know the Lord."

He raised his eyes to the sky, then looked at Jenna. "Wash you, make you clean, put away the evil of your doings from before my eyes. Cease to do evil . . ."

"That's enough scripture, Faithful. I'm not a-harkin' to your words. You seem to be amongst the sinners yourself."

"We're all sinners, my friend. But these here miners worship idols of gold. Woe unto their souls, for they reward only evil unto theirselves. I'm here to help them on their way to salvation. By a simple tithe of their diggins, ten percent of the pouch—a niggardly sum—I hope to build a house of worship right here in Red Man's Bar. I'm following the word of the Lord to build a church in the wilderness." He paused, appearing to wait for a response.

Since Jenna and Blue said nothing, Faithful walked over to Jenna and leaned his body against her leg. Under his breath, he murmured, "I'll pray for your soul, child, haughty daughter of Zion with wanton eyes. I'm not finished saving your soul . . . not finished at all."

Jenna tightened Honey's reins, pulled the bit against her mouth until she reared, then turned toward the camp.

Behind her, she heard Blue say, "I suspect, I'll see you again . . . soon, now that I know you'll be here in Red Man's Bar. Another day, my friend," Blue warned.

"Go in peace with Jesus, brother." Faithful shouted after Blue.

EIGHT

I THINK WE'RE ALREADY on the grazin' lands of the Archuletas' rancho. Can't tell for sure 'till we pick up the road to Rancho San Gabriel," Blue said. "There ain't any more haciendas or farms round. It ought to take a good part of the afternoon a-ridin' before we get to the adobe itself."

Stretched out before them lay vast rolling hills of a lush valley, the grass already burnished from endless sunny days. Here and there, buckeye, madrone, and oak trees dotted the countryside, and willows and chaparral snaked along the rivulets and streams. All along the Guadalupe River, tangled blackberry bushes clung to the banks, and cottonwoods lifted skyward to catch a salty breeze and tease a profusion of noisy magpies. Overhead, an occasional pair of white seagulls sailed by, arcing across the blue on an unseen force.

Jenna, wearing the blue and white gingham dress Darcey had made at Christmas, and a clean, white apron, looked as she did when she crossed the Great American Desert. Now, however, instead of the detested bonnet, she wore a straw hat with a ring of dried flowers around the crown. Her silky, brown hair, not yet grown from the boyish cut, reached almost to her shoulders and hung unattractively straight beneath the hat. In spite of the patchy, dry skin and healing mosquito bites spotting her face, Jenna's magnetic blue eyes and sculptured features, wide brow, and expressive mouth showed her to be a growing beauty.

Eventually, the pair turned onto a path worn from years of pack mules and horses traveling between the ranch and the Pueblo de San Jose. Proceeding single file, Blue watched Jenna riding ahead of him. He thought she held herself straight and tall in the saddle and had a regal air about her.

One day she'll be all growed up with a husband and family, and she'll be a might fine wife for some good man—that is, if she don't get so stubborn you can't reason with her. I can already figure she's got a good hold on her tongue. She don't talk nonsense and don't prattle on like a mired goat. She seems to have a good head on her, but them women can fool you. When they fix on something they want, they ain't reasonable. Blue shifted his thoughts back to his own young wife, dead for so many years. *Jenna ain't anything like my darlin' girl, not so gentle and soft spoken. No sir, she rides a horse like a general.* Blue chuckled to himself. *If it wasn't for that captivatin' smile, she could have growed up a man.*

Jenna observed everything—the land, the low, blue hills in the distance, the smell of rich earth, the rhythmic call of the seagulls. She watched the clouds shape-shifting into an Indian headdress, a fiddle, an old man's foot. She marveled at the swift colony of swallows, soaring, arching, curving with a single wing, a single mind. A red fox, backlit in sun, trotted through the grass following the scent of hidden quail eggs. His intrusion flushed out prairie hens and pheasants that flapped into the air with a squawk and a spray of feathers. Once again, the endless land thrilled her as it had when she held Israel's hand and walked on the prairie.

Though the day was hot as an oven and Jenna baked under her hat, the heat couldn't dampen her enthusiasm for the magic around her. In the hours without conversation, Jenna finally felt resigned to what lay ahead and decided to do as Israel would have expected, to make the best of the situation. It wouldn't last forever. After all, she was still a Daggett, strong enough to face any hardship. She had overcome other problems, other losses, the pain of loneliness. She could handle this, too. Besides, it was time to stop being angry with Blue. She would give him the scarf she had made for him at Christmas to show him she had forgiven him. He was, after all, doing what he believed her papa would want.

Jenna broke the silence. "Blue, that pueblo of San Jose is nothing like Sapling Grove. I didn't expect town would be made from adobe, just like Captain Sutter's Fort. The funny little mud houses surely must dissolve in the rain and wash away."

"They've been here near a hundred years, stood under three flags— Spanish, Mexican, and now American. That adobe is tough as stone. That's what Rancho San Gabriel is made of—thick walls of adobe, a kind of mud and straw brick plastered over with lime and painted white. Makes a good house—cool in summer, warm in winter."

By late afternoon, as the sun dropped low and sculptured the hills in long shadows, Jenna saw Rancho San Gabriel in the distance at last. A cluster of low adobes, including the main house quite large, lay close to the river in a grove of willows, oak, and every kind of sweet-smelling tree. Blue and Jenna rode past orchards heavy with apricots, pears, apples, peaches, plums, cherries, and stubby trees with pendulums of dusty green grapes poking out beneath broad leaves and curly tendrils. Fields of corn in straight rows stood in a tangle of pumpkin vines, ripe squash and gourds, onions, and peppers.

Indians in white cotton pants and tunics tied with red and blue sashes at the waist and around their heads, bent over harvested peppers and carried them in baskets on their heads. Others waded in irrigated rows of garlic and beans.

Everywhere Jenna looked, she saw something exciting, something moving with color or light. She had not expected the bustle.

Cooking smoke rose from the house, filling the air with the delicious smell of roasting corn and sizzling meat. In the shade of a large bay tree, a group of chattery women shucked corn and rubbed the kernels into baskets. Three noisy dogs ran alongside the horses, yapping at the strangers and snapping at the horses' hooves as they rode up to the front porch. Geese and chickens, pigeon-toed and flat-footed, scattered in all directions honking and squawking, and a startled mother cat with swollen teats slunk under a wooden cart.

The last of the sun struck a profusion of deep fuchsia bougainvillea arching over the porch and cascading like a waterfall of blossoms down the side of the adobe. Strings of red, shiny peppers drying in the sun hung from the eaves of the veranda and dangled over the roof.

Blue and Jenna dismounted in front of the door as two young Indian boys, barefooted and dressed in loose pants and tunics of crude weave, ran up and led the horses to a hitching post. No one came out to greet them.

Jenna brushed the dust from her face, shook out her skirt, took a breath of courage, and started toward the house.

A rider came up behind them. *"Buenas tardes,"* a woman said. "I am Doña Juana. You are Señorita Jenna Daggett. I've been expecting you. Señor Quigley Gump, we meet again."

The doña sat sidesaddle on top a giant black stallion, the largest horse Jenna had ever seen, so black and shiny that blue lights rippled across his muscles as he moved. Ornate silver decorated his bridle and harness. Solid silver formed his stirrups and saddle horn.

The doña looked down at them from her high place, composed and aloof. She did not make them feel welcome. Dressed in a white silk blouse, full-sleeved, and a black silk skirt tied at the waist with a long, wide yellow sash, she looked cold and austere. Soft, black leather boots with silver toes and silver buttons showed beneath her skirt. A black *vaquero's* hat, tied under her chin, sat squarely on her head and rested on a black chignon at the nape of her neck.

"Come closer. Let me see you." The doña took the point of her riding crop and slowly lifted Jenna's hat away from her face. She looked sternly at Jenna, moving her black eyes around Jenna's face and down to her dusty boots, then half-smiled in an unfriendly manner.

"I'm pleased to meet you, Doña Archuleta," Jenna said, straightening her hat and looking into the doña's strong face. She did not want to weaken her own expression and thought to herself, *I must meet this woman with equal strength or she will destroy me.* Jenna lifted her chin and straightened her back.

"Are you a good teacher, little American girl?"

"Yes."

"Can you teach me to read and write American English?"

"Yes, I am a good teacher."

"We shall soon see."

They stared at each other.

"Can you teach me Spanish?" Jenna asked, with a somewhat impudent tone.

The doña smiled ever so slightly. "If you are bright, you will learn by living here."

"I am bright." Jenna never looked away.

"Your pitiful clothes deceive you."

"They are all I have."

"You Americans insist on looking like brown field mice."

"We work in the fields . . . like your Indians, only for our *own* farms, not for someone else," she added.

Again, the doña smiled. "Like peasants, you mean."

"To own our own farms."

"You have quick answers, *chica*. Perhaps I will call you *ratoncita*, little mouse."

"My name is Jenna."

Jenna glanced at Blue, who smiled broadly. She could see pride in his eyes. He knew she would not be pushed around easily.

"Then I shall call you Jenna. You may call me Doña Juana. Please feel welcome. You may stay as long as you like, Señor Gump. Your rooms are ready on the courtyard. Jenna, your room is at the far end on the right. I will meet you in the *sala* for late afternoon tea, after you have washed. Marta and her daughter, Luisa, will be your personal servants.

"Ygnacio, Luisa's *padre*, is a house servant. Ygnacio came to my family from the San Jose Mission twenty years ago. We do not treat our Indians like you treat your Negro slaves. We treat them with respect."

Jenna flushed with anger. Her family did not believe in slavery. Israel said it was the crime of mankind. He always talked about "free states" and about never letting slavery into the Far West. Had she been braver, she might have asked the doña why her Indians worked like slaves and lived in crude beehive houses made from the tule grass.

Ygnacio, who had been watching from the porch, nodded his head and gestured for the pair to follow him through the tiled hallway past the *sala* to the interior courtyard. He said something in his native tongue to an unkempt girl about eight years old, who smiled timidly and darted across the courtyard ahead of them. She opened a blue-painted door and leaned shyly against the wall to watch the strangers. Ygnacio led Jenna into the dim room with a shuttered window opposite the door.

Jenna stood in the doorway trying to conceal her excitement. Her very own room! It was a place at the end of some long journey, a journey longer than the crossing on the Oregon Trail or struggling on the American River. It was a new beginning, a new freedom. As she looked around the small room at the simple, neat furnishings, she wondered what secrets she would have in this private place of her own. She wondered who she was to become.

Ygnacio opened the shutters. There were no glass windows, only two bars plastered into the stucco. A fresh scent of apricots from the trees outside her window rushed into the rooms. "Luisa!" Ygnacio called.

Luisa, the shy, scraggly little girl, entered the room, carefully lifted a water pitcher from the washstand, and scurried out the door.

"Well, this is a mighty nice room, ain't it, Jenna? Better than most. Didn't I tell you it was a fine place?" Blue said.

"Oh, Blue, it *is* nice! I even have a fireplace!" Jenna said, running her hands over the cool beehive adobe molded into the corner. She sat on the wooden bed covered in a light wool blanket and sank comfortably onto the mattress. A feather pillow and comforter lay across the bed. A crude wooden table and a chest stood against one wall, and on the other, sat an armoire with red and yellow flowers painted in a field of blue.

Jenna walked around the room, touching the ornate pair of candelabrum, a lantern, and a leather chair. She marveled at two brightly woven rugs on the planked floor, and a decorated chamber pot by the side of the bed. A silver hand mirror, heavy ceramic washbowl painted with colorful birds, a towel, wash rag, and a thick square of mustard-colored soap were neatly arranged on a wooden table.

Everything in the room delighted her, even a painted statue of the Virgin Mary resting serenely in a small alcove recessed into the wall, and two glass votive cups flickering on either side of the Blessed Mother.

The room smelled slightly smoky, damp, and moldy. The mud walls would dry when a cross breeze circulated between the open door and window. But for now, the moist coolness was refreshing to Jenna after the hot journey through the valley.

"Blue, it is so different from our frame house in Sapling Grove. I wish Papa were here to see this place. Mama might not like it, so bare and all, but Papa would. Mama would have liked the courtyard with all the flowers. Papa would have loved all the land. And Solomon! I can just see him with these animals."

Luisa returned carrying the heavy pitcher of water, placed it on the washstand, and again timidly leaned in the doorway. She looked at Jenna with her large, timid eyes, and when Jenna smiled at her, she ran into the courtyard.

"Will you come often to visit me, Blue?"

"Of course, girl . . . whenever I can. You won't be here forever; just long enough to grow up a bit, get some learnin'."

"And Darcey and Pearle? Will they come one day?"

"One day, I'm sure. They ain't that far away—maybe a week or so. Now let's wash up for the doña. I'll hang around a few days till you get used to it here—let my horse rest up."

Jenna had very little to unpack and put away—an oversized coat, a nightdress, some toiletries, Israel's hat and harmonica, a Bible, and her beloved shell box that once belonged to Martha Jane.

The doña had changed her clothes into a tiered, indigo silk dress with high black lace ruffles at the neck, along the split sleeves, and at the hem of each tier. The sleeves were full and lined with cream-colored satin. Over her shoulders draped a small silk scarf of deeper blue, embroidered with cream and red roses on the points. A black lace *mantilla* fell gracefully over her head and below her shoulders.

Once again, Jenna was struck by the strong beauty of the aging doña.

Her eyes, black as obsidian, scornful and teasing, matched the dangling beaded earrings. Heavy eyelids were beginning to fold around the eyes; under her lower lids a permanent dusky tint evidenced her ancient Moorish past. She smelled of the fresh oil of lemons, as did the *sala*.

The doña sat stiffly in an ornately carved chair, her chin tilted upward. She looked at Blue and Jenna down the straight line of her nose. "*Siéntense*," she commented, gesturing for them to sit down.

Blue and Jenna felt strange sitting on the edge of thin-legged chairs, and Jenna suspected the doña knew full well of their discomfort, but did nothing to put them at ease.

"I'm not accustomed to Americans, as you know. But they are moving into Alta California in great numbers . . . into our country very quickly. They will try to take our land. I will stop this, first by my legal rights, then by my rifle. We have already found you Americans squatting on our lands to the west, stealing our cattle, killing and selling the hides and meat."

"I'm sorry to hear that Ma'am," Blue said, balancing his cup of tea awkwardly.

"The Americans are uncivilized. They believe in slavery, the men are thieves, and women work like mission Indians."

Jenna could feel her face bloom with angry splotches. "We are not thieves! We came to build homes and own farms. How do we know whose land it is? You have so much!"

"The ranchos were given to us by our fathers, who served their king, their government, the military. They were officers and cadets and *soldados distinguidos* who lived at the presidios in Monterey and San Francisco. Our boundaries are marked. Your government must honor our grants, respect our heritage, and leave our branded cattle alone!" Doña Juana rose from her chair and paced back and forth, her frustration and anger obvious in each agitated movement.

"We are cattle people. Our business is in hides and tallow, which we sell to foreigners. It is a huge business, a way of life. To take our land is to destroy us." She stopped, leaned forward, and with a cold voice locked behind her teeth, she snarled, "I will *not* be destroyed." The doña returned to her seat, poured another cup of tea, and sat back, apparently satisfied she had made her point. "More tea, Señor?" she asked pleasantly.

"I don't think takin' your land is our aim, Doña Juana." Blue said. "We won a war with hardly no resistance . . . hardly a shot fired, marched right into Mexico with no bloodshed. A lot of you folks even like us bein' here . . . right friendly. No one has said anything about takin' your land. In fact, they talk of honorin' your boundaries if you can prove you own it."

"We'll see, Señor Gump." The doña pronounced Blue's name "Goomp."

Jenna did not like the doña. She straightened her shoulders and said, "I don't think this arrangement will work, Doña Juana. I will be leaving with Blue tomorrow." She stood up.

"Nonsense! Sit down!" the Doña commanded.

Jenna remained standing.

"I see you are stubborn. I like that." She smiled haughtily. "From now on when you wish to excuse yourself, you say, *'con permiso´*, and I will grant your leave."

"I have no wish to stay here. Blue? Take me with you."

Blue hesitated. "I think you two ladies need to get better acquainted. I might step out and check on the horses . . . *con permiso*, Doña."

"Yes," she said. Turning to Jenna she added in a softer voice, "Jenna, stay . . . *por favor*, please. Sit for a moment more."

Jenna sat down on the edge of the chair. "Why do you want me to stay?"

"Because you have much to gain here, many opportunities, an education. Because you are useful to me. Because—maybe I like you. Because—you're not afraid of me."

"Maybe I do not like *you*, Doña," Jenna said strongly.

The doña laughed out loud. "Nor should you." She laughed again. "I have not been nice. If you do not like me after one week, then go back to your life as a prairie dog and dart into your hole when a shadow passes over." She rose from her chair.

"We'll start tomorrow morning with my lessons. I have books to learn to read and write English. You will teach me. Tonight we will eat late with some guests from Rancho Santa Teresa. You will meet Señor Faustino, my *mayordomo* who manages the rancho." She started to leave. "Oh, yes. The dressmakers will begin fitting your wardrobe tomorrow—a morning, afternoon, and evening dress, a party dress for our fandangos and rodeos, perhaps a gown for formal occasions. We'll order silk and velvet booties, *mantillas*, scarves, sashes, capes. Luisa will bring you some copies of *Godey's Lady's Book*. You will look at the most recent fashions and select ideas that are reasonable and suitable for your age, none of those silly American bonnets, and only moderate stiffening in your petticoats. I will approve of what you wear. I do not know yet what to do about your hideous hair. It is a disgrace to your sex!" The doña whirled out of the room, leaving behind the scent of lemon.

🌱 🌱 🌱

During the following week, Jenna and Blue, accompanied by Luisa, her mother Marta, and sometimes the doña, acquainted themselves with the busy activities of the rancho—the many Indian servants who cooked, made grape wine and cheese, ground corn, laundered, worked the fields and the irrigation system, and tended the sheep, goats, horses, and milk cows. They met many *vaqueros* and rode into the countryside to see the great herds scattered over the vast land. Jenna whirled in circles of dressmakers, weavers, and spinners whose fingers never stopped as they created elegant shawls, laces, and *serapes* embroidered with intricate designs.

When Blue said goodbye to Jenna, he did not see resignation in her eyes, or sadness, or the little girl on the Oregon Trail. Standing before him in a white, ruffled, muslin morning dress, her bare arms exposed, he saw a young lady with sharp eyes, an intelligent face, a confident smile.

"I will stay as long as it suits me, Blue. For now, I'm going to learn about ranching and cattle. Doña Juana isn't too awful. In fact, her outbursts of irritation are funny to me now. She's not nearly as gruff as everyone believes. I think it's a show. Underneath her strict manners is someone quite different . . . maybe someone kind of lonely. I wonder why she never married."

Blue hugged Jenna. "If you need me, send a note to the Empire Hotel in San Francisco. They know me there or where I'll be. Or maybe you can send a note to Hattie's Bar. I still have some business up there."

Blue instantly thought about Darcey, wild and strong, her wiry red hair blazing in the sun, a throaty laugh bursting from a most desirable pair of plump lips, and the easy swing of her ample frame. God! He could still smell her soapy skin.

Jenna broke his reverie. "What are you going to do, Blue?"

"I've got some plans I'm a-thinkin' on. Maybe San Francisco, maybe Sacramento—don't know yet."

"Doña Juana said we were going shopping in Monterey soon. She wants to pick up some more material from China, even Boston . . . and kid shoes and gloves. And she wants to buy a real sewing machine she saw in a magazine. Imagine it, Blue! I've never been dressed up before, but I like it—I really do. In these little shoes, I feel like dancing!" Jenna laughed and twirled in circles. A silent breeze blew her sun-bleached, slippery, corn-silk hair around her face. And that's how Blue left her and thereafter always thought of her.

🐚 🐚 🐚

Jenna gradually settled into her new life at Rancho San Gabriel. The shy little Luisa followed her around like a puppy, bringing fresh water, helping her mother clean the room, change the sheets, dry and puff the mattress wool, lay out Jenna's clothes. On her own, Luisa brought fresh bows of eucalyptus and sachets of dried mint to sweeten the room. Often Jenna found a single rose from the garden lying on her satin pillow. Since the two girls could not speak together, they smiled and said, "Good morning."

One hot afternoon, Luisa and Jenna sat under a giant bay laurel in the courtyard and made large, brightly colored paper flowers, which now bloomed in clay pots in Jenna's room.

Another day, Luisa took Jenna's hand and led her to the back of the kitchen. She pointed under a wooden barrel lying on its side to a wiggly mass of kittens, their eyes still stuck tight and their newborn mews crying for nourishment.

Jenna wanted to have her as a friend, not as a servant, but both the doña and Luisa's mother, Marta, continually scolded Luisa for not keeping a proper place. She was ordered to stay with the Indian children and to enter the courtyard on orders only. Luisa kept her distance but smiled adoringly at Jenna. Jenna always found ways to break the rules in order to enjoy Luisa's company. She was the only playful diversion for Jenna other than her horse, Honey, and the animals around the rancho.

There was always something to do—some wonderful, new experience for Jenna. During the hot, lazy days, she learned to love the quiet hours set aside for the siesta. She spent these precious minutes reading, studying Spanish, writing to Darcey and Pearle, or walking along the winding silver river, lush with oak and manzanita and thick shrubs of blackberry and wild grape. She often lay under the willows, always in the company of the three skinny dogs, and watched the ducks paddle lazily by the banks.

In the evenings, when the sun at last sank below the hills and the earth cooled, Jenna sat in the courtyard with the doña and guests that always came from somewhere—a nephew or niece, cousins, an old priest, a soldier, a retired *alcade*, travelers on their way to the coast or to distant ranchos. The people were gay, full of laughter and music, always ready to sing or dance to guitar or violin, or to tell stories long into the night. She found the Mexicans more lighthearted, more playful than her friends and family in Sapling Grove, and she longed to communicate better with them. Jenna's friendly smile and open manner were enough for family and friends to welcome her into their lives and the world of the rancho.

Jenna always enjoyed the visitors. They were a happy break from the rigid routine of the rancho and too many slow days she spent alone. Sometimes, guests arrived at the door—travelers who came with greetings or a letter of introduction from friends of the Archuletas. Sometimes, complete strangers needing food and shelter rode up to the adobe. The doña welcomed everyone, as was the custom of her father. In every guest room, a cup of coins placed by the bed helped a traveler and possibly spared any embarrassing questions.

Jenna did not care for the doña's brothers. Both men, lean and good-looking, arrogant and flirtatious, brought roughness to the table, drunkenness and vulgarity to the courtyard entertainment. Still, the ladies didn't mind their poor manners and flirted back at them with more sparkle in their eyes and more provocative dancing.

Jenna admired the freedom of the dancers, the quick footwork, the fetching tilt of the head. Even the youngest girl, confident of her beauty by adoring family, lifted the ruffles of her skirts and teased the onlookers with coquettish baby eyes.

Most shocking of all was the doña herself, who, persuaded by the guests, danced the sensual *bamba* as evocatively as a young woman. She placed a glass of water on her head, lifted her skirts above her knees, stepped into a hoop, and with supple movement of feet, legs, and thighs in rhythm with a Spanish guitar, inched the hoop above her knees.

Jenna often wondered why the doña remained unmarried.

She saw flashes of youth and gaiety quickly turn to austerity and coldness, or her genial laughter on one day fall into silence the next. Sometimes the bitter curve of the mouth completely altered her Spanish beauty, and on those days, the servants, and even Jenna, stayed out of her way.

The doña watched her male guests ogle Jenna. Her brothers, especially Bernardo, were noticeably attentive, tossing the girl side-glances, engaging in double-talk about her young, lithe body and fair skin.

Jenna was certainly a beauty—quick witted, a fast learner, a young colt of a girl who might need severe training, a reining in, before her passions became too strong and overpowered her good sense. It would be best to turn her into a Catholic. If she was not careful, some man might take away her fire . . . he might lay her down under a cathedral of stars, lift her skirt, find the place where she ached and burned, ignite her over and over, then leave her . . . smoldering her youth away.

No, it would not do to allow a fire to start burning in such a young girl. She could speak from experience.

On the other hand, why should she care at all? Jenna was an American, probably as plain and passionless as the American women coming into her country with their granite faces and stiff bodies. No, American women were those who did not know ecstasy.

One morning, after Doña Juana and Jenna finished their classes, the doña said, "We are going to Monterey. There are several reasons for me to go. I will buy a sewing machine. I will stay with my sister at the home my family built twenty years ago, and I will attend to other affairs as well."

Jenna sucked in her breath. "Monterey! Oh, Doña Juana—Monterey! I will see the ocean!" Jenna had heard about the wonders of this exciting town since she arrived in California, especially the grand parties and beautiful women.

"Also, I have received an invitation to a formal ball . . . from the Americans. You understand, I am an Archuleta. The military governor at the Monterey Presidio has called a convention to discuss plans for California to become part of the United States. People from all over Alta California are attending, including old Spanish and Mexican families. I do not like the Americans, but I am going anyway."

"But Dona, why are you attending if you hate us so?"

"You are such a child! You know nothing about politics. I want you to see foolish men strutting about believing they are important. I want to show you how to pluck their cock feathers from their tails and wear them in your own hat. I will show them the map of the Archuleta rancho borders and once and for all ensure our land grant."

"When are we going?" Jenna asked excitedly.

"In two days, enough time to finish your peach ball gown. You will have to wear my white kid slippers until we can buy a pair for you."

"I am so excited, Doña Juana!" Without thinking, and unafraid of a reprimand or scolding, Jenna rushed over to the doña and kissed her cheek. Jenna smiled as the doña, obviously startled, appeared flustered by Jenna's spontaneous gesture.

"Sit down! Compose yourself! We are still in audience!"

Jenna returned to her chair quite subdued, but knowing her eyes were betraying her excitement.

"Let me explain. The Archuletas have been a powerful and influential family since the beginning of the first colonies. Along with my two brothers and only living sister, who is married to an American, I have much land and cattle. One day, the Americans are going to need our land. My foolish brothers may compromise with foreigners, but I never, *never* will.

My father gave me eighty-five thousand acres of my own along with this first adobe in the southern part of the rancho. We have been the principal suppliers of tallow and hides to the East Coast of the United States for forty years. I have lived under two flags . . . and now a third. Know your enemy, Jenna. Always know your enemy."

"I have no enemies."

"Surely you do. Every soul has something that someone else wants, that he would take from you."

Jenna lowered her eyes. "Well . . . perhaps one enemy."

The doña stopped talking and seemed to wait for her to speak.

Jenna looked up feeling hot splotches flush her face. She took a breath. "Where did you learn English, Doña?"

Doña Juana seemed taken back by the abruptness of the question. "I told you. My sister is married to an American. I learned from him. Remember, I was born and raised in Monterey. There were always English-speaking foreigners about." The doña suddenly walked over to her desk on the pretense of straightening her papers.

"But you were too young."

"I was eighteen."

"There must have been other Americans or Englishmen around for you to learn so well."

With her back to Jenna, Doña Juana said quietly, "Yes, there was one . . . an Englishman who lived with us—my brothers' tutor before my father sent them away to school, one to Peru and one to Mexico. My sister and I were not allowed to learn, to have an education," she said bitterly. She turned back to Jenna. "We girls were raised to be mothers. Our duty was to the church and daily prayers to appeal to the saints and the Holy Mother for the good of the family. My mother died on her knees praying to the Archuleta patron, San Gabriel." She crossed herself mentioning his name. Again, she turned her back. "I learned English by sitting in the corner of the room listening to the English lesson. Professor Coney let me stay and sometimes talked with me in the garden in the evenings." She suddenly changed her tone. "You have permission to leave now. I have too much to do to talk idly. Prepare yourself for our leave." She scowled. "Oh, your dreadful hair! You must wear a mantilla at all times!"

"*Con permiso*, Doña Juana."

"*Tienes mi permiso*, you're excused. And by the way, don't kiss me again. I don't like it."

"Yes, Doña." Jenna hurried out of the room, trying hard to hide the happiness tumbling inside her.

🌿 🌿 🌿

Señor Faustino, the mayordomo, told Jenna she could not ride her own horse, Honey, to Monterey. Jenny understood that her loyal pony had done more than her share of traveling. It was apparent that she was tired—too tired for journeys to destinations even as close as Monterey, two days away. Honey would retire and graze with the cattle. From now on, Jenna would ride Solana, a beautiful straw-colored palomino with creamy mane and tail, a once wild horse that raced over the meadows full of sunlight.

Doña Juana insisted that Jenna ride Solana sidesaddle and rest her satin-slippered foot in a gold-braided loop that hung from the saddle horn. In her ruffled, white muslin dress and sheer scarf over her head and shoulders to prevent sunburn, Jenna felt foolish, as though she were dressed for a party rather than for a journey. This time, she would not argue with the doña, but one day would tell her she refused to ride sidesaddle.

There were many others accompanying them. Marta and the dressmaker rode in the *carreta* pulled by two teams of oxen. They would share the cart with supplies on the way back. Several *vaqueros* rode alongside a team of pack mules loaded with hides. They would spend one night at a rancho and arrive in Monterey by mid afternoon the next day.

The first night, the entourage stayed in a rancho close to Mission San Juan Bautista, resting the animals and exchanging an ox that was coughing and appeared to be sick. They would pick him up on their return trip.

The next afternoon, Jenna noticed a change from the terrible heat of the valleys to cooler, breezier air. Close to the horizon, the sky lightened into a mist and she heard the faraway sound of the surf and the barking of seals. The ocean breezes carried the odd odor of fish, something new to Jenna, and she stretched in her saddle to peer over rises of sand dunes that blocked her view of the sea.

Suddenly, the blue expanse of ocean lay before her, the most thrilling sight Jenna had ever seen. The ocean! She felt the same exaltation as she did on the vast western plains; she had the same urge to run with the wind, fly with the birds.

Jenna filled her lungs with this new world, breathed in the beauty of Monterey, the rolling hills that led to the coast, the pine-covered forests, the white sand and rocky cliffs, the sea spray crashing against islands of sculptured rocks and stones jutting out of the water. Overhead, seagulls soared through the sky with noisy cries. Around the gracefully sweeping bay lay perhaps a couple of hundred whitewashed adobes with red roofs. Most of them were one-story, but there were a few two-story houses higher up on the forested hills. The fort, which was the Presidio, and the imposing Customs House, were built on the rocks and faced the bay and the anchored ships.

The doña waited for Jenna to ride up next to her.

"That two-story house on the hill," she said, pointing, "that is the Archuleta home."

"Oh, Doña Juana, it is all so beautiful! How could you ever have left this place?"

The doña sighed. "I often wonder that myself," she said and rode on ahead.

Monterey was more than Jenna had imagined. Carts and horses, even buggies, clip-clopped through the square and down every street. People from all over California, many fresh from the gold camps, crowded into the plaza, walked along the beachfront, and gathered in fragrant gardens around the plaza. Jenna saw every kind of person imaginable—sailors and traders, bearded trappers, ladies with parasols, gentlemen in fine clothes, Indians, Chinese, and other foreigners from distant ports.

The air was charged with the excitement of the upcoming celebration after so many weeks of drafting a state constitution and of arguing over the problems of slave states verses free states. Music filled the air—spirited pianos from the cantinas, strolling bands of Mexican singers—along with shouts of rowdy men behind the walls watching a cockfight or playing *bolas criollas*. Many curious spectators gathered outside Colton Hall, where men debated objectionable clauses in the new constitution, blundered through deliberations, and ultimately established a broad, liberal, free and independent state on the shores of the Pacific.

The Archuleta home, a gracious Spanish adobe overlooking the bay, accommodated family and guests in a grand style. Jenna loved the veranda, which covered the length of the house and opened onto the sea, capturing the salty breezes and the pungent fragrance of cypress.

Over the next few days, Jenna socialized with guests and family members, including Doña Juana's younger, softer sister, Helena, and her American husband, Erin Cassidy. Helena, with her long, thin face, was not a striking beauty like Doña Juana, nor did she portray the Archuleta arrogance that flashed in her sister's eyes. She seemed open to friendship and hospitality and received compliments from male guests for being a perfect wife – docile, undemanding, a showpiece of good taste.

Jenna did everything she was supposed to do to please the doña. She went to mass, wore the *mantilla* all day and evening, took a proper siesta, and smiled congenially while the family conversed in Spanish beyond her comprehension.

Throughout the following day, during the afternoon siesta, the family's gathering for coffee and sweets and conversation, and into the late evening hours weighty with heavy food and thick peach brandy, Jenna found every excuse to walk on the veranda to gaze at the ocean, hear the crashing waves, smell the sea salt and fishy air. The mystery of the deep, endless water pulled her like a magnet, and she longed to escape to the white beach and put her toes in the bubbly surf.

But going out unchaperoned was absolutely forbidden. The beach was considered an unhealthy place, she was told, full of garbage, unsavory characters sleeping off too much grog, or even vicious dogs that ran in packs. Even more dangerous were unpredictable tides or waves that could surprise an unsuspecting visitor. Jenna was told she must not venture out alone. She really had no time for such adventures, anyway, for there was so much to do to prepare for the upcoming ball. But early the next morning,

Jenna could not resist the temptation.

The cold, rolling fog that hovered on the coast, whispering around the adobe and floating like fine, spun threads through the pines, only heightened the enchantment, and Jenna, without explanation, grabbed a shawl and ran behind the house out of sight and down the hill to the beach. At last she was free!

She threw off her shoes and shawl and ran like a new colt to the water's edge, startling a group of sandpipers, which skittered away, moving as one mind like the inland swallows. Seagulls rose into the mist screeching and scolding, circling like phantom birds above her head. Jenna laughed out loud, delighted at the emptiness, the bubbling water, the heavy salt air that wet her bare arms and face and wilted her white gauzy dress. She whirled with her arms outstretched, picked up her long skirt, and ran and skipped like a frisky horse as far as she could, parting the boiling clouds.

Wet sand spattered her legs up to her thighs, and strands of seaweed slapped at her ankles. She ran until she was breathless, then flung herself down on her back, laughing and panting. Jenna didn't care that she was covered from head to foot with fine sand.

Without warning, a large wave crashed and sent its watery tongue deep into the beach, lapping up shells and tangles of slimy kelp, lifting and sucking Jenna into the hungry sea. She tried to grab at the shifting sand, which offered no support, and to dig her heels into the ooze. She cried out. For a moment, the water drained back and she struggled to her knees, but another relentless wave caught her again and she clawed at the loose sand that slipped beneath her.

Suddenly, Jenna felt the grip of two strong hands grab her under the arms and lift her out of the greedy water. The man, waist deep and strong enough to resist the pull of the current, waited for the water level to lower, then strode out of the water dragging bands of seaweed around his legs.

"There you are, lassie, safe and sound," he said in an Irish brogue. "Steady now." He put Jenna safely down in drier sand a good distance from the water's edge.

Jenna looked up into the smiling face of a handsome man with a tousle of black, curly hair and sparkling, deep blue eyes looking like the ocean, itself, at sunset. His grin was playful and seductive, his manner the same.

She did not recognize him as the Irishman in Red Man's Bar whose gold had been stolen and who had spared the Mexican woman from a flogging.

"I think you saved my life, Sir. Thank you!" Jenna said. She quickly regained her poise, like a cat that instantly knows when it is out of danger.

"Perhaps I did," the man said with a gentle laugh. "Are you all right now, little lady?"

"Yes. I'm surprised, that's all. It's the first time I've seen the ocean. I didn't realize how quickly the waves can change."

"The sea is fickle and unpredictable . . . like a woman. That's why the sea is referred to as *she*, you know."

"No, I didn't know," Jenna said, looking at him squarely, studying him. There was something familiar about this man that she couldn't explain.

The man picked some kelp from Jenna's hair and presented it to her as a bouquet. "For you, lassie."

Jenna laughed. "It was lucky for me you saw me. How did you ever see me in this fog?"

"Well, I confess, I'd been watching you for awhile, running along the beach, twirling like a dancing fairy, a sprite . . . or like a lovely wispy seed. In fact, I said to myself, 'Danny, there's a fairy for sure . . . come all the way from Ireland just to tease your senses.' I haven't laid my eyes on such a sight for a long time. When I first saw your shawl and slippers, I said, 'Well, now, there must be a lassie for those fine clothes,' and I followed the footprints in the sand. Then way down the beach I saw you, whirlin' and spinnin' and laughin' and skippin', just like a sprite you were. That's what fairies do sometimes, don't you know. Now I see you're no fairy at all—more like a drowned rat. Come now, I'll take you home."

"No, no, please. I'm just a short way from here . . . and well, I'm going to have to face the doña unless I can enter through the servant's quarters. She warned me about the sea. I'm going to be in trouble as it is. If you don't mind, Sir, I'd rather go alone."

"All right then, I'll walk you back to your clothes and you hurry home and dry off quickly."

Jenna put the shawl around her shivering shoulders. "Thank you again,

Mister . . .?"

"McDaniels . . . Danny McDaniels, at your service." He bowed low and flourished an imaginary hat.

Jenna smiled and curtsied in her dripping dress. "A pleasure to meet you, Sir. And even more a pleasure not to have drowned!" She turned and ran up the hill to the house feeling peculiarly excited over her encounter with a stranger called Danny McDaniels.

In back of the house, Jenna met Marta, who threw up her hands, warbled off a string of Indian words clearly stating her shock and displeasure, then rushed Jenna to the bathhouse next to the kitchen. The cooks clucked their concern as they heated water for a warm bath and fed Jenna hot sweet coffee with foamy milk and a crusty French roll with butter and honey.

In the hands of so many attendants, she became helpless to their fussing, especially with her hair. After much discussion, none of which Jenna understood, the women began to work on her hair. Jenna felt subdued as one woman rubbed a soft pomade through her stringy hair, heated a curling iron, and proceeded to curl ringlets all over Jenna's head. With deft hands, she pulled them into a delightful bouquet of bouncy curls at the back of her head, leaving a few perky springs around her face and forehead. Another lady looped several bands of blue satin ribbon around the curls and poked in some snapdragons here and there. The dazzling effect thrilled Jenna. She could barely recognize herself.

I'm pretty after all, she thought, looking at herself in a hand mirror. "Papa was right. I look like Grandmother Daggett!" She patted her curls. "I'm going to show Doña Juana. Thank you, thank you!" she said, hugging Marta. Jenna dashed from the room and into the *sala*, where a serious family discussion was being held. "*Perdon*, excuse me!" she said, backing out the door.

"Come in, Jenna. We are finished. There's nothing more to discuss," Doña Juana said coldly. Jenna could see that the doña was holding in her anger. She'd seen that dark look of impatience and frustration in their classes together. "Come, Jenna. We're going shopping." She marched out of the room with Jenna following.

The doña, so far, had not commented on the hairdo. It was not until they were in the courtyard gardens that the doña turned and looked at Jenna "Yes. Much better. Your hair is too fine to wear a high turtle-shell comb. They're far too heavy. Still, you must wear the *mantilla* in the *playa* and for evening . . . and, of course, for the ball tomorrow evening."

🌿 🌿 🌿

The following day, parades, bands, bullfights, picnics, fireworks, and the waving of flags celebrated California statehood. Throughout the morning, the delegates trumpeted their final speeches before the official signing of the documents admitting California into the United States as the thirty-first state. Delegates from all of California, forty-eight in all, had bypassed the territorial stage because of the region's explosive population and unanimously consented to making California a free state—"The Thirty-first State of the American Republic."

Crowds of patriotic Americans, curious foreigners, and Mexicans who only saw opportunity, cheered the new government, some even waving flags. Bayard Taylor, reporter for the *New York Tribune*, wrote, ". . . the Empire of the West, the commerce of the great Pacific, the new highway to the Indies, forming the last link in that belt of civilized enterprise which now clasps the world, has been established under my country's flag; . . . in all the extent of California, from the glittering snows of the Shasta to the burning deserts of Colorado, no slave shall ever lift his arm to make the freedom of that flag a mockery."

Before the final signing of the constitution and the closing of the convention, each delegate contributed twenty-five dollars so all Monterey citizens could participate in a ball and feast. By mid afternoon, the delegates had signed the constitution. Mr. Steuart, the chairman, gave the signal for the American colors to be raised in front of the government buildings. The crowds waiting outside broke into wild hurrahs. A moment later, the first gun ever to be heard in the state of California boomed from the Presidio, and echoes reverberated from one hill to another until they were lost over the sea. After nightfall, the streets and plaza shimmered with lanterns and vibrated with shouts and song and wild dancing.

Inside Colton Hall, citizens important to the new government, officials and representatives, men of power and influence, glittered in the ballroom, which had been converted from the assembly hall. Overhead chandeliers burned brightly, casting a romantic glow on the walls decorated with fragrant pine boughs and American flags and a peculiar picture of George Washington, painted by a local artist who had difficulty matching the subject's eyes. A four-piece band—two guitars and two violins—squeaked and whined lively waltzes, quadrilles, and contradances, and dark-skinned beauties whirled with fairer ladies in full skirts of satin, rich brocades and velvets, gauze, and lace.

Doña Juana, elegantly dressed in red silk and black lace, sat with the Archuletas and cast a critical eye on the merrymaking. Her sister and brother-in-law, however, joined in the ever-popular "Turkey-in-the-Straw," a tune so catching that even Doña Juana tapped her toe under her skirt. She often looked over the rim of her feathered fan, which Jenna thought she used to hide a slight smile. Jenna also noticed that many gentlemen looked at the doña with admiration, nodded a greeting, introduced themselves, or attempted polite conversation, but they quickly withdrew when they felt her contempt.

Jenna overheard the doña say to her sister, "Tell me who are the important men in the government—ones sympathetic to the Spanish . . . *then* I will be friendly."

But on this happy night, Jenna could not be concerned with what the doña thought of the Americans. She was bursting with excitement like the stars of fire rockets against the black sky. Once again, the women servants had fashioned Jenna's curls, this time with wide, green velvet ribbons and burnt-orange flowers. She refused to wear a *mantilla*. Her silk peach dress with a deep hem of fluffy gauze fell in soft folds over a full crinoline. The whole dress was trimmed with green velvet ribbon and embroidered with green vines of ivy. Jenna's pale shoulders, bare and graceful, her slim waist, and shapely figure made her look older than her fifteen years. She was not aware of the gentlemen who looked her way in appreciation.

The hall began to fill with a motley collection of townspeople, sailors, ranchers, and men and women from every station of life.

The doña turned to her sister, Helena. "I thought this was a ball for the select families. I can't tell delegates or officials from anyone else. The whole of Monterey is wandering in and out of here as they please . . . some riffraff as well."

"Sister, dear, we were *all* invited. That's the American way of doing things. Erin says it is a good government. He says they've even outlawed dueling. Imagine!"

"But not lynching, I understand."

"And women can control all property that they owned before marriage. That means our Archuleta home here in Monterey is still in my hands. And so is the Rancho San Gabriel in your name. You do have proof of the land grant to the Archuletas, don't you?"

The doña frowned. "Our brother, Bernardo, has it in his possession. Remember, I only own one-third of the original land grant, the house, and the cattle, but the Archuleta brothers still have authority over the management of the land. I resent the family questioning my ability to run an efficient rancho. They have no right to interfere!"

Her sister looked quite blank and shrunk behind her fluttering fan. "Well, I can't speak for the family. Those are decisions for all of us."

The two sisters looked straight ahead and said no more.

Suddenly, Jenna jumped to her feet. "Captain Sutter!" she called out excitedly. "Captain Sutter!" Seeing her old friend, large and congenial as ever, made her smile happily. She remembered Sutter's Fort and the generous man who reached out his hand to help her and so many other pioneers.

"Why, Bright Eyes, my little friend! How grown up you are! I scarcely recognize you, Jenna. What a wonderful surprise to see you, and on this very joyous occasion of California statehood!" He opened his arms and Jenna flew into them, hugging the rotund girth and catching the strong scent of whiskey.

"Oh, Captain Sutter, I'd heard you were gone forever, and the fort— well, it's not the same; I'm glad you're back from Europe."

Captain Sutter smiled at her with his open, friendly face, but behind his eyes, she thought she saw sadness. Something had changed.

"Yes, the fort is not the same place. It served its function, I guess, but now my son is taking care of matters."

"Your son, Sir?"

"Yes, from Switzerland. My whole Swiss family is coming to America soon . . . when my affairs are in order. It's been fourteen years." There was no sparkle in his eyes as he spoke. "But today is a joyful day for me. Imagine, we are a state now. The people did come to California after all—my personal dream fulfilled. There's little else for me to do but sit in the sun."

"Captain Sutter, you'll never sit still."

"I won't if you'll finish this waltz with me, and, of course, with the doña's permission," he said, taking her by the arm.

Jenna and the Captain enjoyed the last whiny strands of an off-key waltz.

"You must visit me someday at Coloma on the American River."

"And you will visit me at Rancho San Gabriel?"

"Yes, I will indeed. And if another visitor comes to the fort looking for you, I'll be sure my son knows your whereabouts."

"Visitor?"

"My son did not know where you were when a man came looking for you. He did not leave his name, and I know no particulars."

A visitor. How curious; Jenna had an uncomfortable feeling. She thought of the doña's words: "There's always someone who wants something you have!" The pocked face of Reverend Squibb floated into her memory. Would he always come into focus when least expected, making her heart race and her hands turn cold with anxiety?

At midnight, supper was served downstairs—turkey, roast pig, beef, tongue, patés, fruits, cheeses, wines, liquors, and coffee. The Archuletas and Cassidys dined together, with the doña quite suddenly in the company of Reginald Potter, a toady, red-faced lawyer with blustery, witless humor and clumsy manners.

As Jenna finished the last of her meal, a noisy threesome—two women and a man—entered the dining hall. Jenna stared. The brash man, his black curls tousled and vulgar, escorting two painted women who laughed too loudly, was Danny McDaniels, the man who pulled her from the grasping sea. Jenna wanted to disappear. It was too late. He and the women walked directly toward them. Jenna held up her fan to cover her face.

"Cassidy, old friend. What say, three cheers for the Irish!" Danny McDaniels raised a glass and swallowed the amber contents. "And a fine time it is!" In spite of his crooked grin, he still looked disarmingly handsome to all the women who dared to peer at him from behind their fans or handkerchiefs.

"This is your family, I take it," he said, trying to kiss the doña's hand but losing his balance. "And bless me," he grinned, "if it isn't the little fairy herself!"

Jenna held her fan to hide her face from the family, placed her finger to her lips, and shot a threatening glance at Danny.

He threw back his head and laughed out loud. "I beg your pardon, lassie. I must be mistaken. This lovely creature is a princess, not a fairy at all . . . not a sea fairy who spins in the morning fog and makes the surf churn with hunger."

Erin Cassidy intervened. "Daniel, come by the house this week when the spirits aren't with you, and we'll take a swim in the sea like old times. We've got to keep the Irish together in this new government. To the Irish, Danny?" he asked, escorting Danny toward the door.

"To the Irish!" Danny shouted. He left without introducing the two women.

"What a crude man," the doña said. "Ill-mannered—a typical foreigner."

Jenna didn't agree. There was something about Danny McDaniels that made her want a lock of his black curls to keep between the pages of a treasured book. She could not explain the mystifying "moth wings" quivering in her breast.

The dancing and festivities lasted all night. Jenna danced waltzes, quadrilles, and rounds; in spite of glares from Doña Juana, she danced "Skip-to-my-Lou", "Pig-in-the Parlor", and "Bounce Around". Excitement reddened her face and relaxed the springy curls which had been so carefully formed for the party. Doña Juana forbade her to dance the "Weevily Wheat", a disgusting reel only crude Americans would like.

Before dawn, the Mexicans honored the custom of their festivals and broke the *cascarones*—eggshells filled with gold and silver confetti. Jenna whirled into the floating glitter, catching it in her curls and on her moist skin.

Finally, it was time to go home. As Jenna was leaving, and before she could turn around, the teasing voice of Danny McDaniels whispered in her ear, "Hurry and grow up, little fairy."

NINE

URING THE NEXT TWO YEARS, Jenna's friendship with the doña grew deeper—a friendship more of respect than love, for Jenna suspected Doña Juana believed her authority would be lessened if she showed affection. Now, however, a healthy tension, a playful game of wit and argument, kept the pressure around their relationship and kept them both on their toes. Jenna knew deep down that the doña liked her and enjoyed her company. The feeling was mutual.

Jenna also knew the doña took pride in teaching her the manners of the Spanish aristocracy and the ways of the Catholic church. However, the older woman's advice, concerning the proper behavior for a señorita in the company of men, broke from convention. If she had her way, she would teach Jenna to be a spinster—cold, aloof, and feared.

"Keep your back straight and your head held high," Doña Juana would instruct. "Act like a queen and you'll be treated like one. And look directly at a man. Lowering your eyes to appear demure is silly and dishonest— unless it serves a purpose. And another bit of advice, Jenna; always speak your mind. You will soon discover men are childish and easily manipulated—*tontos utiles*, useful fools."

Doña Juana insisted that Jenna accompany her everywhere: to San

Jose to visit friends, to her brother's rancho, to the Missions San Jose and Santa Clara, to every fiesta, baptism, birthday, Saint's day, special mass, and rodeo in the area, to Monterey to shop—but never to Sacramento, the gateway to the mining camps.

Often the two of them rode the stallion and palomino over the large acres of land, both enjoying the freedom of the vast, rolling grasslands. Sometimes they surprised a coyote or bear, deer, even a wild pig that stayed close to the tree line on the hills. Their horses, belly-deep in tall grass, flushed out pheasants, quail, and partridges that tried to keep the riders from their precious eggs. Jenna now rode straddling the saddle, a wining point for her. Reluctantly, the doña had agreed to order a special, heavier riding skirt and pantaloons made for Jenna's outings. Jenna always suspected the doña envied her when she split away into a wind-blown gallop across the meadows.

Jenna avoided the areas where cattle had been slaughtered for their hides and fat. The putrid carcasses, left to rot in the sun, were a feast for wildcats, bears, coyotes, vultures, and vermin. No humans wanted the meat. Only a grassy graveyard of bones, skulls, and horns remained for the land to consume. To Jenna it seemed like a terrible waste of life . . . but it was the business of the rancho.

Jenna's life on the rancho was like living in a cocoon, a cloistered place. Everywhere, California was sprouting tent cities, some stone structures, inventive businesses and services, newspapers, laundries, hotels, post offices, dress shops, and shoemakers. But Jenna scarcely felt the change.

On lonely, reflective days, she rode Honey a short way along the river and talked to her like an old friend about what seemed to be a very long time ago. She enjoyed remembering her family and people on the crossing. Many times, she remembered the lovely Indian woman who stole her bonnet and gave her the small, leather pouch. She always appeared in Jenna's thoughts as a messenger of hope or strength. Jenna couldn't help substituting the Indian woman for the Virgin that the doña insisted she pray to.

Even though Doña Juana objected, Jenna visited the Indian women who lived on the premises in their small, stick, beehive houses with their children and laboring husbands. They harvested the vegetables, ground corn for the cooks, made soap and honey, gathered seeds, and helped gardens and irrigate the crops. They furnished the ranch with baskets and adobe bricks for patching crumbling walls and making additions.

The children always gathered around Jenna, begging for caramelized sugar. Gradually, her visits became opportunities for playing games, teaching English ditties and nursery rhymes. Before long, Jenna held classes for the children under a large oak tree. She started by drawing letters in the clay soil with a stick, then one morning she asked the doña if she could buy materials, slates and primers, so she could teach them in earnest.

"You have better things to do with your time, Jenna."

"I can think of nothing better to do than to teach them. They are eager and quick, especially Luisa. I have too much time," she argued.

"Then next week, I will ask your tutor to give you more work, more reading. You do not practice the piano enough, your needlework is disastrous, your painting is clumsy, and your Spanish merely adequate. You do not yet know catechism or spend enough time in prayer and contemplation."

Jenna flushed. Must she always have to stand up to the doña's unreasonableness? "It is enjoyable and worthy teaching the children reading and writing—in *English*," Jenna said firmly.

"The children are only your toys, your dolls," the doña said spitefully.

"I wouldn't know—I never played with dolls," Jenna said, suppressing her irritation.

"Excuse me, I forgot. The Americans do not play; they only work like dogs. You probably never had a doll—only a broom or a scrub brush to play with. Am I right?" She fluttered a peacock feather fan in front of her face, a technique she used whenever she wanted to conceal her delight in a cruel remark, or hide an unexpected emotion.

The doña's device did not work. Jenna saw the self-satisfied smirk on the older woman's face. Her mouth hardened into a tight line. "I had a doll—one my very own mother made for me—but I lost it in a river crossing. You would never understand such things!"

"Lower your voice or I shall dismiss you at once."

Jenna had not finished. "Whether you like it or not, the Americans are coming here and they speak English, not Spanish. You would keep these Indians ignorant, tied to you. You see them only as your property."

"How dare you! I do not condone slavery!"

"Nor do I!" Jenna snapped back.

"*Vayase*! Get out! You are excused. Your impertinence and disrespect are beyond tolerance. Go to your prayers and ask forgiveness for your behavior. *Vayase*!"

Jenna hurried from the *sala*, immediately sorry she had been so disrespectful to the doña, but angry just the same.

That evening, Jenna did not eat with Doña Juana, but asked Marta to bring her some soup from the kitchen. She did not feel like eating much, or sleeping, or praying, or even writing to Darcey and Pearle.

Jenna picked up Martha Jane's pearl box and emptied its contents on the bed—Nettie's locket, Israel's harmonica, a lock of Martha Jane and Solomon's hair, Miss Little—"Pearle's river stone"—the Indian woman's small beaded pouch, and a sprig of dried prairie sage carefully wrapped in a piece of cloth. She had opened the little box countless times, always slipping into long-ago memories of the smallest things—spilling a bowl of spoon bread batter, or smelling her mother's apron, fresh and full of sunshine.

In her mind's eye, she had gradually changed Martha Jane's deep frown into a look of devotion or concern; she'd softened her sharp voice and distant eyes, and changed the downward curve of her mouth upward into a gentle smile.

Tonight, Jenna slipped Nettie's locket around her neck and remembered her mother's brief touch. "If you don't mind, Nettie, I'm going to wear your locket for a while. You won't mind, I know. When it moves on my skin, it feels alive, like a heavenly touch."

The doña's solitary dinner was tasteless without Jenna's company. Even the sweet strawberries, sliced into blood-red hearts, made her ask herself, *Have I become so cold and heartless over the years? Is Jenna right?* She called Marta into the dining room. "Take a bowl of strawberries and cream to Jenna, and tell her I will arrange for a dozen slates and primers—and to be on time for our lessons in the morning."

The next morning, Jenna apologized. "I'm very sorry, Doña Juana. Thank you for the strawberries . . . and the slates."

Often, Doña Juana would watch from a distance as Jenna announced "school" by ringing a dinner bell. The children would run for the oak tree—two or three, sometimes a dozen or more shouting, "teacher, teacher." Many times, a mother or old grandmother would sit with them, listening while working on a basket.

The doña smiled to herself.

She is becoming more palatable, certainly more refined and graceful than any other American. My influence has been agreeable. I like her energy and occasional defiance, a bit like mine when I was her age. I, too, never wanted a siesta or to say my prayers during the heat of the day. I wanted to run to the stream, ride my horse with the wind.

She must think me a fool for not knowing what she does. No matter. I believe she is more content than when she arrived, perhaps even happy at the rancho, here with me. I wonder if it is dangerous to teach the Indians how to read and write. I wonder. I will ask Saint Gabriel and then decide if Jenna should continue to teach my workers.

🌿 🌿 🌿

One spring morning, as Jenna sat by the river on a grassy bank, dry at last after the winter rains, she saw a rider approaching, a young man, perhaps a *vaquero*, but wearing a crumpled felt hat instead of a *sombrero*. She was curious. The rider had a familiar way about him, a loose, easygoing motion in the saddle. She stood up and shaded her eyes.

Could it be? she thought. *No, impossible.*

But as the rider neared, she knew who it was and joy flooded her eyes. "Harke! Harke!" she cried, lifting her skirt and running toward him.

Harke jumped off his horse and ran to her, grabbing her around the waist and swinging her in circles. "Jenna! I thought I'd never find you."

They clung to each other laughing, the past and present joy compressed into a single moment. Jenna stood back and looked at him—tall and blond, no longer a lanky youth, now strong and solid. His shy, boyish smile was the same, but time had graced him with confidence. His eyes reflected kindness and gentleness. Harke was a man.

"You are beautiful!" he said. "All grown up, and even more beautiful than I ever imagined you to be . . . and so *tall!*" He placed his hands on her shoulders and for moment wanted to pull her close to him and tell her he had never stopped thinking of her.

"We have so much to talk about, Harke. Oh, how I've missed all of you and thought about Mother Boyles, Hannah, the twins, and Emily and Dr. Polley. Please tell me about everyone."

They sat in the grass under a tree noisy with nesting orioles while Harke told Jenna his adventures of the last few years. Mother Boyles had died before the wagon train reached Oregon. She died peacefully in her sleep and was buried in a pretty grove of aspen trees. The Polley family bought a farm that was doing fine, and Dr. Polley enjoyed a decent practice as a country doctor. The twins were growing up healthy, going to school and doing their share of the work.

"And Hannah?"

Harke's face clouded. "Hannah didn't like it much in the Wilamette Valley. In fact, she hated it, Jenna. Never could quite adjust to the idea. But, of course, she was sick when we first got there." He dropped his eyes. Jenna knew he wouldn't speak of her pregnancy.

"Harke, I know all about it. I know she was carrying a child when I left," she said softly.

Harke looked up. "Yes . . . it was terrible sad. She bore a fine boy, Samuel. One morning before he was even a year old, we found him . . . dead. He was never sick a day, a rosy boy. Never sick. We couldn't understand it. Shortly after, Hannah ran away—full of grief, I expect," he said without conviction. "We ain't seen her since. Such a strong baby to die so sudden." As he spoke, the joy fell out of his face.

"She must have been grieving awful." Jenna felt a coldness grip the back of her neck. There was something sinister in the story, a ghost of something Hannah had once said to her, but Jenna couldn't remember Hannah's words and the sensation slipped away.

Harke didn't answer.

"Poor, dear Hannah," Jenna said.

"She didn't know for sure whose child it was!" Harke blurted out. "She brought a bastard into the world . . . a blameless, fatherless child who had no love from his mother. *My* mother gave him all he had. Hannah wouldn't even feed him like a woman is supposed to do."

"Oh, dear."

"She cared more about her looks and having a good time. She never cried a tear when little Samuel expired—not even when we lowered his tiny body into the ground. I can't forgive her for that."

Jenna took his hand. "I'm sorry, Harke. I'm so sorry."

"I don't care much if I see her again, but Mama is sufferin' so. I came to California hoping to find Hannah. I know she's here, somewhere—folks have seen her . . . for awhile in San Francisco. She'll hook up with whoever will dress her fancy and give her a good time.

"Someone said he thought she had headed north to the Feather River and the gold camps. I've been looking for her for over a year, off and on. In the meantime, I got to make a living, so I hired on with a group of miners east of Coloma on a daily wage—twenty dollars a day, which is good pay, and we're still moving tons of pay dirt.

"I don't like mining much. I worked a small claim for awhile and did right well, but it's too crowded for me. You'd never understand the life of a miner unless you been there yourself. I put away a small savings."

"That's fine, Harke." She didn't tell him that she knew about mining camps and standing for hours in cold water with sharp stones tearing flesh away from the hands and shoveling dirt to find "the yellow."

"One day, I'd like to buy me a farm . . . some land."

"How did you ever find me?"

"Captain Sutter, himself, told me where you were. He lives in Coloma. I went to Sutter's Fort two years ago looking for you, but there wasn't anyone there except Sutter's son. He'd never heard of you, of course. I gave up on ever seeing you again." He leaned over, held Jenna's face in his hand, and gave Jenna a kiss on the cheek. It was not a self-conscious kiss, rather one of friendship and happiness of finding her at last.

They laughed together like they had when Jenna was a child.

"Oh, Jenna, I do love you, you know that. I guess I always will." This time he cupped her face in both hands and for a moment the idea of a kiss, not as friends, crossed both of their minds.

A curious, shimmering green hummingbird darted into the picture, fluttered in one spot like a frozen jewel close to them, and stared with its ebony eye. Satisfied, it darted away.

Jenna lowered her head so that no kiss could happen.

The two of them spent the morning together talking about adventures and people on the Oregon Trail and the strange twists and turns of their lives.

Jenna told Harke about her dear friend, Blue, "Quigley Gump," she had said with amusement.

After a small success in mining, Blue decided he preferred staying on the road. He had started a transportation business, the Sierra-Pacific Stagecoach Company, and for awhile he was the only driver between San Jose and San Francisco. After so many people complained about fleas and slow horses, Blue bought a handsome coach, red and black with gold lettering, and two teams of fine horses. He was making a good living, and recently he had expanded his line to include Monterey, Jackson, and Placerville.

"Why, he even carries the mail to the miners and back to the post office in San Jose; sometimes he carries their gold dust to a bank . . . all for a fee, of course. You'd never know by talking to him, but I wouldn't be surprised if he became a rich man—if he isn't already."

I can't believe I missed seeing him, Jenna. What good news. Old Blue was the best of men. Too bad he ain't married and got himself a brood of youngsters."

"He's been like a father to me . . . looked after me when Papa died and when I ran away. He still comes to see me when he can, but he's seldom free."

Harke had been puzzled for many years about Jenna's running away from the wagon train so unexpectedly. He had always suspected something had been very wrong with Jenna after she began living with the Reverend and Cora, but he never could have imagined Jenna's nightmare, nor that any man, especially a man entrusted with men's souls, could possess such wickedness. The truth of the situation would have been beyond belief. The farthest he or anyone could stretch the imagination was in thinking the Reverend and Cora were too strict in the demands of the Bible and the constant recitation of scripture.

"I wonder where old Reverend Yellow Tooth is now?"

"He's in California, up at Red Man's Bar on the American River. I heard from some friends that he's built a meeting house." Jenna passed on the information with little expression.

"Why didn't you say goodbye when you ran away, Jenna? I doubled back for half a day looking for you to bring you back. Then Hannah told me it wasn't no use. You'd made up your mind to go to California, to follow Blue. She told me the Squibbs didn't do right by you. I guess I understood, after awhile."

Harke sensed a coldness, a deadness in her. She had thrown up a stone wall between them, isolating a part of herself, hiding the sunshine and warmth that had been there only moments before. He decided not to pursue more about Faithful.

"And what about you, Jenna? A pretty girl like you ought to be a-thinkin' on marriage and starting a family," Harke said, pushing a long strand of blond hair out of his eyes.

He still couldn't tell her he had never stopped thinking about her, that sometimes when the dew on the fields were awakened with sun, he could still smell the morning in her hair. One day, he knew he would find her and hold her in his arms.

Jenna laughed. "Marriage? Oh, my, not yet. Heavens, no! I'm still studying with a tutor. I have dreams, lots of them all mixed up. Sometimes I want to go to a university somewhere. Maybe one day own land and great herds of cattle, or start a business. Sometimes, Harke, I think our journey on the Oregon Trail made me want to be a gypsy and travel far away, even to China. Marriage is a long way off!

"Besides, right now Doña Juana still needs me. She's getting old—nearly forty-eight, I'm guessing. She'd never tell me her age. The Archuletas say she's getting too old to manage Rancho San Gabriel, too old-fashioned in her thinking. I don't agree. She's clever—smarter than her brothers—and is a fine lady."

"So you will stay here for awhile? You wouldn't consider a home of your own?" Harke blushed and looked away. "Some day?" He was testing her response and sensed that Jenna understood the meaning behind his question.

"My destiny is unclear," she said gently. "Maybe one day . . . maybe never, Harke. Families come together and grow to love each other, only to be destroyed by some violent stroke of fate. Everyone scatters; everyone ends up buried alone. Families suffer."

"Not all families, Jenna. You had some awful luck." He took her hand.

"I don't think I'm supposed to have a family, or else mine wouldn't have been taken away. Does that make sense, Harke?"

"No, Jenna, it don't. Every woman needs a family, children, a man to love her and take care of her. She wasn't created to be alone."

Jenna didn't answer and remained expressionless. She stood up. "Harke, you will stay a few days, won't you?"

"I'm sorry, Jenna, I have to get back to Coloma. But maybe one night wouldn't hurt anyone."

"Good! Now we must hurry back to the house for the noon meal, *almuerzo*, and meet the doña. She doesn't like it when I'm late."

That evening, Harke and Jenna sat in the courtyard under the watchful eye of the doña, two traveling priests, and Luisa, who never took her eye off Harke.

The next day, after a full meal of roast chicken, beans, and rich grape wine, Jenna rode with Harke to the entrance of the rancho to say goodbye to him. He drew his horse close to hers and, without hesitation, leaned over his horse's neck, drew Jenna to him, and kissed her—a long, overdue kiss that took her by surprise and sent a tingling charge down her spine to her toes.

"Bye, Jenna. I don't know when, but I'll be back," he grinned. "Yep, you can bet a poke of gold, I'll be back!" He whirled his horse around and galloped away in a cloud of yellow dust.

Jenna watched until he was out of sight, then started slowly back to the house, still feeling the soft sensation on her lips. She'd crossed a threshold into a new, secret place where she'd never been before, where she was a stranger, frightened and exhilarated at the same time. She slapped the reins on Solana's neck, kicked her flanks, and took off away from the house across the meadow, yellow and wild with blooming mustard.

🌿 🌿 🌿

A stranger on horseback, passing by Rancho San Gabriel on his way to Santa Cruz Mission, delivered a letter to Jenna in exchange for a substantial meal and a mug of strong ale. The letter was from Darcey.

Jenna ran to her room, followed by Luisa, who had caught her excitement. As Jenna started to shut the door, she saw the hurt on Luisa's face.

"Not now, Luisa." She showed her the letter, then pressed it to her heart. "A letter . . . from dear friends. We'll hunt quail eggs later."

Luisa lowered her head and walked slowly into the courtyard, pulling a large pink camellia from its show place, and crushing it in her hand.

Jenna sat by the window, where a patch of sunlight fell across the small table. She wanted the moment to be special while she read her precious letter.

Dear Jenna,

I have not written for such a long, long time because I am so busy with the boardinghouse. At night, I can hardly keep my eyes open. Sometimes, after cleaning up the dishes, I fall asleep at the table before getting to bed. Please forgive me. Just in the past week, my load seems lighter. The miners are saying this gulch is running dry, and many of them are packing up and moving on south of here. There's rumors that some men are turning over as much as twenty dollars a bucketful! I don't much care. I'm doing real good where I am serving stew and flapjacks. I run a respectable house here. No spitting on the premises, and I don't serve spirits. Miners will eat almost anything after being on the river all day. Pearle isn't doing so good. She had another bout with the ague last winter, poor child. She nearly rattled her brains out shivering so bad. Now, she seems weak and quiet, don't smile at all and stays to herself. A doctor's wife in Red Man has been teaching her and passing time with her that I don't have. The Reverend Faithful Squibb is seeing to her Christian education—even takes her with him sometimes when he goes preaching. She don't take to the Bible much. I wish you could visit. It would do Pearle a world of good. She's been so lonesome for you. I'm glad your life on the ranch is a happy one. We've missed you. I'd hoped to visit you many times, but it didn't work out. It seems I never stop workin' and cleanin' mud out of Hatties Place. Sometimes I'm still bakin' long after midnight for breakfast the next morning.

Do you see Blue much? I hope he's well and doing good in his business. When you see him, tell him my gold tooth is fine. Take care Jenna, until the day the Lord sees fit to cross our weary paths.

Love, Darcey

Jenna could hardly finish the letter after seeing the words "The Reverend Faithful Squibb." Her panic collided with the joy of hearing from Darcey. The thought of Pearle alone with Faithful turned Jenna cold and made her nauseated. She did not have to guess—she knew Pearle's fate was the same as hers. "Oh, Lord, if you exist, please take care of Pearle!" she cried out.

Suddenly, she needed someone or something to understand her anguish, and she snatched the statue of the Virgin Mary from the shelf. "Mother Mary, if you have any power, protect Pearle from all wickedness." The painted eyes looking heavenward seemed lifeless, unreal. Jenna squeezed her eyes tight and whispered, "Are you hearing me?" She waited, hoping to hear some words of reassurance from a mysterious source. "Are you hearing anything I say?" she said angrily.

This isn't fair. Not Pearle, too! Oh! Oh! What can I do . . . now?

"Hear my prayers, Blessed Mother." Jenna fumbled through her dresser drawer to find the rosary the doña had given her. She fell on her knees. "Hail, Mary, full of grace, the Lord is with thee. Blessed art thou among women, and blessed is the fruit of thy womb, Jesus. Holy Mary, Mother of God, pray for us sinners, now and at the hour of our death." Jenna breathlessly rushed through the beads with her eyes squeezed shut.

She stopped abruptly and let the slippery beads slide through her fingers and coil in her palm. "I can't do this—I just can't. I must go to Hattie's Gulch!"

Jenna wiped her face and went to speak to the doña.

"Come in, Jenna," Doña Juana said. "I was about to send Luisa for you."

Jenna entered the lemon-scented *sala* and was surprised to see a young man rising from his chair.

"I would like to present my nephew, my brother's son, Enrique Archuleta. He has just returned from the University in Lima, Peru. Enrique, this is my ward, Señorita Jenna Daggett."

Jenna flushed at the unexpected meeting of a man, especially one so young and handsome.

Enrique smiled, bowed low, and kissed Jenna's fingertips. As he raised up, his eyes followed her body, lingered on her breasts, then her mouth, then fastened on her eyes. He smiled with approval. Jenna burned.

"*Con mucho gusto*, Señorita Jenna."

"*Igualmente*, Señor Archuleta," Jenna managed to say.

Enrique turned to the doña. "My esteemed Aunt Juana, you did not tell me your young ward was so disarmingly beautiful." He walked a circle around Jenna, which made her flush again. "I've changed my mind, Auntie. I will stay longer than I had first intended, perhaps for the summer . . . perhaps longer. My father is right. Rancho San Gabriel is enchanting, more than I had expected."

Enrique fixed his eyes on Jenna in a way that made her feel vulnerable, unsure of herself. His voice was strong and commanding, as powerful as his eyes, as sensual as his smile.

To Jenna, the man's presence charged the *sala* like a giant magnet storm. His every gesture ignited the air, spinning an invisible dancing energy around her that made her skin tingle.

She was slightly afraid of him. He had drawn her into a vacuum with him, shutting out everything else around her. All she could see was the hypnotic face, the strange, startling blue eyes of a man intense and powerful.

Jenna walked slowly toward him as though she were being pulled by a cord. She was surprised at her boldness and at the growing excitement in her as she stood in front of him.

"You will like Rancho San Gabriel this time of year," she said, not taking her eyes away from his. "And the horses, too, so full of spirit."

"Jenna," the doña snapped, breaking the spell that clearly drew the two of them together. "Sit down now and join us for café! You had something you wanted to discuss, did you not?"

"Doña Juana, I have an urgent request, but I prefer a private audience with you. I would not want to impose my personal concerns on this rare visit with your nephew."

"Please, little lady, consider me invisible." Enrique selected a cigar from an ornate humidor on the table.

"Go ahead, Jenna. I'll decide if it is urgent," Doña Juana said.

"It's about my friend, Darcey and her daughter, Pearle. I've spoken of them before. They would like for me to visit them . . ."

"Is someone sick or dying?"

"No, madam."

Enrique blew a stream of smoke from his lips. "It doesn't sound urgent to me."

"Nor to me, Jenna. Please sit down and be courteous to my nephew. As I told you Enrique, Americans have no manners."

Jenna looked over at Enrique. He had not stopped looking at her with his enigmatic eyes.

"Well, it is such a glorious day, not to be spoiled by my personal concerns," she said, hoping to sound poised and adult. "Thank you for including me in taking afternoon coffee." Jenna posed herself on a dainty chair, straightened her back and lifted her chin. She smiled quietly at Enrique.

The doña looked at Jenna with a mild disgust.

And so it begins, the first flutter in the heart, the small butterfly wings that brush softly at the soul, awaken the sleeping Eros, then, without warning, turn into sharp knives.

The little fool. What does she know of the ways of men, especially the Archuleta men? All of them charming, beautiful to look at, cruel. God forbid, she and Enrique—together! God, forbid it!

It was not until Enrique excused himself, leaving Doña Juana and Jenna alone, that her ward verbalized her request to visit Pearle and Darcey for a few weeks.

"Absolutely out of the question, Jenna. I will not allow you to return to those evil mining camps. They are ungodly places, full of foreigners—*gringos* and *Los Chinos*, American scoundrels."

"Blue—Señor Gump—will take me there and leave me in the care of Darcey. I'll be very safe, I assure you."

"What kind of woman would behave in such a manner? This Darcey . . . she is not a proper chaperon at all. I won't hear of it!"

"You forget, Doña Juana, I have been in the camps already, under Darcey's care. I am one of the 'American scoundrels'."

The doña noted how defensive Jenna seemed. She could always arouse Jenna's ire when she spoke against someone or something the girl loved. "And you came to me to get away from such bad influences. Jenna, I only want what is best for you. You have grown into a young woman, no longer a little girl. At this age you should be accompanied."

"I won't be gone long, only long enough to see my American family. Please, Doña Juana, I must go. Little Pearle needs me now. She's so small and dainty, like a bird. Doña, I beg you. She may even be dying!"

Jenna sounded so anxious, the doña answered, "Let me think about it and ask San Gabriel what he advises. I will give you my answer after the siesta."

She already knew she was going to give her permission, but delaying an answer kept her position of authority. Privately, she feared Jenna might want to return to her people, her "kind", and she desperately wanted to keep hold of her as long as possible. Jenna had become like a daughter, a source of joy. She did not want to lose her.

On the other hand, she had sensed the instant chemistry between

Enrique and Jenna. It might be better, after all, to let Jenna go at this time, to distance her from her brother's son. Why did he have to come back to California? Why couldn't he have stayed in Lima and left the Archuleta family in peace?

That evening, the doña spoke to Jenna. "I've prayed to San Gabriel. You may leave as soon as you like and stay with your friends no longer than six weeks. I expect you to be accompanied by Mr. Gump. We will make arrangements for you to leave on his stagecoach from San Jose to Placerville. Then, I expect him to ride with you on horseback to your destination. If he can't arrange to do that, you will not be able to go."

"He will do it! I'm certain of that. Oh, thank you, doña!" She threw her arms around the doña and kissed her cheek, as she sometimes did when she was excited; but this time, the doña did not reprimand her or pretend it was nonsense. She had grown used to Jenna's joyful, affectionate outbursts and wondered how she could ever live without them.

Enrique met Jenna in the garden. "I'm disappointed you are leaving so soon . . . just as we were getting acquainted."

Joy radiated through Jenna. She could not tell if her feelings rested entirely with the prospect of seeing Darcey and Pearle, or the fact that Enrique would be at the ranch when she returned.

"Yes, I'm disappointed, too, but I must go."

"Would the doña mind if we walked to the pond? The evening is cool, not yet dark; I want to look at you in the twilight."

Jenna lowered her eyes. "You'll have to ask permission. It is her way."

"It is the Archuleta way, for certain."

Jenna was caught between the desire to be with him and fear of being foolish in his presence. He was sophisticated, mysterious, proud. Something about him frightened her. For him to ask her to stroll in the garden was a compliment beyond words.

"Go on, but take Luisa with you," the doña said sharply. "And take a lantern. Come back to the house when it needs to be lighted."

Luisa happily tagged along a few feet behind Enrique and Jenna.

Enrique offered his arm, an act of courtesy that allowed them to touch.

The intimacy made Jenna feel hot all over. As they walked toward the pond, she felt the splotches bloom on her neck like night flowers.

The pair strolled around the pond accompanied by Luisa and three genial, wagging dogs. Enrique threw a stinging stone at one of the hounds, causing it to yelp. He threw another stone at a family of ducks, scattering them in all directions. Jenna, certain Enrique was only playing with the animals and not intending to hurt them, overlooked the incidents, and only remarked, "Poor things."

As they sat on a bench by the water, faint coral faded on the horizon, and the evening light silhouetted the feathery trees. Stars popped out one by one, and Luisa lit the lantern.

"Even in this gray light, I can see the shine in your eyes, lovely girl— little fairy lights like fireflies. Do your eyes shine for me, or someone else?"

Jenna, uneasy and self-conscious over the compliment, turned her head away from Enrique. He had made her beautiful, desirable. It was a new experience. "Maybe my eyes only reflect the lamplight." She smiled but dared not look at him.

"I don't think so." Enrique gently took her chin and turned her face to him. "Your eyes betray you, señorita."

"We must go back to the house. The doña will be cross if we don't go now."

"My aunt is an old spinster. She knows nothing of a man's sentiment. I can handle the old woman anytime."

Jenna turned to go. "It is a question of respect. Luisa?"

Enrique took her arm. "Then I will go because *you* have asked, not her. We will have many opportunities to walk by this pond in the evenings. Until your return, I will be only half alive, Señorita Daggett."

🌿 🌿 🌿

In a short time, Jenna had heard from Blue and confirmed their arrangements to meet in San Jose. She would go by coach to Pleasanton, then Sacramento and on to Placerville, and finally to Red Man's Bar and Hattie's Bar.

Although she was excited to begin her journey, she found herself thinking more about leaving Enrique. When he left for a few days to inspect the doña's herds and the boundaries of her land, she missed him and the excitement of being in his company. She missed not saying goodbye.

During the journey, Jenna wanted to sit next to Blue in the driver's seat, but he told her it was bad business policy. Besides, the dust would cover her pretty traveling dress and blow her hair every which way. "We'll have a chance to catch up on matters when we ride to Hattie's Bar. We will stay at good hotels and eat our meals together."

Jenna resigned herself to sitting inside the coach with another passenger—a stout man who slept most of the time, or scowled and looked at his pocket watch over and over.

She was glad to have the privacy to think, to dream, and to relive the time she had spent with Enrique. She missed his touch on her arm, his lips brushing her fingers, and she often lingered on a memory . . . when he kissed the nape of her neck. She could still feel his warm sigh on her skin and the sensation of autumn leaves fluttering on her spine. He had tried to kiss her then, but Luisa's staring stopped them.

The stout man got off in Pleasanton, and the next morning Jenna was joined by a bird-like woman and her gawky daughter. Jenna pretended to sleep rather than answer the incessant questions from the unattractive pair.

Late in the second day, Blue entered the southern outskirts of Sacramento, a town noisily stretching along the river and stretching across land where Jenna, Darcey, and Pearle had picnicked in purple clover only a short while ago.

Sacramento had grown with scarcely a plan, from a stack of shanties here and there, to streets lined with new buildings—hotels, restaurants and gambling houses. Signs announcing a play or an opera plastered the new opera house and theater. Shops with false fronts, liveries, and newspaper offices lined wooden walkways, and everywhere churches rose above the dust to save Saturday night sinners, heathens, and painted ladies.

Through the jumble and hustle, Jenna could see a substantial town. She marveled at what eager builders men were.

If there was space, man wanted to erect something on it, his mark, his monument. He wasted no time. The women stood in the shadows quietly civilizing the place, demanding churches and schools and homes reminiscent of those "back home."

The Forty-niners had carved out a new life from the wilderness, one of high energy and optimism, a roughness and playfulness, a cockiness. Those who had crossed the plains, or survived the ocean voyage around the tip of south America, or tramped across Panama through jungle heat, were a rugged, self-reliant breed. Boom towns such as Sacramento blossomed from their spirit.

Suddenly, the coach jerked to a stop. Jenna could see people running toward the coach. Blue jumped down. Jenna looked out the window to see a woman lying in the street.

"I seen it," someone shouted. "She walked right into the path of the horses. You couldn't have stopped, Mister."

Jenna got out of the coach.

"She's dazed but ain't hurt, thank God!" Blue said. "Lady? Lady? Are you all right?"

The woman sat up, but appeared quite confused.

"You walked right into them horses," a by-stander said.

"Does anyone know this woman?" Blue asked.

"That's Annie, one of them Hallelujah Girls from the Hallelujah House at the other end of town," a man said.

"Ain't she the deaf one?" someone asked. "Probably didn't hear the coach a-comin'. She's all ginned up . . . full of spirits."

"Help me get her into the coach," Blue said. "I'll take her home."

The bird-like passenger got out of the coach, ruffled and twitching. "Well, I declare! This stage line will have no more business of *mine*! No doubt that woman is full of vermin of every kind. Take down my trunk immediately! I won't go another step with that woman in the coach. Emma," she snapped, "don't look at that woman. Turn your head away!" She forced the gawky girl's head around as Blue and another man helped the bewildered woman into the coach.

Blue spoke to his unhappy passenger. "We're only two blocks away from your stage stop, Madam. Allow me to take you there."

"I don't care! My daughter and I won't ride with the likes of her."

"Suit yourself, Ma'am," Blue said, climbing into the driver's seat.

Inside, the woman, still stunned, lay back on the seat, her head lolling to the motion of the coach. In the corners of her closed eyes, globes of tears formed and rolled down her cheek.

Jenna straightened the woman's bonnet and brushed away the dirt and small stones that had stuck to her grease-painted face. The woman opened her eyes, and the two of them looked closely at each other. Through the makeup, Jenna caught an image of someone she knew.

"Zelda? Is that you? Zelda?"

The woman squinted as if she were trying to focus her eyes. "It's no use talkin', lady. I'm deaf." The woman concentrated on Jenna's lips.

"You *are* Zelda. I'm Jenna!"

"You're mistaken. I'm Annie," she said and turned her face away.

Jenna took her chin, gently turned her face around, and looked into the confused, puffy face. The woman smelled of spirits and sickness; her eyes were dull, except for a flicker of recognition.

"What happened to you, Zelda?"

"He broke my eardrums, he did. Beat me so bad I lost my hearing."

"Luke, you mean, Luke."

"Yes. I ran away, caught a wagon train of men what called theirselves 'The Buccaneers.' Gold seekers, they was. I worked for my passage, with all of them."

"Oh, Zelda, I'm sorry. I'm so sorry."

"I ain't Zelda. She's dead. I'm Annie, only half-dead. Forget you ever seen me." She shut her eyes and stayed that way until the coach stopped. She never looked at Jenna again, not even when Jenna pressed a twenty-dollar Mexican gold piece into her hand.

Jenna did not tell Blue that the unfortunate woman was Zelda. It was not that she distrusted Blue, but rather that she felt protective of a woman whose tragedy was too deep to whisper about.

As Jenna had matured, she had developed a bond, a deep connection with the women who had survived the westward journey—in fact, any journey—women like Darcey, the emigrants who staggered into Sutter's

Fort, even the doña.

Women seemed to be like the fireweed that refuses to die, to be destroyed. She remembered Emily Polley telling her about the wild, indestructible plant. Out of the ashes, destruction, or calamities, it still grows. Sprouting through displaced soil or charcoal rubble into the sun, a tiny seed of life flowering into magenta spikes, spreading, announcing that all is not despair.

The fireweed is a survivor—like a woman.

On the morning stage to Placerville, the last stop, Blue picked up a woman—tall, angular, and olive-skinned—whose pensive face intrigued Jenna, a face that already showed the skeleton beneath the skin. Her eyes crouched behind heavy lids like hooded monks.

"I'm Jenna Daggett," she said. Jenna had had little desire to talk with the other passengers, but she was curious about this one.

"Pleased, I'm sure," the woman responded, her thin skin stretching into a cadaver smile. "I'm Sylvia Flores."

The two women gradually eased into conversation.

"I'm going to Placerville to be a laundress at the hotel there."

Sylvia's story was like that of so many emigrants. She had traveled west on the Oregon Trail with thousands of others in 1851, and followed her husband to the cold, reckless mining camps where he tried his luck at mining along the Feather River.

"He done well," she said. "We even built us a wooden house and I fixed it up nice. My man was handy with hammer and nails—made us a fine bed and chest, table and chairs, Paulo did. But somehow, he went astray . . . started going to the gamblin' house, spending our money on every fool thing and drinkin' every night. One night, he come home sick, sick as any man could be. He got a hold of a tainted can of oysters. It's what killed him . . . dead, the next day."

"What a sad story, Mrs. Flores."

" 'Paulo, I said, what in tarnation did you eat? Your bile is black as coal!' It was, you see. That's how come I knew he was poisoned. 'Oysters' was about the last word he spoke."

"I'm so sorry. What a sad time for you," Jenna said.

The woman looked out the window with no expression.

"He was hardly cold in the ground when a group of vigilantes, all of them crazy on spirits, come to the house and called my husband out. They kept calling him a greasy Mexican. 'Come out here, you greasy Mexican,' they'd shout. They kept talkin' about him stealin' a horse. Paulo wouldn't steal no horse. Anyways, when he wouldn't come out, bein' already dead and all, they torched the house. I ran out the back and up the hill into the trees and hid. I watched the house burn to the ground, and the outhouse, and chicken coop . . . and my cat, Mittens. Funny thing, them thinkin' we was Mexican. We're Italian stock. We've been American for two generations." She stopped talking, leaned her head back on the seat, and shut her eyes.

Another fireweed, Jenna thought to herself, and let the woman sleep.

In Placerville, Blue stopped long enough to go to a bathhouse, change into a clean shirt, trim his beard, and go to the barber.

"My, my, you look nice," Jenna said. "You'd think you were about to meet the Queen . . . or maybe a lady friend." Jenna smiled slyly. It was obvious that Blue still carried a torch for Darcey, ever since the day Blue and Jenna rode out of Hattie's Gulch.

Blue smoothed his trimmed beard and said, "Only a time for a shirt change, my girl, nothing more."

As they rode into Red Man's Bar, Blue began to talk excitedly. "Look at the changes here. Wooden buildings are scattered all over the place, and, by golly, there are more saloons than customers."

"I saw three women talking in front of a store."

"Any of them wearing beards?" Blue joked.

"And look, Blue, there are even plank sidewalks in some places. I bet the women are happy about that in the muddy time." Jenna remembered the women's mud-caked skirts on the Oregon Trail.

"Looks almost like a town now, don't it?"

The three miles to Hattie's Gulch had filled in with small cabins, a livery, a blacksmith shop, the doctor's house, several makeshift canvas houses, and a meeting house, presumably the one built by Reverend Squibb. The sign outside said, "Assembly of Salvation—Welcome All Sinners." Neither Jenna nor Blue mentioned Faithful's place as they rode past, but both made note of it.

There were no individual men panning along the river. Placer mining had given way to cooperative ventures with companies of men working the rockers, sluices, long Toms, even a stamp to crush chunks of rock hacked out of the mountain.

At last they rode up to Hattie's Place and dismounted. The outside looked nearly the same, but on the inside they met with a pleasant surprise. Red calico cloth printed with small yellow flowers covered the windows and three long tables. It also lined the shelves and dressed the wide doorway that had once led to Hattie's bedroom, now an eating area. Each table held a hurricane lamp and a bouquet of mountain daises. A cozy wood-burning stove sat at one end of the room like a fat jolly man, and on the scrubbed, planked floor coiled two rugs of many colors. A smell of fresh bread wafted in from the outside. The kitchen was now a separate building behind Hattie's.

"Anyone here?" Jenna shouted.

They heard a loud, joyful shout from the kitchen, and Darcey rushed into the room full of nonsensical whoops of delight, throwing herself into the bodies of her guests. She squeezed Jenna with such happiness she could scarcely breathe. Without hesitation, she grabbed Blue and kissed him hard on the cheek.

Jenna had forgotten the warmth Darcey radiated, the atmosphere around her—like the delicious aroma of bread baking in the oven. Darcey's full figure had grown rounder and fuller, her face broader, rosier—a picture of well-fed joy, a woman of friendly laughter and fun.

Blue, once again, fell into her openness, her easy embrace. Darcey made him feel good all over, something he had not expected. She disarmed him completely, scattering all shadows of shyness into the happy atmosphere. She made him believe that he was the source of her joy.

What a fool he'd been to allow so many years to pass without seeing her! He had imagined a courteous, "Nice-to-see-you-again" greeting, one that was cautious, cool. Not so with Darcey. She brimmed over with her good nature, inundating them with more hugs, squeezes and special approving looks at Blue. He'd been wrong to play it on the side of indifference. The firm, fleshy feel of her lingered against his chest, his arms, and hands. He wanted to fold into her largess.

What a woman, he thought.

"I've been expecting you for days, and here you are at last! I'll put the coffee pot on and show you around. I had an additional room built for Pearle and me. You'll stay with us, Jenna. Blue, I figured you'd have a tent."

"Where is Pearle?" Jenna asked.

"She's out doing her lesson with Mrs. Clark, the doctor's wife. She'll be coming along shortly. She helps me serve the men. I hired a cook, Mrs. Baily, who helps me three days a week. She makes good stews. Gives her something to do while her husband is on the river."

"Has Pearle grown up?"

"She's grown some, Jenna, but not like she should—still a fairy child, thin as a reed. And that bum leg of hers slows her down and gives her trouble once in awhile. But she never complains when she's in pain. Maybe you being here will put some roses in her cheeks." Darcey's tone had changed. She could not hide her concern.

"Now let me make the coffee and dish you up a bowl of sweet rice pudding. You must be plumb starved. We have so much news to catch up on. Blue, I heard from Jenna you were doing real good in the stage business and I'm happy for you. You look wonderful!"

When Darcey swished off to the kitchen, Blue watched the wide, easy swing of her ample hips before carrying Jenna's things to the bedroom, another room bursting with red calico. He smiled to himself. *That Darcey is a real comfort, she is, a mighty fair handful.*

Never had a more jovial threesome eaten rice pudding, sliced cold beef, molasses brown bread, and coffee. They laughed till the tears flowed talking about the girls' adventure as miners, Darcey's red beard, the days of living in disguise.

In spite of the fun, Jenna felt anxious about Pearle. "Is Pearle always this late?" she asked.

"No, not always. Sometimes she goes to her 'special place' under a tree somewhere close by. That's where she writes her little stories and letters to you. She used to call it her 'hidey hole' when she was little. I don't know what she's hiding from except her own imagination, but she still goes there. I'll go out back and call her. She'll come if I call."

Jenna knew what Pearle was hiding from. Oh, how she wished she, herself, had had a place to hide. "Let me call her. If she hears my voice, she'll come running." But before Jenna could leave, Pearle limped into the room.

"Jenna! Blue!" Pearle threw her arms around them and held on tightly. Jenna was struck by the change in Pearle. She was thinner and taller than Jenna had expected and was not very pretty because of her gray-white skin, transparent as an insect wing. Her blue eyes were dull, lifeless. There was little energy about her.

Something had gone out of Pearle, like a life-force robbed or sucked from her, a dry child hanging on a spider's web. Her spirit seemed to have fled or locked itself away behind shut doors. Jenna's heart was heavy. She immediately knew the silent despair.

She wondered if she and Pearle could find that special trust to speak of Faithful Squibb. She wondered, too, if she would have the courage to tell Blue of her suspicions. No one could believe the extent of the vulgar invasion of her own body, and to suggest Pearle was suffering the same abuse was an accusation beyond belief. Even though she had told Blue that Faithful had "hurt" her, she was never certain he knew the nature of that hurt.

It had taken a long time for Jenna to believe that she had not been the sinner. The Reverend Faithful Squibb was the evil one and Jenna hated him. Now Pearle would have the same stomach pains, the fear of sleeping, the guilt, the shame, the numbing memories.

The next few days were happy ones. Jenna, Pearle, and Darcey felt close, like sisters. At night, they returned to their old habit from their time at the fort, sitting on the bed telling stories in the glow of the lamplight, laughing and eating pudding or pie, cookies, and warm milk. Jenna missed this kind of closeness on the rancho. She missed Darcey's goodnight kiss and Pearle's colorful stories, so full of wisdom and fantasy.

When the lamp was out and Darcey sang, as before, in low, soft tones, Jenna ached with a longing she couldn't explain; and when Pearle and Darcey slept at last, Jenna saved a precious, private moment to see the enchanting face of Enrique, leaning so close to her that their lips brushed. In her imagination, she held her face up to his and let him kiss her, a long kiss like one exchanged between sweethearts. Jenna smiled to herself and nestled farther down into the covers.

🌿 🌿 🌿

While Jenna spent many hours with Pearle, Blue and Darcey also found time alone together. Each day they grew closer, becoming more intimately involved in each other's lives.

One morning, they followed a deer path above the camp into a high meadow. Blue carried a picnic basket and Darcey, wearing a red calico dress made from the same material at Hattie's Place, carried a jug of lemonade.

"You see, Blue, how the miners are clearing out? Last night I served only ten dinners besides ours. I think it's time Pearle and me leave and find another place," Darcey said, spreading out a red calico cloth on the ground.

"You must have bought a wagon load of red calico bolts," Blue laughed.

"Well, I nearly did. I sold some of it to the other ladies nearby, so now we *all* have red calico dresses, bonnets, aprons, curtains, and the like."

"You fixin' to leave the camp now, Darcey? Have you finally proved you can take care of yourself?"

"It's been hard, Blue, I admit that. But I made a good deal of money. I have enough in the bank in Placerville to open up a fine new boarding house somewhere else—maybe even a rooming house. Pearle isn't doing very good here. She needs a regular school and other children her own age." Darcey unwrapped a loaf of crusty bread, keeping her face turned away from Blue. "I got a place in mind already."

"Where's that?" Blue asked indifferently, picking up a fat piece of fried chicken breast and biting into it. He noticed Darcey wouldn't look at him, but kept her gaze averted, as if suddenly shy or worried.

"About thirty miles south of Placerville, at Jackson. It's growing fast, I hear. Miners are really taking out a big percentage of gold. It's a nice place, and there are other females about—a church and school, stores, and nice houses going up every day. You'd like it there, Blue."

"I know Jackson already. I'm a-thinkin' on expanding a line there."

Darcey brightened. "Oh, Blue, we'll see a lot of each other!"

"Yep." He chewed a mouthful of chicken and said nothing more.

"You would like that, wouldn't you?"

"Like what?" Blue said, swigging down some lemonade.

"Seeing a lot of each other."

"Yep, I suppose so," he said without much emotion.

"What's the matter with you, Quigley? You gone funny on me?"

"Nothin' the matter. Just enjoyin' the chicken and the fine day. Good chicken, Darcey."

"You old goat! I thought you'd ask me to marry you. We've been courting all week!"

Blue was stunned. He could hardly swallow his food. "Well, now, look here, Darcey, how'd I figure you was a-thinkin' on marriage? I can't figure you out. One minute you're all smiles and wigglin' around me, and the next minute you're a-talkin' business, buyin' or buildin' a boardinghouse. I don't call that a solid basis for a-gettin' hitched."

"Why can't we do both?" Darcey said, crawling on her hands and knees over to Blue. "I'd run the boardinghouse, where we'll live, and you can keep on driving the stage or hire on other drivers. You could have a line to Jackson. It could work Blue. Think about it. You'd always have a nice place . . . a warm bed to come home to."

Darcey's massive, wiry, red hair, bushing out from its tied ribbon and backlit by the sun, made Blue weak with love for her. In that moment, he thought she was the most beautiful sight he'd ever seen. She was a fire goddess, and he was completely in her spell.

"Well, say something, Blue. You don't look very bright. I'm proposing to you!"

"I ain't even kissed you."

"Well, whose fault is that? I've given you a thousand chances all week. You must be dense as an old bone. Kiss me *now*, then!"

"All right, I'll just do that." He wiped his mouth with the back of his sleeve, reached over, and kissed Darcey's plump, willing lips.

"I think I'll just do that again," he said. "My God, you're a woman! You are mighty fine to look at, too! I think I might just spend the afternoon eatin' chicken and kissin' you for dessert."

"Well, finally! I've been trying all week to get you to kiss me, all but standing on my hands and waving flags, but you're about the most thick-headed man I ever met. You just kept talking about the weather and the bread pudding. You still haven't said anything about getting married."

"I'll tell you a secret. I come up here to Hattie's Bar over a year ago to see you . . . and I did. You was a-talkin' and a-laughin' with the customers, especially one fella, and, well, I figured you had a beau."

"I haven't had a sweetheart here, Blue. That's the truth. And you left without paying me a call!"

"Yep."

"Lord God, what can a woman do with a man like you?" Darcey leaned her face close to Blue. "So now, what are we going to do now that I *am* asking you to marry me?" she said.

"We got to think this through a bit, don't we?"

"Why? You and me and Pearle can look over Jackson right away. As soon as we find a suitable place, we'll get married. Meanwhile, I won't say anything to Pearle."

"I'd say that sounds fine, mighty fine. How about some dessert?" Blue said, leaning over and kissing Darcey again. He put his arms around her, nuzzled her hair, and breathed in her sweet, soapy smell. "Now you said something about keepin' me warm. Would you be a-feelin' a bit chilly now? I know I am."

"Oh, for Heaven's sake, I was talking about making you a feathered quilt," she teased.

"As long as it's big enough for two."

Darcey didn't answer. She looked at Blue again, this time as a future husband, a mate, a partner, a man, someone she could wrap her large arms and legs around, a body she could curl into, skin to skin, flesh to flesh, breath to breath.

"I made you a present," she said, taking a wrapped package from the picnic basket. "Your engagement present."

Blue unwrapped the paper. "Lord Almighty, a red calico shirt, like the tablecloth! I can't wear that shirt! It's got little yeller flowers all over it. I'll look like a . . . like a schoolmarm!"

"You can wear it to church on Sundays, like the other husbands. The flowers wash out after a couple of scrubbings."

"Well, much obliged—I guess."

The two of them spent the next hour lying next to each other under a pine tree looking up through its branches at the blue sky and enjoying the strange new "oneness" they felt. The wonder of belonging to someone thrilled them. Their sides touched—arms, shoulders, legs, hips, thighs, bare feet—the first intimacy, the clothed expression of loving that would soon follow, the affirmation of deep love and friendship they felt for each other.

TEN

I'VE NEVER SHOWN ANYONE my special place, Jenna, not even Mama," Pearle said as she and Jenna scrambled up a steep part of the mountain behind Hattie's Place. "I used to call it my 'hidey hole' because one day I startled a doe and her fawn who darted out from under the low branches of the trees. When I peeked under the branches, I found a little room, a chamber that could hide the little family. I've been coming here for a long time."

"Do you hide here, Pearle?" Jenna asked.

"Sometimes . . . I mean, sometimes I come here to pretend or write stories. Sometimes I fall asleep here." Pearle stopped outside of a lovely group of three trees that had grown close together, their gracious branches intertwined and bending to touch the ground. "Here we are. Come in, Jenna."

Jenna crawled under the branches into a fairy room, cool and cozy and perfectly hidden. Like Pearle, she was enchanted by the secrecy of the place.

"I feel like a forest animal myself—so safe," Jenna said. "The ground is as soft as a bed. I love your 'hidey hole', Pearle."

The girls talked as they ate day-old muffins and apricots Jenna had brought from the rancho. After awhile, Jenna said, "It's kind of like a little church inside here, don't you think?"

"No, not a church." Pearle frowned.

"Do you go to church, Pearle?"

Pearle pretended not to hear the question. "Do you want to make up a story, Jenna? I'll start, then you keep it going." She wiped the juice from her fingers on the hem of her skirt and picked up an apricot seed. "Once upon a time there lived the tiniest fellow inside an apricot pit."

"Let me start, Pearle," Jenna interrupted. "I'll tell you a story—a secret really. Did I ever tell you I got to know Reverend Faithful Squibb during my journey west?"

Pearle looked at her blankly and said nothing.

"I was your age, Pearle, when my family died. The wagon company voted to have me be under the care of Faithful and his wife, Cora. Do you want me to keep going?"

Pearle's face was expressionless as she stared at Jenna. "If you want to," she said, burying the seed in the moist earth.

"I didn't like him, not at all. I still don't like him."

"I don't want to talk about him anymore. Let's make up pretend stories," Pearle said.

"No one would believe my story about Reverend Squibb, so I never told anyone—until now." She took hold of Pearle's hands. "He is not a nice man, Pearle, even though some people think he's a godly person. I know, and I think you know, that he is an evil man."

Pearle's face became tight with emotion; her cheeks trembled and small dimples appeared under the strain.

"He did terrible things to me, Pearle . . . such painful and torturous insults to my small body that I wanted to die. He made me do sickening things to him, so horrible I thought I would never be clean again, never be able to eat food. That's when I ran away and joined Blue."

Pearle put her face in her hands and did not look at Jenna.

"It's all right, Pearle. I understand. I know you were forced to be with him. You have no choice when you are a little girl. You trusted him, as I did once. He told you he would hurt you if you ever told on him, didn't he?"

Jenna put her arms around Pearle.

Pearle began to shake and sob uncontrollably. "It's all my fault. I'm going to Hell, I know. I'm a sinner, Jenna—a terrible person. He said I could never get to Heaven without first doing what he asked me to do. He said God would never hear my prayers. He said I was crippled because God did not love me."

"Listen to me, Pearle. It's taken me years of shame to understand I was not the one at fault. God loves you. He created you because you were a wonderful idea of His. Faithful made me feel dirty and sinful. He even tried to make me think I asked him to do those terrible things to me. He is full of lies. You must *never* go near him again. Do you understand?"

"Mama sends me to him. She thinks he's good."

"Darcey doesn't know, Pearle, but I think we should tell her."

"Oh, never! He said if Mama knew of my sin, she would send me away to an orphan's home. She would not want me."

"Do you believe that of *Darcey*, your own mother?"

"Sometimes she gets so busy, I think she's glad when I'm not around."

"That's not true! Darcey loves you more than anything in this world."

"Promise me you won't tell her, Jenna."

"I can't promise you that. The man is wicked. He must be stopped. He will hurt other children who come into his life. Don't worry, Pearle. We'll stick together."

"She'll never believe me. She thinks everything I say to her is a pretend story," Pearle sniffed. "Once I told her I didn't like the Reverend and that I had seen his underwear and she scolded me for lying. I was only seven."

"Never you mind about it anymore. You stay away from him and church, no matter what it takes. Do that, Pearle. Promise me."

"I promise," Pearle said.

Pearle's secret had to be told. Jenna waited for the right time, then told Darcey the entire story about Faithful Squibb and what she knew was happening to Pearle as well.

Blue walked into Darcey's kitchen in time to see her fly into a rage. "I'll kill him! I swear I'll kill that beast!" she screamed. Darcey threw herself down on the table, cried and clenched her fists, pounded her temples, cursed.

He raced to her side, placing a bracing hand on her shoulder. "My God, woman, what is it,? What's got you so riled?"

Rage burned through him as Darcey related the awful story she'd just heard from Jenna. The girl had told Darcey the entire truth about Faithful Squibb and what she knew was happening to Pearle, as well.

Blue headed for the door. "Take care of Darcey, Jenna, he snapped, "I'm a-goin' to pay the Reverend a call—one I should have made some time ago. Don't you fret now, Darcey. We're a-leavin' this here place right away. I got just one thing I have to do."

He felt his fury coil and throb in his bowels, his body turn cold, and his eyeballs bulge and sting—primitive readiness to destroy an enemy. He had only one thought riding toward Red Man's Bar—justice, in whatever form it would take. If he did not find the Reverend at the meeting house, he would wait for as many sundowns as necessary to confront this man face to face.

Blue did not have to wait. The Reverend was in the back room of the meeting house heating a pan of beans on a wood stove.

"Well, well, what a surprise. You never know what sinner is going to walk through the door to find peace in his soul. Come in, Brother Blue. Want some beans?" Faithful Squibb said.

"I didn't come a-lookin' for peace, Faithful. I come a-lookin' for justice." Blue's heart was as hard as stone.

"How's that, Brother? Someone has betrayed the Lord and you're acting as judge. Well let me tell you, there is only one judge to settle the score. Sure you don't want some beans?"

"I'm a-talkin' about a couple of children—little girls that you have . . . had your way with. You know what I'm a-sayin'."

"Nonsense, friend." Faithful went over to the stove and put a log in the fire. "I think your own wicked thoughts is stirrin' up trouble. Ain't that right, Brother? You want to touch a couple of sweet little virgins yourself?" he said, opening a can of peach preserves and spearing them with a paring knife.

"You son-of-a-bitch! You touched them little girls, and I'm a-takin' you to the sheriff. If he ain't around, I'm tyin' you to the whippin' post and lettin' the vigilantes decide what to do with you."

"You ain't carrying a weapon. I ain't obliging you, so how you figure on getting me to cooperate is an interesting proposition. You're in a house of God, you know," Faithful said, without moving from behind the table.

Blue lunged toward the table, tipped it on its side, and backed Faithful against the wall. The Reverend raised the paring knife to strike, but Blue held his weak wrist and the knife clattered to the floor. In one quick movement, Blue hit Faithful on the jaw and knocked him to the ground.

"There's no spine in you to fight. It's like a-fightin' a wet bed sheet. Get on your feet! You're not worth puttin' blood on my own hands. Get up, now, and march out that door." Blue leaned over to pull Faithful by the scruff of his neck.

Suddenly, the sharp crack of gunfire split the air and a burning pain blasted into Blue's pelvis. Faithful had concealed a gun.

Blue staggered backward, then fell, hitting his head on the corner of the stove. The world turned black.

Blue did not see Faithful run out the back door. He lay unconscious while a few miners gathered and speculated about the gunshot. By the time they entered the meeting house to find an unconscious man, Faithful was long gone.

The first man in the door bent over Blue and listened to his heart. "He ain't dead, but his head is bleedin' bad. Someone go find Reverend Squibb and tell him there's been a-shootin' in the meetin' house. I'll get Doc Clark. Is this here a man from Red Man's Bluff or from up river?"

The men scattered quickly, announcing the shooting. The miners stopped their work and crowded around the door to hear the verdict of the man's fate. "Is he killed?" "Who done it?" "Anybody seen a fight?" the men questioned.

Blue was carried to the doctor's house and laid out on a work table. Mrs. Clark cut away the bloody pants and the doctor examined him, probing and pushing the torn flesh to find a lodged bullet.

Blue had been hit in the pelvic bone, shattering it like a china plate. "That dern bullet tore him up bad, real bad. I can pick out the fragmented bone around the flesh and keep the wound clean, but that's about all. It looks to me that the bullet is probably still in him, too close to the spine to go searching and traumatizing the wound further. Poking around in there could leave the man paralyzed.

"One thing is certain. He don't have a reliable pelvis anymore. Now it's up to nature to heal him," the doctor said as he wiped blood from his hands. "It's his head that worries me. He's got a concussion and will have to be absolutely quiet. He's goin' to be laid up for quite awhile."

Mrs. Clark said, "I believe this is the friend of Darcey's who's visiting her. I'll send someone up to Hattie's to tell her. My, my, what terrible happenings go on in these camps! Man just ain't civilized. I suppose he was trying to rob the Reverend or something strange. Looks like a decent sort, and he isn't a foreigner. You never can tell, can you?"

🌱 🌱 🌱

Blue heard Darcey's voice, as if from a great distance. "Blue? Blue? Can you hear me? This is Darcey. Wake up, now, darlin'. You can do it. I think he's coming around, thank God!"

Blue groaned with pain. He opened his eyes, still so unfocused he could only recognize voices, not faces.

"Don't you up and die on me, now," Darcey said. "We got too many plans. Do you remember?" She kissed his cheek and squeezed his hand.

By midnight, Blue was awake but in great pain. Darcey had propped up his pillows so she could spoon strong beef broth into his mouth.

"The word is out that it was the Reverend that shot you. Someone said they saw him flee."

Blue nodded weakly. "He done it, all right."

"The vigilantes have already gone after him, moving in both directions along the river. Some are looking in the woods. They'll catch him, Blue. They're getting a 'Wanted' poster printed in Placerville. It won't be long. I want to see that man hanging from a tree! I don't much care for hating someone, but after what he did to you and Pearle and Jenna, I'd shoot him myself if I could."

"I didn't figure he had a gun," Blue said hoarsely.

"You're going to be laid up a long time, Blue, not able to walk or ride a horse for awhile. But Pearle and I will come visit you as much as we can and cook you special meals. Mrs. Clark is a kindly nurse and says she don't mind looking after you. This room is for patients just like you." Darcey wiped a rivulet of broth off Blue's chin.

"I don't know what I'm going to do about the stage company. I'll lose it if I don't keep a-goin' somehow."

"Jenna had an idea of locating a fellow who is working on the river up at Coloma, just outside of Placerville—a Harke somebody. She says he knows you and just might take off mining to drive for you. There are plenty of miners who are sick of this life and would like to earn a wage. You can rest easy on keeping the lines going."

"Harke Polley is a good boy. He would be the best man for any job. I'll pay a fella to ride up there and fetch him."

"Jenna knows the company he works for. She'll write a letter and get it to him right away. Don't you fret about a single thing, Blue. Just get well fast so we can get out of here! All of a sudden, I don't think I'll live long enough to leave this gulch. It's like it's closing in on me. I can hardly breathe," Darcey said, going over to the fly-speckled window. "My, there sure is a jumble of men, horses and wagons, and all kinds of equipment on the move," she added, pensively.

"You still want to go to Jackson?" Blue asked.

"You bet!" Darcey picked up Blue's rough hand and kissed his fingers.

"With me, I mean?"

"I won't go without you. I might go early and look for a place to set up business. The sooner we can leave here, the better for all of us."

Blue smiled. "I'm sorry this whole thing happened at this time, Darcey. I was a-thinkin' on packing you up and moving you myself. Maybe I'll be a-walkin' by the time you're ready to leave. That Harke boy is a reliable young man—someone I can depend on. I guess he'll have to be the one to take Jenna back to San Jose. She's a-fixin' to leave in a few days. I'm stuck here for awhile."

"We'll take care of everything. You just rest now," Darcey said, patting his cheek.

"It's a good thing I got a good-looking redhead to look after me." Blue shut his eyes. He hurt all over and thought, after Darcey left, that he'd ask Mrs. Clark for more laudanum.

🌱 🌱 🌱

Harke rode into Red Man's Bar on the evening of the fourth day. One word from Jenna was all he'd needed to quit mining and come to her aid.

The truth was, he hadn't stopped thinking about her since he kissed her. He was more than happy to do what he could to help her and her friends, to be the man of the hour, maybe even a hero to Jenna. Besides, Blue had always been good to Harke. On several occasions they had hunted together on the plains. Harke thought Blue was a man of good sense and honor. He'd do what he could to help him out.

As Blue gained strength each day, he and Harke worked out the stage schedules and details of comfort and safety that had gained Blue's line a good reputation.

Darcey and Pearle took to Harke quickly, embracing him as their friend. Darcey looked at Jenna in a saucy way. "That Harke is a fine young man, just the right age to court a smart girl. I'd say he's a catch. Wish I was a little younger and you can bet he'd never outrun me."

"And if I was older and didn't have a bum leg, he wouldn't outrun me, either," Pearle said, laughing. Her spirits had improved over the past two weeks.

"He's a good friend—the best. I'm lucky to know him. He's always been there to help me, even when I was little. I think of him as family . . . a brother. I can't imagine him as anything else," Jenna said, carefully folding her clothes and packing them in her bag. "I'm glad you like him. It makes it even more like family—all of us together. I wish you had known my mother and father and baby brother, Solomon. Isn't it strange, how we all lost our own loved ones but found each other? I think of you all, Blue and Harke, too, as my other family. I will miss you so much!"

"You mean I have a big brother now?" Pearle asked, her face lighting up for the first time in a long time.

"I suppose so. Why not?" Jenna said, hugging Pearle.

"Will he protect me, Jenna?"

"Of course he will. That's what big brothers do."

"Then I shall go find him and give him a big kiss and tell him he's my brother now," Pearle said airily and went outside to see if he was nearby.

"Don't go far, Pearle. We're walking to Doc Clark's after lunch to take Blue an apple pie," Darcey said.

That afternoon, the bellows of disgruntled pack mules tired of their heavy burdens, resounded throughout Red Man's Bar. Into the camp had marched the grizzly, white-haired mule driver Ebenezer Cootz, carrying his rifle and shouting commands to a bound prisoner, a strange-looking woman in a red calico dress and bonnet.

The mules stopped and puffed out their lips. The prisoner, with a rope around her neck and around one leg, was tied to a mule and was forced to stop when the animal did or be strangled by a sudden jolt. People circled the prisoner.

"I brung in the ugliest female I could find—a bride to the highest bidder," Ebenezer cackled with a loud, dry laugh. "Ain't nobody interested in a good poke?" He laughed again.

The miners peered closer, trying to see the face inside the bonnet.

"That's the Reverend!" someone shouted.

In moments, an excited crowd had Faithful tied to the whipping post.

"I seen him hiding behind a rock down by the river. At first I thought it was a distressed female . . . a mighty ugly one, but a woman just the same. I was about to give her a hand, when I got suspicious. That red calico was from Red Man's Bar, and I knew a man was on the run from here . . . shot someone. The closer I looked, the more I seen this here was no woman, but a man with yeller teeth and smelly boots. I got my helper, Jesus, to tie him up and I brung him in." Ebenezer patted the rump of his mule then spit for effect. "Who's in charge? I figure there's goin' to be a hangin'. Whippin' ain't strong enough."

A man stepped forward. "I'm on the committee. I'll gather up what men is left in town and we'll have a talk with this here 'female.' There ain't no question about him shooting an unarmed man. He's guilty. Everyone knows that."

"Hang him!"

"You can't hang a preacher! Someone shouted. "Give him a good lickin' and boot him out of town."

"He tried to take an unarmed man's life. Hang him!"

Faithful looked at the crowd and raised his voice to the heavens. "Strike 'em down, Lord. Bring them every foul disease! Turn this here river into blood! Cover them with pox, bubble up their mothers from the graves! Curse them all . . . all sinners, sons of Satan!"

He kept ranting until someone said, "Bring the wagon. This man's crazy. That tree over yonder is the one we used last time. Anyone disagree with his sentence?"

"What about a trial?" someone shouted.

"He just had one!" a vigilante shouted. "Hang him in his dress. He's as low as a sneaky female. Let him die like one." The men cheered with approval. Their word was law.

Darcey, Jenna, and Pearle, hearing the shouts, had stopped outside the doctor's house.

"Maybe they've brought Faithful in," Jenna said. "Please, Darcey, can we go see?"

A rider galloped past shouting, "Hanging! There's going to be a hanging! The Reverend is about to swing!"

From up the river, men stopped their work and, along with the girls, rushed into town. By the time they got there, they heard the deathly silence after the shouting, the stillness of finality. The girls stopped and clutched each other.

Faithful Squibb was in the last moments of squirming at the end of a rope. His red calico dress blew gently in the summer breeze. The sun shifted on his distorted face as the body swung back and forth, the taut rope squeaking in rhythm to the sway. The branch from which Faithful hung creaked under the diminishing bounce until, at last, the body hung lifeless, soundless.

Though his mouth remained open in his final moment, no blasphemies, scripture, words of confession, or pleas for forgiveness gurgled from the black hole.

"Take off your hats, men. We just hung a preacher for God's sake," the vigilante said.

"It's been seven minutes. Let's cut him down."

"Not yet. That Chileño last month took eleven minutes."

"Come on, girls. We've seen enough," Darcey said. "No matter how awful he was to you, we must ask God to forgive him. I've never seen a hanging before. Even when he took his last breath, I couldn't help wondering what he saw . . . what he thought. Death is so . . . quiet."

🙢 🙢 🙢

Eventually, Blue was able to sit up straight in the bed and move his leg slightly. To others, his spirits appeared to be good. In spite of his ordeal, he seemed happier than ever before. Darcey pampered him with rich desserts and fussed over him like a mother bird waiting for her fledgling to take wing.

But Blue was full of smiles and witty remarks only when Darcey was around; when she wasn't, he worried about being as strong as before and privately cursed the intense pain close to his spine.

Jenna left Red Man's Bar feeling confident of Blue's complete recovery and relieved Faithful had met his Maker. Now, he would have to deal with all the wrongs of his mortal life, she thought.

Harke and Jenna rode to Placerville, where Harke took over the responsibilities of the Sierra-Pacific Stagecoach Company. He seemed to take on an even greater maturity in the process. Jenna thought for the first time that Harke was somewhat handsome.

She liked being with him and playfully teased him. With Harke, she could be the girl of the vast plains, free and full of far horizons. They clearly enjoyed each other's company, sometimes riding side by side without talking, often just smiling for no reason at all.

Sometimes she wondered if living with the doña had changed her, restricted her spirit, denied her the companionship of an American friend, someone like Harke. But for this moment, she pushed such thoughts out of her mind and enjoyed being with her dear companion.

In Sacramento, Harke and Jenna stayed in a newly built hotel. That evening two black men, a brother team, thrilled guests with a fiddle and a banjo, music so fast and happy that everyone danced into the morning. Devil music, the guests called it. Jenna and Harke danced until their faces shone and their clothes felt damp.

Outside on the porch, they caught their breath and let the night air cool their skin.

"I've never had such a good time, Harke, *never!*" Jenna said, still laughing over the last lively polka.

"Those boys play music like I've never heard before. I couldn't even see their hands, they moved so fast. I think that banjo is like they say—the Devil's instrument, makin' you dance and jump like crazy folks. My toes are still tingling. I could dance all night—never sleep or eat."

Harke grabbed Jenna's hands. "We've always danced good together, Jenna. Don't you remember all the times on the trail . . . you and me dancing to Blue's fiddle and your papa's harmonica?"

"Oh, yes. I think about the crossing often . . . the good times."

Impulsively, Harke took Jenna in his arms. "Marry me, Jenna!"

Jenna pulled away. "What? Oh, Harke, you don't mean that. We're *friends*. Please don't change everything. I'd die before I hurt you."

"Why not marry me? I love you so . . . since I can remember. I could never love anyone else. I'd make you happy. *Please*, Jenna. At least think on it."

Jenna's joy changed to concern. Standing before her was one of the dearest people in her life. The long shock of blond hair, damp from dancing, fell over his forehead in a boyish way. She gently brushed his hair back in place. "Oh, Harke, don't love me that way. Love me like you always did before."

"Jenna, I've always loved you more than a friend. We're right together.

You know we are."

"I'll think about it, Harke," she said, lowering her eyes, but even at that moment, she knew Harke was not the one for her. How could he be, when she thought only of one man—Enrique Archuleta. She could never tell Harke that each mile they traveled toward San Jose was a mile closer to this enigmatic man who invaded her thoughts, thrilled her dreams.

"Goodnight, Harke . . . dear Harke. I'll see you in the morning."

🌿 🌿 🌿

Jenna had expected Enrique to meet her at the stage stop in San Jose, but instead, it was Ygnacio driving the open carriage with Luisa and a smiling group of coppery Indian children from Rancho San Gabriel. The children grinned happily as Harke assisted Jenna into the seat behind the driver.

"Goodbye, Harke," Jenna said. "You will come to visit me soon, won't you?"

"You can bet on it." Harke cocked his head and grinned at Jenna in an appealing, boyish way. "Don't say 'no' just yet, girl. Keep a place for me a might longer. Maybe one day you'll have a change of heart."

"Goodbye, Harke," she said as the carriage began to move.

"Goo-bye . . . goo-bye . . . goo-bye," the children called out, imitating Jenna and giggling with high spirits. When Harke was out of sight, the children settled down to eat juicy plums, drippy peaches, and sweet plump grapes all the way home.

Enrique was not at the house when Jenna arrived. Her heart had been pounding with the expectation of seeing him, but Doña Juana explained that he was out with the *vaqueros* until evening.

"It will give you time to clean up and join me for tea. I have some things I want to discuss with you in private," Doña Juana said in her usual crisp way. Jenna thought the doña appeared strained, not especially happy to see her.

At tea, the doña, as usual dressed in silk and wearing a *mantilla*, poured a cup of strong tea for Jenna, asked a few courteous questions about her trip, seemed to listen politely but with disinterest, and finally spoke frankly to Jenna.

"Since your absence, there have been some changes at the rancho, none which please me, but over which I have no control. My esteemed brothers have taken control of my rancho in a very subtle way. I own the land and the cattle, but they are in charge of the operation of the rancho. My opinion and vote do not count. They have chosen to dismiss Señor Faustino and to put my nephew, Enrique, in charge of the rancho's operation. He is now the manager of Rancho San Gabriel, the *mayordomo*. I do not agree with their decision. I do not like Enrique. He does not like me. But there you have it."

Jenna frowned. She knew what the doña feared most was losing control of her property. Still, Jenna was very excited knowing Enrique was now a permanent part of the ranch. She felt confused, divided in her affection for the doña and her undeniable fascination for her nephew.

"Doña Juana, forgive my intrusive question, but why don't you like Enrique? I should think he'd be a fine *mayordomo*—even though I'm sorry Señor Faustino was dismissed."

"I do not want to talk about my nephew. He is my brother's son. My reasons are my own. I only say this. I watch you turn into a . . . coquette, whenever he is around. I know he is charming and handsome, but do not be deceived. He is an Archuleta male, headstrong and cruel. He will get what he wants. The family will stand behind his sins against God. I warn you, Jenna. Stay away from Enrique." The doña's eyes were as cold and black as the onyx earrings dangling from her ears. Her disdain for Enrique was obvious.

Whenever the doña became disagreeable, Jenna thought her strong beauty and intimidating manner weakened her, aged her. She did not want Doña Juana to become like the gossipy widows who gathered into black clumps in the gardens or on the church steps to whisper their disapproval of the young people. "I can't promise that, Doña Juana."

"I see. Then we shall have to talk at a later time when you are not so blinded." She gestured to Jenna that she was through talking with her and wanted her to go.

"Please, Doña Juana, tell me what are Enrique's *sins against God*, as you call them." Jenna sat stubbornly, refusing to leave. She thought her question would expose the doña's unreasonableness.

"You will find out in time. He is only part of my problem. Can't you understand what my family is doing? They have sold off much of their share of Archuleta land for profit, even gambled some of it away. Now they want my property for themselves so that they can break it down into small units to sell to the Americans. God knows how many foreigners have claims and illegal titles on Archuleta grants.

"My brothers have been deceitful, especially Bernardo—even selling some land twice. No one can prove anything. It's all mixed up, and that Land Commission is not straightening anything out yet." The doña's voice was becoming more shrill by the minute.

"Gold has brought too many people here. The *Yanquis* have an insatiable appetite for gold, for what belongs to us. They truly believe God has directed them to take whatever it is they want. They are coming in such numbers that my way of life is over. It's *over* I tell you! The Californio's days are gone forever.

"The big ranchos are selling off their land for high profit. The old families are in debt from their own foolishness and now taxes. Some Californios are selling before the squatters come and simply take what they want for free. We have no protection. Our own people have dirty palms. The only boundaries that are safe is where the old land grants are clearly established, witnessed, and in the archives.

"My brothers have all my proof of boundaries in their possession. They have the map and the signatures of the vouchers. They are going to reduce my land to nothing. They will sell off my cattle, of that I am sure. I will be left with nothing, no means of support except what they choose to give me. I will live like one of the old aunts dressed as a black crow, giggling like a simpleton at the babies or sitting in the patio—a stone statue shat on by birds."

The doña blew around the room like a sudden summer thunderstorm. "I won't have it! This is *my* land and *my* cattle! I must find a way to protect it!" Suddenly, she stopped and looked at Jenna with, what Jenna thought, was a strange expression.

The doña quietly sat down and poured another cup of tea. "Did you know I smoked *cigarillos*?"

"No—no, I didn't." Jenna was surprised at the change in the doña's manner.

"Well, I do. I am going to smoke now, if you don't mind. I hope it doesn't shock you."

"No, it doesn't." But it did surprise her.

The doña lighted a thin black *cigarillo*, inhaled a deep breath of smoke, and sat back in her chair. "I want you to go to Monterey with me as soon as possible. I want you to bring your most beautiful dresses. I will write to my sister and tell her we are coming for a visit."

Going to Monterey was always exciting, a chance to buy the latest slippers, gloves, ribbons, bonnets, and imported fabrics. But at this moment, Jenna did not want to leave the ranch and Enrique. She had missed him terribly over the past month.

"So soon after my return, Doña?"

"Yes. Immediately," she said harshly. Then, in a pleading voice, she added, "Do this for me, Jenna."

Jenna did not understand the doña's urgency, but she wanted to please her. After all, now that Enrique was going to manage the ranch, she would have many hours to be with him. "I'll be ready to go when you say the word."

"*Bueno*," the doña said, pressing out the fire of the little cigar in a saucer. She squeezed an oily lemon rind on her hands to block the smell of smoke. "You're dismissed."

As the afternoon shadows crept across the valley, Jenna saw the *vaqueros* galloping toward the adobe. She ran to the corral, straining to see Enrique among them. In the distance, she saw him riding Solana, her palomino, and sucked in her breath at his handsome appearance.

Enrique galloped up to her, pulling Solana's reins tight. The horse's body was running with sweat, her mouth hung with strips of foamy saliva, and her eyes were wild.

Jenna's joy at seeing Enrique shifted to concern for her palomino. "Enrique, you have run her too hard. Poor thing. She must be dried off and groomed right away. Why did you do that?" Jenna tried to calm the trembling horse, who kept tossing her head and blowing out her cheeks.

"And so, my beautiful lady, you prefer to greet the horse instead of me." Enrique jumped from the horse and picked Jenna up in his arms. "Now you are flesh and blood, not a dream in my head." He kissed her roughly on the mouth and stood her on her feet. "Come with me to the corral. One of the men will attend to your precious horse. Now say hello to me."

"Enrique, you cannot ride my horse ever again. Look at her flanks! You've cut her with your spurs!" Jenna's felt her cheeks grow hot. How could he be so cruel?

"She's slow and stubborn. I don't like her anyway. Now stop worrying about the stupid beast and look at me. Tell me what you see."

Jenna stared at him. She was breathing hard, angry on the one hand and thrilled to see him at the same time. "I don't want to look at you. You've hurt my horse."

"Nonsense. A little rough riding is good for her. You've turned her into a pussycat. She's not hurt. Now look into my eyes and tell me what you see. If you don't see a man in love with a beautiful, desirous woman . . . then you are blind. Look at me, Jenna." With slow, deliberate hands, he turned her face toward his and kissed her gently on the lips.

Jenna sighed. That single, soft kiss blew away her anger and she felt completely captivated once again.

Doña Juana's impatience to leave for Monterey was obvious. The older woman sat elegantly in her fashionable new buggy, surrounded by trunks and an entourage of attendants, scowling at Jenna. The girl turned away from her, ignoring the drumming fingers as she gave Enrique one last look and tender smile.

On the road, the doña once again expressed her dislike for Enrique.

"Why do you hate him so? He is nothing but nice to you, Doña Juana."

"You are wrong, child. He is toying with me. We both know what he is all about. It is an act. He only pretends to like me because he's after my property." She hissed through her teeth. The two of them rode in silence.

The intense August heat filled the black-hooded buggy, and the stagnant

air, heavy with the smell of garlic and rotting carcasses, nearly suffocated
them. Jenna wondered why the odor was so strong when the cattle had been
slaughtered for the hide and tallow months ago. She shuddered, thinking
that maybe a bear or mountain lion had attacked a helpless calf. In any case,
she did not feel like discussing it with the doña, who had become quite
stony.

Jenna hated the butchering of the animals even though she knew it
was the rancho's business. By the time they returned from Monterey, San
Gabriel would be preparing for the roundup, the slaughter of hundreds of
animals, the rodeo, fiestas, the cruel bull and bear fights. The southern end
of the ranch would be strewn with putrefying carcasses, their red, bloody
flesh blackening in the hot sun, the sickening stench carried for miles on the
breezes.

At last, Doña Juana spoke. "What if I told you your wonderful Enrique
was a criminal?" she blurted out.

Jenna's eyes smarted with anger. "I wouldn't believe you."

"I thought not." She appeared to be waiting for Jenna to say something,
and when she did not, the doña smirked and said nothing.

Jenna resented her secretive, vicious manner, and decided to let her
suffer in her own silence. Jenna would not utter a word to her all the way to
Monterey if need be.

Finally, the doña spoke. "The family doesn't know that I know about
Enrique's past, but I do. He was rushed out of the country so quickly that
he was never charged with the crime. Our powerful family saw to that. But
I know what I know." She looked straight ahead, her jaw set firm, her lips
tight.

"I don't want to hear what you have to say against Enrique," Jenna said
angrily. "You have tried to turn me against him ever since I met him. You
won't succeed. I'm in love with him!"

"Well, then, you leave me no choice but to tell you why Enrique fled to
Peru. He and another boy drowned an Indian boy in the river . . . held his
head under water . . . all for their own amusement. Enrique was fifteen at
the time. The Indian boy was only ten years old."

The blood in Jenna's face had drained. "I don't believe you! You are wicked!" she said fiercely. "Stop it this minute or I will jump out of this buggy!"

The doña said nothing, and they rode many more miles without speaking. Finally, the doña said, "I'm sorry, Jenna. I should not have involved you in a family secret."

🌱 🌱 🌱

Every morning, Monterey lay under a cloud of fog, turning the moss that hung from the cypress trees into swaying phantoms. By midmorning, the taunting ghosts gathered and retreated out to sea; the sun broke through the misty trees and evaporated the stubborn specters that tried to linger.

Jenna thought Monterey a magical place, but not even the beautiful days and wondrous harmony of the waves could soften the rigidity of her hosts and the perpetually strained expression worn by the doña. Jenna felt great tension when she was with the older woman. Unfortunately, she was required to spend her mornings involved in business affairs with Doña Juana.

As soon as work had ended for the day, Jenna would escape the house. On some occasions she, the doña, and her sister, accompanied by the carriage driver, rode horses through the pine forests down to the sea and along the coastline. Other times, Jenna would walk on the beach alone, collecting shells and reflecting on the odd turn of events in her life.

Her thoughts always turned to Enrique. She rejected the idea that he had actually drowned an Indian boy.

It could not be true! Doña Juana was being vicious. She was trying to poison my relationship with him. But, why would she try to do that? Maybe her own loveless life had made her cold to young love. Yes, that must be the problem!

Still, the doña's accusation against Enrique left Jenna confused and unsure of herself. She was like the wave rushing to the beach, retreating, rushing again, retreating. As hard as she tried, she could not rid herself of her unsettled feeling. The waves offered her no wisdom. They seemed fickle and indecisive, under the control of a larger force.

After a day of rest, the doña's purpose in coming to Monterey became clear. Dressed in the most appealing European fashion of the day, including a small English morning bonnet, the doña looked strangely Anglo—a curious fact, Jenna thought. Jenna had rarely seen the doña in public without the pride of her *mantilla*, her heritage.

Though the doña was in her middle years, she carried herself like a young girl, her movements decisive and quick. She was still the dark-eyed beauty with fair skin, strong countenance, an air of intelligence, purpose, and cunning. When the doña entered a room, people took notice, straightened their backs, and stood tall.

She and Jenna marched into the office of the Land Commission. "I am Doña Juana Maria de Archuleta, the daughter of Colonel Joaquin Raphael de Archuleta from Rancho San Gabriel. I've come to confirm my claim with this office and place on permanent file the boundaries of my third of the original land grant—approximately eighty-five thousand acres." The doña looked down her straight nose at the bureaucrat behind the desk and waited for a response.

"Yes, Madam," he said. "Let me repeat your request."

"There is no need to repeat what I've said. I have a letter here with the names of my family and my request clearly stated." She handed him a sealed envelope. "Once my land is placed on file with your office, I intend to give the title to Jenna Daggett, my ward, including sixty thousand head of cattle, the adobe structure, the natural spring, and the water rights on the Guadalupe River that runs through the property. I will act as Miss Daggett's legal guardian and trustee."

Jenna was flabbergasted. "Doña Juana, what are you saying? Do you know what you are doing?"

With the coldest glare Jenna had yet seen, the doña answered in Spanish, "Listen and be quiet. This is business. I'm doing this for my own protection. You will understand later. Say nothing more. Only support me. I need you for this transaction."

The officer smiled pleasantly. "There should be no problem, Madam, as long as you can produce proof of your ownership. You can imagine how many hundreds of people—especially *your* people—are making claims they own land." He gestured to piles of documents and bound books showing his overload of work.

"I can draw you a clear map. I have stated in the letter those witnesses who marked the borders with my father and vouched for him. I am an Archuleta. My word alone has always been of the highest honor." Jenna watched Doña Juana lift her chin and swell her chest, a reminder of the aristocrat's proud heritage.

"I'm afraid that is not good enough, Madam. You see, the United States government, under the direction of the Department of Interior, has set up this Land Commission to collect, collate, and bind those documents and maps that firmly establish and verify professed grants of land."

"My grant is honorable, Señor," the doña said acidly. "The Spanish government gave my father his rancho in 1818 for his many years of service to the crown and for risking his life in a strange land since 1798. He was a gentleman and an officer serving at both the Presidio of San Francisco and Monterey. There must be a record somewhere." The forcefulness of the doña made the officer speak softer and slower, but with equal animosity.

"I'm aware of your frustration, Madam. I hear it all the time. The fact remains, you have no concrete proof to give me. You Mexican people have a habit of illegal conduct—forgery, perjury, false claims, overlapping claims, false witnesses, lying, and stealing cattle. The corruption reaches clear to Mexico City, to the highest officials in your government."

The doña shot out of her chair and threw her beaded purse down on his desk, scattering papers and tipping over a glass of water.

"How dare you insult me!" she shouted.

Jenna broke into splotches. She'd seen this kind of tempest from the doña before. It was a matter of moments before she would begin throwing whatever she could lay her hands on. The official stood, brushing the drops of water from his coat.

"Please, Madam, forgive my candor. We certainly can conduct our business more civilly. It is the American way, you see. The Mexicans will have to be Americanized. It is the price of progress. I realize you have been used to doing things in a more casual manner. We must have order after so many years of chaos."

Jenna froze, waiting for the explosion. Instead, the doña sat down, stiff and steaming like a copper teapot.

"Perhaps you should contract the services of a lawyer to help you. We have many fine ones here in Monterey. It is quite possible the Archuleta grant is already on file. As for your inheritance—well, you need some kind of proof. That is not my job. You need to go through the courts, through the American legal system."

"It will take too long. I haven't the time. I must do this transaction now, immediately."

"I'm sorry, Madam. My advice is to find a lawyer." He stood up. His business was over. "I wish you success, Madam Archuleta. It has been a pleasure meeting you and Miss Daggett. Good day."

The doña raised her chin again, looked down the straight line of her nose, and threw the official the iciest look of contempt she could create. She and Jenna left quickly and got in the waiting carriage.

"Doña Juana, please explain what is happening. I don't want your land. It's *your* land, your precious rancho. What are you thinking?"

"Jenna, this is perhaps too much to explain, but if you care for me at all, you must trust what I am doing. I need you more than ever."

"Yes, Doña Juana—of course I want to help you."

"I am giving you the land and cattle to keep my brothers from destroying the rancho . . . and *me*. If it is secure in your name, an American, they can't take it away and they can't sell cattle that no longer belongs to them. They can't take my home and reduce me to nothing. I am outsmarting them at their game of wickedness, their certain actions, by making my property—excuse me, *your* property—secure in the government offices of the Americans before they make a move.

"If they have already swindled settlers by selling land that has been sold before, I doubt they will want to produce the map they hold as proof of our bequeathed portions. I can't be sure. They are such greedy fools. This transaction—and I assure you there will be one—will be our secret, Jenna. We will live just as we are now, but with new papers—filed with this ridiculous Land Commission. I can't wait out the years it will take to straighten out all the corrupt claims. Do I have your word, your loyalty, Jenna?"

"Yes, Doña—but I can't be responsible for your land. I'm too young to be an owner of such wealth . . . aren't I?"

"It will be your land on paper but my land, in fact, until I die. In only a few weeks you will be 18 years old, the legal age to own property, and no longer under my guardianship. Then you, not my brothers, who want to destroy me, will be the owner of Rancho San Gabriel. For now, your age matters little—a small fact that can be dealt with. I will get my way. You'll see."

Jenna stiffened. "Surely . . . Enrique wouldn't . . ."

"Stop, Jenna!" The doña interrupted. "Enrique is Bernardo's son. If I die, he stands to inherit my third. He's part of the conspiracy. Why else do you think he pushed out my loyal *mayordomo*? Now he's in a position of power and control. He has eyes and ears everywhere. I know this is hard for you to accept, especially since you have feelings for Enrique, but think for a moment. You will see that what I say makes sense."

Jenna fought the idea of Enrique being part of an evil plan to take over Doña Juana's property, part of any unkindness. Could she have misjudged a man she loved—or thought she loved—certainly a man who held a kind of power over her? Perhaps the doña, a frustrated spinster, was mistaken. On the other hand, the doña was not a foolish, hysterical woman, but rather keen and intuitive.

Jenna's thoughts tumbled with doubts. She felt weak and vulnerable, not like a Daggett at all. The secrecy distressed her, but she owed so much to the doña, she would do as she was asked and keep the matter in confidence.

"My sister is entertaining guests tomorrow night for dinner," she said. "I think she should ask that toady little lawyer, Reginald Potter, to dine with us. He is easily charmed by a smile . . . like a Saint Bernard drooling for a bite of beef. I know he fancies me. A rich Mexican lady might be of special interest to an aging widower."

ELEVEN

A T SIESTA, Jenna lay on her bed in her petticoat and camisole, completely exhausted. The ocean breeze from Monterey Bay filled the room; the sound of waves crashing against the protruding stacked, black boulders, barking seals, and screaming gulls soon put her into a deep sleep.

She awakened refreshed, washed in a basin of cool water, and dressed for dinner. Since the day had been hot, she wore an airy yellow skirt and white ruffled blouse like the Mexican *señoritas*. The skirt showed her trim ankles beneath a lace petticoat, and the flowing blouse fell off the shoulders, exposing her creamy skin. Jenna felt more comfortable in the loose silks than in the pinched East Coast fashion of the day.

Around her waist, she tied a brocade sash—red, with a black silk fringe. Its vibrant color matched the garden roses at her breast and encircling her chignon. Deep red garnet earrings set in intricate gold work dangled from her ears, and a gold cross the doña had given her lay at her throat. In case the doña thought she looked too bare, Jenna carried a white shawl to wear at dinner.

When she entered the *sala*, the guests were already enjoying polite conversation, especially Doña Juana, who was engaged in animated discourse with Reginald Potter, the lawyer. Helena, Doña Juana's sister, always the perfect hostess, introduced Jenna. As Helena took her seat, Erin, her husband, came in from the veranda laughing heartily with another gentleman.

Jenna stared at the robust gentleman whose gaiety filled the room the minute he entered. Danny McDaniels, the curly, black-haired Irishman who stole her youthful heart the day he rescued her from the ocean current, stood before her smiling broadly with mischievous, Celtic blue eyes.

"And so we meet again, Miss Daggett. A young lady now, I see. Indeed, a fully grown-up young lady." He kissed her hand. Jenna could not believe that her heart skipped a beat and she felt momentarily like a little girl. She returned his smile quickly and easily.

"Yes, Mr. McDaniels. It is a pleasure to see you. I might add, you also . . . have grown up?"

"If that is a question, the answer is no—not at all." He laughed, turned to his host, and said, "I think she's referring to my little parlor game with Irish whiskey. I tell you, Miss Daggett, the wee spirits play terrible tricks on the Irish."

Dinner was announced.

"May I escort you into the dining room?" he asked, offering his arm to Jenna. "What brings you to Monterey, little lady?" he inquired, pressing her arm slightly against him. Jenna resisted the temptation of pulling away. His gesture could easily be interpreted as friendly, not seductive; but the lingering side-glance was clearly flirtatious.

Jenna decided to let him play his game. She would remain poised and somewhat aloof. "The doña is here on business and shopping. And you? Do you live here, Mr. McDaniels?"

"No, I live in San Francisco, the devil's playground." Danny winked at Jenna and pulled her closer to him. "I am here on business, as well, Miss Daggett; however, I always find my pleasure, especially when I have a delicious lassie at my side. Erin is my close friend. We go back to the early days here when we had mud on our boots, blisters on our hands . . ."

"And Irish whiskey in your bellies." Jenna, shocked at her forwardness, covered her lips. What was it about this man that made her want to be glib, even rude?

Danny laughed good-naturedly.

"I apologize, Mr. McDaniels. I didn't mean to say that."

"Didn't you, now?"

"What I meant to say was . . . I meant to ask you what your business is. Do you think me rude in asking?"

"Not at all. Most ladies don't ask such questions, but then, you are not like most ladies. I am in shipping, transporting goods—commerce. I started out panning gold like everyone else, and then, well, the luck of the Irish was with me, you know." Again, he squeezed Jenna's arm against his body.

Jenna flushed. *Danny McDaniels, if you don't stop looking at me with such wicked eyes, I shall not be able to profess indifference. In fact, I will want to kiss you.*

Danny was the main attraction at dinner. He told story after story of his misadventures, each one more clever than the last. The guests laughed freely. He had a way of turning a phrase, surprising the amused dinner guests with remarks just at the edge of acceptability, yet he offended no one.

Jenna could not stop watching him. From time to time he looked at her over the rim of his wine glass, sent her a special toast, and smiled at only her.

He was an outrageous flirt. Jenna knew that, but still she found herself unable to eat, chew her food, or swallow without being aware of his penetrating, playful eyes. She felt naked and wished she'd worn a different blouse. His gaze seemed to touch her skin like caressing fingers—fingers that slipped below the neckline of her blouse, over her breasts, down her spine, and over her soft abdomen.

His relentless gaze made her feel self-consciously beautiful and desirable, like a temptress . . . which she did not want to be. As the evening progressed, the meaning of his glances became more obvious, less playful. With every gesture, he said he desired her. Even when she tried not to look at him, she knew he was looking at her and felt embarrassed. She prayed no one else was aware of his deliberate game to unsettle her.

It surprised her how much he resembled Enrique with his black, curly hair, his appealing mouth, and blue eyes. But where Enrique seemed prideful and arrogant, Danny appeared to be playful, carefree, shrewd. She could not quite trust either one of them.

When dinner was over, at last, and the men began to assemble in a separate room for cigars and brandy, Jenna took a moment to say to Danny, "Mr. McDaniels, you made me feel ridiculous with your arrogant looks across the table. I'll thank you not to ever do that to me again. I am not a mouse to be toyed with. I am not someone to amuse you. I find you vulgar and ill-mannered! I hope I never have the pleasure of being in your company again!" She turned on her heel and rushed out of the room, feeling his amused chuckle burn the back of her neck. Clearly, he was unimpressed with her confrontation.

Early the following morning, before the family stirred to the smell of coffee, fried corn tortillas, and black beans, Jenna found herself running barefooted down the sloping path, through the misty forest toward the beach. In spite of her words the night before, she hoped she would see the enchanting Daniel McDaniels again. In fact, her heart was pounding with the mere idea of it.

Perhaps it was for that reason that Jenna dressed as she had on her first encounter with the handsome Irishman. Her hair was loose and free-flowing, and her white muslin gown floated around her slender body like the fog itself. Now, however, Jenna was no longer the young fairy child, but a young woman whose passion rounded her breasts and thighs, carved a desirable, statuesque shape, long, strong legs, and rhythmic, supple gestures that moved like seagrass or willows in the wind.

The beach was empty except for an unwieldy pelican and a few waddling gulls. Disappointed, Jenna walked down the long stretch of sandy shore toward a quiet cove. The teasing surf crawled up to her toes chasing her higher up the gentle slope.

She stopped and looked in a clear tide pool at the living drama of two clumsy hermit crabs, a dainty fish, and a garden of enticing sea anemones waiting for a passing morsel to draw into their flowering mouths. She poked her finger into their hungry centers to feel the soft lips close around it and toyed with a crab too big for its shell, wondering if she, too, had outgrown her old self and needed a larger space, something new. Like the hermit crab who occupied a snail's shell—someone else's home—she was beginning to feel the pinch of confinement. Jenna picked up an abandoned periwinkle shell and put it in her pocket and was about to leave when she looked up to see a rider galloping toward her along the edge of the water.

"Hello there," he shouted. It was Daniel McDaniels, smiling, looking down at her.

She held her breath.

"I knew I'd find you here, little lady, looking every bit the sea sprite. Give me your hand. Come, come . . . I'll take you for a run down the coast."

Jenna didn't hesitate. In one strong motion, Danny bent down and pulled her onto the horse in front of him. She threw her leg over the horse's neck, gripped with her knees, and with Danny's arm tight around her waist, they galloped away in a spray of water. Jenna's delighted laughter was carried by the whipping wind and twisting spindrift. She had never felt so alive, so exhilarated. Feeling Danny McDaniels' strong body next to hers, rocking to the horse's stride, made her want to ride forever.

They rode into a quiet cove, leaving the waves of the open sea to crash against the gateway of rocks. Danny jumped from the horse and reached up for Jenna. He slowly slid her curvaceous body down the length of his until their lips met, then kissed her long and passionately. Jenna could scarcely breathe, but she did not resist. He picked her up and carried her away from the wind, laid her on the soft, dry sand, dropped down beside her, and pressed against her, kissing her hungrily.

She turned her head. He was forcing his passion on her; a familiar feeling of fear began to strangle her. "Please, Mr. McDaniels, let me up!"

He pulled away grinning and let her sit up. "Don't be so shocked. You act like kissing is a disease. I have no intention of deflowering a little babe, but I thought a kiss would start the day out fine. Don't you agree, Miss Daggett?"

"You are *no* gentleman, Mr. McDaniels," Jenna said, brushing the sand from her arms.

"You're absolutely right, lassie. I'm no gentleman. Never forget that. Never."

"Why do you always anger me? I want to like you. For a moment, I thought I did. Now you've spoiled it all again. I think I hate you!"

"No, you don't—that's the trouble. You came to the beach looking for me just as I did for you. You're mixing up your surprising urge to see me with, shall we say, passion . . . yes, Miss Daggett, passion that lies just below the surface, like a little seed just poking up through the earth. Ah, Jenna, I still feel you warm and trembling, pressed between my legs moving with me to the horse's gait. I've kissed a lot of lassies, even little seedlings. You were not resisting, lassie—not at all."

"Take me home!"

"That I will, but let me remember you as you are now, as I have remembered you whenever I ride this stretch of beach—a woman like the ocean wind, streamers of hair blowing wild, a strong body, tall and firm. Not a soft kitten to be cuddled, not a porcelain vase to be handled gently— no, not you, Jenna. You are the fiery reds of the sunrise."

Jenna picked up a rock and threatened to throw it at him. "Take me home! And don't ever speak to me with that familiarity again. You must think every woman who looks at you believes you're some kind of a god. I think you are disgusting. I'm ashamed my family knows you."

"I'll take you part way, then you can walk. I don't want to ruin your reputation . . . or mine, for that matter. But let me tell you, Jenna Daggett, one day you will come to me. And one day I'll call on you, and you will open your door for me wide, very wide—a warm and friendly bit of hospitality with a burning, fragrant, delicious hearth. I can wait. You'll call on me, maybe sooner than you think."

"I prefer to walk," she said, shaking out her dress.

"Come on, now, I'm not going to bother you anymore, I promise. I even apologize for my bad behavior. Right now I have a hungry appetite for breakfast. Ah, what a glorious day it's going to be! Don't you agree, Miss Daggett?"

Jenna didn't answer, but in spite of her anger, she, too, thought it was going to be a fine day.

As she ran up the stairs to her room, she paused at a niche in the garden wall and genuflected to a statue of the Virgin. "Blessed Mother, if I have sinned, well, forgive me. It's too late now." Jenna held the small periwinkle shell in her hand and kissed it. She would put it in Martha Jane's shell box, for it now was a treasure, a memory. Something she did not want to forget.

Danny had watched Jenna run up the path from the beach to the house until she disappeared in a grove of cypress trees.

Ah, Jenna, you pretend to be a cultivated garden flower. Let me warn you, lassie, you are ready to be picked.

Danny took off his boots and removed his morning shirt.

There are too many garden flowers—common, wilting. No, lass, you are all the metaphors of the sea—a succulent flower moist with sea spray, enduring waves that try to tear you from the cliff, an open ruby blossom wide as a mouth and drawing life into your lungs. One day I will know the sculpture of your body moving like a white dune. I'll taste your salty skin. I'll drown in you.

He plunged into the charge of a cooling, salty wave, then broke through the curl, exhilarated.

🌱 🌱 🌱

The doña went to see Reginald Potter alone that afternoon and returned in high spirits. Mr. Potter had found a record of the original land granted to Joaquin Rafael de Archuleta in 1818, a legitimate document that had been in the archives of the Monterey Presidio for years and among the first to be documented and bound by the Land Commission. The map clearly defined the boundaries of the Archuleta grant—two hundred and sixty-three thousand acres of land.

As Jenna and the doña sipped rich chocolate and nibbled sweet biscuits out on a sunny patio, the doña said, "My sister will be pleased to know the family land is recorded, even though her only interest in it is for my well-being. She was given the Monterey property, her third of her father's inheritance, which includes this house and grounds to the beachfront. Now, all I have to do is prove my third of the agreement.

"I drew Señor Potter a clear map showing the row of western hills, the turtle-shaped mounds on the east, the river and spring, structures, the three oaks to the north, the arroyo—but that's still not proof of ownership, they say. My sister's property is no safer than mine except that she's married to a *gringo*, an American. The Americans will play favorites. They think of Mexicans as a conquered people."

"Maybe your sister has some kind of deed or something that proves she owns this property."

"Let me remind you, Jenna, she knows nothing of my plan to thwart our brothers. I'll ask her when we finish our chocolate.

"By the way, we are going to Mission de Carmelo this morning. I expect you to attend church with us and light candles to the heavenly saints. I'm asking Saint Jude to intervene and solve my problem. I suggest you light one to Santa Lucia to guide you . . . in your romantic ventures. She protects young girls . . . virgins."

Jenna's cheeks grew hot with embarrassment as she recalled her encounter with Danny McDaniels. His rude words still burned in her mind. She had thought of little else. Could the doña possibly know her feelings, read her mind? Could the whole world see the awakening within her, the unexplained yearning that made her tremble?

"Aye, Jenna, you make too much noise when you place your cup in the saucer. When the two objects come together, it should be a union of grace, not the noise of a stable boy shoeing horses." Doña Juana placed her cup noiselessly in the saucer to prove her point. "Don't rush, but keep in mind our busy morning. I will speak to Helena at my first opportunity."

🌣 🌣 🌣

The three women, returning from the Carmel Mission, sat in an open buggy pulled by a pair of unhurried horses. The carriage road to the house meandered through a forest of graceful cypress and scented Monterey pines. Sunlight slipped through the trees onto the women, rippling their silk dresses like watery pools and splashing their hair and skin with moving dots of light. The sea stretched below them, sky and water, blue meeting blue.

"Of course my property is secure, sister," Helena said. I have a title back at the house, and I recall I also have father's letter to me before he died, stating his wishes that I have the Monterey property. Erin has it among his papers."

Jenna drifted in and out of the sisters' conversation, indifferent to the business of their property. Instead, she let the splendor of the day, the gentle tug of the horses, and the soft air enfold her in its enchantment. Sometimes, the face of Danny McDaniels floated before her, then changed into Enrique's. She couldn't hang on to either one, and at that moment it didn't matter. It was the day, itself, that made her feel so gloriously happy.

Back at the house, Helena presented Doña Juana the important family papers. "Here is my title and the letter from father, " Helena said. "You will be happy to know he clearly states his intentions, dividing the land between you, Bernardo, and Juan. It's all in his handwriting," Helena said, handing the letter to Doña Juana.

"A letter of intent?" The doña grabbed the letter from her sister and read it.

"It's not a will or anything like that, just a personal letter to me. It was written two years before he died. Look at the date—1825."

"May I take this with me to see Señor Potter? It is the only proof I have that he intended to divide the land three ways—not a legal title perhaps, but persuasive." Doña Juana folded the envelope carefully. "And with little extra enticements . . . may be *very* persuasive. The Land Commission needs something in its possession to justify a claim."

The meeting with Reginald Potter was successful. After examining the letter, he agreed it was valuable evidence and more proof of ownership than many of the other vague land claims the commission had accepted as valid.

"I am going to record your portion of the property as legal, Madam Archuleta. You will have a document on file, along with your father's legal map, your drawn map, and this letter. Consider the matter done, except perhaps a dinner with me," he said, smiling coyly. "I will draw up your deed. Now, as far as reassigning the title to Miss Daggett, I see no problem except her age. Since you are naming her as owner of the said property before your death, and until she becomes of age, you must act as trustee. She will not be in full charge until she is an adult in the eyes of the law— age eighteen."

The doña smiled. Jenna would be eighteen in only a few weeks. "And if anyone should try to take my land from me—rather, from Jenna—it would be against the law, a violation?"

"That is correct, Madam," Mr. Potter said with an official air.

"Will you be able to complete the paperwork before I leave for San Jose?"

"Within the week, assuming there are no obligations or conditions attached to the transaction, such as insisting Miss Daggett become a Catholic, fulfill servitude, and so on."

"There are no such obligations," the doña said.

"Bring Miss Daggett in for her signature. I will have the document in my possession to verify our transaction and complete the papers."

"And a receipt of all fees and taxes?"

"Indeed."

"Thank you, Señor Potter," the doña said, rising from her chair and extending her hand to be kissed. "I look forward to our dinner together."

🌿 🌿 🌿

The three happy dogs who usually welcomed everyone to the ranch did not rush out to greet Jenna and the returning entourage.

"Luisa found all of them dead out in the meadow," Ygnacio said as he helped Jenna from the buggy. "Someone shot them," he added, without changing his expression.

The news angered Jenna to tears. Why would anyone shoot her three little friends who had accompanied her everywhere? She knew no one at the ranch thought of the dogs as pets, not living creatures with personality and humor, but rather the host for millions of biting fleas, a nuisance under the horses' feet. The dogs had survived like the wild animals by eating the carrion left in the meadows after the slaughter of a steer, yet they hung around the barns and house wanting the company of man—indifferent or cruel as he may be. But Jenna loved them, giving them treats from the table and always a kind word. The dogs, in turn, had filled many lonely hours.

The ranchos in the area eagerly awaited the roundup of the cattle at San Gabriel. The doña had a reputation for putting on the best rodeo, the greatest games, hosting the most exciting events for miles around. She welcomed everyone at the three-day fiesta.

The men slaughtered the animals, skinned their hides, sliced off the fat to boil into tallow. Under swarming clouds of flies, the stench and bellows of the frantic animals, the women chatted gaily and prepared sumptuous food, placing it on long tables under the trees.

The *vaqueros* strutted in black pants and gold braid to show their skill with the *reata*, catching a horn or hoof of an animal, throwing it to the ground to break its neck if it happened to be the one selected for dinner. They bit the ears of captured wild mustangs to keep them under control before releasing them into a race. They played games, burying a chicken up to its head and trying to grab it while hanging from the saddle of a racing horse.

Jenna could not stand to watch the cruel games in which animals were always the victims. The men cast their bets and shouted as cocks tore each other apart, or cheered as a captured grizzly bear was tied to a bull and both began fighting for their lives until one or the other dropped dead, leaving the victor to bleed to death. Jenna always wanted to run to her room to shut out the screams of the animals, the vulgar shouts of the men.

"Silly woman! How you cry and carry on over the animals. They have no souls," Enrique chided. "They are created for work, for food and human needs. You are being foolish. It is as nature intended. All *gringos* are soft as women! Now they are outlawing our traditions, trying to destroy our culture. I dare them to come to the rancho to stop it. Come now, Jenna. I insist you watch the games," he said pulling her arm.

"No, I don't want to watch. It saddens me that the cruelty, the torture, brings you such pleasure, Enrique. I'm glad we're outlawing your vicious games, and other nonsense as well. It is monstrous. I'll have none of it!"

Enrique's eyes flashed. "It is too bad you have such pale blood. I thought you had more fire. I did not think you were a typical *gringa*."

Jenna withdrew from the fiesta and dancing. When she first moved to the rancho, she had thought the festivities were very exciting, a happy diversion from the long, uneventful days. But now, they represented the celebration of a people from whom she felt alien.

Increasingly, Jenna had become aware of the Mexicans' resentment of the Americans. The two cultures clashed, neither one respecting the good of the other. The Californios were made to feel like a conquered people, more like the Indians than fine old Spanish and Mexican families. Although some Californios intermarried and spoke well of the new system, the Archuletas were not among them.

Jenna was caught between two cultures, admiring them both, yet seeing the growing hatred on both sides. She was sorry they did not want or understand the new laws. The Spanish often settled their arguments in a duel or a quick flash of a knife, or sometimes the dons of the families settled the disputes. It had worked for decades. In between the hostilities of Alta California, the neighbors danced and sang and rode their horses. They embraced large families from great-grandparents to babes, all part of a warm network of love and pride.

The Americans, on the other hand, cut off from eastern family ties, eager for land, gold, or opportunity, had to form a new pattern of survival, a lonely, independent, highly energetic and imaginative one.

Day by day, Jenna grew more restless. Though she still believed she loved Enrique and his flattering attention, she wanted something more in her life. Her loyalty to the doña had kept her at the rancho longer than she had intended. Now she longed to leave, at least for awhile. Besides, Enrique spent most of his time away from the place, riding or gambling or gaming with the *vaqueros*.

But what could a woman do on her own except housework, laundry, dressmaking? Even those jobs were now taken over by the Chinese. Letters from Darcey and Pearle, even Harke and Blue, contributed to her turmoil, making her homesick.

🌿 🌿 🌿

In Jackson Darcey had bought a fine house for boarders, a respectable place with good furniture and linen tablecloths. She intended to have the finest place in town and a clientele that contributed to Jackson's growth, a community that might become the county seat.

She planned to move from Hattie's Bar in the spring and predicted that by that time, no one would be left there or at Red Man's Bar. Any shacks or shanties would fall by the next winter and, in time, no one would know the mining camps had ever existed.

By spring, Darcey hoped Blue would be better. His recovery had been slower than expected. Walking caused great pain along his spine, and the doctor concluded that a splinter of bone had worked its way into the area. To make matters worse, Blue could not bend, lift, or sit for very long without great discomfort. He'd grown thin and discouraged, saying, "I'm only half a man, Darcey. Why do you put up with me, girl?"

But to Darcey, Blue was all man, her man, and she attended to him whenever she wasn't cooking. Business had dwindled as the miners packed up and moved on. Once again, Hattie's old bedroom behind the red calico curtain was converted into sleeping quarters, this time to accommodate Blue. Darcey could look after him in her own way and keep his spirits high by speaking of their future together in Jackson.

Harke paid periodic visits to Hattie's Bar, entertaining them all with his adventures driving the stagecoach and encouraging Blue with news of a growing business. Pearle, always so happy to see him, snuggled beside him to hear his stories, or often led him to her favorite places above the river, where she read him her stories and poems or shared her private dreams. He had become her big brother, her connection with the outside world, the romance of life in the towns, pretty ladies in lovely dresses, flower boxes, and fine carriages. For Harke, Pearle had become the sister he had lost in the swell of California boom towns.

🌿 🌿 🌿

Jenna withdrew from many activities on the rancho, even afternoon coffee with Doña Juana, claiming she did not feel well. The fact was, she had little appetite, felt listless and anxious. She longed for a change of place, a defined purpose and time to sort out her troubled thoughts.

The secret she carried of being the owner of the Archuleta estate lodged in her stomach like a sharp stone, subtly driving a wedge between herself and Enrique. The lie closed a door to the romance that once had thrilled her, consumed every waking thought, every dream. If part of the doña's plan was to discourage her relationship with Enrique, she had succeeded, and Jenna resented it.

Moreover, she realized she had been gullible. The doña had outsmarted her. Doña Juana was a woman utterly self-serving, capable of almost anything to get her way.

As for Enrique, he had little time for her except when he chose to be amorous and charming. There were days when Jenna didn't see him at all. He clearly preferred spending his leisure hours gambling, betting on cockfights, playing dominos, racing—playing any game where his machismo was involved. It was not until she expressed her desire for a change that Jenna managed to attract Enrique's attention.

"I'm going to tell the doña that it's time for me to find a place for myself," Jenna told him. "I've thought of going to Jackson to assist my friend Darcey open her rooming house. She can use the help, and it will give me a chance to think about my future."

Enrique's face turned dark. "And leave me and the rancho? I can't believe you could think of doing such a thing. Haven't we told each other that we are in love?"

Jenna remembered the day Enrique uttered those words to her. He had approached her as she was taking Honey out for a short afternoon ride down by the river. Being alone without the watchful eye of Luisa, the pair's game of flirtation that had been carefully controlled, ignited into a passionate embrace.

Jenna had fallen into the spell of his kisses, yielded to him openly, not caring if it was wrong to return his passion, wrong to be alone with him, wrong to want him. He told her how he longed for her, loved her, that she was more important than the air he breathed . . . and then he held her wrists.

"Tell me you love me, or I won't let you go. Tell me, Jenna. You speak with your fiery, cat eyes; you move your body in ways that show me you want me; you kiss me like we are man and wife."

Unable to free her arms, she felt the moment turn cold. She couldn't say she loved him. Enrique forced her arms behind her, then pressed the arch of her back into his lower body. She felt his hardness, familiar and insulting.

"Tell me, Jenna. Say it!" Enrique had demanded, squeezing her wrist tighter.

Just to be released, Jenna had said, "I love you, too, Enrique . . . only don't force me. *Never* force me again!" His eagerness had repelled her, her wrists burned. She had regretted her part of the intimacy.

Standing before her now, Enrique's demeanor was one of hurt pride and anger. "You care more for your friends than for me. I've told everyone in the Archuleta family that I'm going to marry you. I've been waiting for the right moment to ask you to be my wife."

"Then why haven't you asked me?" Jenna asked, not certain she believed him. "You have a peculiar way of courting, Enrique."

"My soul burns for you. I ache when I'm not with you. You are all the beauty in the world to me," Enrique said, gently holding her chin and looking deep into her eyes.

Jenna was not convinced. She had grown used to his flowery words. They no longer sounded poetic or sincere.

Enrique's face was tense. "You must know how I want you. One day I will inherit this entire rancho. I will be a powerful don. We will spend our years together, a hard fist of the Archuleta family. I want to give you my name, my power. I love you, Jenna," he said, his eyes welling with tears.

Jenna froze. It was as the doña had said. Enrique was waiting to inherit Rancho San Gabriel. How angry he would be to know the truth, that she held the deed. The rancho was hers, not his. What a clever woman the doña was! She had manipulated the entire land transaction to suit herself alone, protect herself, and in the doing, to prevent Enrique from marrying her. He would never marry a woman who owned his land. He would turn against her, perhaps hate her.

"Jenna, I know you love me. Let us pledge to each other now, right now, with this beautiful oak tree as our witness, that we will be man and wife. Marry me, my dearest love."

Enrique's sincerity, his pleading, his astonishing subservience, confused Jenna. She felt a surge of love for him. In that moment, he had discarded his macho, arrogant manner. He seemed rather like a child, a boy full of apology and humility.

"I need you. I'm only half alive without you. I'd die if you said 'no' to me. I could not live . . . nor face my family."

Jenna was moved. Enrique had completely disarmed her by his emotion. He had always been so confident, the one in control. Now she was the strong one.

"Give me time to think, my dearest," she said. "This is too sudden to answer. I must be certain." Her head was pounding. She was caught in a web of deceit. "Perhaps if I went to Jackson for awhile, to think . . ."

"I would die without you here, but if you insist on leaving . . . if I could have your answer before you leave. Oh! What can I do to prove my love?" he said in a burst of anguish.

"Let me have a few days to collect my thoughts, Enrique."

"You will say yes. I know it, *Señora Archuleta.*"

𝇇 𝇇 𝇇

During the next few days, Jenna avoided Enrique and did not join the doña for afternoon coffee. She often heard the two of them arguing over ranch business, the doña's voice shrill with shouts. She would hear the *sala* door slam and an enraged Enrique gallop away on his horse, no doubt digging his heels into the poor mustang's flanks.

Jenna struggled with her dilemma. At times she felt honesty was the only way to handle the situation. She would insist on a meeting and tell them both what needed to be said. She was the doña's pawn, Enrique's possession. She did not feel like a Daggett.

Sometimes she talked herself into thinking there was a solution. Enrique would be reasonable, even forgiving about the betrayal. After all, if they married, he would be a patron and run the rancho just as if he owned the deed. What difference did it make? She would become an Archuleta and still be true to the doña's wishes. And the doña . . . eventually she would trust Enrique, see his good, overlook his arrogance. But, of course, she knew in her heart this outcome was ridiculous. The situation was much too volatile.

How she regretted putting her signature on that deed! Perhaps the best thing was to leave, go to Jackson, perhaps find a teaching position somewhere, even San Francisco. Jenna's easy life had suddenly become complicated. Whichever way she turned seemed to be a betrayal to the doña or Enrique. She knew one thing—soon the Archuleta brothers would know they had no authority over the rancho. For now, the deceit and cover-up about the ownership of Rancho San Gabriel was a game played by liars, and she was a principal player. She had to speak with the doña immediately.

Jenna opened the heavy carved doors to the *sala,* flooded with low afternoon sunlight, and found the doña slumped in her chair, her arms dangling lifelessly at the sides. Something was wrong. Jenna rushed to her. She had seen too many deaths to deny the signs—the peculiar angle of the head fallen to one side, the mouth agape. The doña was dead.

"My God, my God! Doña Juana! Oh, Lord!" She pressed her ear against the silent chest. Searching for a single throb in her neck and finding no life she ran from the room, calling for Marta.

"She must have had a stroke or heart attack," Jenna said, sobbing. "I can't believe this. She seemed so well."

The Indian woman nodded her head. "I'll call Ygnacio to carry her to her room. She must not be left unattended for the bad spirits to enter her open mouth. We must send for the priest quickly."

"Yes, yes—old Padre Ortega. He'll come. He's loyal to the doña after all the years she's taken care of him and supported the old mission."

"Luisa!" Marta called. "Go to the corral and send a man to find Señor Enrique. He will have to ride to his father's house to tell them."

In minutes, word had spread throughout the rancho. The field-workers and the women and children gathered in a solemn group outside the door of the rancho. The older women were on their knees repeating prayers for the salvation of the doña. They had pulled their shawls over their heads in respect for the doña's departing soul, and to ensure that any evil spirits hovering about would not take their own souls away.

"Oh, hurry Enrique. I need you," Jenna said to herself as they laid the doña on her bed.

Jenna gently closed the doña's open mouth and folded her hands across her chest. She looked at the stranger on the bed, no longer the doña at all, but a doll, a casing, a piece of wax. Without life to animate the body, spark the light in the eyes, hold the tissue in place, the face distorted and the body turned into a useless, unfamiliar vessel.

Jenna held the doña's cold and stiffening hand. How strange and powerless she looked, but still, her lifeless countenance had frozen with a look of pride. "I wonder where you are, Doña Juana. Are you in this room watching me? Are you somewhere in between this life and another? Do you see Jesus and all the saints? Maybe you will meet my family— papa, mama, and my little brother, and Nettie, my little friend. I can hardly remember any of their faces now, they died so very long ago."

As Jenna smoothed a loose strand of hair back of the doña's ear, she noticed one of her black onyx earrings was gone and had left a droplet of dried blood on her lobe.

"Oh, dear, I must find that other earring—probably it's on the floor by the chair or on the stairs. She will want to be buried in the earrings she wore all the time . . . and her black lace *mantilla*. It is the way I think of her, the way I shall always remember her."

🍂 🍂 🍂

Enrique comforted Jenna, holding her while she grieved, reassuring her that all was well. "Tia Juana is with the Lord, we can be sure of that. Not a more noble lady graced this land," he said, stroking Jenna's silky hair.

Jenna looked up into Enrique's face. "Oh, Enrique, I owe so much to Doña Juana. We had our differences, but we understood one another. I loved her, I truly did." She walked over to the doña's high-backed chair and ran her fingers over the carved wood. "I feel she is still sitting in this chair. Her presence is still so strong."

Enrique moved quickly across the room and took Jenna by the shoulders and sat her down in the doña's chair.

"Stop it, Enrique. What are you doing?" She tried to stand up, but again, Enrique pressed her down.

"Sit there, Jenna. I want to see you as the doña of this rancho. Soon you will be, my love."

Jenna felt weak. Was this the time to tell him she owned Rancho San Gabriel? "Please, Enrique. This is sacrilegious behaving this way. I don't want any part of it. This is the time of mourning, praying for her departed soul."

"Come now, Jenna. Don't be a hypocrite. What do you know about faith?" Enrique gave a sardonic laugh.

Jenna stood up. It was true what he said. She had never really lived up to the doña's expectations to become Catholic.

Enrique pulled her to him and took a fistful of hair at the back of her head. Jenna froze. She had to get away from him. "If you will excuse me, Enrique," she said, removing his hands, "I'm going to take a siesta. I need to rest so I'll have enough energy to handle all the preparations for our many guests."

Taking on the role of patron, master of the rancho, seemed easy for Enrique. He moved about the house and grounds with an air of authority, supervising the servants, managing the funeral arrangements, even suggesting the painted design for the wooden casket.

The cooks kept busy preparing food for the expected stream of guests. Family, friends and neighbors would soon arrive to pay their respects, and stay for a holy communion service. Some would spend the night.

Rooms were cleaned and freshened with herbs, outfitted with the traditional small cups filled with "guest money" to help the travelers pay their expenses. The Indian women took the mattresses down from the loft, removed the damp wool and prayed the rainy season would let up so the rare show of sun would help to air and dry the bedding. Even a few hours of sun lessened the strong odor of mildew.

Marta and her friend prepared the body, dressed the doña in peacock blue silk, and carefully draped her black *mantilla* over her head and around her bloodless face. In death, as in life, the doña's countenance gave away no secrets of her spinsterhood, no sorrow, no regrets. She remained beautiful and arrogant, as cold polished marble.

Unable to find the missing onyx earring, Jenna suggested a pair of pearl drops the doña favored. Jenna placed the single onyx earring among her precious memories in Martha Jane's shell box.

They laid Doña Juana's body in a casket lined with white satin and discreetly tucked eucalyptus, dried roses, and sweet basil around her body to disguise the smell of death. The body was laid on a table in the *sala* for the guests to view. The Indian women placed tied bundles of bay leaves and sprigs of mint throughout the room and filled vases with sprays of chrysanthemums. Candles flickered in the dim light, throwing curious shadows on the white adobe walls.

The family had decided not to bury the doña alongside her father at San Jose Mission. Not only was the mission too far away, but there were also reports of desecration of the graves.

By the following evening, the old padre from the mission rattled up to the rancho in a *carreta* drawn by a swaybacked horse, carrying his only bundle—a silver chalice wrapped in an alter cloth. He would perform the holy communion for the family and mourners.

Padre Ortega stayed mainly in the *sala*, hoping to obtain a few coins for special prayers and *novenas* to comfort the mourners and to assist the doña into Heaven. When no one was about, he warmed his thin bones by the fire and nibbled sweet biscuits that he kept hidden in his robe. Sometimes he wandered back to the kitchen for a bowl of beans or cornmeal or soft pumpkin and "a little boiled beef, easy to chew." To the amusement of a few mimicking Indian children hiding behind a trestle of vines, he would sit by the kitchen at a rickety table under the poplars, gumming his food so vigorously that his chin rose up to meet his nose, then sop up the last soupy mixture with bread and crumble the crusts for the noisy gander.

The padre had buried the doña's father and attended the Archuleta family's births, deaths, baptisms, and first communions. He had heard their confessions and blessed them throughout his life until the Mexicans secularized the missions. Though many priests returned to Mexico or moved to the towns, those too old to leave remained and depended on the charity of loyal families. The doña continued to tithe to the church and supported Padre Ortega for years. The rest of the Archuletas ignored him and thought him a pest. They were among the throngs of California Catholics who found piety less interesting.

The old padre had remained at the mission saying his prayers, listening to a few confessions and assisting a younger priest now and then. He'd cultivated a small vegetable garden and made leather sandals and pouches to sell, but mostly, he shuffled in and out of the dark rooms, rattling inside his foul robes, and muttering about the sins of the Catholics who had forgotten the church. Behind the thick adobe walls, he'd grown thin and putrid, and his teeth had fallen out one by one. His robe smelled like mice nests. He was as crumbly as the missions themselves.

Throughout the day, the padre watched the Indian children running and tumbling around the rancho, the busy servants coming and going across the courtyard, and enjoyed listening to the chatter of the cooks. He took pleasure sitting under the dripping eaves of the porch, watching puddles grow into small ponds and the protected hanging columns of peppers and garlic blow slantwise in the wind. He listened to the friendly conversation of the geese and watched the flapping wingspread of the ducks preening themselves in the rain.

By the end of he week, the padre's skin looked firmer and less pasty. The seamstress had made him a new robe of lighter wool so that his old, patched heavy one could be washed and mended. Still, he never bathed, saying, "Our Lord frowns on bathing. After all, didn't the holy men wander in the waterless desert for forty years?"

🐚 🐚 🐚

The doña was buried in the churchyard in San Jose under a cold, sobbing sky. By the time everyone returned to the rancho, Jenna felt chilled. The *sala* provided a welcome warmth with its glowing fire. She asked Marta to bring a pot of hot tea for her and brandy for Enrique and Padre Ortega and anyone else who cared to join them.

While they were attending the funeral, the furniture in the *sala* was put back in place. The votives and blackened candles were removed. The sconces and candelabrum were refurbished with fresh tapers. The doña's room looked the same once again, except for a large terra-cotta vase of bright paper flowers made by the children. The splash of red, yellow, purple and pink blossoms defied the somber mood of death still lingering in the shadows.

Jenna walked around the room readjusting a small rug, a footstool, and the lamps. She picked up a needlepoint pillow to place it on the settee. Hooked on the back was the doña's missing onyx earring! A shiver crawled up her spine. She scarcely wanted to remove it, to touch it, for it was there without reason. As she carefully unhooked it, she noticed with horror a small droplet of blood on the threads. How could the doña's earring be hooked to the pillow? And why was there blood, as well?

Enrique's hard boot heels sounded on the tiled entryway. Jenna quickly pocketed the earring and replaced the pillow. She had to think about the implications of her discovery, but for now, she knew only one thing.

She was frightened of Enrique.

Oh, Lord, could it be possible that the doña did not die of heart failure, but by someone's hand? How quick and silent it would be to place a pillow over the doña's face from behind her chair. Surely, she would have struggled, violently struggled, turning her head, twisting from side to side, tearing her earring out of her ear as she attempted to free her face from suffocation.

Enrique entered the *sala*. Jenna held her breath.

I must compose myself. I must not show my fear. He must never know of my suspicion—no, more than that—my conclusion. Enrique is capable of great cruelty. He murdered Doña *Juana!*

She turned her back to him and faced the fire.

"My dearest," Enrique said, coming up behind her and encircling her in his arms. He slowly turned her around and kissed her. "It is over, my love. Auntie is at peace; the guests are leaving. We are soon to be alone, like a man and wife; nothing now stands between us and our marriage. We will make plans for summer."

Jenna looked at him and tried to smile. She must not show him fear.

"Don't you see, Jenna. I am the patron, the owner of Rancho San

Gabriel," he said, taking her hands to his lips.

A feeling of panic swept through Jenna's body like a sudden gust of wind. She wanted to draw her hands away for fear Enrique would feel her tenseness and her revulsion at the tip of his wet tongue wedging in between her fingers.

"Man and wife, Jenna. I'll make you know the power of my love."

Jenna lowered her eyes and noticed faint scratches on the back of one hand—three lines that ran up to the wrist. She looked up to see Enrique carefully watching her.

"You are wondering about these scratches. A stubborn young cow tangled herself in the chaparral. I had to free her."

"I've asked Marta to bring tea and brandy. Padre Ortega will join us," Jenna said, turning to face the fire.

"That old, toothless fool. I don't want him here. I want to be alone with you. I'm tired of having him about. He annoys me with his constant stories of the great days of the mission when Catholics were devoted," Enrique said, imitating the priest. "I'll send him on his way."

"Oh, Enrique, not yet. I've asked him to stay a few days—at least until the weather breaks. There is so much rain and mud . . . and fog. He might get lost in the fog. Please, Enrique."

"As you wish, for awhile longer. I'll be gone anyway. I need to go to my father's on business matters. There is much to do."

"How long will you be gone?" Jenna inquired.

"Long enough to discuss business with my uncles. No bastard *gringos* are going to outsmart the Archuletas. We have our own ways of doing business. Be patient, dearest. Soon you will have the name Archuleta and all the power that goes with it."

Jenna's mind was spinning. At that moment, she didn't dare tell Enrique she owned the property, the house, the cattle. *All of it was hers.*

He would know soon enough. And then what?

Enrique was a violent man. Looking into his blue eyes, she wondered how she could have loved him, why she had not seen his cruelty. The doña had warned her. She wondered, too, if Enrique was capable of hurting her, as well, if she was going to be an obstacle that had to be removed to get what he wanted. She slipped her hand into her pocket to be sure the onyx earring was secure, closed her fingers around it and felt its cold, hard, black message from the grave.

🌼 🌼 🌼

A few weeks after the funeral, the padre said to Jenna, "I think I must stay throughout the winter and return to the mission in late spring . . . to comfort you, Señorita Daggett, and the family, as well. We all need to say daily prayers for Doña Juana de Archuleta in case she has not quite made it into Heaven. But then I must return to plant a garden. Meanwhile, my Indian family will look after the cow and feed the birds. What do you think about this arrangement?" he asked with a childish smile.

"I think it is most generous of you," Jenna said. "The doña would be proud to have you stay in her home."

"Then it is settled," he said, cracking a lipless smile across his face.

While Enrique was away from the rancho, Jenna gathered courage and strength. She rode Solana for hours across the wet meadows under overcast skies. With every step, her anger at Enrique grew. She could never prove Enrique killed the doña. She, herself, would stand more to gain from her death.

There was no one to investigate such crimes. Matters concerning theft or murder were settled by vigilantes in the mining camps. But their interest did not include problems between Mexican families. The families settled the matters themselves, sometimes quite severely. She could not face the Archuleta brothers with an accusation against Enrique.

Eventually, the truth about the deed would surface. Then she would face them all. The Land Commission and American law would surely side with her. If the Archuletas wanted the land, they would have to fight for it. The Americans were in control now. She was part of the new power. The Archuletas had lost. Their corruption and foolishness had caused their own downfall. This land was hers, and she was going to keep it. It was time to be a Daggett. Israel's words came back to her. "Be strong! Don't ever, ever give up!" She would have to face Enrique with the truth.

The opportunity to confront Enrique came sooner than Jenna had expected. On his return, he was angry that the padre had made no plans to return to Mission San Jose.

Jenna straightened her shoulders and stood tall. "I told him he was welcome to stay as long as he liked. He is an old, lonely man, Enrique, and clearly enjoys the activity of the rancho. He doesn't harm anyone. He loves to putter out by the kitchen making sandals and pouches for the children, and he's making a fine *reata* for you. What's wrong with letting him stay?"

"I don't want him here. I told you that!" Enrique retorted. "He's to leave immediately."

"No, he's not leaving," Jenna rebelled. She could feel the red splotches surfacing on her neck and face.

Enrique flashed. "What do you mean, woman? Who are you to dictate the rules of this house? *I'm* the authority here. This is *my* house. You have no decisions here."

Jenna hesitated, then thrust forward like a lance. "You're wrong, Enrique. This is *not* your house, or your ranch, for that matter. It is *mine*. I have papers to prove it. I am the doña of this house. Doña Juana gave it to me. The proof is in Monterey at the Land Office."

Jenna's words struck a severe blow, knocking the wind out of Enrique, leaving him speechless. He stared in disbelief at her unemotional face, searching for a lie behind her cold eyes. "What are you saying? You are lying!" He raised his hand to strike her.

"Don't you touch me!" she shouted at him, "or I'll have you hanged!"

He stopped, his open hand in midair. They stared at each other, tied together like the bear and the bull by an invisible rope. He could see that Jenna was not afraid of him. Her piercing eyes convinced him she held a new kind of power, one he did not understand.

Enrique saw something in Jenna he had not seen before. Could it be that those icy eyes could see into his conscience, read his thoughts, know his deeds? It was a look of defiance different from the expression a man would have. He could read a man's face, understand his swagger, his stiff-legged strut, his maleness; he could smell the animal instinct to fight, intuitively know the moment of extreme tension and danger, the split second before violence. But a woman? He could physically crush her in an instant, that he knew, but he sensed another power in her beyond physicality, equal and unsettling. Something she knew gave her voice authority. Yes, she knew something, maybe something about him, and she was a *gringa* who knew *gringo* law.

"You may think you own this rancho, Señorita, but you are mistaken. This is Archuleta land, *my* land. You will never claim it—*never*! You are a liar and a thief. You let me ask you to marry me and share my life here, all the while scheming with the doña against me—against the Archuletas, her own brothers. You must think I'm a fool! You must have laughed behind my back while you were taking what does not belong to you. If you were a man, your throat would be cut from ear to ear. I leave you, Jenna Daggett, with this: You are my enemy! From now on, you will be afraid to close your eyes at night, afraid to walk to the pond or ride your horse alone. We Archuletas have laws of our own . . . our own justice. You will regret your actions."

"Don't threaten me, Enrique."

"I am not threatening you. I'm telling you."

"You don't frighten me."

"Don't I? We'll see." As Enrique stormed out of the *sala*, he turned to hurl a final curse. Jenna had her back to the hearth to warm the chill on her spine. The fire blazed behind her, casting a giant shadow.

🌱 🌱 🌱

Jenna arranged for Señor Faustino to manage the rancho once again. He and his wife and children were happy to return to his old house, one built especially for him when he became *mayordomo* years ago. With his guidance, Jenna began the task of understanding the operation of the rancho. She was anxious to ride the perimeters of her property before calf branding and the roundup, for she needed to know exactly what she owned.

While she waited for the weather to clear, she felt anxious and impatient, often pacing the damp rooms. To pass the lonely hours, she played dominoes with Padre Ortega by the fire and helped Luisa and the other children with reading and writing.

Señor Faustino had reported to her that he thought the herds looked light. "I'm guessing we are about two thousand head short, and there are very few calves. We can account for a few stolen animals from squatters, but I'm certain Señor Enrique is simply taking them, herding them onto his father's land. He's helping himself."

Jenna's problems were just beginning. As she and Señor Faustino rode the meadows in the southern section of the property, Jenna saw for herself the squatters' farms. She had known they were there, but did not know how many families were taking land that didn't belong to them and claiming it for themselves. They were everywhere, some with fences.

"What do I do, Señor Faustino? There are so many of them."

"I don't know, Señorita. They won't leave, and they meet our men with guns. They fire over our heads. Some say they have been here for three or four years and have paid taxes to the government. One man claims he has bought the land. Others say they pay rent and can prove it. They show me paper I cannot read. Every time I check the land or cattle, more squatters have settled down, more cattle are missing.

"These *gringos* are hostile. They do not understand that empty land is not for the taking. They say the American government wants the land taken care of, cultivated, improved. They say they came to California to homestead. They did not know anyone owned the land. Now they say they are going to fight to keep what is theirs. They consider you and me the trespassers. One family has fenced in part of the stream and does not allow our cattle to drink. There is no law, Señorita, to protect your herds."

"You mean, they simply put up a nice house and plant crops and nobody stops them?"

"*Sí.* There are too many of them now."

"I'll go to Monterey and speak with Reginald Potter. Surely I can stop them. This is against the law!"

"What law, Señorita? You need much money to fight in the courts. You will need much money and armed men to fight the Archuletas. But you are American. Maybe you will have better luck than the Californios. They are losing their land. Many old families now live in small houses in the pueblos. Once they were rich. Many are selling quickly before the squatters take it all. Some owe too many taxes to the Americans and now they have no way to pay it back without selling off many acres to keep only a few. The land cannot support the big herds, so they are being sold, too. It is very sad, Señorita."

"Do we owe taxes, Señor Faustino?"

"*Sí,* Señorita. Doña Juana refused to pay any money to the *Yanqui.*"

Jenna felt helpless. She owned land that was draining away like water from a leaky bucket. She owned cattle being driven onto the Archuleta brothers' land without any way to stop them. The taxes had accumulated for so many years that she had no authority against a squatter's claim, especially one who was paying the taxes. She must take steps to right these wrongs.

"Señor Faustino, I want a new brand for the remaining herds. Make it JD for Jenna Daggett. If anyone takes a single steer with my brand, he will be a thief. Americans hang cattle thieves."

TWELVE

D ARCEY SMILED TO HERSELF as she placed a large bouquet of peonies on the washstand. The perfumed, pink flowers looked cheerful next to the pink and green wedding-ring quilt and made a welcoming touch for the new boarder, due to arrive anytime. Darcey was highly pleased with the effect her decorating ideas had created in her beautiful, new rooming house, Higgins House. She had carefully chosen wallpaper, curtains, bed covers, and small rugs to carry out a different color scheme in each of the upstairs bedrooms.

Sarah Abrahms, an aging mother with hair like a bird's nest, had the blue room. Her middle-aged twin boys, Thaddeus and Tobias, occupied the green room next to her, a more spacious chamber with two corner windows curtained in lace. Across the hall in the raspberry room lived Gilmore Jameson, a piano player at the Bonanza Saloon. He came and went at all hours and sometimes slept during the day.

Blue occupied a smaller bedroom papered in a fleur-de-lis stamp of apple-green and yellow. He thought the room better suited a group of dance-hall girls but didn't dare say so to Darcey. She had picked it especially to "brighten his dreams."

Blue's room was appropriately separated from Darcey's, on the floor above her chamber. Until they were married, Darcey wanted no one to think her relationship anything but respectable.

At night, he lay alone in his bed and thought of her just below him, a few stairs away. He listened to her singing in the dark, or sometimes he heard the splash of water as she bathed her naked body. He desired her, yearned to be next to her. But how could he marry such a magnificent woman when he was still so helpless to do a real man's work?

And then, too, was the other problem—the horror of his softness, his limpness since he was shot. The humiliation was more than he could bear. Darcey had been patient and loving. Surely she was wondering why there had been less talk of marriage since moving to Jackson. "It's all right, darlin'," she had said. "We'll marry when you are well. As long as we can be together and close, I'll wait for you. Do hurry, though."

Darcey was so caught up with running Higgins House, Blue sometimes wondered if she had time to think about anything else. The boarding house was an immediate success in Jackson. The rooms rented quickly, and additional boarders filled the tables. Darcey's reputation for good food kept her tables full. Despite the back-breaking work—ironing, washing, or baking past midnight—joy showed in her springy step and the swish of her skirts as she moved about the house.

Blue often sat in the parlor watching her, admiring the roundness of her form, the milky whiteness of her skin. He covered up his frustrating limited physical activity by keeping busy and being as useful as possible. He not only managed the business end of Higgins House, but also handled the books and payroll for the Sierra-Pacific Stagecoach Company. Blue did odd jobs around the place, looked after the pair of buggy horses and two wagon mules, worked in the garden, used his carpentry skills whenever possible, and drove the buckboard the short distance to market for supplies.

He was still unable to ride a horse, a fact that made him feel lost. A man without a horse was unnatural, unmanly. In fact, a man without a horse could hardly be called a man at all.

Harke continued to drive the stagecoach for Blue, and with the added

line from Sacramento to Jackson, he was able to keep in continual touch
with Blue, Darcey and Pearle. They had become his family.

After keeping company with the colorful swaggering stage drivers—the
heroes of stable boys, the fear of the meek—Harke developed a new
personality. He learned the gift of gab and was quick to discuss affairs
of state, love, philosophy, religion, the weather, any manner of trivia that
suited his customers.

Passengers often paid with items rather than a small coin, and so Harke
now looked like a true captain of his craft, wearing a nice slouch hat, a pair
of high-cuffed gloves, a fine pair of boots, a silk handkerchief. He often
wore patterned gauntlets and a creamy-white hat and prided himself that he
could "drive like hell," keep up with the most notorious drivers, and still
keep his sobriety and be courteous to the ladies. Harke often thought about
Jenna and wished she could see him dressed so fine and know how worldly
he had become.

Pearle loved Harke more than anything in her world. Between visits, she
wrote in her private journal, "My beloved brother, I'm rushing to grow up
now, because I want to be with you forever. Oh, Harke, I know I'm not too
pretty, but I pray you will wait for me."

🌱 🌱 🌱

Soon after Higgins House opened, Laveda Lovelady arrived on its
doorstep with a mountain of baggage—bulky trunks, hat boxes and
bundles, a rolled rug, and a brass lamp post. The coach driver struggled
through the door lugging an ornate Chinese chest and carved chair, a large
vase with paper ferns, followed by Blue carrying a bird cage with a pair of
stuffed lovebirds tipped over on their bills.

"Stage props," Laveda said, smiling sweetly, opening and closing her
large chocolate eyes fringed in feathery lashes.

The people of Higgins House stood on the porch gawking at the
new boarder directing the wagon's unloading. She flitted like a worried
hen gathering up her chicks exclaiming, "Oh, do be careful. Be gentle!
Watch that you don't scratch—don't drop the lamp! It is vital to my Moth
Dance."

Laveda shimmered in a rose taffeta dress with an apron pulled seductively to the back in a flounce of tiers. The white plumes of her fashionable hat bounced with every turn of her head. Darcey thought the hat a bit gaudy, worn only by a silly or capricious woman, but she had to admit that Laveda looked charming in it. It suited her grand entrance. Darcey also wondered about the massive chignon of dark brown hair coiling at the nape of her neck. Loosened, it would certainly fall below her knees . . . maybe clear to her ankles.

Tobias and Thaddeus pushed and bumped each other as they vied to haul Laveda Lovelady's possessions to the second floor, arguing like children over who would carry the bird cage. When the last of her luggage was taken to her room and the weary driver compensated for his extra work, Laveda stood in the hallway surrounded by her first audience in Jackson. She was obviously accustomed to center stage.

Rolling her soft eyes heavenward, sucking in her breath, and clasping her gloved hands to her breast, she looked like a painting of a saint—*perhaps the Virgin herself*, Darcey thought.

"My, my, how dear you all are to greet me this way. I feel so welcome, so at home already. Now, let me hear your names, and we'll get over our shyness right away. I know you're Darcey, the proprietress, and this is Pearle, your daughter. Now, who is this handsome man?" she said, cocking her head coyly.

"Blue. I'm, well, just . . . Blue."

Darcey took his arm possessively. "His name is Quigley—Quigley Gump."

"Quigley! What a divine name. My favorite uncle was named Quigley. It is a name of such character, such strength."

Blue blushed. "Y . . . yes," he stammered.

A small, knobby woman stepped forward. "I'm Sara Abrahms and these here are my two sons, Tobias and Thaddeus."

The two men smiled like schoolboys. "Take off your hat, Tobias," Thaddeus said, elbowing his twin.

"Oh, you boys are just what I'm looking for to help me build my Little Theater—that is, if you've got the time or if you're not working for someone else," Laveda said.

"The boys is helping me build an emporium here in Jackson," Mrs. Abrahms said with a slight coldness in her voice. "The boys won't be able to help you, I'm afraid." She tossed a warning glance at the two men as if to say, "Keep your mouths shut!"

It was not the first time Darcey had noted Sarah's controlling look at her sons. There was something suspicious about this family. The "boys," as Sarah called them, had gray hair sprouting at their temples and peppering their wiry beards. Where did they come from and where was the father? This little lady, hard as a sack of nails, ruled the twins and directed the building operation in town like a sergeant. She had told Darcey that her husband had accidentally shot himself in the camps at Gold Hill. The Abrahms had come west to farm like everyone else, but got the gold fever. "We done right well with the boys working alongside their papa, but none of us is cut out for mining."

Darcey had learned long ago to keep her nose out of other people's business, especially in the mining camps. Many people went by first names only, untraceable names, nicknames. In a society where gold was a man's best friend, names didn't matter much, nor did a man's past. One learned not to be curious. Still, Darcey wondered about the Abrahms and the secrecy around the emporium.

Darcey had also noticed that Mrs. Abrahms had hired many Chinese to construct the building, and suspected she was paying them low wages.

When Darcey asked about them, Sarah Abrahms explained, "Them Chinese never eat when they work. It's the way they was made, ya see. Any food but rice don't set well in their stomachs, ya see. Only one bowl of rice a day is all they need. They was made different from white people. They don't even sweat like regular people. Why, they can even see in the dark . . . like a cat, ya see. But they work harder than any other human and they keep to theirselves."

Darcey turned her attention away from Sarah Abrahms and looked hard at Laveda.

This lady is so stuffed with airs she's about to burst her buttons. Inside her boots, she's got bunions same as the rest of us. But she is a pretty one,

*appealing, too. Blue is already acting like he's got a mouthful of pudding he
can't swallow. And he's grinning all lop-sided like Tobias and Thaddeus.*

Laveda sighed. "Your house is lovely, Miss Higgins. Oh, it's all so
charming. I tell you, finding a home like this after all my travels is a joy,
simply a joy. I can't tell you how grateful I was to hear you had room for
me."

She ambled into the parlor and cast an admiring glance around the room.
"You would never believe some of the horrid roadside inns and hotels Lola
and Sue and I have inhabited on our shows throughout California. Of
course, it goes without saying how comical some of our stages have been.

"Living on the road is so dreadful. I love being in a place of permanence.
I just couldn't face staying in the hotel here in Jackson. It suited my
accompanist, but not me. As soon as I get settled and establish my classes,
I'll build a quaint little cottage and studio for myself."

Darcey, followed by a parade of the household, showed Laveda the rest
of the place—the bathing room off the kitchen, the outside laundry area,
and the gardens. She explained that a Chinese family did all their linens and
how the boardinghouse functioned.

While they chatted, Darcey said to herself, *she's another mysterious
one, naming herself Laveda Lovelady, waltzing in here like she was Lola
Montez, herself, claiming she's been traveling around with the famous
dancer and even performing at the American Theater in San Francisco
with Lotta Crabtree and Lola and Susan Johnson!*

"Miss Higgins—I assume it's Miss since I didn't see a ring—I'm simply
dying of thirst and would be most obliged for a cup of tea or a lemonade.
But first, I would like to change out of these dreadful traveling clothes.
Maybe Mr. Quigley Gump could help me upstairs with my satchel."

"I'll do it," Tobias said, grabbing the bag.

"That's not fair!" Thaddeus said, tugging at the satchel. "She asked
me!"

"Stop it, boys! Go on, Tobias," Sarah said. She turned to Laveda. "My
boys aren't too bright. They mean well, though."

"Don't you fret, Mrs. Abrahms. They're sweet, and I love the attention."
Laveda flounced up the stairs in a swish of crisp taffeta and a swirl of

bobbing plumes, leaving Darcey, Blue, and Pearle in her wake.

🦋 🦋 🦋

Laveda Lovelady was an immediate sensation in Jackson, a whirlwind of gossip among the ladies, the object of sly winks by the men. She threw herself into a frenzy of activity, contracting workers to build her Little Theater, a small, wooden structure with a stage and wooden benches. She announced her arrival in the Jackson newspaper as a great event. She solicited pupils to learn singing, dancing, and elocution and set herself up at the hotel for performances.

The warm, dry weather allowed her to perform on a wooden platform next to the side porch. By placing it against the stairs, she could incorporate a dramatic entrance and exit and flutter up and down the stairs in her chiffon-draped arms, which moved like moth wings.

The Jackson newspaper reported:

> Miss Laveda Lovelady's performance on opening night of "When Wings Flutter Heavenward," was a sensation unlike any stage debut before seen in our fine town. The Moth Dance was as spectacular as the famous Spider Dance of Lola Montez. Jackson is fortunate to herald the graceful gifts of a rare beauty. Daughter of a Hungarian nobleman and raised in an atmosphere of European royalty, Miss Lovelady is a true courtesan. She has played the world stages and since coming to America, has not only befriended Lola Montez and her protégé, Lotta Crabtree, but just completed a tour of the California mining towns singing and dancing her way into the hearts of America. She has lived and entertained with the San Francisco Bohemians and now plans to live in Jackson between tours. Although her singing voice was perhaps not as controlled in the higher ranges, she, none the less, sang with such emotion on "How Should I Leave Thee?" and "Where the Quinnebaugh Flows," that there was not a dry eye in the audience.

Everyone in Jackson had turned out for her opening night. Laveda shocked the people of the town, especially the ladies, by wearing long, pink tights over which floated dusty blue chiffon tiers layered and split, revealing her thighs as she danced.

Even more spectacular was her hair, crowned in a wreath of flowers, loose and falling in a river of brown crimped waves down to her calves. She moved her head to let the massive hair undulate like a river, cascade over her breasts, and drape in coils around her arms like snakes.

The finale of her performance was a huge success. She portrayed a moth, fluttering too close to the stage lamp, singeing her wings. Unable to fly and suffering pain, the moth began to slowly die. Laveda looked up at the sky with round, pleading eyes before crumpling in a heap of supposedly burned, dusty blue chiffon wings.

The townspeople shouted and applauded. Miners jumped to their feet and threw gold coins and Mexican dollars onto the stage. While the women clapped and smiled mildly and pulled their dull shawls around their shoulders, the men flushed and sweated and avoided the sideways glances of their wives.

Blue had been among the first on his feet throwing coins and shouting, "Bravo," until he caught Darcey's cold stare.

Unlike the other women, Darcey did not object to Laveda's daring costume, nor to her exciting performance. She did, however, object to her constant fluttering and cooing around Blue. Everything he said seemed to delight her and she broke into bell tones of laughter. As his confidence grew, Blue appeared to work at witty remarks and harmless teasing that he knew would please Laveda.

Darcey listened to her ringing laughter throughout the house, especially in the upstairs hallway whenever Laveda happened to encounter Blue coming or going, which happened more often than could be attributed to coincidence.

Once, as Darcey was about to carry fresh towels upstairs, she overheard Laveda ask Blue to open her stuck window, and Blue replied, "With them pretty filly eyes pleadin' at me, I can't say no."

The twins, as well, seemed to think they were comedians. Laveda acted as if she appreciated their jostling for attention, their buffoonery and childish ways.

While Higgins House resounded with Laveda's theatrics, Gilmore

Jameson, the piano player, was seldom around. Darcey had heard the rumor that it was not respectable to have a piano player at the boardinghouse.

The women frowned on him and his profession and thought it disgraceful to have his influence in a house where a young girl was growing up. A man like that would surely bring the sins of the saloon, card playing, and drink into the home and possibly taint the child and destroy the dignity of the place.

Darcey paid no attention. She liked the young, fair-haired, mild-mannered Mr. Jameson and even bought a piano for the parlor. Many evenings after dinner, before Laveda had arrived, Darcey sang her Irish songs, accompanied by Mr. Jameson. Blue played his fiddle, and the boarders sang and sometimes danced. Darcey and Pearle entertained everyone with a duet, "Whistle, Daughter, Whistle," and Blue made everyone laugh singing in his growly voice,

> *"Had a dog and his name was Blue,*
> *Bet you a dollar, he's a rounder too.*
> *Every night just about dark,*
> *Blue goes out and begins to bark . . ."*

Higgins House bubbled over like a happy pot of blackberry jam. Darcey had set the tone for the kind of establishment she wanted. The conventional ladies of the town be damned.

Pearle, enchanted with Gilmore Jameson's quick fingers moving up and down the keyboard, begged him to teach her how to play, how to read the notes and play popular songs. He spent time with her, encouraging her, bringing into her life a new excitement—the wonder of sound and harmony.

All the joy or sadness she had expressed with words now assumed another form of escape from inside of her. Whenever Pearle was not in school or doing her chore of serving meals at the boarding house, she patiently learned simple pieces and quietly picked out melodies on the keyboard to fit her poems.

Still small as a waif, always a little pale, timid, and retiring, she created within herself a world of great joy. Her deep inner beauty poured out of her eyes and caught people off-guard. When engaged in conversation, she listened so intently and looked so directly into their eyes that, without effort, people would soon fall under a spell of peace and confidence. Pearle saw the world in a special way. Beauty surrounded her thoughts, and when she limped about in her heavy, built-up shoe, she seemed to wear that beauty around her shoulders.

Even Harke had noticed her quiet dignity and felt touched by the deep well of her spirit. He enjoyed her company, her sweetness. "Come, little sister, read me one of your stories, or a poem," he would say. But lately, it was harder to say "little sister." Pearle was no longer a child but an intelligent and gentle young lady. In her quiet way, she held a powerful place in the world.

🍃 🍃 🍃

With Laveda's arrival, Darcey lost some control over the atmosphere of the boarding house. Laveda, without trying, simply dominated the establishment. Her entrances and exits, her tinkling laughter and easy amusement, her charming conversation, wit, and tales of life in Europe enchanted everyone.

She entertained in the evenings, singing alongside Darcey. She taught the boarders "ditties" she had learned in England and in the mining camps, and even charmed the cook into making *Magyar Gulyas*, Hungarian goulash, and Seven Chieftain Tokany. "It's really just stew with sour cream, my dears, but simply divine," she said.

"She eats like a bird," Darcey complained to Blue as the two of them drove the buckboard to town for supplies. "Why, she even told me meat made a woman *coarse*; it's food for men, not women, she says. I'm tired of her directing the kitchen to make more rice and noodles for her special digestion."

"Well, I suspect she hasn't much room in that little stomach of hers." Blue regretted having made the remark. It was a confession that he'd noted Laveda's superb hourglass figure.

"She's laced-in like a trussed turkey. No wonder she can't swallow!" Darcey retorted.

"Uh-huh," Blue said, trying not to show his amusement at Darcey's fussing.

"And if you look closely, she's got a slight mustache. It really spoils her looks, don't you think?"

"Didn't notice." Blue shook the reins to show indifference, thinking, *I believe my girl, here, is a might jealous.*

"She don't ring true, Blue. Something funny about a woman who don't give her real name. Laveda Lovelady! Be honest, Blue, don't you think she's hiding something?"

"Not much in them pink tights," he snickered.

"Be serious. She's about as Hungarian as . . . as these mules," Darcey said, gesturing at the animals pulling the wagon.

"Uh-huh," Blue mumbled.

"I can tell you're taken with her."

"Me? No, I ain't. What gives you that notion?" Blue said, acting a bit offended.

"I don't know. You've changed somehow."

"How?"

"You comb your hair different, your beard is shorter. You smile a lot in a kind of sappy way, like Tobias and Thaddeus. And you're singing louder than before, stomping your heels and acting like you're ready to break into a jig."

"Well, maybe I am about to. The fact is, I'm better these days, kind of like I could do a bit of dancin' again."

They rode along in silence, but Blue smiled all the way to the store.

On their return, they passed the Abrahms' nearly completed building, the "emporium," as Sarah had called it, and stopped to watch some workmen carry in a large oblong mirror.

"Hold on, Blue. I want to see what's being unloaded into that emporium. That mirror doesn't make any sense at all. It looks like a saloon mirror."

As they watched, the men unloaded a piano, several iron and brass beds, some velvet sofas, and a few gaming tables.

"Well, there you have it, Blue. I've never seen the inside of one of these ill-repute places, but I've just seen the outside of one. Mrs. Abrahms isn't building a store at all. She's building another saloon, or gaming hall—with extra female services. I know it, Blue! She's no farmer's wife at all. I bet she's called Madam Sarah Abrahms. Just imagine, Blue, I've got someone *under my roof* who deals in . . . well, in all kinds of sin. That's her emporium!" Darcey set her lips tight and let a scowl deepen the line between her eyes. Blue put his arm around her.

"Now, Darcey, she's minding her own business and causing no trouble at all. She don't look like a woman of the evening, but a nice older lady with two sons. Maybe you're a-jumpin' to conclusions," Blue said, trying to console her.

"I swear, Blue, nobody is who they say they are anymore. Next you'll be telling me you run with Murietta and his outlaws. I can't trust anybody."

"You can trust me," he said, giving Darcey a squeeze.

"Can I, Blue? You haven't said anything about getting married since we moved to Jackson. Things haven't changed between us, have they?"

Blue tensed. "It was you who didn't want to get married until you was settled here. You've been busy with the boarding house, Darcey. I've been a-workin' on your books and my business a-tryin' to expand the lines, a-tryin' to keep up with the Wells Fargo Stage Company. The timing's been all wrong," he said, looking straight ahead.

"We're still sweethearts, aren't we, Blue?"

"Yep, I guess so," he said, but he could not hide the doubt and hesitation in his answer. He loved Darcey and longed to hold her in his arms, in his bed. He had dreamed often of seeing her next to him, her red hair spread out on the pillow or hanging loosely over her bare shoulders, feeling her naked breasts against his body, her fleshy legs wrapped around him. Sometimes he exchanged Laveda for Darcey, but quickly returned to Darcey's familiar image.

🍃 🍃 🍃

One night when Darcey turned out the lamp, she lay on her bed without drawing the sheet over her. The summer night was warm, and outside her window the crickets thrummed their love songs. The ceiling above her creaked as Blue walked across the floor and sat on the bed. She listened to the thud as one boot dropped and then the other. Darcey listened to the crickets' insistent throbbing song and an annoying moth battering blindly against the walls until she fell asleep.

Dawn eased away the night and brought with it a soft, persistent rain. Darcey had slept fitfully and awakened with the sheet twisted uncomfortably around her body. It was too early to start the coffee and too late to sleep soundly. She threw off the covers and lay on her back, listening to the sound of raindrops tapping on the porch. She passed her hands over her fleshy breasts, soft naked belly and thighs.

Above her, Blue coughed and rolled over on noisy springs.

Darcey smiled. *The old dear. It just isn't normal him being there and me being here.* Impulsively, she got out of bed, and without putting on a robe or slippers, she quietly tiptoed up the stairs and slipped into Blue's room. The rain pattered on the roof and dripped off the eaves outside the window, enclosing the room like a cozy cocoon.

Blue lay under the rumpled blankets on his side, his hair like thatch matting on the pillow. His bird-nest beard tucked under his chin. A low snore, more like a lion's purr, rumbled contentedly from his den of covers as he dozed.

Darcey took the side of the bed with the most room and crawled under the sheet, tucking up behind him until she fit snugly like a puzzle piece or a broken pottery shard placed for mending.

"Move over, Blue, you're taking all the room," Darcey whispered close to his hear.

Blue's eyes popped open, but he didn't move. He waited, listening, questioning his fuzzy senses. It was unmistakable—the pressure along his back and curving around his buttocks and into the back of his knees.

"Move over, Blue."

Without turning, Blue reached back with one arm to feel what he thought to be a body. "Darcey?"

"Good morning, Lovey. I thought you'd like some company," she said in a soft, throaty voice. "Were you expecting someone else?"

Blue turned over, facing the woman in his bed, looming large and soft and smelling so sweet. He put his arms around her and held her close. Neither spoke, but together they rocked in the joyful comfort of loving one another.

"This feels just right, Darcey," Blue said at last.

"I know, Blue. It's nice."

"Mighty nice . . . like it's supposed to be this way."

"I agree."

"I ain't too old for you?"

"No! You're not mad at me for coming to you this way, are you?" Darcey asked.

"No! I wanted this for the longest time."

"Me, too. But I couldn't wait forever, you know."

"I asked you once before to come with me, if you remember, and you said no. I wasn't sure after that. And then the shooting and all . . ."

"Hush! No more excuses. The fact is you're a stubborn old goat who needs a little prodding."

"I need a little proddin', all right!"

The two of them began to giggle like children, stifling their snorts in the bed covers. Blue did not know when the shaking from laughter turned into the stirrings he'd thought were gone forever. He slipped into Darcey— complete, powerful, grateful.

"Darcey, if we don't do something about this, we'll be sinning on a regular basis, maybe two or three times a day. There won't be no proprietress around to manage the place. What say we get married?"

"And you can move down into my room. Pearle is nearly fourteen. She can move upstairs into this room and use the spare room off the kitchen if we have paying guests."

"When?" Blue asked, raising up on his elbow and smiling broadly at Darcey.

"As soon as I can bake a white cake and call a preacher. How about next Sunday?" Darcey said, smoothing Blue's pointy hair.

Blue pulled Darcey closer to him. "This proddin' ain't half bad," he said, squeezing Darcey's ample waist.

Darcey laughed happily as she climbed out of bed. Her wiry red hair spoked out like Medusa's snakes. Blue thought she was magnificent.

"I could stay here all morning just lying next to you and listening to the rain . . . and proddin'." She kissed his forehead. "I've got to get coffee and biscuits started. See you at breakfast, darlin'." She shut the door quietly.

Blue lay on his back with his hands behind his head. "Darlin'." It sounded nice. Blue grinned. "Darlin'," he said aloud. "I'll be darned. No one's ever call me that before, not even my mother. She called me Quigley."

THIRTEEN

J enna and Señor Faustino sat on their horses in a steady spring rain surveying the carnage. Before them, hundreds of JD branded cattle lay dead, many of the cows about to calve. Some animals died quickly from a gunshot; others, only wounded, died in agony; and still others, thrown to the ground with a *reata* looped around their feet, were left with broken limbs to die. Jenna knew the way the *vaqueros* worked. The butchery became a game under the Archuletas' direction. The sight of the senseless slaughter sickened her.

"This is Enrique's revenge, his way of punishing me," Jenna said, holding back her angry tears. "He is a monster, Señor Faustino, and I don't know how to stop him. I'm glad Doña Juana is not alive to see this horrible massacre, this barbarism."

"I'm sorry, Señorita. I don't know how to stop him either. It isn't certain he did it, unless he used our own *vaqueros* against us. Otherwise, how could he come onto the property, fire hundreds of shots, and ride away without our men knowing about it?"

Jenna sighed. She was tired of the entire Archuleta family, their land, their customs, their greed. She wished she did not own Rancho San Gabriel.

She had gone to Monterey and talked to Reginald Potter explaining her plight. He merely shook his head and said her circumstances were indeed sad. His best suggestion was to hire a lawyer to bring the matter to the attention of the courts. He would be glad to handle her case, but it would take considerable money and time.

Jenna knew that the Mexican way of settling disputes, their loyalty to each other, their suspicion of anything American, made his suggestion a poor one. Mr. Potter reminded Jenna that she still owed thousands of dollars in unpaid taxes, a matter that would have to be settled before proceeding. He suggested he might be able to help her in this question of back taxes—for a percentage of the amount saved, of course. Perhaps she could sell the land . . . he had friends.

"And the cattle? Where would they graze? How would they find water?" Jenna had asked. She did not like or trust Reginald Potter. He must think her a fool.

"Sell the cattle, dear child. I might be able to take them off your hands as well. We could negotiate a fair price. Think about it," Mr. Potter had said, all the while rolling a pencil between his moist, white fingers.

Jenna considered Mr. Potter's proposition. If she sold everything—the land, the cattle—she could leave Rancho San Gabriel forever. She could let Enrique take it all. Or she could fight for it, outsmart him somehow, beat him at his own game.

By the time of spring calf branding, it was clear her herds had diminished severely. Enrique had simply helped himself, driving her cattle onto his land.

Jenna knew her role as doña of Rancho San Gabriel was considered a farce among the Archuletas. Nevertheless, the rancho appeared to run smoothly. The Archuletas had kept the tradition of the rodeo, the fandangos and fiestas, races, bull, bear, and cockfights, which her *vaqueros* attended. But Señor Faustino's suspicions about the *vaqueros* were right. She did not have their loyalty. They did not like working for a *gringo*, especially a woman.

The proof of their disdain came one afternoon as Jenna and Luisa were driving back from San Jose. Two of the rancho's men galloped up alongside of her—one on either side of the buggy. Their brazenness, flushed faces, and loud voices made it clear they had been spending the afternoon with a bottle of tequila.

"*Buenos dias, Señorita*," one said, leering at Jenna.

"Good afternoon," Jenna replied with a cold, distant voice like Doña Juana used with the *vaqueros*.

"Have you been shopping for sweet treats, señorita?" the other asked, taking hold of the horse's bridle.

"Please let go and move away. You're making the horses nervous," Jenna commanded.

Instead of moving away, the other *vaquero* took hold of the bridle of the other horse. "Did you buy some whiskey for us?" he slurred. The drunken man swayed in the saddle.

"Go away!" Jenna said firmly.

"No whiskey? Did you buy some sweet treats and you are hiding them under your skirt?" The men laughed at the joke. "We hear you carry sweet treats between your legs, Señorita."

Jenna pulled the reins, stopping quickly. Without hesitation, she stood up, lashed the buggy whip at one and then the other, snapping the stinging whip at their necks and faces as hard as she could. Her horses reared, knocking one of the men off his horse into the dirt. The other man fell back laughing at his friend as Jenna rode off quickly.

It was clear that while the *vaqueros* lived at her ranch, they were still loyal to Enrique. Jenna was placed in a precarious position. If the hands decided to desert her, she would have difficulty replacing them.

🌿 🌿 🌿

There had been little rainfall for the past two years. The grass turned to straw early, a dangerous dry tinder making the ranchers nervous. A spark and a hot wind could destroy thousands of acres quickly.

One night, Jenna awakened abruptly from a sound sleep as though hands had shaken her. She sat up in foggy confusion.

"Papa? Is that you, Papa?" The feeling of Israel faded quickly from her consciousness, and she sat in the darkness feeling oddly frightened.

Awake now, her nostrils picked up the distinct smell of burning grass. Jenna ran to her window and opened the shutters. Smoke hovered in white, ghostly streamers in the black sky. She ran to the front of the house. Before her was the sight she had always feared. Fire! All along the horizon to the south and west was a line of flames licking the night. In places, a long tongue of flame shot high into the sky as a lone manzanita ignited. Red sparks hurled into the air, blowing into dry spots and starting new fires.

Moving quickly and shouting, "*Socorro! Socorro!*" Jenna ran to awaken Señor Faustino and his family, then to Ygnacio, Marta, and Luisa. She pounded on Padre Ortega's door. "Padre! Padre! Wake up! Fire! The land is on fire."

The padre, sleeping soundly, did not respond. Jenna ran around the outside window and banged on the shutters. Padre Ortega unhooked the latch. "What is it, child? Are you ill?"

"Fire! You must hurry. Ygnacio is bringing the wagons. Come!"

In moments, the rancho erupted into a panic with people running in all directions, their arms overflowing with belongings they considered precious. Jenna rushed into the *sala* and unlocked the chest where Doña Juana kept her box of gold and silver coins, some precious jewels, and a few worthless promissory notes to her father. Jenna tucked it under her arm and ran into the courtyard.

"Set the horses loose!" Jenna shouted. "Louisa, awaken all the Indians, and grab your cat. Marta, don't bother with any more of my clothes. Take care of your own things. Señor Faustino, warn the *vaqueros* in their quarters. We need them to fire a path around the house."

"They've gone, Señorita."

"What?"

"*Los hombres salieron.* I'm afraid they have gone over to Enrique's and the fire is their farewell. They're trying to burn you out, Señorita. We can do nothing except hope the wind changes. This fire is going to destroy thousands of acres—precious grazing land, precious food for the animals. It is moving fast, coming this way, toward the house. A line of fire has erupted below the eastern hills. We are quickly becoming surrounded, trapped. We must hurry! The best thing is to save only your most valuable things. I'll load the wagons. Ygnacio will load the buggy with a few items. We must move out quickly now, away from the smoke."

"Yes, yes, of course. First, I must get Honey and Solana."

"I have tied Solana to the back of the wagon. Honey, well, she is in the range with the cattle. Hurry now, Señorita! The cook, and some of the Indian women and children are waiting in the wagons."

Already, the fire wind was spiraling across the meadow, a scorching dragon's breath sparking other fires. Devil flames danced like madmen, open-mouthed, frenzied. The sky glowed red in the south like an inferno.

"Satan's Hell!" the padre shouted. "Can't you see? It's Lucifer leading a revolt of the angels!" He climbed into the wagon carrying his altar cloth, wine, chalice, and a pair of silver candlesticks. "We'll all go north to the mission, a safe haven. Surely the fire won't reach that far. Maybe it's time for me to leave your gracious home, Señorita Daggett."

"It will be stopped on the west by the river," Jenna shouted above the crying babies, yanked so unforgivably from their cozy beds. "I'm certain Enrique has built a fire barricade in front of the Archuletas' section. This fire was no accident. Oh, God forbid the animals get trapped!"

The wagons rolled out of the rancho past the orchards and fields, the rows of corn, the Indians' homes. They pulled onto the road leading to San Jose, where they met other ranchers, their families, and workers fleeing the frightening fire. Jenna looked back at the adobe, so vulnerable, and wondered if it would still be standing when she returned. She clutched the things she valued most—Martha Jane's shell box and Israel's harmonica and old leather hat.

A small, frightened rabbit hopped under a manzanita bush to hide from the monstrous wagons. Jenna wondered where it would hide when the fire roared across the land.

Columns of smoke slanted across the coral sky. Underbellies of boiling clouds glowed a sickening yellow-green, the color of bile.

Jenna held her breath as the cornfields burst into crackling fire. Flaming stalks and red sparks shot in all directions driven by the erratic fire wind. Suddenly, through burning, watery eyes she saw a band of people silhouetted against the wall of flames, running and stumbling.

"Wait! There are people trying to get away. They'll never outrun this fire! We've got to go back for them. They'll be burned alive," Jenna shouted above the din of the frightened horses and wailing children. "Stop, Señor Faustino!"

"The fire is moving too fast, Señorita. We haven't time. We must save ourselves."

"*Please*, Señor Faustino. Stop and wait for them," she pleaded, pulling at the reins.

"Our wagon is full. We have no room for them," he said, struggling to keep control of the horses.

"Stop at once or I'll jump out!" Jenna shouted and stood up precariously.

Señor Faustino pulled the reins of the horses, who tossed their heads and snorted with fear.

"Help me wave down other wagons. They can take some of our people with them."

"I'll go back with you, Señorita Daggett," Padre Ortega said. "I've been in the fight with *El Diablo* my whole life. The coward is showing himself to me, to all of us true to the faith. I speak with God's authority. I will shout the Apostolic Creed in his face!" He shook a heavy candlestick above his head, "*Vayase!*"

The women and children got out of the wagon and one by one found a place with someone else—a *carreta*, wagon, or buggy. Solana carried three children easily.

Jenna, Señor Faustino, and Padre Ortega turned back into the wall of thick black smoke and blowing cinders.

They came upon the small group of Indians Jenna had seen through the clouds of smoke, a family whom Jenna recognized as part of the rancho. The father and mother each carried a small child. The head of one of the infants wobbled on its tiny neck like a lifeless baby bird. Other children of various ages stumbled behind the adults, their hair and naked bodies gray with ash. One child pulled a bleating mother goat, blackened with soot, its full udder swinging with milk.

Once in the wagon, the Indians coughed and caught their breath. They had been trapped by the fickle, shifting, thick smoke, which felled one child. The small boy lay dead across his mother's lap, a fledgling child who would never fly. None of them spoke, but grief clawed through their eyes. Jenna's eyes stung with angry tears. Enrique was a murderer. This senseless disaster was his fault, and she hoped he would burn in Hell for it.

Father Ortega mumbled his prayers over the dead boy, hoping the Lord would receive the heathen child out of Purgatory into Heaven even though he knew it wasn't possible. Sometimes he, himself, wondered where the souls of innocents really resided. Limbo was such a nowhere place.

Could he remember the prayers to get a heathen child out of Purgatory, one who came from a family of heathens who really didn't understand the Catholic faith? After all, they were children, too, and insisted on making the Virgin Mother into a corn doll with black corn eyes.

🌿 🌿 🌿

The fire, whipped by the fickle wind, first in one direction, then the other, consumed everything in its path. After three days, the wind reversed direction, the fire turned back on itself and burned out, leaving the blackened earth smoldering and smoking as far as the eye could see. Thousands of acres had burned, taking with it the fine old adobe that Doña Juana had fought so hard to protect.

Jenna's worst fears for many of the animals came true. Frightened and confused cattle had moved up against squatter's fences unable to find a retreat. Their charred bodies were found crowded against fallen and tangled barbed wire. Jenna never found her beloved Honey.

Those animals that had moved to the south were safe, but now faced starvation. There were too many left to graze on the scant grass. Jenna was desperate. Enrique had defeated her.

"Señor Faustino, I don't know what to do except sell the cattle quickly, or maybe drive them toward the coast. I've got to think. I've got to salvage something."

That night, lying in the dark room of San Jose Hotel, Jenna cried bitterly into the pillow. Her rage against Enrique tore at her insides like a fierce animal. She felt like the tied bear at the rodeo fighting the bull, only this time, the bull was not tied and was free to gouge, to rip, tear, to destroy like all the Archuletas, like the lawless land.

Such a waste! That poor child. All those animals!

Suddenly, Jenna had an idea. She jumped out of bed and looked at the first light of the morning. She knew one person who might be of use to her—Danny McDaniels. He dealt in commerce and shipping. At least that's what he had said.

By morning, Jenna was packed and on the stage to San Francisco.

🌿 🌿 🌿

The doña had never taken Jenna to San Francisco. "It is a vulgar place," she had said. "There are few women of respect, I hear. Even the women who speak my tongue are unchaperoned. Countless Chilean women have come in boatloads, as well as female Chinese slaves with no morals at all. Do you know, Jenna, no one attends church or holds mass or speaks with our dear saints? And women can actually divorce their husbands! They do it on a whim with no conscience at all. It is shameless, I tell you! Everyone is openly hostile to the Mexicans, to all foreigners. Erin tells me there are gangs of outlaws who call themselves The Hounds who murder for a pocketful of coins, and no one, not even the authorities, stop them. It is a town of sin and corruption, violence, earthquakes, and disease. No! I will never set foot in San Francisco! It is a curse—God's punishment to the hateful *Yanqui*!"

Jenna was certain the doña was speaking of the early days, because now, from the stagecoach window, she saw an exciting town with stone and brick buildings, some as high as five stories. There were churches, hotels, theaters, restaurants, office buildings, and a fine courthouse. In the square, Jenna saw handsome coaches in black and gold, an omnibus, prancing horses, gentlemen wearing eastern clothes, and women in daring fashions Jenna had never seen except in magazines.

She had heard of young women wearing bloomers and short skirts, but the idea was just too ridiculous to be true. But here in San Francisco, the women wearing the peculiar full pants, and "hats" instead of bonnets, walked confidently on the street—alone or on the arm of a companion. No one seemed impressed. Everyone was too busy going somewhere, not sauntering, as in quiet Monterey. And the women, especially, moved with a freedom and surety that Jenna liked. They walked as though they knew they were a rare sight in San Francisco. They knew they were desirable, whether common or beautiful. Married or unmarried, the women commanded respect.

"I will buy some bloomers immediately," Jenna said to herself.

In spite of the dryness of the late summer, the streets held pockets of deep mud, quagmires left over from the rainy season. Some streets and walkways were planked with wood; others were cluttered with stepping stones of wooden crates, barrels, old stoves, broken wagons, and garbage. Although many surrounding hills were sweet with wild, ripe strawberries, the town smelled of fish and manure, stagnant marshes, oil and smoke from the ships.

As Jenna checked into the Saint Francis Hotel, beautiful and glittering in polished brass and crystal, she saw a woman walk by wearing a Turkish costume of yellow bloomers, a black tunic with gold braid, and an outlandish red turban. Jenna couldn't help staring. Other women, many speaking French, wore elegant dresses with such long trains trailing behind that one had to wait until they passed in order not to step on the hems. Jenna wondered how the women managed in the deep mud that was everywhere.

In time, Jenna learned that these tasteful, showy women were high-priced companions for an evening, often skilled gamblers, bright conversationalists, full of wit, unafraid to show themselves publicly or to speak their minds. By contrast, it was easy to pick out the wives of the minister, doctor, the professional man, if not by their more conservative dress, then by their straight backs and straight noses.

Jenna was surprised by the large number of Chinese filling the streets, scurrying about in sandals, carrying bundles. In their single braids and Chinese coats, they walked apart from the rest of society, quietly and quickly delivering or picking up laundry, then returning to Washerwoman Pond, where they scrubbed and boiled the shirts, starched and ironed in the open air. Few outsiders bothered to add up the endless coins—too heavy for pockets, too numerous for pouches—which grew into small, hidden Chinese fortunes.

Jenna's room in the Saint Francis was a surprise. The furnishings were adequate, the mattresses of good quality, and the sheets on the bed a rare comfort. The walls and ceilings, however, were made of stretched canvas, and Jenna knew she would be certain to share the intimate sounds of restless, snoring guests in the next room.

From her window, she could see the glittering bay dotted with ships, the surrounding hills, and parts of the city. There was something unique about San Francisco—an energy, a hot-temperedness, and still a geniality. It was a pot ready to boil over, a town in a hurry to grow up, get rich, restore order, do good works, enjoy culture, test convention—a town impatient with itself. Jenna immediately fell in love with the place, sure that, at least for a time, her destiny was unavoidably tied up in its magic.

🍐 🍐 🍐

San Francisco was now a metropolitan city that had grown in only five years from an uninviting, unpopulated village of mud huts and tents to a place where waterfront property had soared from $27 to $10,000 per lot. The handsome citizens crowded fashionable eating houses, theaters, fine restaurants, and fancy stores. The newly rich, still rough around the edges of refinement, frequented gambling houses and saloons to play billiards, tenpins, or faro. Though Lady Luck was fickle, San Franciscans only laughed and placed their last pouch of gold on the gaming table.

The year before Jenna arrived, the drought had seriously hurt the miners in the Sierras. Insufficient rain made it impossible to wash out the gold in the mines and streams, making mining unprofitable. Many men had given up the surface mining and had come to San Francisco with other skills and desperate need for work. They swelled the population to nearly sixty thousand inhabitants, mostly young, energetic men.

As Jenna looked out over the city, she could see the Wells Fargo Building, the handsomest building in sight, and wondered if Danny had his office there.

She wondered where he was at that very moment and what he was doing. She imagined a chance encounter on the street and her casual greeting, then shifted the scene to a rider finding her alone walking on the sea-grass dunes. She had often relived Danny's aggressive kiss in Monterey and sometimes dared to imagine more until her heart beat fast and she chided herself for being foolish.

"Danny McDaniels is out there somewhere," she whispered, "and tomorrow I'll begin inquiries. There should be no problem finding a man in shipping and commerce. I'll go to the Custom House on the wharf. If they can't tell me where he is, I'm certain any single woman, any saloon keeper, any Irishman, anyone who likes rousing good fun, will know the whereabouts of Danny McDaniels."

Jenna smiled to herself. Tomorrow, she would don her most stunning outfit and pay him a call. She would tip up her chin just a bit and walk like the French ladies. After all, she had a business proposition to make and must look like a woman who knew what she wanted.

Early the next morning, Jenna dressed in a handsome tan and copper taffeta striped dress that complemented her cluster of light brown curls. She carefully chose a turquoise jacket and tan hat with a wide turquoise ribbon that wound around its crown and fluttered behind like a pair of birds. Aquamarine earrings matched her eyes, open wide to the excitement of San Francisco and the prospect of seeing Danny.

In the hotel dining room, she ate a fresh crisp French roll and drank a foamy cup of coffee with steamed milk for breakfast, then asked for directions to the Customs House.

The coastal clouds had burned off early, leaving the city under a sparkling blue sky. Against the advice of the desk clerk, she decided to walk.

"Watch where you step, Madam. There is a great deal of construction going on and the streets are uneven."

"Thank you," Jenna said, smiling. She had known about the cluttered, muddy streets and wore comfortable boots.

The day was fine and Jenna high-spirited as she headed for the wharf. Pounding hammers and whining saws, whistling workmen, and the clip-clop of horses created a symphony of sound. A laugh, a song, a shout, a baby's cry floated out from open windows. Dogs barked at passing freight wagons with wobbly wheels, and a practicing soprano and a struggling violinist shattered the crystal air.

Jenna crossed to the old square where a crowd stood silent. Suddenly, two pistol shots startled a rooftop of seagulls, which scattered like angels above a body lying on the ground. Jenna moved into the crowd. The spectators around her shifted and whispered uneasily at the death of a man who had agreed to a duel, agreed to live or die on a particular sunny San Francisco morning.

"Well, that's that," a young whiskered man said to his friend. "The French haven't got no sense of humor. He wasn't the only man making comments in the bathhouse about the Frenchman's wife. Lots of men knew her as Rosette, not Paulette, the wife of a French dignitary. Why, I heard about her in Nevada City three years ago. They said she had the sweetest red rose tattooed on the sweetest bum a man ever seen. It was a work of art, folks said. Can't see why a man would get so hot under the collar about art."

Jenna watched in horror as some bystanders carried a young man's body away. Only moments ago he stood tall, full of future, and in a split second, millions of lives resounded and changed course. When a single man falls, everyone vibrates.

Jenna turned and hurried toward the Customs House, picking her way through debris, empty barrels and boxes, rotting planks, and foul-smelling heaps.

"Yes, I know Danny McDaniels," the custom official said. "Everyone about town knows him. If he's not in his office in the Wells Fargo Building, he's at Foley's with his Irish boys. You'll find him."

Jenna took a horse-drawn omnibus back up the hill to the Wells Fargo Building. She wanted time to compose herself before meeting the man she'd thought about since she was a very young girl. She had kept the periwinkle shell she'd picked up on the beach that wild morning in Monterey, and had placed it in her shell box among her treasures. Jenna often pressed the small periwinkle to her lips, recalling Danny McDaniel's kiss. It was smooth and warm, a symbol of something yet to be discovered.

The office of *McDaniels, Murry and Hemeon—Commercial Enterprises,* was on the third floor. Jenna walked nervously into an outer waiting room and announced herself to the clerk. The young man opened the door and ushered Jenna into Danny McDaniels' office. She straightened her shoulders, lifted her chin, and swept through the door with an air of authority.

Danny rose quickly from his chair, came over to Jenna, and took both her hands in his. "Miss Daggett! Jenna!" he said, kissing her fingertips. "What a pleasure to see you again . . . stunning as ever, I might add."

Standing before her in an expensive coat with a brown velvet collar, he looked trim and manly, more handsome than she had remembered. His black curly hair lay neatly in place, far different from the tangled, blowing curls she had recalled so often. But his bright eyes, still playful and exciting as the sea, could not conceal his boyish, free spirit. Danny was every bit the impish man with an Irish brogue who charmed and teased and turned the coldest heart into a bowl of warm cream. Jenna knew she must be careful not to fall under his spell.

"Mr. McDaniels," she said, withdrawing her hands and tilting her chin upward. "It is also a pleasure to see you." She acted as formal as she could to keep a respectable distance between them, but her excitement at seeing him again was hard to contain. What was it about the company of this man that made her feel daring, haughty, desirous? How much easier it would have been to follow a deeper instinct, to burst into the smile bubbling beneath the surface, to rush to him with the joy she felt.

"And so you have come knocking at my door, as I predicted, young lady. Had I known you were in San Francisco, I'd have arranged a horse ride along the coast to the Point. You do remember our ride together, don't you?" He sat on the edge of his desk smiling at her.

Jenna thought to herself, *What a conceited, forward, egotistical man. I will not allow him to fluster me and turn me into a child!* She would have to resist that same captivating smile that once had set lose a flight of birds in her chest. *But not this time*, she thought. *I've got to be strong.*

"I hate to disappoint you, Mr. McDaniels, but this is not a social call. I've come on business, and I need help—if not yours, then someone else's.

"Well, well, well. 'Tis a business matter from a lassie. Forgive my misreading your intentions. Please sit down. I did not realize you were an entrepreneur."

"Please don't patronize me, Mr. McDaniels. I have come to you for help. I am hoping to find that I can trust you. If you think I'm in the wrong office, I'll leave immediately."

Her sincerity impressed Danny. Jenna had a specific purpose. He would put away his teasing for the time being. "I did not mean to be insensitive to your mission. Please tell me what is in your pretty head." Danny returned to his desk chair, prepared to give her his attention. Still, his eyes wandered carelessly over her statuesque body, her well-formed breasts and trim waist. While she spoke, he found himself distracted by her wide, expressive mouth and lips he felt certain could drive a man mad. As he had suspected, this sprite of a girl had grown into an exciting woman, one he would have one day, by God, wrapped around him, skin to skin.

Jenna told him the incidents leading up to ownership of San Gabriel, the doña's death, her involvement with Enrique and the Archuletas, their deceit and cruelty, the fire, the squatters, the desertion of the *vaqueros*, the slaughter of the animals, the impossible land taxes, her distrust of Reginald Potter, and her desire to be as far away from San Jose and Enrique as possible. "I want out of it all, but I'm not a fool, Mr. McDaniels. I want to recover my losses, take what is mine, and convert it into money—a lot of money."

Danny listened with keen interest. "What do you propose to do? As you said, you must decide quickly before your cattle grow sick or weak or are senselessly butchered. The grass will grow back by spring. The land can recover—a dead cow can't."

"I intend to divide the land into three-hundred-and-sixty-acre parcels and sell them."

"And you want me to sell your land for you?"

"Not at all! I intend to do it myself."

"You?"

"Of course. A woman can sell acres of land as easily as a man. Why should I pay anyone, including you? Excuse my directness, Mr. McDaniels, I'm aware a corrupt lawyer may take more than a healthy percentage, why not you as well?

Danny laughed. "So you think I might take advantage of you? As I recall, you're not an easy one."

"I did not mean to imply . . . I meant to say…"

"I'm sorry, Lassie. Let's get back to business. Dealing in the sale of property is usually a man's job; women have not customarily done this kind of thing."

"And do you think it something a woman hasn't the brains to do?" Jenna said coldly.

"On the contrary. I like women who have the spirit for business." Danny liked Jenna's fiery manner and her sharp tongue. Even more pleasing was her tall, handsome frame, her strong, deepening voice, pleasing to the ear—unlike so many women with high, shrill tones that cut like broken glass. "How can I help you? I don't deal in the buying and selling of land, anyway."

" But you do deal in commodities and in shipping, as I recall."

"Yes, that is true."

"I want to sell my remaining cattle for meat, not hides or tallow. I want to feed and fatten them for market. The Americans love beef. The miners will pay anything for a thick, juicy steak. I believe I could sell one head for seventy to eighty dollars."

"Seventy dollars! That's a very expensive dinner. It's almost robbery," he said, lighting a cigar. "How many do you have?"

"After the butchery, the fire, the theft, and the squatters helping themselves, my *mayordomo* estimates I have close to forty thousand head."

Danny blew a cloud of smoke into the air and smiled. He quickly calculated over two and a half million dollars and instantly saw an opportunity taking shape.

Jenna's expression did not change. "I need slaughterhouses along the coast, distribution points to the interior towns. I need pack trains to make runs quickly, before spoilage. I can drive the herds north on the grassy corridors along the coast, and then I need cattle transported by ship to Sacramento and Los Angeles. I need people to make good sausages, canned meat, dried beef.

Some of my land in the extreme south was left unburned, but not enough to support the herd. When the grass grows back, the remaining cattle can roam freely. There are no fences, no laws to stop free ranging. I am willing to risk my cattle being stolen right under my nose. The Archuletas have no respect for another man's brand, least of all my JD cattle. The Archuletas plan to destroy me any way they can. I must act quickly, Mr. McDaniels. Can you help me or not?"

Danny sized up this shrewd, young woman standing before him. No, this was no kittenish female with tiny little mews on her tongue. This was a lioness, a huntress who was stalking something big. "You want to start a business. I'm interested," he said.

Jenna walked slowly to the window, then turned around and faced him directly. "If you want a partnership, you will have to buy shares of stock. I will be the major stockholder. Otherwise, I'll simply pay you handsomely to get me started, build the slaughter facilities, and find the right men to keep the herds breeding healthy and multiplying. I intend to do my share of the work and keep my finger on the business. What do you say, Mr. McDaniels?"

Danny looked into Jenna's intense face, her determined blue eyes flashing now with pinpoints of green emeralds. He was not only struck with her proposition, but her grandeur. This was a young woman of character and determination, quite obviously a challenge, someone to be reckoned with.

He tried to recall the wispy fairy-child spinning on the beach like a milkweed seed. He searched for something soft, pliable—something he could hold or mold, flatter, cajole. Danny suddenly realized he possessed no resources to control this woman. She had him at arm's length.

"I'll have to think about this, discuss it with my partners. Perhaps tonight you would join me for dinner at La Chaumiere, one of San Francisco's superb restaurants. I would be honored. We could talk over more details and become better acquainted. I usually like to know a business partner well before I commit myself. Danny flashed one of his most seductive smiles hoping to disarm her.

Jenna stood up. "Thank you for the invitation, Mr. McDaniels, but I must decline. I have other matters to attend to," she said coolly.

Danny watched her drop her gloves. As she stood up, her hat fell slightly to one side and a strand of hair fell from its prim place over her eyes. She flushed as she brushed it back.

He grinned, noticing her awkwardness and embarrassed smile. "I see you have wee bit of mud on your hem . . . and your walking boots, as well."

Jenna looked at her hem and shoes caked with mud. Her muddy footprints covered Danny's office.

He smiled again and waited for her to comment. Instead, she straightened her back and raised her chin.

Ah, he thought to himself, *this gorgeous lassie is not so perfect after all. She has a soft spot, a way in.*

"Goodbye, Mr. McDaniels," Jenna said, walking to the door. "You needn't see me out."

"Jenna!" he said, walking toward her. "You forgot your purse."

"Oh, thank you, sir." She turned away.

"And your parasol," he said, grinning broadly.

Jenna flushed into red splotches. She could always feel them spring to the surface of her skin. She felt foolish, caught in a web of her own playacting. There was nothing to do at that moment but break into one of her open, irresistible smiles. "Have I left anything else, Mr. McDaniels— my head, perhaps?"

"Not yet," he said.

Jenna rushed out of the office, her heart pounding, her mouth dry, and with something like a joyful squeal locked in her throat.

🌱 🌱 🌱

While Jenna waited for Danny McDaniels to make his decision and work out plans with his partners, she explored San Francisco. She thought it must be the most exciting city in the world. Jenna loved walking through the streets, browsing in the fashionable stores, finding exotic clothes, hats and furnishings, tapestries, oriental rugs. Jenna noticed how shockingly expensive everything was. It seemed to her that people bought luxuries on a whim, carelessly spending their fast fortunes on gambling, mining, speculation, investment. She'd heard that if a man lost a fortune overnight, there was probably another awaiting him the next day.

Jenna hired a driver to take her around the city and into the hills to see the luxurious homes, some as resplendent as stone castles. They belonged to millionaires born out of the richest gold strikes.

"This here area is called Rincon Hills, ma'am," Jenna's driver said. "These folks have forgotten they're no better than the rest of us, just got lucky somewheres. I always say, 'be nice to folks climbin' up the ladder, so's you'll have friends on the way down.' "

Jenna thought if Danny McDaniels decided to do business with her, someday she would buy a fine home in the prestigious Rincon hills.

The thought of returning to rancho life no longer held any magic for Jenna. She did not want pastoral quiet or long days of loneliness. For a while she thought of moving to Jackson to live close to Darcey, Blue, Pearle, and Harke. How she missed them all! Now that Blue and Darcey were married, she felt they were even more of a family to her. But Jackson was far away and quiet compared to San Francisco.

Now, she was swept up in the rushing human current, easy laughter, quick decisions, good-natured tolerance of eccentricities, and fierce independence, possible in San Francisco. A man backed up his words with honor or a duel, or quite inexplicably shrugged off the entire argument with a friendly drink of ale. A woman did not hide. A corrupt man's days were short, unless he was in the police force or the struggling government.

"Ya' see that building over there, Ma'am?" Jenna's driver said as they drove around the city. "That's where the Vigilance Committee took the law into their own hands and hung two murderers right out them second-story windows. Charlie Cora and a man named Casey—cold-blooded murderers they was. Charlie Cora killed a U.S. Marshal. Casey shot a newspaper editor sittin' at his desk. Must have been near eight thousand of us signed up and was issued arms to get some law in this place. We stormed up the steps of the police department and demanded the release of them two murderers. Then we hung 'em where everybody could see."

"Are you a vigilante, sir?" Jenna inquired.

"Me? Don't know where ya' get that idea. I ain't sayin', but if I was— and I ain't sayin', ya' hear—I'd be mighty proud of it. Yep, we hung that rascal, Cora, and run his girlfriend or his wife, Belle, right out of town. She married him on the same day he died—became a bride and a widow on the same day. Anyways, I hear she's gone. Are you new here, lady?"

"Yes, I am."

"Well, you better learn where not to go. Pardon me for sayin', but there's women who shouldn't wander in certain neighborhoods, leastways they taint their reputation. Take Belle Cora for example. She's got a house over here on Dupont Street. Her business ain't legal, ya' understand, outlawed only last year, but no one pays no mind. Her business is as active as ever. Some other beauty has taken over her place. Excuse me, Ma'am, for mentioning them ladies."

"I want to drive by Belle's place, driver, and then onto Portsmouth Square, the Mission District, the wharf, Market Street. I want to see what you call Sydney Town. I want to see it all," Jenna said. "I'll pay you well for your trouble."

"If you say so, Ma'am. But I ain't responsible if you see things a lady shouldn't see. And I ain't takin' you to where the Sydney Ducks is known to hang out. They is the meanest men alive, escaped Australian convicts from Botany Bay. Why, they club people to death, raid their establishments, threaten good folks. I'd hate to be a Chinee. Them Australians see a Chinee and they go crazy. They beat 'em to death in their sleep like they was bedbugs. Well, where to?"

Surely the man is exaggerating. Men aren't that uncivilized.

"I'd like to start with a drive on Pacific Street, then to Sydney Town. Jenna sat back in the seat, smiling.

What a city of extremes! I think I belong here.

❦ ❦ ❦

Danny, his associates, and Jenna celebrated their partnership by dining at one of San Francisco's finest French restaurants, La Chaumiere. McDaniels, Murry, and Hemeon Enterprises had agreed to start a corporation with Danny as the president. Jenna was the major stockholder, owning fifty-five percent of the stock, and the chairman of the board. Danny and his rich partners would divide the remaining stock between them. Jenna would initially capitalize the company with a bank loan based on the value of her sizeable herd.

Speculation was in the hearts of all San Franciscans, including bankers. People were willing to take risks. There was no reason for a fledgling business not to succeed immediately. Cattle were proving to be a very profitable enterprise. And, of course, her land, which she would sell off gradually, was a potential fortune.

Jenna's immediate task was to arrange for the first portion of cattle to be driven to the coast and to maintain the unburned section of land for the remaining smaller herd. Danny would take it from there, setting up the slaughter business and the transportation of cattle and meat. Later the other two associates would establish subsidiary meat companies which would produce dried and canned meat, sausages, and meat by-products. JD Meat Company was well on its way.

Jenna faced the task of selling her land, as well as joining forces with Señor Faustino, to hire *vaqueros* needed to tend the smaller ranch in the southern section of her property. Señor Faustino would continue his role as *mayordomo*. She would see to it that an appropriate adobe be built for his family and a bunkhouse for the men as well. With good luck and protection against Enrique, the herd would multiply by spring.

Throughout the evening, Danny repeatedly toasted Jenna. "To a new San Francisco beauty." With each refilled glass, his toasts became more frequent and flowery.

> *"The stars stand up in the air*
> *The sun and the moon are gone,*
> *The strand of its waters is bare*
> *And her sway is swept from the swan."*

"Come, gentlemen, to our queen . . . To a sea sprite . . . To a lady on horseback."

The partners, a bit quizzical, nevertheless raised their goblets to Jenna, who flushed and lowered her eyes. The more Danny drank, the more pronounced became his Irish brogue and the more hilarious his Irish stories. They rolled off his tongue with ease, a gift that even enlivened and enthralled patrons at the surrounding tables. The gentlemen laughed heartily, and Jenna, embarrassed by the casual manners in a public place, restrained herself from laughing out loud.

She couldn't take her eyes off Danny. His every gesture, his cleverness, his humor charmed her. *Oh, if I were a man, I'd laugh 'til my sides ached*! It would be unseemly to laugh like a man, especially in public in the company of men, and so she covered her face behind her napkin, her laughter bubbled happily like a pot of simmering strawberry jam. Danny was adorable even though he was flushed and bright-eyed with wine.

When the party stood up to leave, Danny made one parting toast to Jenna.

> *"She's more shapely than swan by the Strand,*
> *She's more radiant than grass after dew,*
> *She's more fair than the stars where they stand*
> *'Tis my grief that her ever I knew!"*

🌸 🌸 🌸

Jenna rented a room in the Bay View boardinghouse, a rich home in a nice neighborhood, and made plans to take a steamer to Monterey. She needed to discuss the selling of her land with Reginald Potter. From Monterey, she'd take the stage to San Jose. "A step at a time," she said to herself. "It will all fall into place in good time."

Everything was moving quickly and easily until she spoke with Reginald Potter.

"What do you mean I have no land!" Jenna said angrily. "You have my deed on file—right here! My signature and the doña's—and *yours*—are on dozens of papers—on the deed. You have a description of the claim, a letter from the doña's father, maps, everything you said was necessary to be secure in our claim!"

Reginald smiled and wiped his wet hands on a handkerchief. "My child, I'm saying there are *no* papers on file here, *nothing*. I've looked for them, of course, but, unhappily, there are no records at all. Perhaps you took them with you by mistake."

"They were filed in *this* office, in those big, black books. You know that!" Jenna shouted. "You are cheating me, Mr. Potter!"

The lawyer stood up, red-faced. "How insolent you are! There are no records in this office or on file in the courthouse. I'm not accountable for others' errors!"

"The doña trusted you, trusted the Land Office and the American system to protect her. If you've lost those records, how can I prove anything? Who would believe me? I have nothing!" Jenna stormed around the office.

"You have no other records, madam?"

Jenna placed her hands firmly on Reginal Potter's desk and shot him a fierce look, a weapon she had seen the doña use many times. "I told you already. *Everything* was burned in the fire!"

"My, my, what a dilemma. If neither you, nor our office, nor anyone else can prove your ownership of a rather unduly large estate, and you've paid no taxes, and there is no deed, I'm afraid there is nothing to be done."

Jenna was unable to speak. Her outrage over the corruption and deceit of Reginald Potter left her in shock.

"I'll ask my clerks to make a page-by-page search of the office. Of course, we've done that already, but to reassure you the papers are not here is our duty."

"I'll have you arrested!" Jenna said, leaning over his desk and pointing a finger into his face.

"On what grounds, Madam?"

"Theft! If I find you've sold a single acre of my land, I'll have you thrown in jail!"

"Oh? May I remind you, Miss Daggett, the land is no more yours than it is mine. It is no one's. Anyone can own it. Do you want to buy it back? I'm certain the Land Office could accommodate a three-hundred-and-sixty-acre parcel, if it has not already been spoken for. So many people are interested in the Santa Clara Valley. As a matter of fact, it seems likely your remaining herds are grazing on someone else's property. You could be severely fined for trespassing." Potter's mouth curved into an unfriendly smile. He tapped his pudgy fingertips together with apparent satisfaction.

"I will find a way to uncover your fraud, Mr. Potter."

"Perhaps the Archuleta family can help you?" His chuckle vibrated his fleshy cheeks.

Jenna thought the comment peculiar. Could it be that he knew the Archuletas would never help her? Was that why he was so sure of himself? The property could be sold off by anyone—Reginald Potter, the Archuletas. After all, the Archuletas had an original map showing the property divisions among the brothers and the doña. What use were documents in this confusing land issue when any corrupt official could make deals or alter the truth?

Was there a conspiracy between Mr. Potter and the Archuletas? She would have to consult Erin. Perhaps, as the doña's American brother-in-law, he could help.

But when Jenna spoke with Erin, she discovered that he, too, was unsympathetic, indifferent, and unhelpful. He avoided looking directly into her eyes and acted nervous and irritable. Even when he extended an invitation for her to stay with him and his wife, Helena, the gesture was lukewarm. Jenna declined, saying she had business to attend to and would be leaving for San Jose the first thing in the morning. She decided not to tell him about her enterprise with his friend, McDaniels.

"I'll see what I can do for you, Jenna," Erin said. "Mr. Potter is a hard-working man, a personal friend of mine. I know he's swamped with land searches, but I'm certain he's given you every consideration."

Jenna's conversation with Erin left her even more convinced she would never own that land again. He and Helena could be taking advantage of her, as well. They might even be in partnership with Reginald Potter in the sale of Archuleta land. In any case, there was no reason for them to give her any special consideration. She had never been more than a house guest to them.

Jenna only spent a few days in San Jose. Everything about the place aggravated her bitter feelings toward the Archuletas. She also didn't want to delay her return to the rancho. She knew she needed to work fast to protect her only remaining asset, the cattle.

Jenna had another task ahead of her, as well—helping Señor Faustino, Ygnacio and their families start a new life. It was the least she could for her steadfast friends.

Before she left San Jose, she made one last stop. While the matter of her lost land appeared to be over, Jenna sought out the sheriff, relaying to him her belief that Enrique and his loyal *vaqueros* had deliberately set fire to her land, that they had stolen her cattle and harassed her.

Even as she spoke to the Mexican deputy, she knew she sounded to him like no more than a hysterical woman who had no business questioning the actions of the Archuletas, let alone any man at all. She was out of her proper place, a meddling female who should be home with her babies or at church confessing her sins—the sins that hung on her and all women like a net of cobwebs.

"Sí, Señorita. We will do what we can to help you. You can expect a full investigation. We will get in touch with you if we have any news to support your charge," the deputy sheriff said.

Exasperated, Jenna left the office knowing nothing would be done.

As she crossed the street to the hotel, Enrique stepped in front of her. With an exaggerated bow, he said, "*Buenos dias*, Señorita Daggett. What a pleasure to see you, and looking so lovely. Your dress must not have burned in the fire." He smiled in a cruel way, a smile she had seen when the bull gored the tied, terrified grizzly.

"Move aside, Enrique. I can't bear to look at your face." Jenna tried to step around him.

He took hold of her wrist and squeezed it to the point of pain. "You will look at me, my sweet Jenna. See in my eyes the Indian in me, the Archuletas. You are afraid. Do you know, standing here right now, I could snap your wrist in two? Tell me, what should I do?" His eyes had narrowed like a wild cat focusing on its kill.

"Let go of me this instant! You do not frighten me, Enrique, nor do any of the Archuletas. You are powerless. You are weak! Your only strength is in a family that hides you, or the *vaqueros* who do your dirty work."

Enrique's face twisted into a look of insanity, a hatred that terrified Jenna, but she stared at him without backing down. She felt certain he would break her wrist.

"I will tell you this, Miss Daggett, the Archuletas get what they want. We have unfinished business. You have something I want . . . between your legs . . . not because it is so damned precious, but because you American women keep it a hidden treasure. Maybe I should cut it out and hang it on a flagpole for the world to see? What do you think, Señorita? Or maybe I should feed it to the dogs. Keep your legs crossed, pretty lady," he snarled before loosening his grip.

The assault made the bile rise in her throat. Jenna ran to the hotel, into her room, and retched into her chamber pot. She could hardly wait for the stagecoach to carry her away from the evil she felt still clinging to her.

🍃 🍃 🍃

The winter months in San Francisco were the coldest Jenna could remember. She wore wool next to her skin, drank hot tea, and stood close to the hearth fires. The chilling dampness crept through the buttonholes of her coat, up the sleeves of her cape, and down her neck. Even the bone-white moon glowed with hoarfrost through the veil of clouds.

But while winter dashed stormy waves against the shore and rocked the boats in the bay, Jenna and Danny built the JD Meat Company. They also developed an unspoken passion and fascination for one another that surely would have erupted by now, except for one problem. Danny had a woman, a mistress whom he'd possessed for several years.

Jenna had heard rumors from her full-breasted landlady, Mrs. Dewberry, that Danny, "that no good Irish devil," flaunted a dark beauty, taking her to public events, even to the theater, without the slightest conscience, "a shameless man, a shameless woman, who keep San Francisco under a cloud of indecency." Jenna thought it best not to tell the woman that she and Danny McDaniels were business partners.

"The authorities should run the two of them out of town like they did that Belle Cora woman," Mrs. Dewberry had said, swelling her chest like a thrush.

"Tell me what you know about this woman, Mrs. Dewberry," Jenna asked. She would not admit to herself that she was jealous. She was only interested in the welfare of the company.

Mrs. Dewberry, appearing delighted to pass on the gossip, leaned closer, pressed her face into Jenna's, set her jaw firmly, and rolled her eyes. "They say she gambled like a man. In fact, she ran the roulette table at a popular saloon on Sansome Street. Everybody knows she worked at Belle Cora's place and was 'friends' with the most prominent men in town. Rumor has it that Mr. McDaniels got so jealous he pulled her out of Belle's and built her a fine home on the hill, a mansion. I'm told it's furnished with the finest things—gilded mirrors, exquisite china, and silver. She don't care how much anything costs. They say she's got a gold comb, brush, and mirror set.

Some women say Mr. McDaniels is so crazy about her he'll do anything for her, even bring her a breakfast tray in bed, mind you. He's admittedly very handsome, but a rogue, nevertheless." Mrs. Dewberry took a deep breath. "Some folks say he killed a man over her, knocked him out cold in Portsmouth Square. The man died a few days later as a result of the fight, making that devilish Irishman a murderer in my book!"

"A very interesting story," Jenna said without showing any expression. "And they live together in a house on the hill?"

"Oh, my no. He just 'keeps' her there. Isn't it scandalous?" She didn't wait for an answer. "Haven't you seen her about town? She's very haughty—rides around town in a black coach with a pair of white horses with silver-studded harnesses. And the horses wear white plumes! Isn't that the limit? I don't know what is the matter with some people. It's just a matter of time before we women take matters into our own hands and send them both packing."

Jenna's curiosity about Danny and now, this bold woman, consumed far too much time in her thoughts. She looked for the fine rig whenever she was in the streets; she created an image of the "dark beauty," a composite of San Francisco's beautiful French women.

In her imagination, Jenna even dressed Danny's mistress in fine clothes, sometimes in a sky-blue velvet gown, at other times in a deep maroon brocade and an ermine-trimmed cape. She couldn't help competing with this stranger, wanting Danny to see her as desirable as she imagined his concubine was.

Flirting was not something Jenna could do. It was awkward, unnatural, ridiculous. She had watched the Mexican girls move sensuously in their loose clothes, short skirts, and bare-shouldered blouses, but she had never dared imitate them. They tossed kisses and easy glances without self-consciousness in a delightful game of flirtation that everyone played. Even the smallest girls learned the rules early and smiled at the constant applause and shouts of "*Que linda! Que bonita! Que preciosa!*" They grew up believing they were beautiful and desirable. The American women, especially Martha Jane, were starched and crisp, sturdy and erect, did their duty, and kept clean kitchens and clean children. Jenna could never compete with a mystery woman, especially one who knew how to bare her shoulders.

She wondered why Danny McDaniels expressed his obvious interest in her. Talking business kept the flames down, but not the heat. She desperately wanted to be in private with him, yet feared it at the same time; over and over she relived the scene on the beach, the windy ride on the coast, feeling Danny's breath on her neck, his kiss. In the privacy of her thoughts, she was safe to show unrestrained desire, to kiss him back with unleashed passion, but the scene would quickly change when her heart beat fast and the ache between her legs began to throb. She was, after all, a lady.

As for Danny, he smiled with satisfaction, and at Foley's saloon he'd wink and say, "Well, me boys, I've got me a virgin wigglin' and squirmin' on the end of my line. Won't be long now when she'll be lyin' on a buttery platter waitin' to be eaten."

One afternoon Jenna was certain she saw the backs of Danny and a woman entering a restaurant. The woman wore a tasteful, cream brocade dress with a long, embroidered train. Beneath her hat, long black curls shimmered down her back like rippling water—a daring hairstyle, not the fashion, not neatly twisted or braided into a bun. Whoever she was, she took pride in her river of curls and wanted the world to know it.

Jenna said to Danny during their next meeting, "Did I see you going for lunch last Wednesday at Henry IV with a lovely young lady?"

"Possibly," he answered but did not elaborate, and Jenna did not pursue the matter.

🍃 🍃 🍃

Mrs. Dewberry was not only a valuable source of information, but a woman stuffed with "good works"—women's charities, cultural and civic clubs, literary and sewing circles. She glowed with self-importance. Jenna thought her a kindly sort, a bit tedious at times, but nevertheless, one who had carried a God-fearing code across the plains and planted it firmly in San Francisco. She was admired by many for her contribution, her energy, and her devil's food cake.

The Dewberrys invited Jenna to the American Theater for the opening performance of *School for Scandal*. "We have a box, you know—very good viewing. You must join us to see San Francisco at its best," Mrs. Dewberry said. "Our theater is as good as any on the East Coast."

Waiting for the curtain to rise, Jenna looked at the gaily dressed people taking their seats, rustling in expectation of a good performance. She scanned the box across from her and at that moment saw Danny McDaniels and his companion just settling into their seats.

"Well, look there, Jenna," Mrs. Dewberry said, pursing her lips. "There's that Irishman I was telling you about and that woman. Do you see the lady in the plum-colored dress?" She raised her opera glasses, as did others in the audience. "Rogue!" she exclaimed, handing the glasses to Jenna. "At least he's got sense enough to keep her discretely in the back row. Don't he remember it was just this same situation that got Charlie Cora killed?"

Jenna adjusted the focus on the small, pearly glasses.

Mrs. Dewberry whispered loud enough for others to hear. "Charlie brought an immoral woman to the American Theater and sat her in plain view for the world to see, pretty as you please. No respect for the community and decent folks. Well, my dear, he refused to leave even after the marshal politely asked him to remove himself and that Belle woman. Well, that Irishman better not flaunt his lady or he'll end up on Cemetery Hill."

In the dim light, Jenna could see the woman was a beauty. She could also see Danny McDaniels lean over and whisper something that made her smile.

Throughout the first act, Jenna, more interested in Danny and his companion than the play, let her eyes wander over to his box. She had to get a closer look at the woman sitting next to him, looking as elegant as a queen. There was something familiar about her, something she could not put her finger on.

Danny and his friend did not leave their seats during intermission. It was only at the end of the play that Jenna had an opportunity to meet the couple face to face. She cleverly maneuvered through the crowd, followed by the Dewberrys, until she was close enough to say, "Good evening, Mr. McDaniels."

Mrs. Dewberry stopped and gasped, then quickly turned her back.

Danny seemed momentarily taken off guard. But with his typical broad smile and casual manner, he returned the greeting. "Good evening, Miss Daggett. What a surprise to see you here. May I introduce my companion, Lilly Jordan. Lilly, this is a friend of mine, Jenna Daggett. We have mutual friends in Monterey."

The two women stared at one another, both wide-eyed, unable to speak. A long, awkward moment passed until Jenna said, "Miss Jordan, it is a pleasure to meet you. Did you enjoy the play?" Jenna choked on her words, swallowing the name, *Hannah Polley.*

The woman calling herself Lilly Jordan was Jenna's childhood friend and confidante, Hannah—beautiful, exotic Hannah, who had crossed the plains in a straw hat, stealing buttermilk to keep her skin white. This was beloved Hannah, who had hugged Jenna like a sister on their parting at Fort Hall, the friend who had danced with her under big night skies, woven wildflowers into wreaths to wear in their hair, who had collected buffalo chips under hot sun, gathered buckets of hail to keep the butter cool and chill a glass of citric acid. This gorgeous, aloof woman standing before her was her closest confidant, who had splashed in the streams, picked wild blackberries, counted graves, stood by her side when she buried her family . . . who had shared so many secrets.

Before her stood Hannah Polley!

Jenna wanted to embrace her with the joy she felt, but Hanna's warning expression stopped her. Hannah assumed a cold indifference, a blank face never suggesting the two women knew each other. Jenna remembered that Hannah could always keep a secret better than anyone. She had cultivated the art of lying convincingly, starting with Emily Polley, the dearest mother in the world, Doctor Polley, and Harke. No one ever caught her in her deceitful games, and she got whatever she wanted.

"Yes, thank you, I enjoyed the play. It's one of my favorites." Hannah squeezed Danny's arm and began moving toward the door. "Nice meeting you," she said, and tossed Jenna an ironic half smile.

Jenna watched them slip through the door, then turned to find the Dewberrys standing with their backs to her.

"I'm sorry," Jenna apologized. "Forgive my rudeness."

"Indeed." Mrs. Dewberry answered coolly. "How could you lower yourself, Jenna, to speak to those two disreputable people? After all I've told you, I must confess I'm shocked and disappointed."

"That gentleman is a friend of my deceased guardian's brother-in-law. I've known him in Monterey since I was a child. As a matter of fact, it would have been rude of me not to speak. He was always a gentleman in Monterey."

"Then he doesn't carry his reputation with him!" Mrs. Dewberry swelled her bosom and teetered out the door on her tiny high-heeled shoes.

Jenna did not feel she needed to defend her greeting any further. Mrs. Dewberry's rigid propriety would peck holes in almost anything if given the chance. She had changed her mind about the gossipy woman. Mrs. Dewberry wasn't a woman generous of spirit at all, nor one of good deeds. She enjoyed chewing on the small pellets of life and digesting them with gravelly stones.

Jenna was far too excited at seeing Hannah to be concerned with Mrs. Dewberry's scolding. She would call on Hannah at her house on the hill as soon as she could find out where she lived. Surely, any coach driver would know her residence.

FOURTEEN

I KNOW THE HOUSE, MA'AM," the coach driver said. "It's on California Street. Are you sure you have the right party? That place don't hold the best reputation."

Jenna didn't answer. She was far too excited to see Hannah to be troubled by tongue-wagging. Nine years had passed since the two girls parted, years intense with growing up and belonging to an era of gold hysteria, boom and bust lives. Everyone in California had survived something: the journey around South America or through the jungles of Panama, or overland on the trails, some through the Sierras or deserts, untested, ending in death and unfulfilled dreams; but life went on and the men and women used their ingenuity and spirit to overcome the odds.

Jenna wondered how terrible Hanna's life could have been for the Polley's adored daughter to end up with a new identity in San Francisco. Doctor Polley's practice must have thrived in the far west since doctors were scarce and highly valued. Emily Polley was a saint and Harke, a strong, loyal brother who would have protected her from any kind of trouble. Hannah had every advantage.

Why, then, did her reputation mean nothing to her? What made her value riches over her own body . . . or did she enjoy her acts of intimacy with strangers? Did she choose that life, or was it chosen for her? Remembering the squirming weight of Faithful Squibb, smelling his unwashed body and putrid breath, made Jenna's skin crawl with revulsion. How could anyone place themselves willingly under a man who merely wanted a vessel to fill with semen?

Surely, the physical act of love would be different, bearable, even wonderful with a man one loved. Jenna tried to shut out the intrusive vision of Danny and Hannah lying together. Beautiful, captivating, selfish Hannah had what Jenna wanted—the attention of a man who made her tremble, who filled her with desire. Hannah knew all his secrets, shared the most private part of a man and woman's life. She knew him skin to skin, mouth to mouth.

Jenna slammed the window on her thoughts and visions. It was better not to think about these things at all. For now, it was sufficient to be close to Hannah. In a strange way, it made her feel closer to Danny, like a mouse in a pocket or a flea in the ear.

When the buggy stopped in front of a large, tasteful house, Jenna's conflicting emotions—love and jealousy, curiosity and trepidation, fought against each other. How could she be so sure and unsure of herself at the same time?

"Please wait, driver. I won't be long," she said.

A tiny Chinese man bent over like a cane top escorted Jenna to the parlor to wait. Though the room sparkled with showy riches and gaudy accents, the space was suffocating and austere.

Hannah glided into the room still wearing a morning gown. Her black hair fell carelessly about her shoulders.

"And so you have come to see who I am. Please sit down, Jenna. I can't say I welcome your visit, but it was only a matter of time, I suppose, before you would have discovered me. I'm easily noticed, quite visible. You have a lot of courage coming to this house."

Jenna looked at the woman before her, still the same wild beauty, exotic as night, powerful as fire, but cold and distant as the stars. "I've thought about you often, Hannah," Jenna said, looking directly into her eyes.

"And now you see." Hannah eased herself onto a divan and arranged the folds of her dress, a silk parrot-green dressing gown tied loosely at the waist. It fell open at the chest, casually revealing a red, silk camisole.

Jenna felt uncomfortable at Hannah's lack of propriety. Surely, she did not receive guests dressed in this manner. On the other hand, she was an unannounced visitor.

"My, how curiosity gets the better of us," Hannah went on. "Are you satisfied?"

"No, not yet. There have been too many years, too many memories for me to simply brush away as if they never happened. And I don't think you can forget so quickly yourself."

"You'd be surprised how quickly I can forget. In my profession it is an art. You know about me, I presume?" Her acid smile momentarily distorted her beauty.

"Yes."

"And you came to see me anyway." Hannah sneered. She stared coldly at Jenna, then pulled from her pocket a peacock-feathered fan which matched her gown, spread it open like an the tail of an amorous bird, and lightly fanned herself.

"Once we were good friends," Jenna said, still looking intensely at Hannah.

She smiled. "You used to worship me. I led you around like a puppy."

"You were older, prettier. And I admired your family. But I never wanted to be like you." Jenna stiffened. Hannah did not want to be friends.

"It is clear you are not." Hannah gave a sardonic laugh.

"You know Harke has been looking for you for a long time. He's here in California—around Jackson."

"I know. That's why I changed my name." She folded the fan and tossed it aside. "I did not want to be found," she added without emotion.

"But your mother, Hannah . . . your family. They must still be grieving for you."

"Come now, Jenna. Don't throw pitiful sentiments my way. I hate them." Hannah reached for a box from which she took a small burl pipe. She ceremoniously tapped in some tobacco, pressed it with her finger, and lit it, drawing deeply several times. Blue smoke filled the room.

"My mother is a realist. She came to terms with my absence long ago. Her God follows her everywhere, you know, even to the privy."

Jenna knew that Hannah's every gesture and her rude manner, was a deliberate attempt to shock her.

"I never belonged in that family," Hannah continued. "I was separate from everyone, always. The Polley women never could get their noses out of cooking pots and furrows of dirt to see another kind of life. My nature, my desires, my dreams were opposite theirs, but I was expected to mold to their little brown ways, like some kind of prized custard.

"I would have died if I'd stayed in Oregon. I don't regret leaving, and Mother—well, it is better she think I drowned myself, grieving over the death of the baby." Hannah kicked off her satin slippers and tucked her legs under her like she had as a young girl.

Jenna looked at the stranger, so indifferent and selfish. What else could she say?

"What more do you want to know? How I got here? That's a shocking story I'll spare you. The army men have always been good to me." She had clenched the pipe in her teeth when she spoke, which made her voice sound calloused.

"You are happy then?" Jenna asked.

For a fleeting moment, Hannah's eyes changed. "I'm wealthy," she answered. "Happiness and wealth are the same for me. Am I satisfied? There's never enough."

"And Mr. McDaniels. What about him?" Jenna tried to sound matter-of-fact.

Hannah laughed. "He's a fool, no different from the others in my life who paid to 'keep' me. Every man has a weak spot, and I'm a master at finding it."

"And using it?"

"Yes." She smiled.

Jenna stood. "Hannah, I came here hoping to be friends. I guess I made a mistake."

"Sit down, Jenna. Oh, don't be stubborn. Sit down. This is like old times."

Jenna hesitated. Hannah's commanding voice made her rigid.

"All right, *please* sit down. Don't be difficult. This is fun. I know I've been rude to you." Hannah smiled in a playful way, the same manipulative way that had always made Jenna do her bidding.

Jenna didn't move one way or the other, trying to decide which way would keep her in control of the situation.

"Come now, Jenna. You're not made out of cream cheese. I haven't offended you, have I? You seem far too strong to let someone like me bother you. Sit down, please." Hannah seemed sincere, even pleading.

Jenna sat down again but remained poised on the edge of the chair as if ready to depart.

"I have no friends in San Francisco—no female friends, that is. They don't like me here, and frankly, I don't like them. They are dull as dishwater. When I first came here, I made a hundred thousand dollars in two years—before I even learned how to gamble. Pretty good, don't you think? I became rich off many of the women's husbands and even richer at the gaming houses.

"In fact, I'd made enough money to leave and start a new life, but San Francisco and I just fit. It was a love affair with the place from the beginning.

"Years ago when I had more conscience, I tried to give back some of my wealth. I thought if I donated the money to build a hospital, one especially to help women, I'd have enough respect to live another kind of life. Well, I was wrong. The *Alta* even wrote that the city should not want charity from a woman of easy virtue. The laugh is, the editor was one of my best customers.

"I decided to stay just to remind the 'Christers' who they or their husbands were. Belle and I planned many a fancy party with champagne and fine food. We sent engraved invitations tied with white satin ribbons, and the men surely did join us for a fine evening."

Hannah looked smug. "No one wanted my dirty money, but they got it anyway—in a roundabout sort of way. Isn't it a laugh? The money came out of the pockets of upstanding men, husbands, and fathers. I never needed to court dirty miners. I waited until they were rich and clean and wearing velvet coats. I don't care what people think."

She stretched out on the couch and put a pillow behind her head. She drew on her pipe with enjoyment.

"I don't believe that altogether; otherwise, you wouldn't have tried to build a hospital, one to help women. Oh, Hannah, what a grand idea that was!"

"I was building a monument to myself, that's all. It was another way to poke the ladies in their self-righteous posteriors."

"I don't believe that. Once you were as distressed as I was about people, especially women who were hurt. Remember Zelda?"

Hannah's face softened. "Yes. It is women like her who I wanted to help. In my profession I see many beaten women who fell into prostitution because they had no way to survive. Many ran away from abusive husbands and had no place to go. Women have died in my arms, full of broken limbs and bruises, smashed faces, torn-off ears, burned or mutilated breasts and privates. I've buried them with my own money. It's the least I can do. If they have children, I give them some money, no names attached."

"Oh, Hannah, that is good of you, and there is no monument behind your generosity."

Hannah didn't answer. Finally she sighed and said, "Yes, I remember Zelda." She stood up. Jenna's audience was over. Hannah's cold facade had melted, and now a weariness dulled her eyes and softened her face.

Jenna gently placed her hands on her old friend's shoulders.

Hannah turned her face away. "I will not speak to you on the street. I advise you do the same."

"I will do as I please, Hannah."

"Will you tell Harke where I am?"

"Yes. He's my dearest friend."

"Tell him, 'hello,' but not to bother acting brotherly or heroic. I won't be around for several months. I'm going to Europe in the spring to shop. Mr. McDaniels has promised to take me to Paris and Florence. I love Italian art, don't you?" Hannah had resumed her cold distance.

Jenna smiled, hoping to disguise her reaction to the news that Danny was taking Hannah to Europe. She could not understand her feeling of betrayal. After all, his attentions to her were never more than superficial flirting.

"By the way, you must be well off yourself. You look . . . expensive. By chance, did you find a rich miner?"

Jenna thought she detected irony in Hannah's question. Could she possibly suspect her feelings toward Danny?

"No, no miner." Jenna did not care to discuss her life, her past nine years. Even through hard times, her own life had been full of wonder and irony; it was too precious to toss off in a few casual remarks as the two women said goodbye.

"Goodbye, Hannah," Jenna said. When the door closed behind her, something else closed inside her—a sweet childhood memory of days of innocence.

Hannah went to the window and drew aside a corner of the curtain and watched Jenna walk down the path to the coach.

She's attractive in her own way. There is something aristocratic about her, the way she walks and holds her head high. She still has that wide brow and a strong, graceful curve of her cheek. And blue eyes that study me. No, this woman is not easily intimidated.

Hannah did not want Jenna, or anyone else for that matter, intruding in her life. She did not want or need friends, especially childhood friends— particularly Jenna, who could resurrect memories of sad-eyed mothers and the wail of a bastard baby.

She closed the curtain and drew back into the dim room. Hannah suddenly felt very alone. There had been a time when friends and family surrounded her, adored her. She had grown out of their rich soil and bloomed like a glorious cactus flower, unreachable, enticing. Once she had embraced Jenna as a friend.

Hannah poured herself a thimbleful of brandy and let the sweet liquid burn in her mouth. Jenna was a good person, not a fool or pious; a fit-looking lady, cultivated, not easily dominated. It wouldn't do to have a friend the likes of her. How could anyone . . . how could Jenna understand her world of delicious, twisted shadows?

✿ ✿ ✿

Jenna wrote to Harke at Jackson telling him she had seen Hannah. As delicately as possible, she told him his sister was unmarried, but living alone, supported by a man of means:

> Hannah has made a great deal of money on her own and lives as a wealthy woman. Dear Harke, I know it distresses you to hear of your sister's fall from respectability, but she is not to be condemned. I suppose she did what all women must do one way or another—survive. I'm sure one day, she will see the light and settle into a life of propriety and good deeds.

Jenna decided to keep secret her acquaintance and visit with Hannah, at least for the time being. It gave her security, a kind of control, stopped her runaway emotions where Danny was concerned. Because she possessed intimate knowledge of her partner, she could make better decisions and handle herself appropriately.

She reasoned that what he did in his private life was his own business. He was no different from every other man, except he was more decent, in fact. Hadn't he, after all, persuaded Hannah to leave her bordello and gambling life? Danny was a moral man, even if he kept a woman. He dared to take Hannah's arm, show her in public.

In Jenna's mind, he was not a "rogue" or scoundrel. In fact, he was even more fascinating to her than before, and sometimes Jenna's heart raced just standing next to him. Still, because her hidden knowledge gave her an advantage when dealing with him, whenever a remark passed that sounded flirtatious, Jenna smiled or playfully retorted to deflect any meaning behind it.

One afternoon, as Jenna was leaving Danny's office, he took her arm, turned her around, and pulled her toward him.

"Don't," she said quietly but firmly. Her conviction stopped him cold.

"You're driving me crazy, Jenna! You have since you were a wee child. Maybe it's because I couldn't have you then, but I let you grow inside me, take shape and form. I allowed my senses to touch and taste and feel every part of you. I want you, Jenna!" He put his mouth to hers.

Jenna pulled back. "Stop it, Danny. Please. You want what you can't have. You want whatever pleases you for the moment—a glass of burgundy, a run on the beach, a fine cigar. You're a man with fleeting obsessions. You buy whatever you want."

"You're different from the others, Jenna. I can't stop thinking about you. And don't tell me you have no interest, no feeling. I'm too experienced, Jenna. I can read your eyes. There are times I can read your thoughts. You hold me at arm's length, not because you're such a lady, but because you're afraid you might not be one. You're afraid our touching will start a fire."

Jenna couldn't stop now. Danny had provoked her. "It is common knowledge about your friend Lilly Jordan."

Danny walked over to a cabinet and took out a bottle of brandy. "I've known Lilly a long time," he said, pouring the amber liquid into a glass. "She's of no concern to you or anyone else." He took a long drink. "Jenna, this is part of a man's life that is never discussed. I'm surprised you even brought her name up. Most women would have never been so bold."

"I'm not most women, Danny. I did not intend to sound judgmental. We are business partners. It is best we keep it that way."

Danny didn't answer. He drained the glass and poured a second drink. "Jenna, my lass, you are as cold and hard as this brandy glass, but just as transparent." He raised his glass. "To my business partner!" He deliberately lingered, savoring the taste of the liquor on his tongue. "Sweet, so sweet— warms the soul, Miss Daggett."

Jenna started for the door.

"By the way," Danny said, "I need to discuss my plans at our next board meeting. I'm planning a business trip for several weeks in the spring—to Europe."

"Yes, I know," Jenna said, glancing at him as she tossed her head. She left Danny with a most quizzical expression on his face.

🌼 🌼 🌼

Mrs. Dewberry's favorite organization, the Benevolent and Relief Society, was planning a *soiree*, a masked ball, always a popular event in San Francisco. They hoped to raise money to build an orphanage for the many children whose parents had died by accident, infection, smallpox, cholera, fevers, or exhaustion. There would also be a facility to house desperate women or mothers with children until they could find work.

Jenna agreed to help Mrs. Dewberry write invitations to the "right sort," society's select, the prosperous and influential.

"We'll sell some tickets at the door, too, but the invitation list will prevent riffraff from coming. As a member of my committee, Jenna, you may invite your guests as well. It's going to be a lovely party. There will be a door prize and raffle, champagne, and a surprise that is too exciting for words.

Miss Creed has promised to sing 'Is It a Sin to Love Thee?' We have a fine little string orchestra that plays lovely quadrilles. I think the violinist is Mexican, but he's not too dark looking.

"It's such fun wearing masks. I have one made in iris purple silk and ecru lace with chips of amethyst. It matches my ball gown perfectly. Last year, I wore a green satin one with peacock feathers. No one guessed who I was, but I was the talk of the ball."

"I can imagine," Jenna struggled not to smile, averting her head as she blotted the ink on an invitation.

"Do you know, Jenna, I have nearly twenty ball gowns. How many do you have?"

"Enough," she answered. Jenna thought about the one formal dress salvaged from the fire that she'd carried to San Francisco. Since Doña Juana's death, she'd had little need for formal wear. Only in Monterey did she dress elegantly. She decided she had better find a good dressmaker.

Jenna glanced outside at the sunny garden full of rhododendrons. A breezy spring afternoon had obliterated the last of winter's cold and she decided to take a stack of invitations outside to address. Sitting in the gazebo, she pulled out an envelope and wrote in her neat pen:

To Miss Lilly Jordan
and Mr. Daniel McDaniels
No. 7 California Street
San Francisco

She smiled as she sealed it. *This will be a surprise to a great many people, including the recipients of the invitation. Mrs. Dewberry may not like my expanding the guest list to include my two friends, but she will like their generous contribution to the cause. Hannah will come, of that I'm certain.*

When Hannah read the invitation she laughed contemptuously.

This is rare. No doubt a mistake. I am not on any guest list, nor is Danny. Is it possible that Jenna is behind this? Perhaps this is her mean little spirit hoping to run me out of town. These very same charitable women helped to run Belle off. This is someone's idea of a joke, but I think I may get the last laugh.

But Jenna, darling, if you think Danny will ever want you for more than a bit of amusement, you're wrong. You don't know him. You'll never understand him as I do. I wear Danny like a second skin. He's my dancing bear, my helpless marionette. He's my chameleon twin who changes colors at my whim, at every change of my nightdress.

🐚 🐚 🐚

The large reception room of Saint Mary's Hall provided a perfect place for the *soiree*. Every kind of formal attire, San Francisco style, could be seen, which meant the rich looked grand and those who struggled with respectability looked a bit motley as they mixed and matched, borrowed, and copied the pacesetters the best they could.

Jenna had a gown copied from a French fashion magazine—a white and black lace dress with intricate beadwork in pearls, black jet, and crystal. Her matching mask, black and white hair plumes, pearl necklace and earrings, gave Jenna the look of a monarch. Like the other women of fashion, her full dress fell gracefully over wide crinolines.

Generous white flounces cascaded down the back of her skirt like a jeweled waterfall. Jenna glittered with every step. Statuesque and graceful, she felt as if she was floating like a blossom on the water. As she moved about the room, Jenna was aware that heads turned to look at her. No one knew who she was, but Jenna saw the admiring looks and felt beautiful behind the mask, even daring and a bit flirtatious. After all, who would know her?

As the guests arrived, Jenna anxiously watched the door. The music and dancing started and still her special guests had not arrived. Perhaps she had been wrong. Hannah was not coming after all.

But when all eyes turned toward the door, Jenna recognized the dazzling couple everyone ogled.

Hannah stood framed in the doorway for all to see. Her black curls were piled on top of her head and crowned in sable plumes and a jeweled topaz hairpiece that made the women suck in their breath with envy. The taffeta shine in her russet dress flashed iridescent gold and green and copper under the chandelier. No one would know her behind the glittering gold dust mask. She was the grandest one at the party.

Danny also looked stunning in his black tail coat, white waistcoat, silk cravat and patent leather boots; however, he was not wearing gloves, a fact pointed out by Mrs. Dewberry.

"And those fancy boots!" Mrs. Dewberry sneered.

"How does he expect to dance without slippers? Well, he don't know any better, being Irish and all. All them folks know is how to jig and stamp their feet."

Many people commented on the handsome couple who spoke so little and were as mysterious as a fairy tale.

Seeing Danny standing alone while Hannah was pursued by dozens of partners, Jenna walked over to him. "Good evening, Mr. McDaniels," Jenna said, smiling in her captivating way.

"Jenna! I've been looking for you. You look like a queen! Do we dare dance? I'll behave myself—not that I want to, you understand."

Jenna flashed a flirty smile. Behind her mask it was easy to be bold. "I'll take my chances, Mr. McDaniels."

They danced the next two dances before the evening's entertainment began. Jenna and Danny stepped out on the veranda while Mrs. Creed, "San Francisco's songbird," sang,

> *"Believe me, if all those endearing young charms,*
> *which I gaze on so fondly today . . ."*

The perfumed night air intoxicated Jenna. "Look at those beautiful rose bushes along the garden path, Danny."

"Not as lovely as you, Jenna, my girl." Danny took a small flask from his pocket and took a deep swallow. "I don't suppose you'd be wantin' a wee swig of the Irish, now, would you." He wiped off the rim with his sleeve put it back in his pocket. "Let me remove your mask. I want to look at your eyes."

"No, Danny. Let's go back inside."

Danny laughed. "You know your eyes tell secrets. We both know it. You've never fooled me, not since you were a young lassie." Danny kissed her lightly on her lips. "There now, a kiss between business partners...no harm done." Danny took Jenna's arm and escorted her back to the party in time for the orator's recitation.

The orator placed his hand on his vest, his deep voice ringing like a steeple bell.

> *"There's comforting thought at the close of the day,*
> *when I'm weary and lonely and sad,*
> *That sort of grips hold of my crusty old heart*
> *And bids it be merry and glad . . ."*

And the poet, his gloved hands clasped over his heart, looked to the ceiling and emoted,

> *"Sinks the sun below the desert,*
> *golden glows the sluggish Nile . . ."*

The guests clapped enthusiastically for the entertainers and shouted and cheered with the announcement of every raffle ticket winner.

"Ladies and gentlemen, your attention please," Mrs. Dewberry shouted. "The last object in our raffle is a surprise, the most exciting part of the evening." Her voice began to go higher and higher as she spoke. "We have, right here, a generous marble statue sculptured by none other than our famous Italian artist, Mr. Benito Pellegrino, who has donated his work for our honorable cause. And he is among us this evening—incognito, of course. We will sell it to the highest bidder! Mr. Dewberry, bring out the statue!" Mrs. Dewberry's voice was ear-shattering.

Two men rolled out a large, draped object about five feet high.

"How exciting it is!" squealed Mrs. Dewberry. "Now, I'll only tell you it is called Trumpeting Cherubs Ascending, a perfect thought for our cherubic orphans, don't you think? Now, Mr. Dewberry will handle the auction."

Again the guests cheered and whistled, unable to repress their rough edges and rowdy nature.

Mr. Dewberry put on his spectacles and read:

> *"If you see the hot tears falling*
> *From a brother's weeping eyes,*
> *Share them. And by kindly sharing*
> *Own our kinship in the skies.*
> *Why should anyone be glad*
> *When a brother's heart is sad?"*

After several more verses, he ended with a smile that showed all his teeth. Everyone clapped, and the ungloved men stomped their boots.

"Let's see them little buggers, mate," someone shouted.

In one dramatic gesture, Mr. Dewberry pulled the drape off the sculpture.

"Ah-h-h," the crowd hummed, then broke into raucous cheers and comments over the two excessively fat and creased cherubs with pointed toes, each one holding a horn to its baby mouth. Their full-blown cheeks ballooned, and one pair of angels eyes, raised heavenward, were decidedly crossed under the ballroom light. A drape of marble encircled the pillar and wound over the swollen bellies, gracefully hiding their private parts.

"We'll start the bidding at a hundred dollars or six ounces of dust," Mr. Dewberry said.

The competition began, but not enthusiastically. Then suddenly, from the back of the crowd, a female voice said coolly, "Twenty-five thousand dollars."

The room silenced, the people turned.

"I bid twenty-five thousand dollars," Hannah repeated.

Mrs. Dewberry looked pale, as if she might faint. Mr. Dewberry said, "Did you say twenty-five thousand dollars?"

"I did. My contribution to the orphanage," Hannah said coldly.

"Madam, how generous! The statue is yours!"

As the people shouted wildly, a champagne bottle passed from hand to hand to the bewilderment of the caterer, and Benito Pellegrino tore off his mask and rushed to kiss Hannah's hand.

"Take off your mask! Let us see who you are!" people said, encircling Hannah.

She walked slowly through the parting crowd. The excited guests hushed as Hannah carefully removed her mask and looked disdainfully at the San Franciscans.

The men exploded into shouts so loud the room shook. "Three cheers for Lilly!" The women of the Benevolent Society did not cheer. Their faces were somber or stricken.

The good ladies from the Society were about to become even more distressed as everyone removed their masks. Pandemonium and laughter broke out everywhere when a number of gentlemen recognized many of the exquisite ladies attending the function as the "fair but frail" women who worked at Belle Cora's before she was run out of town.

The committee women huddled in groups. "This is a disgrace!" Mrs. Dewberry shouted. "Here now," she shrieked above the crowd. Getting no attention, she removed her shoe and banged it on the floor. At last her shrill voice got attention.

"The members of the Benevolent Society have discussed your offer, Miss Jordan. Although it is generous of you, we must remind everyone that this is a Christian organization. It would not be appropriate to accept your contribution."

The crowd responded by low murmurs and a light applause.

"Very well, then, I'll withdraw my offer," Hannah said with indifference.

"Wait!" Jenna said, pushing her way through the crowd to the front.

"I'll match Miss Jordan's bid—short one dollar, of course. The sculpture is hers. You can't refuse forty-nine thousand dollars to build your orphanage. It would be unchristian. Do you believe the money that paid for this party is any less tainted, coming out of the mines, corrupt business transactions, even stolen land?" She turned to the crowd and raised her hands. "Does not San Francisco graciously accept this money?"

The San Franciscans cheered, hollered, clapped their hands, and whooped their approval.

"And who now would not add their tainted money to this offer?" Jenna shouted.

In a rush of laughter and good-natured hoots, the men and French women of easy virtue threw coins at the foot of the sculpture. The evening ended in high spirits.

Jenna stood near the door, watching Hannah move toward her with dignified grace and style. She nodded to her old friend saying with exaggerated courtesy, "Goodnight, Miss Jordan."

"Goodnight, Miss Daggett," Hannah said and gave Jenna a special, secretive smile that only the two young girls of the plains would understand.

"Goodnight, Mr. McDaniels." Jenna had no trouble looking directly into his eyes. She did not care that her fixed gaze sent an amorous message.

"It has been a pleasure, as always," Miss Daggett.

The next issue of the *Alta* had a few words to say about the extraordinary events of the *soiree*.

> " . . . In spite of the success of the fundraising, the conduct of many of those who attended showed little respect for public morals and decorum. Men who have virtuous mothers and sisters should be outraged by those who brought women of questionable virtue to an honorable event. The insult must not be repeated."

Hannah's response to the newspaper article was to place the Trumpeting Cherubs Ascending sculpture on her front lawn, where curiosity seekers could marvel at the ostentation, and the supporters of the Benevolent Society could always be reminded of good deeds and charity.

🍂 🍂 🍂

After Danny and Hannah left for Europe, Jenna tried to tell herself she didn't care that Danny was away, that his relationship with Hannah was of no importance to her. She was, after all, a realist. He had never expressed any interest in her except in teasing, suggestive advances, and attempts to kiss her. There was an attraction between them, but he had clearly chosen Hannah as the woman in his life. Any other female would be a fool to take his flirtation seriously.

Still, no matter how she tried to talk herself out of feeling anything romantic toward Danny, she knew she was kidding herself. She wanted to be with him all the time. Thinking about Danny and Hannah together, the kisses and passion they would exchange, even the strolls in a shady park, aggravated her. Her jealousy was beginning to grow, fed by the fact that she would never let Danny know the truth. She had fallen in love with him.

Jenna also overlooked the fact that Danny had not been on top of her company's affairs as she had hoped. He seemed to have spent more time with the Vigilance Committee, for which he had been an officer.

The Vigilance Committee had been created by restless young men, men like Danny, who had been aroused by San Francisco's lawlessness. They had wrapped themselves in the excitement of armed conflict with corrupt police officials and judges refusing to do their jobs of convicting and trying criminals. They had thrived on the exhilaration of a good hanging, deporting political swindlers, secret meetings, the pomp of parades, and hot cries against corruption. They enjoyed being part of the muscle behind the new slate of elected officials from the People's Party.

With the election of James Buchanan as President of the United States, the Vigilance Committee had disbanded. Buchanan had promised the California Governor Federal troops, if necessary, to establish law and order. There was no longer a need for vigilantes to be the arm of the law.

Jenna remembered standing in a crowd, watching Danny at the head of a parade for the Vigilance Committee. His face had been flushed with pomposity and heroics as he marched with his boys, flowers in their guns and muskets to show they were responsible for ushering in a new order and were now willing to put aside their violent ways.

Now, the saloons were full of the old vigilantes or "me boys," as Danny called them, filling the drinking rooms with old songs and Irish jigs, and keeping the saloon doors swinging. Jenna felt certain that Danny's decision to go to Europe was driven by his need to be distracted, to ease his restlessness now that the Committee was disbanded.

🍃 🍃 🍃

Throughout the spring and summer, Jenna immersed herself in the growth of her new company. After listening to her male partners and their discussions about new business opportunities, she turned her attention to investing in other growing companies.

Jenna was excited by the energy of the male business world, and by quietly listening from the sidelines, she discovered she had an uncanny sense of what was a sound or shaky investment. She had tested her private thoughts against the opinions of her partners and decided she would risk her own money elsewhere. At twenty-two years old, Jenna had proved to be a capable entrepreneur with keen investment instincts.

She turned her newfound business acumen to the cattle industry, realizing she would have to carefully assess the market place. She was beginning to hear of great cattle drives crossing the plains from Missouri and Kansas Territory to the west coast. Before too long, the large profits in the cattle industry would have to be shared, and eventually she might have to sell before there was more supply than demand. She would know the right time to sell.

Meanwhile, she would look into other companies. San Francisco needed investors in order to build roads and bridges, to establish new manufacturing concerns, promote commerce, improve communication and develop land.

Jenna's brief experience living in the mining camp made her realize there was a need for transportation of goods by some means other than mule trains. Why not a railroad?

She had followed the career of Theodore Judd, a visionary who also saw the need for a local train, as well as a transcontinental railroad from New York to San Francisco. At her first opportunity, and even though her partners discouraged her, she bought stock in a small railroad line from Sacramento to the foothills of the Sierras. It was completed with little difficulty and proved to be a good investment. Now Mr. Judd was pleading to build the Central Pacific Railroad, a transcontinental railroad right through the mountains.

"Through the Rockies? The Sierras? The desert? Formidable walls! Impossible!" the nay-sayers shouted. "Who would fund such nonsense?"

But Jenna listened with interest. She had become convinced that the spirit of man could change the face of the earth. Man could move mountains, blast through rock, cross deserts. He could do anything! She believed in the message of Mr. Judd with all her heart and had bought stock in the Central Pacific Railroad.

Her partners, even Danny, believed the establishment of a transcontinental railroad was a very long way off and did not follow her interest. Instead, they had joked with her about her ghost railroad that would have to sprout wings to fly over the mountaintops.

Now that Danny was not around to discourage her, she attended a meeting at the Saint Charles Hotel, where Mr. Judd was going to speak. So far, her stock had not yielded a profit, and no one seemed interested in building the railroad by anyone.

How stupid they are! Jenna thought.

Four very rich and powerful men, known as The Big Four, seemed to dominate the meeting. They would not invest in a railroad, but Mr. Judd convinced them they needed a roadbed or wagon road through the Sierras to Nevada City. After all, gold and silver were coming out of a few Nevada mines, and Californians, as well, needed a good road for the transportation of goods.

Jenna could see clearly what Mr. Judd was doing. If he could not get money for a railroad, he could get it for a road, which would become the roadbed for the future train. Mr. Judd seemed to be outsmarting the Big Four. But later, when Jenna tried to buy stock in the road, there was none left to buy. The men, also, had seen the opportunity, and were going to keep control within their group of four.

"I'm sorry, little lady," one of the four men said, "but this is no business for a female. It is for men only. The stock has already been sold—all of it."

Jenna knew she had missed one of the greatest opportunities for unfathomable wealth in the opening of the West. She turned her sights to the surrounding hills of San Francisco and quietly and steadily began to build a fortune in property. The drought that had brought so many disillusioned miners to San Francisco, had also left many newly built homes, business blocks, and land tracts without buyers. Jenna reasoned she could buy unwanted real estate at a low price and wait for times to change.

The land would always be valuable. She had seen nothing but growing populations as towns and cities sprang up in the span of a few years. The people would come and keep coming. They would need houses and schools, churches, theaters, restaurants. Before they could build, they would have to buy her land.

Business was booming for Jenna, but its demands left her empty and lonely. As she watched the blue sky of summer mellow into autumnal hues, Jenna found herself yearning for a way to fill her personal void.

She longed for companionship, friendship. She needed a change of scene. It was a perfect time to visit Darcey, Blue, and Pearle, the only family she knew, the only ones who cared whether or not she awakened in the morning. She made immediate arrangements to leave by coach for Jackson.

The Sierras were hot and the town of Jackson sweltered under a relentless sun. Dogs panted in the shade of a wagon or on the cool side of a building and scratched wildly at fleas and sores. Tied horses, heads hanging down and eyes closed, switched their tails, shooing nasty, biting, blue flies off their backs. Gnats swarmed in dizzy circles in the middle of the streets, seemingly the only activity in the town.

Jenna loved the slow days of late summer, sitting on the porch with Darcey, shelling peas, or reading stories aloud with Pearle in the shady side of the garden under the trees. It was a time for afternoon lemonade, evening chocolate cake, and mornings of skimming off thick cream to eat with sun-

warmed strawberries. It was a nostalgic time when Jenna's thoughts turned
to fading memories of Sapling Grove. Seeing Darcey and Blue married,
compatible as fresh bread and jam, and Pearle, lovely as a peach, gave
Jenna great happiness, a feeling that all was right in the world.

At night, the boarders joined Jenna and her "family" on the porch for
gentle conversation, a moment of friendship, the sharing of the crickets'
thrum and pause. They all told stories, sometimes those everyone had heard
over and over, but everyone laughed just the same.

The story of Sarah Abrahms and her twin boys, Tobias and Thaddeus,
was a favorite.

"I was right," Darcey said. "Sarah ran a disreputable house called the
Golden Dragon. She had a full-blown business of buying Chinese women
called the Daughters of Joy . . . right here in Jackson! And she was building
that place under our very noses! And living here . . . in *my* house! Of course,
she didn't fool me after I saw the Chinese workers loading brass beds into
her so-called *emporium*. Those two boys didn't know if they were a-foot or
a-horseback half the time. Blue thought she was just a nice, harmless old
lady, but I had my suspicions right from the start. She really fooled Blue,
though."

"No she didn't," he said defensively. "I just respected her as an older
lady what needs respect."

"Anyway, she made a lot of money until they ran her out of town. And
you'll never guess what they found in the basement of that building—an
opium den! She was dealing in every kind of sin imaginable right under our
noses." Darcey slapped Jenna's knee to make her point.

"What about Laveda Lovelady?" Jenna asked.

"Well, I'll tell you about our famous lady," Darcey said and began to
laugh. Blue shuffled his feet, shook his head, and chuckled.

"Our dear Miss Lovelady is no longer with us . . . a sorry end to her
Jackson career. She left sometime ago and took our other boarder, Charlie,
with her as her accompanist, she said. The pair of them are traveling
somewhere in the mining camps so she can do her famous Moth Dance.
Last I heard, they were in Nevada somewhere—Nevada City. I don't think
they'll be back, but she left her brass bird cage with two stuffed birds in

it. It's still up in the blue room, as kind of a reminder to a certain person on this porch that lovebirds have got to be the real thing—not stuffed with cotton."

Blue cleared his throat and grinned.

"Laveda made a big splash in Jackson, throwing her long hair around like a mop, prancing on her toes like she was a burned-up moth and wearing skimpy clothes and tights and batting her eyes at all the men in town. She got so important, men took off their old, greasy hats and bowed and fawned like she was a queen. Why, the men in this town acted like fools."

"Now, Darcey, the men thought a lady of high breeding deserved a little respect, that's all. Remember, she was a Hungarian princess, I think she said."

Jenna watched Blue trying not to smile. He loved to hear Darcey fuss about Laveda, especially when there was a hint of jealousy in her voice.

Darcey slapped a mosquito on her arm. "Poppycock! She was a farmer's wife who read books! And she was about as Hungarian as I am! The only thing she knew about Hungary was they made goulash."

"And mighty tasty it was, too," Blue said, pulling out a pipe and filling it with tobacco.

"Anyway, she started giving singing, dancing, and elocution lessons. 'Lessons in Ladyship,' she called them. A group of us women decided we'd learn a few of her . . . you know, tricks, brush up on some skills. Besides, we thought it was time to show our menfolk we were worthy of hat-tipping, too. But instead of appreciating our efforts, the men got to snickering behind our backs. So we women put our heads together and taught the men a lesson."

"What did you do, Darcey? Tell me!" Jenna said, laughing at Darcey's excited voice.

"We took dancing lessons! Yes, that's what we did!"

Blue burst into a loud laugh, which ended in a cough.

"Hush, Blue. We ladies learned a dance Laveda called Woodland Morn. Everyone had a particular part to portray."

"What was you, Darcey?" Blue asked.

"A swan! You know perfectly well I was a swan. What did you think I was?"

"I thought you was an Arab. You see, Jenna, each lady was something—a bumblebee, a bird, a tree, a butterfly, a bush, a nun . . ."

"Not a nun!" Darcey snapped. "Mrs. Creed was a blackbird."

"Well, she looked like a nun to me. Anyway, one lady floated around waving her arms and blowing out her cheeks. She was the fog." Blue threw his head back and laughed so hard he nearly tipped over backwards.

"No, Blue, that was Mrs. Rogers playing the morning mist," Darcey said, sounding irritated.

"Anyways, the ladies all came out on the stage dressed in colored tights like Laveda's, and pranced around and waved their arms and threw flowers and . . . " he started laughing and wiping the tears from his eyes.

"It wasn't *that* funny, Blue," Darcey said. "The men didn't laugh, I can tell you. They were so embarrassed seeing their wives and the town women up there, they didn't clap, stomp their feet, or throw money. No, sir. They skedaddled home and after that they never cared to attend Laveda's programs for fear they might just see someone they knew on stage—maybe even their wives. They quit fussing over Miss Lovelady. When she saw her splash was over, she packed up and left town. But we women keep our tights and costumes ready just in case we need to remind the men we're also ladies of allure, ladies that need respect." It was Darcey's turn to laugh out loud.

"Go put on your swan outfit and your white tights, if you're so courageous. I still think you looked like an Arab," Blue said, and blew a cloud of pipe smoke into the air.

🙂 🙂 🙂

"Harke should be here any day now," Pearle said, setting the picnic basket down. "He knows you're here. He'll come. Won't it be fine having him around for a few days?"

Jenna and Pearle spread a cloth on a grassy area, a perfect picnic spot with a view. The hills looked smoky in the dusty light.

"Yes, I'll be happy to see him, too." Jenna looked at Pearle's sweet expression. Her quiet gestures and easy, soft voice were as calming as a stream winding through an undisturbed forest. The awkward limp and built-up shoe did not detract from her special beauty.

There was something about Pearle that made Jenna feel certain, sure of herself, balanced in the scheme of things. She had watched Pearle sitting so still in the garden that squirrels ate from her hands, and once a rabbit, unafraid, stopped within touching distance and looked at her. They seemed to exchange a silent greeting, a simple, "Good day. Nice to see you."

Jenna also noticed the face of a girl in love when she spoke of Harke. The deep sweetness in her eyes and tender smile at the mention of his name could not hide her girlish secret.

"You are fond of Harke, aren't you, Pearle?"

"Oh, yes, Jenna! He is good . . . and knows the world. When he rides into Jackson, he is like a knight to me, returning from faraway lands. He always brings me a present. Once he brought me a linen handkerchief from Italy!"

Harke had arrived by the time Jenna and Pearle returned from their picnic. He looked every bit a stage driver with his fine gloves and expensive hat and silk scarf. Jenna noticed the change in him—the confident swagger, the cocky smile and easy manner. He did his best to show off his worldliness and to impress Jenna, including keeping his fine leather hat on at all times until Darcey finally said, "Take your hat off, Harke. You look like you're about to leave any minute."

Pearle, who had been watching his every gesture with admiration, spoke up. "Tell us an adventure, Harke."

"Well, I can't say it was an adventure, but a mighty interesting experience. You'll have to leave the room, though, while I tell it, Pearle," Harke said in a big brother way.

Pearle seemed to deflate like a pricked souffle. "I'm as adult as everyone here. In fact, I'm becoming an old woman before your very eyes! I'm not leaving the room, Harke," she protested.

"Mind you, Pearle, it ain't fittin' for you to hear, what I'm about to mention."

Jenna smiled to herself. *Dear Harke, as worldly as you seem to be, you can't see the young, gracious woman blooming right before your very eyes.*

Pearle's baby face had smoothed into a near-perfect oval, a pale pearl drop with lips full and soft as a rose. The quiet wisdom in her eyes clearly showed she was not a flower that wilted at the blast of high noon heat or an icy wind. She had been through too many hardships and had survived by an inner strength, perhaps a belief in a higher power, or simply by watching the balance and rhythm of nature. She had learned to flow like the mountain stream, to slide around granite obstacles, to eddy, rest, and move on quickly.

Harke shook his head. "Well, I don't understand the way young women of today are allowing theirselves to be exposed to unbecoming conversation, but since you all seem to think it's all right, even you, Blue, I'll tell you a shocking thing I seen, as God is my witness. Don't say I didn't warn you, Pearle."

Jenna smiled. Harke was enjoying being the center of the conversation.

"Oh, for Heaven's sake, Harke, get on with it," Darcey said, slapping at another mosquito.

"I've been over to the west side of the Sierras to Carson Valley to a Mormon settlement there. They're making a fortune in cultivating turnips, of all things! Anyway, I was hired to carry a Mormon man from Volcano, and—excuse me, Pearle—his three wives and five children. One woman was his brand-new wife, a young one. I seen him—excuse me, Pearle—fondle her knees whilst them other two wives looked straight ahead and the kids paid no mind at all."

"Gracious!" Darcey exclaimed. "What did the new wife do?"

"Nothing! She looked straight ahead, too, like the other two wives. It was the darndest thing I ever seen."

"Maybe she had sore knees and he was a-helpin' her out," Blue suggested.

Darcey flashed him an exasperated look. "Honestly, Blue, sometimes I think you're plain dense."

Blue chuckled, looked at Darcey's knees, and winked at her.

"And that ain't all," Harke said. "I seen Joaquin Murietta's head pickled in a jar of alcohol. It ain't funny—I really did!"

"Do you mean that famous bandit?" Jenna asked.

"I mean the worst scoundrel of these parts connected with a hundred deeds of blood. Someone finally caught him—the vigilantes, I'm guessin'. I tell you, drivin' stage will be a whole herd safer from now on." He glanced at Jenna and popped his hat back on his head. "I'm in constant danger on the road as it is."

Harke made Jenna smile. Although he tried to impress her with his manly deeds, to her he would always be her girlhood friend, the boy of the plains whose straw-colored hair blew like dry grass.

One night when Jenna lingered on the porch after everyone had gone to bed, Harke joined her. They talked of Hannah. Jenna felt Harke's pain over his sister, his anger that she had hurt his mother so deeply by running away.

"I have a mind not to tell my folks I know where she is. Mama has resigned herself that Hannah is dead—and as far as I'm concerned, she is."

"Will you go see her?"

"Out of curiosity maybe . . . maybe not. If you see her, tell her you seen me. If she shows any interest, I'll go to San Francisco."

Jenna already knew Hannah had no interest in connecting with anyone in her family. "I'll do that, Harke," she said sadly.

They sat in silence until the beauty of the night seeped into their souls and the sound of crickets singing somewhere in the grass changed their private sadness into reflection and then into the wonder at simply being alive, sitting together on a porch like two pinpoints of light in a vast universe.

"Jenna, you know I still love you, don't you?" Harke said, taking her hand. "Have you changed your mind about me—I mean, being more than just a friend?"

"I will always love you as my dearest friend, Harke. I don't think I could love you in any other way," Jenna said softly.

"What's wrong with marrying your friend? Why, men and women who have never met at all marry and settle down and raise a family. They don't think about the kind of love you're a-thinkin' on. They marry because they are partners. They work together and help the land grow. If everyone married on your kind of love, there would be mighty few marriages. I can provide for you, Jenna. I got enough money saved to buy a farm and land—and, well, we belong together."

"I wish with all my heart I could marry you, Harke, and raise a family. But I seem to be drifting into another current, going in some other direction—and I like it. Right now, marriage is far from my mind. I can't imagine settling down."

"But Jenna, you're getting old! Before too long, women will gossip that you're headed for spinsterhood."

"I can't help that, Harke." Jenna withdrew her hand. "But you know, there is someone who *is* clearly in love with you—I mean, in every way, the way of men and women."

"Who?" Harke asked, sounding incredulous."

"I can't believe you are so blind to this person who worships everything you do or say. Can't you guess? Who makes you feel like the most special person in the whole world?"

"You mean *Pearle*?" Harke shot out of his chair like he'd been stung by a bee. "Pearle? She's still a-growin' up. She's like my little sister! Not Pearle!"

"Yes, Harke, Pearle. And she is *not* your little sister. She's sixteen, a young lady, and one of the dearest people on this earth."

Harke appeared dumbfounded. He sat on the porch steps and ran his hand through his hair. "Are you saying she *loves* me?"

"I am," Jenna said, sitting next to him. "She lives for your visits, writes poetry about you; she even writes secret love letters, which she puts in her stories by other characters, but they are to you. She can't pretend with me. I've played too many games of imagination with her. Besides, all you have to do is look into her eyes to see she's in love with you. It's there as plain as the nose on your face."

"I've never looked at her . . . romantically. I've always felt special with her, important somehow. I make her laugh. I guess I never thought about anyone else but you for a wife. All this time she's been smilin' at me and makin' me nice little presents, I never thought she had a feelin' for me." Harke blew out his cheeks. "I guess I'm not as smart as I thought I was.

Pearle . . . I'll be switched!"

"She's easy to love."

"Yep, she sure is," Harke said, standing up. "If you don't mind, Jenna, I think I'll take a walk. I got some hard thinkin' to do."

By the time Jenna left Jackson to return to San Francisco, Harke and Pearle had announced their engagement with plans to marry at Christmas time.

FIFTEEN

D ANNY RETURNED FROM EUROPE in September. Jenna could hardly wait to see him, but decided to let him call on her. Meanwhile, she controlled her anxiety by working on her pet project: a home she had designed and was building in the lovely hills above San Francisco.

The house was situated among the trees, a park setting overlooking San Francisco and the bay beyond. The foundation was already laid. If good weather held, she'd be in her new home by Christmas. It would be a tasteful two-story affair, smaller than Hannah's house, not ostentatious, but appropriate for a woman living alone with only a small staff. She planned a luxurious garden all around the house and riding paths through twenty acres of her land that might later be developed.

A week passed before Jenna received a message through a young courier to join Danny for lunch. She sent her acceptance and found herself nervously waiting for him to drive up in his fine rig.

Through the window she watched Danny bound up the steps of the Bay View, two at a time, full of high energy and boyish good looks. She heard the door open and the scurry of the timorous feet of boarders disappearing up the stairs or into the dining room.

When Jenna entered the parlor, she immediately felt Danny's magnetic pull. He seemed to reel her toward him like she was a helpless fish caught on a line. The pair quickly escaped out the front door away from the curious eyes of guests, who now peered around corners or sat on the porch like a jury waiting to condemn.

"Where are we going, Danny?" Jenna asked as he helped her into the seat next to him.

"The Seacliff, a new, rather intimate restaurant across town on the ocean side. Perhaps you've heard of it. It's situated high on a cliff. And oh, Jenna, me love, the view is magnificent! You'll love the *bouillabaisse*."

As they approached the coast, the air grew chilly. A wall of fog sat ominously on the water like something alive and waiting to move toward the shore; but Jenna thought the day magnificent as she sat next to Danny, smiling into his sea blue eyes, feeling beautiful. It was rare to be with him alone, without their business partners or a crowd of fascinated people captivated by his entertaining stories.

Danny, too, thought the day a fine one, especially since it was filled with Jenna. He glanced at her, once again marveling at her strong beauty, tall and graceful, with her direct eyes and sensual smile. He admired her strong profile, high, smooth forehead, the straight nose, stubborn jaw, and her slightly open, luscious mouth. The nakedness of her long white neck disappearing downward into the neckline of her dress excited Danny, and he smiled to himself.

Being alone with Jenna could prove interesting. The only thing between them now was a few layers of silk and a few sensuous hours of innocent conversation.

He moved his leg carelessly closer to her, hoping to touch the cool thigh hiding under the petticoats. He grinned broadly. "Tis a fine day, Jenna, me girl," he said, and with spontaneous high spirits, he broke into one of his songs.

"Sweet William married him a wife
To be the comfort of his life.
He married his wife and took her home,
But I think her married a little too soon."

His wife would neither card nor spin,
For fear of spoiling her delicate skin.
His wife would neither bake nor brew
For fear of spoiling her high-heeled shoe.

Sweet William has gone out to his barn
And there he's taken his sheepskin down.
He laid the sheepskin on her back,
and with two little willows went whickety-whack . . ."

Jenna tipped her head back and laughed—a rare, open laugh, reminiscent of the carefree girl who had excited him years ago.

A gust of wind blew unexpectedly into their faces, lifting the brim of Jenna's hat and whipping the ribbons into a frenzy.

"Take it off, Jenna, or you'll lose it in the dunes."

"Yes, a good idea," she said, removing the pins. Another gust suddenly tore it from her hands and carried it into the air, spinning it across the dunes, where it rested and fluttered like a frightened bird.

Danny jumped from the buggy to retrieve it. With each step up the soft sand, he sunk up to his ankles, unable to get a firm foothold. He had just about reached the hat when off it sailed to another dune top. It had taken on a life of its own, teasing Danny to chase it, like a mother bird pulling a predator away from its chicks.

Undaunted, Danny removed his coat and began sneaking up on his prey as if it had a game in mind, one that would end with either him or the hat victorious. Suddenly, the wind snapped it out of a hollow, sailing it over Danny's head and back toward the buggy

Jenna jumped from the rig to corner the mischievous hat, while Danny approached it from the opposite side. Just as Jenna placed her foot on a ribbon, Danny lurched, throwing his body over the hat and kicking up sprays of sand.

"Got it!" he shouted. He held it up victoriously, squinting through his sandy lashes.

Jenna knelt beside him, laughing as she brushed the sand from his face and hair.

"Glory be, the grit is even on me teeth," he said. He stood up, shook his hair, and looked into Jenna's electrifying eyes. Impulsively, he reached for her, pulled her into his arms, and kissed her.

Jenna let the kiss linger, thrilled by its boldness and surprised at herself for not caring where such a kiss could lead her. She wondering if Danny was still playing.

When another blast of sand whipped around them, stinging their bare skin like a hoard of angry bees, Danny let her go and flopped on his back. The spell was broken. "Aye, Jenna, you work up a man's appetite."

Jenna felt relieved. Behind his kiss was mere exuberance for the moment. But his passion had left her wanting more, wanting him to press against her harder. Danny had pushed open doors that had been carefully locked as long as she could remember. The feeling was new and exhilarating. It had slipped out of an illusive dream into a reality with shape and substance.

She laughed and picked up her hat, shaking out the fine sand. "We're a sorry sight."

"I like you this way, with your hair flyin' out of your combs. All women look prettier a little mussed, and even more appealing to the eye when they don't care a damn."

"Then I don't care. And I'm hungry, too."

The rest of the way to the Seacliff, Danny entertained Jenna with stories he knew would amuse her—tales that made his other lassies smile or swoon under his Irish charm. Jenna was no different. Even the filly pulling the rig trotted with a perky high step and arched her neck prettily as if to please her driver.

Yes, this little lassie was ready. He would have her, by God.

He could control his arousal for the moment, but he must have this woman. He thought of nothing else when he was around her. For years, he had imagined her perfect, naked body open, inviting him to ravage her, to taste every part of her. By God, he would have her!

The Seacliff lay perched high on the cliffs above the sea-crashing rocks.

"The view is wonderful, Danny!" Jenna exclaimed, hanging tightly onto her blowing hat. "It's so wild and fierce. The power of the sea is frightening."

"That's why I brought you here. You're like this place, Jenna, but you don't know it. When I'm with you, I feel you have no still water. What runs deep is a torrent, crashing waves against the rocks. No, me love, I know who you are."

Jenna smiled. She could have said the same about him, but only took his arm as they went in for lunch.

How devilish and forward he is. It must be the way of the Irish, and Danny McDaniels is so cocky he believes he can take liberties and get by with them. I should not have let him kiss me like that. I'll be on my guard next time, lest he think me like all the other silly ladies who flutter around him.

The windows of the restaurant faced the open sea, allowing Danny and Jenna to watch a fog bank slowly move closer to shore. They chatted brightly and comfortably, with Danny toasting often to her or the saints, to the President of the United States, to the Irish wee folk, to all the lassies with blue eyes. Then, quite unexpectedly, Danny's mood shifted. His words were shadowed by sentiment and strange, uncomfortable double meanings.

Jenna hoped to bring him back to his carefree self and to rekindle the gaiety. "Danny, tell me about Ireland. I know nothing about your life before you came here."

"There's nothing to tell of interest. My family were clod farmers."

"Clod farmers?"

"Dirt clods. That's all they could grow—the only thing the land yielded." Danny took an extra-large mouthful of beef, piled the back of his fork with a clump of mashed potatoes and peas, swilled a mouthful of wine, and said nothing further.

"Do you have brothers or sisters?" Jenna asked.

"Two younger sisters, two brothers—one younger, one older."

"What are their names?"

"Mary, Leeny, Colin, and Erin. Good Irish names."

"And where are they now, Danny?"

"You aren't wanting to know all the details of my life now, are ye? You know what curiosity does to a cat, for sure."

"I don't mean to pry."

"It's all right, Jenna. I haven't talked about my family in a very long time. They were good people . . . simple farmers, but very bright just the same. Me mother worked herself to death raisin' children with no food and no hope. She was a dandy girl, she was. Danny smiled and called the waiter to bring a whiskey.

"Tell me about your mother."

"Me dear ole mum? She starved to death."

"Oh, Danny, I'm so sorry. I didn't mean to bring up sad memories."

"So did Mary and Leeny. Me da' died of a broken heart, he did—just laid himself down on me mother's grave and asked the angels to carry him away. I don't know what happened to me brothers. Like me, they walked away from the farm lookin' for food. There wasn't a potato left in the whole of Ireland. Everyone starved—except me, lucky Danny, the one who fled to America." Danny shoved another bite of food into his mouth, dropping some into his lap.

Jenna felt great compassion for Danny. All his gaiety clearly cloaked a terrible suffering, one ragged with guilt. "Tell me what happened," she said, "that is, if you care to."

"My older brother, Colin, and I went to Dublin before we went our separate ways, both of us swearing vengeance on the English who'd promised economic reforms for Ireland, but did nothing, the bastards.

They wanted us dead—anyone against the Union. They let us starve. They knew the Irish were dyin' like flies, strugglin' daily for a single bite of food, scratchin' the earth for any kind of withered root to boil into a tea for the wee ones, but they did nothing.

We both joined the Young Ireland movement and got mixed up in agitating and demonstrating, doing what we could to repeal the Union and thwart the pus-sucking British buggers. They got wind of one of our planned risings and brought troops in. Some of us were shot, some were deported, and some escaped.

I never saw Colin again, and young Erin—a good lad, he was—I never saw from the day I left him with some neighbors, the Coffeys. I don't know what happened to him or any of the old friends, for that matter. The Coffeys' farm burned down. I feel certain that Erin must be dead. He was never very strong like Colin and me. But he was me mum's favorite, for sure. The last thing I said to him was, 'Be a brave lad, Erin. I'll come for you one day.' He believed me."

A day that had started out full of fun was now somber, and Danny's spirit seemed as gray and silent as the creeping fog outside the window.

Then, as suddenly as the change of a dance step, Danny smiled and said, "Enough tears for a lifetime. No more Irish sad songs . . . not on a day spent with a lass who doesn't care if she's wearin' a hat full of sand."

Jenna had wondered about Danny's past that had always been a mystery to her. Now that he had spoken about his family, the new intimacy deepened her feeling for him. On the other hand, discovering the other side of the carefree Danny carried with it the price of possibly knowing too much. She had caught a glimpse of the private world, the inner man who covered his memories with amusing stories, high energy, risk, strong appetites, and rowdy friends . . and women . . . like Hannah. He had given away part of himself, a kind of confession that would change the shape of their relationship—for better or worse.

The fleeting thought of Hannah had intruded once again as it had so often in the past. Always hanging between them like the fog bank was Hannah's invisible presence. Not speaking her name, avoiding stories that focused on her and Danny together, clouded an honest friendship and obscured their feelings toward each other.

Even in their discussions about his trip to Europe, Hannah never appeared. Danny spoke as though he had traveled alone. Surely, he knew Jenna was aware he had a mistress. Everyone in San Francisco talked about them and, except for "his boys," thought it was scandalous.

Jenna wondered if he expected her to pretend Hannah didn't exist. She did not want to tell him that his mistress was her girlhood friend for fear he would suspect a conspiracy or feel an invasion of his privacy. For now, she thought it better he not know of her early friendship, and that both Hannah and Danny never discover that she had fallen in love with him.

All Jenna knew was that being alone with Danny this day made her feel like "the other woman," as though she, herself, was the illicit one. Carrying secrets around was uncomfortable for her, like scratchy undergarments or prickly heat. She was not one to hide from any situation, choosing always to be open and direct. Jenna had been forced to keep secrets before—the horror of Faithful Squibb, the knowledge of Enrique's murdering the Indian boy and the doña. She did not like secrets but knew that all people had them, locked them away, and carried them to the grave. Jenna wondered if she could hide her for Danny—if this, too, would remain an undisclosed secret.

By the time they finished lunch the fog had moved silently over the cliffs, engulfing the restaurant and spreading across the peninsula. They stood for a moment on the edge of the cliff feeling vulnerable and precarious as they watched the swelling water curl and crash against the rocks. Jenna's heart pounded with a strange fear, as if she were one step away from a violent end, but as she stood there, she wanted the wind to touch her, to tear at her, rip away unnatural confinement, correctness, conformity, inhibitions.

She removed her hat, and instantly her hair blew out of its soft form. Danny grabbed her and kissed her hard on the mouth, twisting on her lips. This time the kiss was fierce and full of meaning. Jenna did not resist, nor did the passion stop. On the drive home, the strange fog enveloped them in a surrealistic world of gray shapes smudged into a charcoal drawing and vanishing in the mist. Everything was obscure except for Danny and the rhythmic clip-clop of the horses, and the passion that absorbed them.

Danny did not drive Jenna home. Instead, he drove her to his house, and under a blanket of fog carried her up the steps into his bedroom and laid her on the bed. In moments, Jenna found herself as exposed as the rocks, as violent as the waves.

🐦 🐦 🐦

Jenna moved into her beautiful home at the close of the year. She was grateful to have the distraction from her growing obsession with Danny.

As the weeks passed, Jenna's passion for Danny had raged unabated. She, like Hannah, was his lover, but Jenna did not care. Unlike Hannah, she loved him desperately, completely, in ways she never believed possible. To Hannah, Danny was a useful fool who paid her extravagant bills. Jenna asked for nothing except to be with him and to feel him move inside her, to let her love him in return. She quickly dismissed thoughts that she was no more than his whore and even accepted his exquisite gold brooch, a peacock with a fanned tail of tiny diamonds and sapphires.

Danny never mentioned Hannah. Jenna was curious that she had not seen her or her fine carriage and plumed horses about town. Could it be that she had gone? Curiosity led her to Hannah's house.

"She's still gone, Miss," the old, bent Chinese man said. "To England. Back in springtime—blossom time. Maybe yes, maybe no."

Jenna felt uneasy. Was Danny's passion for her simply a means to fill the void left by Hannah's absence? Was she only a substitute, someone with whom to pass the nights and long afternoons?

With no competition, no vying for position, Jenna's romantic madness began to diminish. She had been so involved with Danny she had difficulty keeping her mind on the business and her investments. It was time to get control of her runaway emotions, time to confront Danny with some direct questions. The opportunity arose one afternoon his office.

"I need money, Jenna," Danny said.

A chill went over her body. "Oh?"

"I want to invest in some Nevada mine stock. There are veins being discovered all over the area. A friend of mine, a reliable source, a stockholder himself, believes they're following a vein that gets wider and deeper the farther they mine. He believes all indications point to a titanic vein, Jenna.

"There are rich veins of silver that no one is paying attention to and tributaries of gold shooting off everywhere. Speculators are beginning to make fast fortunes on some of the smaller enterprises.

"My friend is presenting me a great opportunity to buy stock in his mine before the word gets out. I've got to get in on this. Damn! If I'd never gone to Europe, I'd have been in on the first deals. You should be investing, too, Jenna."

Jenna frowned. "I've looked into it, but too late to trust anyone. So many people have been hurt, taken advantage of by bogus companies. In time, no one will support such mining interests for fear of losing everything. With no backing, the mines are sure to close. The entire Nevada operation could fall. You know, yourself, how quickly these smaller companies fold. I don't advise investing in your friend's mine, Danny. It's too risky," Jenna said.

"What do you know? You're still a child in these matters. Women don't have a feel for these things." Danny scowled. "I know what I'm doing. Damn it all, I don't need your advise!" Danny poured himself a shot of whiskey from a decanter and swallowed it down. "Can you loan me money or not?"

Jenna held her tongue. She had thought Danny was different from the men who resented a woman with an opinion, especially a woman who expressed one. "How much are you talking about?" Jenna said quietly.

"Ten thousand . . . or more."

Jenna stared at him. "That's a great deal of money."

"You're good for it! You're a rich woman."

"How do I know this money isn't going for your appetites?"

Danny whirled on her. "What are you saying, woman? What business is it of yours how I spend my money—loan or not!"

Jenna shrank. She had not seen Danny's temper. "I'm sorry, Danny. I was being accusative. Please don't look so angry," she said, trying to appease him. "I was just wondering how you can live so extravagantly, even buying me an expensive sapphire pin and other beautiful things, and then not having money for investments." Jenna was also wondering who was supporting Hannah in England.

"I don't want to say this again to you. How I spend my money is *no* concern of yours!" Danny poured himself another whiskey.

Jenna bristled. "Why and to whom I loan my money *is* a concern of mine. I'd also be concerned if my loan supported your mistress in England!" She stood up to leave, but Danny intercepted her.

"How do you know this, may I ask? I've told no one where Lilly is. Do you spy on me, my dear?"

"Don't be ridiculous!" She tried to step around him.

"You know about Lilly Jordan because you checked on her." He laughed and swallowed the entire contents of his glass. Then, in his charming way, he gently drew Jenna toward him. "I don't care a whit, you know. You're the only one that matters."

Jenna pulled away from him and walked to the window. In the street below, San Franciscans were hurrying through their daily routines. She wondered if they, too, struggled with romantic doubts, lived secret lives, feared loving someone as she did Danny.

He came up behind her, put his arms around her waist and kissed her neck. "Come, now, lassie. Don't be turnin' your back on me, now. You know how I feel about you."

Jenna turned and searched his face trying to read his sincerity.

He gently kissed her eyes shut. "Quit lookin' for a devil, my girl. A woman shouldn't see the whole of a man, for then she wouldn't have a man at all, but a pet. Leave it be, my love."

Jenna felt herself soften, her agitation calm. "Danny, I want Lilly to stay away forever. I live in constant concern that she'll come back and you'll have no more of me. You do love me, don't you?"

"What do you think, Lassie?"

"You've never said so. I want to think . . ."

Danny placed his fingers over her lips then kissed her gently. "Know only that I adore you."

"And Lilly?"

"Lilly is not here. Must we bring her into our world?"

Danny eased her concerns. She felt foolish doubting him.

"Now let's get this business matter settled," Danny said. "Why don't I sell back to you my fifteen percent of the stock in JD Meat Company? You'll feel safer and, well, I need more than ten thousand dollars."

"What do you believe the value of my stock is?"

"It's more than doubled."

"You're right. I'll buy your shares for seventy thousand dollars," Jenna said.

"Consider it a deal!" Danny smiled and poured himself another whiskey.

🍃 🍃 🍃

Within the week, Jenna received catastrophic news. Her cattle in the Los Angeles area were dying from a disease in which their bodies were not only covered with abscesses on the outside, but on the inside as well. Pockets of pus were found in the slaughtered animals, making JD Meat Company's meat unsafe for consumption.

Jenna stormed into Danny's office. "Did you know about *this*?" she shouted, waving the letter in front of him.

"About what?" Danny rose quickly from his desk.

"The Los Angeles division—diseased cattle, that's what!" She threw the letter down in front of him. "Danny, the implications are that you knew about this and turned around and sold your entire business interests out— back to *me*, in fact, to let me take the loss! I can't believe it! Your timing is too perfect for coincidence."

"I would never do such a thing, Jenna. Your opinion of me must not be very high. I'm insulted," Danny said in a controlled voice.

"Tell me the truth, Danny. I've got to know. Did you know about these sick animals before the rest of us?"

"No, of course not! I'm as stunned as you are. Do you think I would know something as serious as this and then deceive you . . cheat you? That's absurd. I thought you had more trust in me than that," Danny retorted angrily.

"It's suspicious, don't you agree?" Her face felt flushed and her mouth dry.

"Yes, it would be suspicious if I were a stranger or a crook. Is that how you think of me?"

"I don't know what to think. Danny, am I ruined? If it is known our cattle are sick, no one will buy the JD brand anywhere. I don't know anything about cattle diseases, about this terrible disease that is killing our animals. That's why we've hired experts in the industry. It's your job to look out for our, rather, *my* interests. If you hadn't been running around Europe, you might have been on top of this situation before the Los Angeles herds started dropping dead!"

"Jenna, sweet girl, you must know I share your shock over the news. This is terrible, a disaster. I'll get on it immediately. In fact, I'll personally go down to Los Angeles to see what can be done. Then I'll make the rounds of all our outlets, to San Luis Obispo, Santa Cruz, and the like. Now get hold of yourself, girl. It's time to think and not act hysterical."

"I'm not hysterical. I resent that remark. Let me remind you, you have nothing to lose here. I'm losing everything. I'm ruined in this business, and you know it. Don't treat me like I'm a china doll. I can handle truth, not lies. I'll do what I can to save myself. I always have. I just have to think. No one will buy the meat; and the hides, they are worthless—all covered with sores and lesions. Those animals will have to be disposed of. It makes me sick! Oh, Lord in Heaven, I hate this business!" Jenna faced Danny again but this time was able to calmly ask, "You didn't lie to me, did you? Tell me with your eyes, not your words. Look at me."

"No, my dear girl," he said, putting his arms around her.

Jenna let him hold her to ease the fear. "I've got to think," she said. "Maybe it's not a total loss. I'm going to San Jose to talk to Señor Faustino while you're in the south. I need to check the health of the cattle there before they are driven to San Francisco and shipped to the slaughterhouses. Maybe we can trace the disease, find the source." Jenna sighed. "Well, let's call a board meeting and decide the best way to proceed."

Before Jenna left the Wells Fargo building, she'd made reservations on the stage for San Jose two days hence, then drove back to her house, full of anxiety. The disastrous news was only part of her apprehension; the thought that Danny might have deceived her was even more disturbing. The coincidence nagged her thoughts until she concluded she must settle the matter in her mind or lose control of the situation. She had to keep a clear head.

Jenna reviewed every bit of conversation with Danny, every subtle gesture, every glint in the eye, to see if she had missed something. She needed to prove to herself once and for all that Danny's word was true—as a friend, a business partner, a lover.

Before she left for San Jose, Danny called on her at home. He did not wait in the parlor as he was asked to do by Jenna's house manager, Sung Moon. Instead, he took the stairs two at a time and entered Jenna's room without knocking. His black curls were damp and tousled, his shirt unbuttoned, and his eyes bright with drink. He shut the door and leaned against it, swaying slightly.

"Danny, what are you doing here?" Jenna exclaimed. His intrusion into her room surprised her. In spite of their intimacy, this kind of action crossed the line of respect. She did not like it. "Can't you wait downstairs? Have you no manners at all?" she said, gathering her robe around her.

"I can't wait," he said. "I came to tell you something Jenna. I love you. I really do love you." He grinned broadly. "I'll make it up to you one day, because I'm going to be so damned rich, those stupid cows won't be more than pigeon droppings." Danny smiled impishly. "Don't be angry at me, my girl, for barging in here. I had to tell you I loved you before you left. I always have, you know—on me *mither's* grave, that's the truth. Old Danny, here, is smart. I've got a nose for gold. I can smell it, my girl, like it was bacon frying in the early morn. Don't look at me like I'm a wanton wretch. I'm telling you, dearie, I'm going to be rich, and you're going to be rich with me. Trust me, Jenna. Trust me."

"Sit down, Danny, before your knees buckle," Jenna said, leading him to a chair.

"Let me hold you," he said, clumsily putting his arms around her like a friendly bear. "Strong as a tree, you are. I apologize for my behavior. You don't deserve this. But Jenna, you don't understand—I had to tell you I loved you before you left. On me *mither's* grave, I love you. There! I said it!" Danny giggled and zigzagged to the bed, sat down, and threw an arm around a bedpost. "I think I'm drunk."

"You are very drunk, Danny. I'm sending you home."

"Let me sleep downstairs, please. Home is on the other side of the world."

"All right, I'll ask Sung Moon to fix up a room and help you to bed."

"On me *mither's* grave, I'm sorry about this. Send for Sung Moon. He's a wonderful man, a fine man, one of the better men in the community. Send for Sung Moon. Maybe he'd like a game of whist before bed. Or send for Ping, his nice old wife, to sing with. Good old Ping. I bet she knows the old songs." Danny flopped back on the bed giggling and began to sing in a thick Irish brogue, *"O, the pale moon 'twas risin' beyond the green mountain, the sun 'twas declinin' beneath the blue sea. When I strayed with me love to the pure crystal fountain, that stands in the beautiful vale of Tralee."*

Sung Moon helped Danny to his room.

"No whist, Sung Moon? No whist, man? Everyone loves a game of whist. Then how about a verse of 'Me Wild Irish Rose'?"

Somewhere just before dawn, Danny entered Jenna's room. In the dim morning light, he looked at Jenna lying asleep, her curved hip, slender arms, and marble shoulders so gracefully placed among the covers. Her long, silky brown hair spread over the pillow like fine, sea grass.

"My God, she's a magnificent woman," he whispered softly. "Can't you see, Danny boy, this one is different. She deserves better." He crawled under the covers and put his arms around her, gently urging her into consciousness. She awakened to his caressing hands.

"I'm sorry for last night, Jenna. Forgive me. What I said, I meant. I love you, girl."

"On your mother's grave?" she whispered sleepily.

"On me mother's grave."

Danny meant what he said, at least for the moment.

🌿 🌿 🌿

"No, Señorita, you can see our cows are good and healthy and we even have forty calves so far this spring that I know of," Señor Faustino said. "The only problem is that new herd of cattle I told you about—the one with the Lazy H brand. There are many of them, a big herd, bigger than ours and the Archuletas, I think. I don't know where they're coming from, but the *vaqueros* say the cattle are grazing on land purchased by a European."

"My land, you mean. I'll wager whoever it is bought the land somehow from my dear friend, Reginald Potter-not only land in this valley, but down around San Luis Obispo, too. The Lazy H brand is showing up everywhere.

Someone is squeezing all of us out with huge herds. I would like to know who this person is."

Jenna wondered if she should sell the healthy JD cattle before word spread about her sick cows. Then she could get out of this hideous business once and for all. It was clear the cows were healthy in this valley. She'd be dealing honestly and would salvage some of what would be certain disaster if she waited. She'd find out the name of the unknown European who appeared to be so eager to become a cattle baron.

🦋 🦋 🦋

Jenna borrowed a horse from Señor Faustino to ride through the shallow valleys and along the low western hills. She wanted to feel the earth, the rhythm of the horse, the solitude, the embrace of earth and sky. The spring morning, the smell of sweet grass and the fields blooming with yellow mustard, brought back a rush of memories.

Her thoughts drifted back to the doña, a bittersweet reflection with sad edges, dry and papery as a treasured letter. She quickly shifted to happy times of meadow walks with Darcey, Pearle, Blue, and Harke. Whenever a meadowlark warbled, she thought of Israel, of her family, and the days crossing the plains.

The sun rose higher, the air grew warmer, and she decided to ride to the spring to cool herself and the horse in the shade before returning. In Jenna's preoccupation, she did not see the figure of a horse and rider on the crest of a low hill. The horseman watched Jenna dismount, cup her hands in the cold water, and drink several times before he slowly moved down the slope toward her.

When Jenna heard the noises of saddle and spurs and the soft snorts of a horse behind her. She turned and froze. Enrique stood before her, smiling in a way that made her freeze like a rabbit caught in the open.

"Hello, Enrique," she said, moving toward her horse and trying not to show her fear. "I was just watering my horse."

Enrique dismounted and took hold of the reins of the horse. "You're trespassing, Señorita." His smile was thin and sharp like a blade.

"This is not your land, unless you've stolen it," Jenna said sharply.

"This has never been anything but Archuleta land. You are the thief, my lying little *gringa* bitch. How clever you must think you are to manipulate the doña into giving you Archuleta land. How stupid you must think we all are! This is still our land, Archuleta property. Do you know what we do to intruders like you?"

Jenna tried not to show any weakness as she mounted her horse. "Give me the reins, Enrique. We have nothing to say to one another. Our business is finished."

"Oh, I don't think so. I told you once before the Archuletas never lose. We keep what belongs to us, and we take what we want."

Enrique grabbed Jenna's arm and viciously yanked her from the horse. She struggled to free herself, but his grip was strong. He pushed her onto the ground and struck her with the back of his hand across her face.

"I'm taking what I want!" he screamed and struck again. His face distorted with hatred as he lunged on top of her and bit through her bottom lip.

Jenna squirmed helplessly like a butterfly on a pin as Enrique forced himself between her legs and into her, violating her with such intensity she thought he was tearing her insides apart.

"I'm not finished with you," he hissed through his teeth. Sitting astride her, he ripped her dress down the middle, exposing her bare breasts and torso.

Jenna weakly raised her hands to fight him, but he struck again savagely, this time so hard she felt she was losing consciousness. The ringing in her head from the blow momentarily blotted out Enrique's raving.

When her head cleared, she felt crushing pain in her face and blood running into her ears and eyes. With one murderous hand, Enrique squeezed her cheeks and chin until her jaw shifted. Her teeth ripped the inner tissue of her mouth and blood spread across her lips.

"I want to leave you with something to remember me by—a reminder that the Archuletas never lose," he said, pulling a knife from his pocket.

In three quick strokes, he carved an "A" on Jenna's abdomen, grabbed a handful of dirt, and rubbed it into the mutilation.

Jenna tried to scream, but Enrique's powerful hand around her neck choked off all air. The deep knife wounds pulsated on her stomach.

My God, what has he done to me?

"This will scar nice and dark—an Indian trick, my lovely. What man will desire you now? 'A' for Archuleta—my calling card."

When Jenna began to vomit, Enrique stood up and, with the tip of his boot, rolled her over on her face.

She heard him ride away before she fainted.

As Jenna began to regain consciousness, she saw the figure of someone familiar standing by her—the Indian woman of long ago, the same Indian angel she'd seen as a child when Faithful Squibb had violated her. A mist blew around the form, rippling a soft doeskin dress covered with colored beads, sometimes obscuring the image in vaporous gray clouds.

When the clouds parted, Jenna could see the woman's face clearly. Her eyes held the same deep love and unspoken message of courage and strength as Jenna remembered from her childhood. She was a life-force, perhaps Life, itself.

Jenna couldn't tell if Indian woman was real or not, but she was there beside her, reaching out her hand and telling Jenna in some way to rise and clean herself, to wash the blood and dirt from her lip and from her stomach, and to clean the blood from the ripped tissue in her vagina. Enrique had raped her savagely, brutalized her like a wild animal.

At last, Jenna was able to mount the horse and ride back to Señor Faustino's. The pain of sitting in the saddle was unbearable with every step the horse took, though she rode sidesaddle. Her lip was swollen and throbbing. Shaking uncontrollably, she tied the reins and let the horse guide her home so that she could keep pressure on her bleeding stomach and her mouth. She was still shaking when she arrived at the adobe.

"You need a doctor, Señorita," Señor Faustino said, lifting her gently off the horse. "You've had a terrible fall. Maybe you broke something."

"No, no, your wife can help me. I'll need something for infection and warm compresses to draw any poisons, and a place to lie down and sleep for a few days. It's all right, Señor Faustino. Please don't worry."

When the señora took off Jenna's dress to wash and mend, she saw the blood between her legs, the bruises from battering, and the knife wound and knew what had happened. She said nothing as she gently bathed Jenna and pressed spider web into the deeper gashes that continued to bleed. She doused the cuts with warm saltwater and tequila, rubbed goose grease on Jenna's lip, and laid strips of raw chicken over bruises and swollen skin to ease the pain.

Señora Faustino worried over Jenna's mouth and the obvious teeth marks. She knew the human bite could be fatal and made a poultice of ground moldy tortillas to kill anything evil. The tortillas were a remedy of her people, who believed corn the gift of life and its mold a healing gift from the One Great Spirit.

Carefully spooning warm skullcap tea into Jenna's mouth, she said, "You are safe here, Señorita. You are safe with your secret. Sleep now."

For several days, cloistered in the small, dark room, Jenna tossed feverishly, slipping in and out of consciousness. Once, she surfaced to find herself being rocked in the comforting arms of a woman who sang soft and low. Jenna struggled through her fever to focus on the vaguely familiar face who soothed her. Surely it must be Emily Polley holding her inside the covered wagon, or maybe Darcey singing to her in their moonless room at Sutter's Fort. Or was it her own mother, Martha Jane, and she, herself, a tiny uncertain infant? Then she became fully aware of the reassuring arms of Señora Faustino humming old melodies rooted in an ancient culture.

Gradually, Jenna's strength returned. She spent long days sleeping and waiting for the painful bruises, torn flesh, and a broken nose to heal. Her lip and jaw took the longest to mend. Enrique's bite was as poisonous as a rattler's. When her festering lip drained its venom, she began to eat soft food.

Lying in bed, she would touch the wound on her abdomen and cry in agony and humiliation. When she gathered enough courage to look at herself, she could see the clean "A" mark at least three inches long—deep and red and angry—and she knew she would carry Enrique's hatred the rest of her life.

She thought of Danny. How could she have lain so joyfully in his arms, her body so willing, and in three days, that same body be so vilified, experiencing such repugnance? What would Danny think when he saw the "A"?

Jenna's rape stirred up monstrous memories of her childhood violation. She'd repressed the feeling of being filthy and worthless and had found a way to carry on with her life and to still love herself. She would have to do the same again. The body would heal quicker than her rage, but Jenna knew there was something higher, beyond her physical existence, an unseen power in her life, a spirit, an intelligence that kept balance and the order of things. She had felt the peace of a loving presence before, something not of this world, a guidance and a strength. Jenna would again turn to this source and trust it.

During the days, as she lay curled in the cool protection of the adobe, she rehearsed her encounter with Danny and imagined various reactions from him. Sometimes she pictured him loving, sometimes grimacing with revulsion. Would Danny be repulsed by the mark of another man? Would he hate her, turn away from her? She would cross that bridge when she came to it.

When Jenna was strong enough to face a world outside of Señora Faustino's gentle care and the small, safe place she inhabited inside the dim adobe, she took the stage back to San Francisco.

Danny was expected to be gone for a few more weeks inspecting the cattle in the south. Jenna hoped her lip would be healed and the blue marks faded by the time he returned home. Eventually, she would have to explain the indelible "A," the Archuleta brand, the unforgivable slashes.

🌱 🌱 🌱

Before Danny returned, the inexplicable knowledge carried only by women began to form in Jenna's mind. A tiny embryo of thought had planted itself and begun to grow, an unfamiliar sensation creeping through her blood, her skin, her nerves, something over which she had no control.

A month had passed and Jenna explained the absence of her menstruation as due to trauma; but after another two weeks, the signs were apparent—

sore breasts, unexplained drowsiness, nausea. Jenna was pregnant.

The whole idea frightened her—the ghastly conclusion that the growing flesh in her might be Enrique's final word, the fear that Danny would leave her forever, the humiliation of facing an unforgiving society and its condemnation for the rest of her life. Most unsettling to Jenna was the glaring truth that the child growing inside her could be either Danny's or Enrique's. She had been with both men in the space of five days.

Her thoughts cut like little knives, her imaginings tumbled recklessly— destructive and humiliating.

What am I to do? Come now, Jenna. This is no time to be faint-hearted. You have a big problem and must spend your energy resolving it. Life goes on —yours, as well as the child's inside. You will have to face this predicament like a Daggett—one day at a time. One solution is to acquire Danny's name—marry him, buy him, if necessary. You'll never know whose baby this is until it is born, and maybe not even then. Oh, God, you never dreamed you'd be in such a situation! Martha Jane was right—you should have been born a man! It would be much easier, uncomplicated.

Jenna reasoned that Danny had no obligation to her. The man could always leave a woman, a wife, travel the seas and silk roads, go to battle . . . and never return. The woman had to somehow survive with her babes. Jenna remembered her own mother's response to an unwanted pregnancy—a knitting needle and a slow death. She would never be like her mother—never. She took a deep breath. What is, simply is. No sense whining now.

Sometimes, Jenna's thoughts turned optimistic, even joyful. A baby! A stranger in her life. A little person was forming inside her who would depend on her for its very life! She thought of Danny. Certainly, this was his child, conceived in love.

Jenna's anxiety shifted to wonderment, to the realization she was like all women everywhere from the beginning of time. She shared a common purpose, understanding and instinct. Her body was a vessel, her breasts a source of nourishment. The word "mother" had always been incomplete, distant, synonymous with rejection. Perhaps now, the meaning would change. The yearning for something she had never had might be fulfilled.

Why should she ever want to be a man! Martha Jane was wrong.

But before she could treasure the sweeter thoughts of motherhood, Enrique's savage rape clouded her mind. The mass inside her suddenly felt as cold and hard as a knife blade. Could she truly love a child conceived in violence and hatred? If her calculations were right, she would know in February.

🍐 🍐 🍐

Danny returned from his trip in high spirits. Although his news of the cattle business was dismal, Jenna thought he was unusually exuberant. Like Jenna, he discovered the Lazy H brand everywhere and agreed it was time to sell out, to get out of the meat business. He had the name of the European, a German, who was buying up everyone's cattle in the region, and was prepared to start serious negotiations with him. Danny had even gone so far as to suggest a price of thirty dollars a head to this German who was clearly gaining a monopoly of the cattle business.

"That's too low! I can do better!" Jenna contested.

"All the cattle in the south are selling for much less than that. You'll be lucky to get thirty dollars. If you want to sell out, we've got an immediate buyer. Jenna, I advise you to do so while you can. Take your money and turn it into winning investments. God, woman, people are making fortunes in Nevada mines. Don't hang on to something that is slipping away. You're losing, Jenna. Let the German have it all. He's going to take it anyway, one way or another. It takes money to make money."

"Maybe you're right, Danny. At least selling now and taking what money I can will give me something to work with. I can still find a way to make my capital work for me. There are plenty of fortunes still to be made." Jenna had not yet given up on the railroad idea. Mr. Judd was intent on building a line from San Jose to San Francisco, and she was already thinking of investing.

"Do as I am, me lass. Invest in the Nevada mines. While I was in Los Angeles, I bought as much stock as I could in one of them—the Bobcat Mine."

"*All* of your money!" Jenna gasped.

"All of it. Yes! When it pays, and it surely will, I'm a rich man—really rich!"

"How do you know your investment is safe?"

"It's backed by a man who hasn't missed yet! If I had more, I'd invest it, too. As it is, I'm broke—flat broke." He smiled happily as though he had already struck a paying vein and playfully kissed Jenna on the neck.

"Let's go somewhere together," he said, nuzzling Jenna. "Would you like to see the Islands? They say they are beautiful and exotic, like my girl. Or England? We'll dine with the king and queen at the palace."

Danny's happiness was contagious. Her news could wait.

🍃 🍃 🍃

Jenna avoided Danny as long as she could, making excuses and telling him she was unwell. Finally, the hurt on his face led to an unavoidable confrontation. They had taken an afternoon ride above town to pick berries and picnic on Strawberry Hill. Lying on his back with his arms behind his head, Danny looked like a schoolboy, happy, relaxed. The time had come. Jenna broke it to him gently that she was carrying a child. Danny responded soberly—all playfulness vanished from his eyes.

"There's more," she said. This time, Jenna hung her head and squeezed back her tears.

"What is it, my girl? I've never seen you cry. You're not the type. Saints be praised, you've got an Irish soul after all! Tell me," he said, lifting her chin and wiping a tear away.

"I need you now—all of you. Your support and strength, your good sense. I can't bear to talk to anyone who is going to overreact or try to make me suffer more than I already have. Please, Danny, let me say all I have to say before interrupting. Promise me."

"I promise," he said, frowning at her intrusive serious tone.

Very carefully, Jenna started her story from the beginning of her relationship to Enrique to the death of the doña. Danny had heard much of the story before, but this time, she told him her suspicions of Enrique's murdering the doña and his threats to her.

"He's capable of murder, Danny, and I think would like to see me dead, certainly punished or destroyed. He's hurt me badly . . . violated my body."

Danny grabbed Jenna's shoulders. "What are you saying, girl?"

"He had his way with me," she said softly and lowered her head.

Danny groaned and put his fists to his temples. "That son-of-a-bitch!" His anger took his breath.

"He left his mark on me, cut my abdomen with a knife—the letter 'A'. I'm scarred for life. If you stay with me after all that I've told you, you will have to share that part of my pain, my humiliation."

Danny couldn't speak. He put his head in his hands and sobbed with such anguish, Jenna put her arms around him. She wondered if he was crying for her or for himself. He looked up, his expression pained, horrified, and threw his arms around Jenna.

"My girl, my poor Jenna. How you've suffered!" The two of them cried together, but this time, Jenna's tears were more of relief than sadness. As Danny held her and stroked her back, she became a child again—if only for a moment. How Danny would work out the problems of her pregnancy was yet to be determined.

When Danny pulled away, his eyes were dark, without light, like an endless tunnel piercing back into a place of shadows, or a cave of primitive emotions kept hidden from the world of reason.

"Enrique's going to pay for this, Jenna. He's going to lose the tools of his trade—if not by me, then by me and my Irish friends. We don't take this kind of thing lightly. He's going to suffer, the son-of-a-bitch!"

"Don't be foolish, Danny. The Archuletas will protect him, hide him. If they know anyone is looking for him, they'll send him out of the country. He's probably gone already."

"Maybe my friends and I will have to tell him *adios* . . . give him a farewell party."

"Have him arrested, Danny. Don't get personally involved. You don't know these people like I do. They take revenge. It will never stop."

"What we do will be our own choice—when and where. You're not a part of his punishment. The Irish have a code all their own dealing with bullies, especially when it comes to harming a young lass. Know this, my girl, he'll never rape another woman."

Danny lay back on the grass breathing hard. Neither spoke. Jenna finally said, "You know this child could be his or yours. You know that, don't you?"

"Don't muddy the waters, Jenna. I have only one thing to think about now. I can't think about a wee bairn."

Jenna walked over to a cluster of strawberry plants and picked a few berries and put them in her basket. She looked at Danny lying with his eyes closed.

"Are you asleep?" she said.

"No, just thinking."

"I can't have a bastard child, you know." She waited for Danny to respond. "Marry me, Danny."

He sat up slowly, still not answering.

"Danny, don't make me beg you. I know this is hard. I'm asking for your name only. If you want me to leave after that, I promise I'll go and never bother you."

"Jenna, I'm going to San Jose as soon as possible. When I get back we'll talk about it. I have no money now, no way to support you. I'm not one to settle down, you know that. Being a family man is the last thing I ever intended to be. It's not in me blood. You know how I am. I'm not fit for married life, especially to be a da'."

"You said you loved me."

"That's different. I do love you, but I can't promise you a life with me. I'm a gambler at heart. I love the risk of high stakes in life. You deserve better."

"Some women like high risks, too, you know."

"I haven't got enough money to pay a preacher!"

"I'll take care of money matters until your mine begins to pay off," Jenna said.

"Women don't pay my way in life. It's unthinkable!"

"I love you, Danny. I'm prepared to be your wife in all ways—a partner. But I'll never stop you or get in your way. I would hope you would love me and this child and accept your family role, but you can live whatever lifestyle you like. I won't interfere. I promise."

"I'll think about it on my way to San Jose. It's better to wait until I get back. Right now, I have a score to settle." Danny spoke through his clenched teeth, and averted Jenna's eyes.

"Don't wait too long," Jenna said, touching her stomach. Already, her waistbands felt tight.

🜂 🜂 🜂

Danny had sold his own house to cover bills and to wait out the endless days of expectation . . . waiting . . . waiting for the Bobcat mine to strike a paying vein. He talked endlessly about other investments he would make once the Bobcat hit gold. Meanwhile, he took on the job of selling the JD cattle and closing the JD Meat Company and all its operations. He seemed nervous and irritable. Jenna noted the dark intensity in his eyes, an expression she had not seen before.

Danny and Jenna were married in late September. Every Irishman in San Francisco toasted the bride and groom, and Danny, without exuberance, returned the toasts, and would end up a very drunk groom stumbling into Jenna's house.

Danny never spoke of the trip to San Jose except to say, "That bastard will never bother you or any woman ever again."

Jenna noticed that at the wedding reception, three Irishmen from outside of San Francisco met with Danny and made a private toast together—not playful, but serious, a bond that had a secret with it. She overheard one of the men say, "Danny, me boy, you wield a good knife. By God, you should have been a bloody surgeon, the way you sliced off his castanets. That will stop the bastard from any more dancing."

Jenna also overheard one of the Irish friends speak of his employment with the JD Meat Company in Los Angeles area and how they dealt with destroying and burning the infected cattle. This was no time to think about Danny and his passion for a quick dollar, his character, his risk-taking nature, or worse yet, his possible deception which was a lingering doubt that never quite disappeared from her thoughts. Learning that one of Danny's "boys" had been working in Los Angeles with the JD Meat

Company, certainly would suggest that Danny knew the cattle was sick before he sold his shares of stock to her. For now, she smiled as the bride of Danny McDaniels, and she smiled because the quickened child, so real now as it moved within her, would have a legitimate birth record—a name. That alone was worth all the money she was spending to keep Danny with her.

🌱 🌱 🌱

In the early months of Jenna's pregnancy, Danny was attentive, taking her to the theater to see billings such as Lotta Crabtree in the play *She Stoops to Conquer*, with a fine English Opera Company and a popular vocalist, Catherine Hayes, in the *Swan of Erin*. They dined and took Sunday drives into the country.

On one such drive, Jenna saw Hannah's polished black carriage and white-plumed horses as they pranced around the corner on Mission Street, their silver harnesses jangling and glittering in the sun. She looked at Danny to see if he, too, had noticed Hannah's carriage; but he kept his eyes forward. Jenna wondered when Hannah had returned and how much of her own money would support Hannah's expensive appetites after Danny's money ran out.

Time moved slowly for Jenna. She spent the last weeks of her confinement retired from the eyes of society. It was unseemly for a pregnant woman to show herself. Jenna wrote letters to her Jackson "family," poems and stories to read aloud at night on the porch.

She read the monthly magazines, *Harpers* and *Atlantic*, and newspapers to keep informed about the growing tensions between pro-slavery and anti-slavery factions, and the election of Abraham Lincoln to the presidency. She entertained herself with the controversial editorials of San Francisco's Bret Harte, stories by Edgar Allen Poe and the poetry of Walt Whitman.

There were too many hours in the day, and she often caught herself brooding about Hannah's return. If Danny was seeing Hannah, Jenna did not want to know, nor did she inquire about his activities. Too often, Danny returned home late, subdued and unwilling to talk about the day's events.

Until it was inappropriate to be seen in public, she helped with various charity organizations, volunteered at the hospital in the women's ward, and spent a lot of time working at the orphanage. Now, even more than before, her heart went out to the children left to survive the illnesses and accidents which still plagued emigrants moving west and left children without families. Perhaps one day, she would be a guardian like the doña.

Jenna realized she was lonely. She felt the lack of a deep friendship with another woman. Darcey and the doña and Pearle had been her friends—Hannah, too, for a brief period. How nice it would be to have a close female friend to share in the wonderful thing happening inside her—all the nuances of pregnancy, the birth, the ideas of motherhood and family.

The women she remembered as a child always shared their lives, knew each other's struggles and triumphs, nurtured each other. They were woven together by invisible threads, a communication system as sure as the "talking wires," and in times of celebration or grief, sickness or worry, the women surrounded and strengthened the one who needed it.

She thought of Emily Polley and the women on the crossing. Emily had attended the birth of one woman's baby girl and Martha Jane's self-inflicted abortion. With all women, she shared the experience of participating in births and deaths, forming the women's a bond of blood. When her nursing duties ended, she washed her hands, dried them on her apron and went on living and baking the bread. Jenna had not yet been called upon to share in that experience.

Her own interests were different from the women of the community. She had learned early to amuse herself and find pleasure in solitude. She had never been the giddy school girl or heavy-shoed matron, the eager young lady seeking a mate, not a laundress, farm girl, teacher, seamstress-not a French *fille de joie*. She seemed not to fit comfortably anywhere. She had not changed from the orphan who sat at the edge of the fandango circle, not fully understanding the dance, the rhythm, the language, the flirtation, the church, the saints, the women.

One Sunday afternoon as she and Danny were returning from the country, Jenna spotted a large dog struggling desperately in deep mud. With nothing under the dog but endless ooze, the animal had slipped up to its neck. Its eyes were splattered closed and its nostrils plugged with thick mud. The animal had given up.

"Stop, Danny! Look there at that poor animal. I must save it!" she said, climbing quickly from the coach.

Danny bounded out of the driver's seat. "Stand back, Jenna! You're in no condition to help."

Holding on to the reins, Danny stepped into the mud up to his knees and reached for the dog's paw. "Back the horse up, Jenna. The dog is big and the mud like a suction cup."

Together, they pulled the hound out of the mud sink, a pitiful creature, chocolate dipped in thick muck. Jenna wiped globs of mud from its nose and eyes with her gloved hand, all the while muttering soft words of comfort. Miserable and weak as the dog was, it wagged its tail.

"I'm taking the creature home, Danny," she said, putting her arms around the dog's chest. We don't care about the buggy. It can be cleaned. So can we."

They lifted the large dog into the buggy and drove home with Jenna embracing it between her legs, not caring about her waiting dress and oversized silk bloomers.

"It's a female. What shall we name her?" Jenna smiled, slipping mud off its ears. "I'll give you a soapy bath, young lady. I should call you Bathsheba. I know, I'll call you Sheba. Do you like that name? Sheba. What do you think, Danny?"

"I think you have a strong mother instinct. You're going to have two babies, one with four legs. Yes, I like the name Sheba. It suits her, and I don't have any friends with that name. Once I named a dog Patty, forgetting it was the name of my great aunt. She stopped knitting me mittens."

For the rest of Jenna's pregnancy, Sheba, a vivacious black Labrador, followed her everywhere—upstairs, downstairs, into the gardens and through the cool, misty forests. Jenna had found her best friend.

🐾 🐾 🐾

In the early morning hours of late February, Jenna went into labor.

Danny waited in the parlor, anxious for the event to be over. He had never planned on being a father, but the least he could do was support Jenna in these critical days. He reasoned that his life would not change much after the baby. Why should it? She was the mother, the one responsible for her situation.

Other women had managed to be virgins until properly married, had kept their legs closed, valued chastity above amorous coaxing and capitulation—even from a rogue like himself. His own mother had waited, resisted temptation. Jenna could have done the same. It was her fault she got pregnant. After all, what decent man would not try to bed a lady? It was his nature to do so.

Jenna knew what she was doing. After all, it was her choice to take a risk. Women knew when they were most vulnerable. How could he know? This baby was her own damn fault, and he was not going to alter his entire life over Jenna's foolishness! She could not expect more from him than he was already doing. He'd been a good actor, comforting her when he felt like cursing. She got the McDaniels' name, quite a concession on his part, especially when she could be carrying a child resulting from a rape—not even his own flesh and blood. He was a fine fellow, indeed, to play this unnatural role.

Danny continued to brood while he waited. Even though he felt sorry for himself on the one hand, he had to admit he did love Jenna in his own way. The woman had always fascinated him . . . of course, not in the same way as Lilly Jordan. Lilly was an obsession, a woman he had never conquered, an unfeeling bitch who took his money without conscience and demanded more. Yet, he could not rid himself of his insatiable desire for her. The haughtier and more venomous she behaved, the more he wanted her, like the poisonous, heady effect of strong whiskey.

Damn her anyway! He had already been with the whore several times while Jenna's clear, maternal beauty bloomed . . . and repelled him . . . and the "A" on her stomach stretched into a bolder pearly letter repulsing him. Its ugly presence was like a third eye, another person watching, taunting, always intruding into his desire to make love to her. He kept it covered when they were intimate.

🌱 🌱 🌱

Jenna was attended by a midwife who moved efficiently about the room preparing for the delivery, smiling and speaking words of encouragement. Her helper massaged Jenna's stomach in downward circular strokes to help the baby's journey. Everything appeared as normal as a sunrise. The baby soon emerged into the light, a new consciousness. Strong hands turned it upside down and whacked it to fill its lungs.

"It's a girl, Mrs. McDaniels—nice and healthy, with all her fingers and toes, and a nasty yell. This one is going to be a howler, I'll bet my bootstraps. Listen to her carry on! She'll get what she wants in this life."

Perplexed at the spanking, Jenna reached for the baby. "Oh, don't let her cry so. Give her to me, poor little thing. How awful to come into this world in such a violent manner!"

"Inflating her lungs, that's all. It's got to be done," the midwife said, handing her the angry, red baby, wet and trembling. Jenna placed her child on her bare stomach, pulled a soft towel over her body, and stroked the fragile back. The baby stopped shivering and crying.

"I'll clean you and the baby and then send downstairs for the mister. He'll be mighty pleased to see you both so healthy. You did real fine, Mrs. McDaniels, like you already had a brood of youngins. Well, some women is made for delivery—wide hips, loose pelvic bones, and joints. Others is so tight it makes a bad time for everybody. Your little girl didn't have to fight so hard—got a nice-shaped head, she does. And will you look at that head of black curls!"

While the midwife chatted, Jenna's own shaking subsided and she relaxed. The ordeal was over. All was normal; she could rest. Somewhere, as she drifted in and out of her sleep, she heard Israel say, "That's my Jenn . . . you did fine, daughter. She's a beauty."

Jenna was aware of the midwife pinning cloths around her middle and padding her to absorb the blood, yet she distinctly smelled the strong fragrance of prairie sage; it was unmistakable. It lingered as she fell into a deeper rest. In her swirling dream, Israel stood smiling in a prairie blowing with sage. Even as she slept, she knew her vision was more than a dream, and after Israel faded and Jenna awakened, the smell of sage lingered so strongly she said aloud, "Sage."

"That's a nice name, Mrs. McDaniels . . . different," the midwife said, taking the baby from Jenna to wash away the birth fluids.

"Yes," Jenna smiled. "It's a perfect name for my little girl. Sage. Sage McDaniels. Does that suit you, Papa?" she said sleepily.

"Beg pardon, Ma'am?"

"It's nothing, I'm just muttering. Can you send for Mr. McDaniels now? I want him to see his baby daughter. And one more thing—could you hand me the shell box on the dressing table? Inside is a locket my mother gave me. I would like to wear it."

For the first time in Danny's life, he was without a clever comment. Staring into the wrinkled face of the tiny baby girl overwhelmed him. Could she be his own blood? Did he dare love her without reservation?

"Looks just like you, Mr. McDaniels," the midwife said.

"You think so?" Danny asked, looking up at her.

"Look at that hair. Of course, it may all fall out and come in blond," she laughed. "They change all the time. Sometimes they look like the mother, then the father, back and forth until they become their own little person. But I think she's going to favor you."

"Well, I'll be," Danny said, tucking his finger in the curl of the baby's fist. "Hello," he said. "You don't say much do you, especially for someone who's completely changed my life."

🐚 🐚 🐚

The birth of Sage appeared to soften Danny's attitude toward being a father. He clearly enjoyed taking Jenna, Sage, and even Sheba on Sunday buggy rides into the square and on Mission Street as far out as the dunes. Danny nodded and tipped his hat to the townspeople, obviously proud of his well-dressed, beautiful wife and baby daughter, ruffled in Irish lace and wrapped in fur.

Jenna thought she must be the happiest young mother that ever was. Even Sheba looked pleased with her charge and sat obediently in the carriage. Rarely was a family pet given such privilege.

Danny tried hard to be a proper father and husband and mostly appeared happy. However, there were dark days Jenna never understood, days when he exhausted himself running up and down the steep hills above the city, evenings when he preferred to be alone with his whiskey, moody and irritable. Often, he stayed away from the house long into the night.

On such occasions, he'd return full of Irish songs and playful affection before falling into a thick sleep. In the morning, he'd apologize for his foolish behavior, saying only, "I'm trying, Jenna—give me time to come around. It's not easy. When the Bobcat Mine hits, I'll be a changed man. Only a few more feet and we'll hit color, I'm certain of it. I hate being supported by you! It's unnatural, humiliating. If anyone knew, I'd be made a fool."

At times, Sage made the situation harder for Danny. She was a fussy baby, chronically cramping after nursing, drawing up her legs in painful spasms. In the middle of the night, when colic gripped the household, Danny grit his teeth and let Jenna deal with the problem. Once he flew out of the house and did not return until after breakfast. Jenna said nothing; in fact, she made no demands on Danny, hoping he would love Sage as she did and accept her as his own daughter.

One night as the world slept and Sage's ear-shattering screams shocked the stillness, Danny could stand it no longer and roughly took the baby out of Jenna's arms.

"Give her to me," he demanded. Throwing an afghan around her, Danny stepped outside into the garden with the screaming baby. Jenna listened to Sage's cries ease and stop. In a few moments, Danny returned with a boyish smile on his face and a sleeping baby over his shoulder.

"You see, Jenna, I have a way with women—even wee ones."

Jenna, relieved and exhausted, placed the baby in her crib. "How did you do it, Danny? You're a magician."

"I told her, if she stopped her maddening screams she could hear the fairies in the garden hiding under the rose bushes singing and carrying on—like fairies do."

"Oh, Danny, thank you. You're wonderful!" Jenna exclaimed, throwing her arms around him.

"I am that," he grinned. "You know, she's kind of cute, that one."

Sixteen

WEEKS GREW INTO MONTHS and still the Bobcat produced nothing. When the San Francisco Mining Exchange opened, Danny and Jenna were among the eager San Franciscans to get involved in the excitement of buying and selling a wider selection of stocks.

Although Danny fought for shares in more of the Bobcat, Jenna put her foot down and insisted they look into more secure stocks. "Danny, we can make a great deal of money investing in companies that build machinery to do the digging and boring, the crushing and smelting. That's the safest money. The mines today can't function without the machines. If a mine fails, another will open somewhere else, needing equipment. Let's go together on this."

"Using your money, of course," Danny said irritably. Buying joint stock with her funds made him curse his weak position. He felt his masculine pride being gradually nibbled away, but he had no choice except to agree with her, at least for now. He consoled himself that soon the Bobcat Mine would pay off and he'd make her investments look like table crumbs. He consented to join her buying stock in a small railroad line between San Jose and San Francisco—"safer stock," Jenna had said.

"Don't you see, Danny, everyone around us makes great fortunes, then loses them overnight. We may never be millionaires of a mother lode, but we can be rich and respectable just the same."

"Do as you like—it's your money," he grumbled.

"I want you to manage our affairs, Danny. It will be *our* money—yours and mine and Sage's. We're a family."

Danny didn't answer.

As time passed, Danny's happy-go-lucky nature changed into one of intense irritability. He spent long hours away from home with friends in town, often saying he was going to a meeting. Danny was turning his restlessness and anger into political fights.

The long arm of discontent between the North and the South had reached the Pacific, and California found itself divided in its sympathies. In the southern part of the state, especially in Los Angeles, the shouts of separatism were louder than cries for the Union. The controversy around slavery had not been settled, even though California had been admitted into the United States as a free state.

Southern slaveholders entering the state had brought their slaves with them and still considered them property, even though the law said otherwise. The pro-slavery faction found its way into the political arena and dominated elected positions in the state, organizing speeches, parades, and rallies supporting the southern states' talk of seceding from the Union.

Men in powerful positions spoke of California breaking away and forming a separate republic. As the tension grew, so did open arguments, duels, fistfights and the gathering of angry crowds.

Danny was in the middle of the fiery emotions rippling through the state, and became an effective speaker for Unionist, anti-slavery sympathies. He joined the Union Club, a group of pro-union men who rallied against the Knights of the Golden Circle, separatists with pro-slavery leanings. Danny had found a place to vent his own frustrations.

"These damn fool separatists are determined to involve California in a war supporting secession and splitting this country in two. I have no use for them, Jenna! They cheered Jefferson Davis over in San Bernardino—thousands of them. They seem to be growing in numbers all the time and must be stopped!

"Now we have *two* senators with southern sympathies, ready to send California money to the South to fight a war against the North. I can't believe it! We were never pro-slavery in this state until these damn southerners flooded in here bringing their slaves. Seems they hold all the elected or appointed offices. Ever since Lincoln's election, they've been steaming under their stuffed shirts."

Danny poured himself a whiskey. "I'll tell you one thing. They're going to be stopped, one way or another. Hear me, Jenna. Never trust these separatists. And don't trust the men that want California a separate nation, a republic on the Pacific Coast. There's big money, power, and special interests behind these men who are doing all the talking."

Jenna saw the light in Danny's eye, one she had not seen in a long while. His cockiness had returned and she found him exciting. She did not like any show of weakness, his moroseness, his days of withdrawal. These were not a Daggett's traits.

She knew Danny felt trapped in a marriage he did not want, and she tried to give him all the freedom he desired. On the other hand, there were days when he seemed more peaceful, happy even, and enjoyed carrying Sage on his shoulders when the whole family walked in the woods. But lately, with his involvement in the Union Club, his energy, quick actions, humor, and glib conversation had returned. The fight, the daring, the risk that spun like a force around him had returned, and Jenna again loved him with fiery intensity. She ignored the whiskey that always lingered on his breath and chose to enjoy his outbursts of Irish songs as part of his charm.

As San Francisco became more involved in the heat of an inevitable war, Danny and his friends organized, orated, and marched behind parades to excite pro-unionists into collective action. Danny's gift of speech ignited crowds, setting them off like explosions of fireworks. With his black curls, wet with perspiration, his coat off, and his shirt unbuttoned, he shouted about a united country and freedom for all men.

"My southern friend, Mr. Randolph, says he speaks for California, and I quote,

*'Far to the east in the homes from which we came, tyranny and
usurpation is this night, perhaps slaughtering our fathers, our
brothers and sisters and outraging our homes. If this be rebellion,
then I am a rebel!'*

"My friends, I say to you this very night, there are slaves escaping an
unforgivable tyranny. This very night, the landed gentry are sippin' mint
juleps on their handsome porches while southern armies are forming to
fight northern brothers.

"The War Between the States will make brothers fight brothers. Already,
Californians are fighting Californians . . . men who were brothers in the
mining camps, who have built this state brick by brick . . . side by side.

"We must unite against secession, build an army. My friends, the
chains of slavery are cutting into the hearts of all of us, and blood is going
to spill here in the West. If it is war they want on California soil, if our
representatives consider us rebels to *their* causes, then I, too, am a rebel!"

The crowd burst into cheers. Danny shouted above them. "Let the
southern sympathizers feel the butt of our boots—kick 'em back to their
southern states and clean up California!"

Again the crowd shouted, and Danny grinned from ear to ear. He loved
the rhetoric, the camaraderie, the intrigue and high drama.

Jenna did not question Danny's activities during the next few months.
Many times he dressed in worn boots, old soiled clothes, a wool cap
or shapeless hat, and fingerless gloves—apparel Jenna had never seen
before.

"You look like a dock worker, a down-on-his-luck miner, maybe a
fisherman, Danny. Where are you going? Please tell me. You know I'm not
a gossipy woman." Jenna felt Danny's excitement on these nights and saw
his blue eyes electric and happy.

There were times she would have liked to be a man, to play their roles of
intrigue. Men could play together in ways women could not. Their type of
loyalty had a dangerous edge, one Jenna understood. Had she been a man,
she would have loved danger just like Danny. But as a mother, with the

binding loyalty of other mothers, she would play out the female role God had given her. She could never risk her own life for a male cause. She had a baby girl to raise.

"Danny, I know you're up to something with your *boys*, as you call them. You've always been open in your protests, but this disguise frightens me. Tell me, please. You're spying or you're planning something that could hurt you. I have to know!"

"Don't be curious, my girl. I'm out with me boys for a few laughs is all."

But Jenna knew it had something to do with the Union Club. War between the states had become a fact. The Confederate states elected Jefferson Davis president of the new nation, and tension was felt throughout the land.

🌱 🌱 🌱

One night as Jenna lay alone in her bed, wondering as usual where Danny was, she heard voices below her window and saw the spill of lantern light on the leaves of the pepper tree. She looked out the window and saw two men carrying Danny in the back door. Sung Moon, standing in his nightshirt, held a lantern as the men entered the house.

Jenna rushed down the stairs and into the kitchen, where Danny lay groaning on the floor; Sung Moon and two men she did not recognize were bending over him. He had been severely beaten; his eyes were swollen shut and his face full of blood. The men said nothing and left quickly when they saw Jenna.

"Danny, what happened? Can you speak?"

"I'm all right, Jenna. I can take a beating, especially from separatist cowards. I need to be cleaned up is all."

Sung Moon knelt down by Danny. "Can you move body, Mister Danny?"

Danny nodded.

"Arms and legs, too?"

"Yes, I think so," he said.

"Mister vomit or pass blood?"

"I vomited."

"No blood?"

"No."

"Mister have broken collarbone. I fix it for you, tape you up good. Don't worry, Missy Jenna."

"Jenna, get my pistol from the armoire in the bedroom. Be careful, it's loaded. I don't think I was recognized or followed, but just in case—there are a few people unhappy with me and me boys."

What Jenna had suspected was true. Danny admitted he and the others had been spying on a group of separatists of the Knights of the Golden Circle who were meeting in secret, raising an illegal confederate army throughout California.

"They've got an arsenal somewhere," Danny said.

Since Danny's face and sympathies were well-known, he had been operating in disguise, hanging around docks and houses of ill repute, gambling houses, and saloons on the Barbary Coast District. His goal had been to get information on the extent of the southern success. To this end, he'd even attended clandestine meetings on both sides.

"Worst of all, Jenna, our own state militia is already infiltrated with men who would join their cause in a moment's notice. That damn Senator Gwin's influence over the new commander of the military forces is clear. Like Gwin, he's a southern sympathizer and turns his head the other way while they arm themselves right under our noses. God knows how many of them have guns—probably all of them—and they're well-organized. We could erupt into open conflict *right here*."

"Oh, Danny, do be careful," Jenna said, washing Danny's cut eye. "Everyone knows you. You were lucky this time."

"The South has already seceded. The North and South are in armed confrontation. We may not be spared from open hostilities out here in the west. War can be anywhere at anytime.

"I hear some Californians are leaving to join the Confederate army, persuaded to fight for southern causes. I tell you, Jenna, we've uncovered a conspiracy here in California. I can send Washington enough evidence to secure a Union army and stop southern infiltration of our state right at the border!

"The South needs gold to carry on a war; they need gold to back their Confederate paper money, and there are some slick men who know how to get it. These Southern rascals make plots and financial deals with corrupt California officials and sympathetic mining companies."

Jenna poured Danny a whiskey and stoked the fire.

"I'm going to Nevada to see what is going on with the Bobcat. Those mint julep southerners aren't getting any gold of mine—and no one else's if I have anything to do with it. Besides, I think it's best if I disappear for awhile."

🌱 🌱 🌱

Danny left for Nevada, once again leaving Jenna alone, this time to care for her toddler. Sage, now walking, flirted with blue eyes that sparkled like sun-rippled water, delighting everyone around her, especially her mother.

One afternoon, Jenna carried Sage on her back into the woods behind her house. Sheba trotted alongside, sniffing the trails of creatures that had recently passed by, running only a short distance ahead of Jenna before stopping to see if she was within protective reach.

"It's the three of us again." Jenna sighed. A threesome, always a threesome.

Well, we'll make do without Danny. He's happier on the road, away.

Walking back to the house, she had a peculiar sensation someone was watching her. She stopped and picked up Sage, listening for a footfall on the sticks and leaves. Suddenly, Sheba caught a scent, raised her hackles, and barked sharply. Jenna saw two men run deeper into the woods and out of sight. When she returned to the house, she took the loaded pistol from the armoire and decided to keep it close at hand.

That night as Jenna was about to retire and Sung Moon began extinguishing the lamps, they were startled by a loud banging on the front door. Instinctively, Jenna reached for the pistol and held it in the folds of her dress. Sung Moon opened the door cautiously. The two men standing there appeared well dressed, but their voices were hostile.

"We want to speak to Daniel McDaniels."

"He not home." Sung Moon began to shut the door.

"Hold on, Chinee. I said I want to see McDaniels." The man pushed open the door and stepped into the hall.

Jenna came forward. "Perhaps I can help you gentlemen." She kept the pistol hidden."

"Are you McDaniels' wife?"

"I am."

"Where is he?" the other man said, stepping into the hallway. "Upstairs?" He took a step toward the stairwell.

Jenna pulled the pistol from her skirt and pointed it directly at the two men. "I do not know who you are, but I want you to leave, instantly. My husband is out of the state."

"Wait, Madam, we are friends of his."

"I do not know which side you are on, nor do I care if you are a friend or enemy. I don't like your manner. Please leave at once."

One man smiled. "She don't like our manner," he sneered and started up the stairs.

Jenna aimed above his head and fired a shot. "Get out or I'll kill you!"

The men backed away to the door. Sung Moon grabbed Jenna's gun and began firing wildly, smattering the glass door panel, firing holes into the ceiling and floor. Sheba barked and lunged at the men. They turned and stumbled down the porch stairs while Sung Moon fired into the air and Sheba chased them to the road.

"Don't come back! Sung Moon is dirty yellow Chinee son-bitch! Sung Moon is crazy Chinee!"

The men jumped into their rig, snapped the reins of the nervous horses and dashed out of the courtyard.

Sung Moon was smiling when he came back into the house. "Yellow-belly cowards," he said, handing Jenna the pistol.

"You're a good shot, Sung Moon. You managed to miss them," she said, smiling.

"I clean up, Missy. You go to bed."

"Thank you, Sung Moon."

"I fix you sleepy tea?"

"It's not necessary. I feel safe with you here."

Sung Moon bowed low, partially hiding a toothy grin.

🌿 🌿 🌿

One afternoon, Sung Moon announced a caller, a lady, waiting in the parlor. Hannah had come to call.

"I hired a coach, Jenna, so as not to spoil your respectable, homey image in San Francisco," Hannah said, striding about the room.

"I'm glad you came, Hannah. Forgive me for still being in my morning dress, but I was pruning some roses. We'll have lemonade in the garden. Is this a social call?" Jenna was certain it wasn't. She knew Hannah had a strong motive for coming to her door, one designed to unsettle her. Jenna straightened her back and lifted her chin to disguise her uncertainty.

"You might say so. After all, we share a lot, you and I." She smirked and shook her long curls like she used to do as a young girl. "I wanted to see your baby. Sage, isn't that her name?"

Jenna flushed. Obviously, Danny had shared their life with her, and Hannah wanted Jenna to know that fact. "I'll have Ping bring her down. She'll be waking from her nap anytime now."

"You look quite married . . . motherly, in fact. It suits you, I think. Better you than me."

The two women sat in a garden blooming with camellias while Sung Moon fixed the lemonade and a tray of biscuits. Jenna carried on small talk, all the while suspecting Hannah's purpose in visiting was not altogether friendly. Her remarks had an acidic tone, overly confident, sarcastic, with double meanings and innuendos.

Jenna was glad when Sung Moon brought the refreshing drink to distract the uncomfortable conversation. Ping carried Sage into the garden and handed her to Jenna. The toddler, dressed in a soft pink smock embroidered with tiny flowers on the hem, smiled and bubbled baby sounds.

"Happy baby, Missy." The lines in Ping's face creased into a wrinkled smile.

"The baby is cute . . . too olive for an Irishman," Hannah said. "They're so wonderfully white-skinned. She doesn't look like you or Daniel at all."

Jenna's heart was pounding in her chest.

Hannah placed one finger on the child's arm. "My mother wondered where I came from. She always thought I had Indian in me—but one never knows all the family mischief. Don't you agree, Jenna?"

"Sage looks very much like Danny. Everyone says so," she answered, feeling the splotches rise on her neck.

Hannah laughed. "My mistake. I've never been much good about babies and family traits. Surely, you didn't take offense at my casual remarks?"

"Not at all." Jenna wished Hannah would leave. She placed her cup of unfinished tea in its saucer, rose from her chair and looked down at her. "I do have things to attend to. I'm sure you understand."

"One thing more," Hannah said coldly. "Daniel is not cut out for marriage, you know. I advise you to keep a loose rein. It's none of my business, of course, but since we're friends, I thought you . . ."

"My marriage is none of your business, Hannah. Your lifestyle is none of mine."

"Quite right." Hannah walked to the door. "Come visit me sometime, and bring your adorable daughter. Sage, isn't it?"

🌱 🌱 🌱

Danny returned from Nevada weary with disappointment. Without acknowledging Sage, who reached out to him with her pudgy arms, he flung his bag on the floor and headed for the whiskey decanter.

"I'm wiped out, Jenna. The Bobcat was a fiasco, a washout. I had a feeling in the pit of my stomach for weeks that something was wrong." He poured a shot of whiskey, drank it quickly, and poured another.

"Oh, Danny, how sorry I am. Tell me about it," she said, putting Sage down. The infant walked over to Danny and grabbed his leg, smiling up into his face and babbling her baby greeting.

"Can't you control her, Jenna? I'm in no mood to be a da' now. Go on, Sage, run along to your mother." He patted her head of massive, black ringlets without real interest.

"I'll have Ping put her down for the night. I thought you'd want to see her first. It's been a month."

Danny flashed her a look that told her not to press him with her personal frustrations.

"The miners working on a vein of clay hit a geyser at three hundred feet. Hot steam and boiling water shot out and caught the crew in a gush of scalding water. The next day, the whole shaft was deep with bodies floating like boiled fish.

"The Bobcat owners fled with whatever money was left—abandoned the whole project without notifying the stockholders. They're deep into Mexico by now."

Totally indifferent to the expensive fabric, Danny stretched out on the settee in his soiled traveling clothes and dusty boots. He sighed. "I think mining in California, the big profits, are pinching out. Those great days of massive fortunes are coming to an end. God! My timing is bad!"

Jenna sat on the edge of the settee. "There must be some other fortune waiting for you elsewhere," she said, trying to be of some support. Her words sounded trite, even to her.

"It's not just the money, Jenna. It's the fight of it all, the game, the chance, the winning and losing. Damn! I'm having a lousy streak."

Danny's words deflated her spirit. She feared the hurt would show through her eyes. Were she and Sage part of his bad luck?

Apparently, misreading her expression, he said in a gentlemanly voice, "Forgive me for swearing, Jenna. I'll try to watch my language." He drew Jenna to him and put his arms around her, a comforting embrace, one shared by partners, not lovers. "I don't know how to get started again—without money."

"You'll think of something, some opportunity."

"My Irish boys are talking about going to Colorado Territory. Mining is going strong there . . . several substantial strikes in the Pikes Peak area and above Denver and Auraria. They're having a gold and silver boom, like California did ten years ago. They're in the first stages of mining—in some places still skimming off the top with panning. The timing is perfect!"

Danny held Jenna at arm's length and looked at her with his aquamarine eyes, bright as ice. "The lads want me to join them—prospect for a mine, start a company. We've talked about it. I've got to go, Jenna. I can't sit here while my boys are off in the wilds. It's why we came to the American West together in the first place. The adventure was a bond of four lads. It's in me blood, girl."

Jenna had thought that in time, Danny would want her and Sage above
all else. It was the way marriages went, but his expression told her it was
not the case. "And what about me and Sage?" Jenna asked in nearly a
whisper.

Danny got up and poured another drink. "I can't support you. I'm not a
good family man, you know that." Through the window of her wide, blue
eyes, he saw her heartbreak, like a shadow blotting out the sun.

"I'm sorry, Jenna. I do love you, that's true. The saints be my witness.
I thought I'd get used to marriage, that I would do a better job than I'm
doing."

"I told you I wouldn't keep you, Danny. That was our agreement."

"I'm not leaving you forever, Jenna. I'll send for you and Sage when
we've settled on a place to mine."

Jenna brightened. "Really, Danny, you want us to join you?"

"In time," he said cautiously. He thought surely a woman of means
who enjoyed the culture and comforts of San Francisco would never want
to suffer the hardships of the wilderness or follow him through the muck
of mining life; but instead, he saw eagerness on Jenna's face. "It may be
months. Could you give up all you have here in California?"

"Oh, yes, my dearest. To be in the Rocky Mountains, with you, would
be a dream fulfilled! I remember seeing the edge of them in the distance
when we stayed at Fort Bridger on the crossing. I can only imagine how
magnificent they must be."

"There aren't many people there yet—only a few women, mostly
scruffy, hard-eyed miners. It's a hard life, girl, with snows so deep they
cover the rooftops. You'd have to live in Denver in the winter and in a
crude cabin in the summer up in the cold camps."

"You forget, I've done it before," she said, throwing her arms around
him. "When would you leave?"

The liquor had given Danny a sense of well-being. He could handle
anything now, even a family. Why not? He was in charge of the situation.
If she was fool enough to want to come, she'd find out soon enough it was
only a life for the toughest men and would hightail it back to California

when the first snowflakes fell. Women were like that. What woman would give up her dainty slippers for muddy boots? He had nothing to worry about.

"The lads are leaving in August, after settling a little matter with the Knights. We figure the Pioneer Stage will take ten to twelve days on the California Overland—the old California Emigrant Trail. We'll buy supplies in Denver, get us some mules, and head west right up into the hills. We'll have a few good weeks of prospecting before the snows get too deep."

"I could join you in the spring, Danny. That is, whenever you send for me."

They talked until Danny's speech became thick and his facial muscles sagged with exhaustion.

He looked at Jenna through unfocused eyes. "There's a matter of money, my sweet. Either we sell the stocks we just bought or maybe you could help me out again."

"We'll talk about that in the morning," she said, guiding him to the stairs. "You need sleep now. You've had a long journey."

As Jenna extinguished the parlor lamps, her momentary euphoria died like the light. Talk of money always lay below the surface of so many conversations she had with Danny, rising unexpectedly like a sea snake— an intruder, once again confusing the lovely pictures Jenna created in her mind.

She did not want Danny to leave, but to hold him at home would have been a slow death for him, for their marriage. She rationalized that a new life in Colorado might bring them together in stronger ways, a place without the distractions of San Francisco's tempestuous diversions of the Barbary Coast, faro tables, and Hannah. She could put aside all the bitter memories of the Archuletas and Reginald Potter, of Enrique and that horror-filled morning by the spring. She could start a new life with her beautiful, capricious daughter, who already showed the flirtatiousness of an Irishman and the willfulness of a Spaniard.

For the next few weeks, Danny's high spirits spilled into the household— the liveliest of times, Jenna thought. They entertained Danny's friends, both married and single, and Jenna hosted afternoon socials with several women. In her own mind, it was a way to say goodbye to California. She knew that for Danny, it was an expression of his perpetual gregariousness and affability, his insatiable desire to keep the party going.

Some members of the Union Club periodically met at the house, speaking in low voices behind the closed parlor door. Danny's unfinished business became clear when a fiery blaze lighted the night sky at the edge of the city. The Unionists had found the arsenal of the secret Confederate army—a cache of arms, gunpowder, and dynamite. What the Bloodhounds—as the Union Club members were called—did not steal, they ignited.

The governor, fully convinced of the threats from those supporting the Confederacy, removed the commander of the state militia and replaced him with a Union general. The militia from Oregon was summoned to keep order, and Washington, fearing California wealth could fall into the hands of the confederacy, issued passports for anyone desiring to enter California.

🐚 🐚 🐚

When August burned its way into the summer, Danny kissed Jenna and Sage goodbye, promising to send for them. "I'll make it up to you, my love—this time for certain."

"Please write me, Danny. Tell me you have arrived safely. Tell me all the news." Jenna knew she wouldn't have long to wait once Danny sent word. A letter from Colorado arrived in San Francisco in ten days by Pony Express. Since telegraph wires now extended from Salt Lake to San Francisco, she could receive a telegram from him even faster.

"I'll be safe, darlin', safer there than here. There are a few people who'd like to tar and feather me around town, but where I'm going, only the Indians are causing problems. But they've never met the likes of four Irish lads, now have they?" Danny let out a whoop of youthful joy and leaped down the stairs three at a time, his hair flying, his coat thrown over his shoulder. He was like a schoolboy free from the day's confinement.

Jenna stood in the road and watched Danny's coach until it turned the corner. He was gone again, but this time he was uprooting, changing his whole life, leaving everything familiar and comfortable—all for some insatiable hunger, not just for gold or opportunity, but for the excitement of the quest, the unknown.

Her papa had been that way, too. She remembered a craziness that sometimes glowed in his eyes, flickering in the firelight, dancing like a pair of wild men waving their arms above their heads.

Jenna thought about how different the values of men and women were. A man would die for an ideal, a belief. He would go to war and die for a comrade. A woman would die for her children. He would sacrifice himself for a cause. She would sacrifice herself for him and her home and family. He would die protecting what belonged to him—a way of life, property and stock, a wife and family. She would die protecting her children, but not her husband . . . or would she?

Men like Danny loved the challenge of the game, and when one was finished, they found another one—a new vein of gold, a better machine, a new war. Women were not allowed to play the game, but only could be bystanders, flag wavers, hand clappers with tiny voices. Women's playfulness, humor, adventurousness, wantonness, desires, passions, their very shouts, were bound like their corseted bodies. Men took chances; women tended the babies.

Jenna walked back to the house. She had spent many hours waiting for Danny to come home and had concluded that for all his impulsive behavior that made him an unreliable as a family man, he loved her and Sage in his own way. It was better to hang on to the ideal of the family—something she never had as a child—than to think she might never have a marriage, a home and a husband.

She did not want Sage to suffer as she had. No matter what concerns whispered at the back of her mind, Danny McDaniels was worth all the doubt. She adored him and would wait. Maybe he would change.

Jenna entered her house, and for a reason she could not explain, slammed the door hard behind her.

This time, however, she was not going to be alone. She'd arranged to visit Darcey, Blue, Harke, and Pearle—her beloved friends—and to stay through Christmas. The timing was perfect. She could be a companion to

Pearle, now in the last days of her pregnancy, enduring the weary hours of confinement that seem never to end. She would be with Pearle at the birth of the baby. Then, after the first of the year, she would begin preparations to leave California, and turn her thoughts to the new adventure awaiting her.

Besides, maybe it was time to disentangle from California. It had been easy selling her railroad stock—the small line to the Sierras. Rumors that the railroad would soon be absorbed by the Central Pacific had driven up the price of the shares. The transaction had made a nice profit, the proceeds of which would help Danny get started in the Colorado Territory. She felt certain she could easily sell her house, property and all the furnishing, yielding a nice profit for her new life in the Rockies. Yes, maybe it was time to go.

Jenna looked at Sage's trusting face, and thought of her own childhood, remembering herself running in the meadows, braiding clover chains, racing her horse to beat the wind. But those carefree days had ended abruptly for Jenna, to be replaced with another culture. The remainder of Jenna's youth had been full of contrasts, strict and religious on one hand, exotic and sensual on the other. It had been spent in a culture that had never fully accepted her.

Jenna was determined to make certain Sage never endured such inconsistencies. She wanted her daughter to always feel loved in profound ways, to be anchored in a family with strong roots reaching deep in nourishing soil.

She would reunite with Danny to make certain Sage had that family, even if it meant following him through all the world's cold canyons. Someday, the three would be together again, have a new start, with friends and miles of Colorado meadows and mountains to explore and call home.

🍃 🍃 🍃

Jenna, along with Sage and Sheba, arrived in Jackson as the leaves began to fall and the late summer sun cast hazy days, quiet and golden.

Introducing her little girl to her dearest friends had been Jenna's dream since the day Sage was born. Sage was a precious child with coy little mannerisms and bubbly laughter that instantly won favor and smiles. She already knew she could be the center of attention by dancing on her tippy toes, twisting until she fell down. She knew, by the inviting, outstretched arms and sweet faces, she could choose anyone she desired to run to and lay her head of tousled curls on a friendly lap.

Blue, especially, coddled Sage, walking with her about the house and through the gardens, picking zinnias, fallen leaves, and bruised cherries from under the trees.

"You're going to spoil that child rotten," Darcey teased, but she, as well, happily carried Sage around, fed her sweets, cuddled her in the porch swing, and sang Irish lullabies until the little girl nodded off.

Pearle felt anticipation and excitement course through her as she watched Sage, thinking that in only a few weeks she would be a mother of a child as enchanting as this one. The little stranger stretching against her inner walls told her daily that he or she was outgrowing the space, waking for longer periods and listening to gentle murmurs, outbursts of joyful laughter—even the muted sounds of music, the vibration of foot stomping and hand clapping.

Pearle and Harke lived in a small house only a few streets away from Higgins House. Every day she walked to Darcey's to be with Jenna and Sage and to help with the cooking, baking, and light ironing.

Her moon-shaped stomach sat high and made her short of breath. For one so small and dainty, the protuberance appeared exaggerated. She only laughed. "I'm proud of my roundness. Why should I hide from gossipers? I'm beautiful! Can't you see, I swallowed the moon? See its holy light?"

It was a glorious time for Jenna. Mornings were filled with Darcey's throaty laughter, hot cinnamon rolls, and steaming coffee. Jenna loved helping Darcey make custards and pies and ginger cakes for the noon meal. The friendship between the women bonded and leavened like the loaves of bread they made daily. Together with Pearle, they filled baskets with black currants, sweet from the higher hills, and made jars of jelly and jam. Together, they peeled peaches and pears, spending whole afternoons with juice running down their arms, as they pitted the seeds and blanched the fruit halves for canning.

The kitchen spilled its delectable aroma of cherries one day, and tomato relish the next. The fragrance of watermelon pickles, string beans, beets, ribbons of cloves, ginger, garlic, chocolate cake, and yeast breads wafted through the house. The women smiled at their accomplishment as the rows of canned fruits and vegetables marched along the counter and filled the pantry shelves.

Sage, the delight of the boardinghouse, played on the floor with pots and wooden spoons and patted leftover dough into cookies over and over until the ball was black with dirt. Sticky from sampling the sugary syrups, she would cry and hold up her small, dirty hands to be washed.

Often, the women went to a secluded spot by the river where Sage waded and splashed, and Sheba bounded time and again into the water to retrieve a stick. On these special afternoons, they could rest or carry on breezy conversations before preparing late tea for the boarders. It seemed the work never ended.

Jenna said very little about Danny, only that she was gloriously happy and soon would be leaving for Colorado. Darcey knew Jenna well enough to detect Jenna's uncertainty about her marriage.

There are too many excuses, Darcey thought as she observed Jenna's drawn expression. *It is a strange coincidence that I met this enchanting Irishman, Danny McDaniels, at Hattie's Place—he and his rough Irish friends. I thought he was a devil then with his captivating smile and ways to make a heart stop, even make an old girl swoon. Jenna got caught in the beam of his eye, the web of his charm and wit.* Darcey remembered with some embarrassment the tingle he'd sent up her own spine.

Darcey was also curious about Jenna's modesty. In the past, the women had helped wash each other's hair, scrubbed backs, poured hot water into the tub around soapy bodies. There had been no shyness between them then, even after Jenna had become a woman.

I guess people change, Darcey thought. *They become more reserved. Still, something just ain't right.*

One afternoon as Jenna, Darcey, and Pearle sat lazily under the shade of a large eucalyptus by the river hemming table napkins and Sage napped between them, Pearle murmured, "I keep wondering if I have a baby boy or girl kicking inside. Look there at a foot or fist pushing my stomach."

Darcey placed her hand on Pearle's round stomach. "It's got to be a boy by the way he's carrying on in there. On the other hand, your face and jaw haven't taken on a masculine look and you haven't grown a mustache, so I guess it's a girl."

"There's one way to find out," Jenna said, unwinding a long piece of thread. "You tie your wedding ring on the thread and hang it over your tummy. If it moves in a circle, it's a girl; if it swings back and forth in a straight line, it's a boy."

Pearle lay on her back and hung the ring over the horizon of her belly. "It's not moving at all. It's just a dead weight," she said softly.

"Concentrate, child," Darcey said, "and don't go gettin' dramatic. There, it's moving now . . . like a boy."

"I'd love to have a little boy, a miniature Harke," she said, stretching on the blanket like a contented cat. "God will bless me with just the right one."

"Well, I'm happy I got a beautiful girl," Jenna said, running her hand gently over Sage's black curls.

Darcey thought Jenna might open up about her marriage to Danny. "And Danny? Was he happy to have a little girl?"

Jenna did not change her expression. "He said he would be happy with either one. Just to be sure that a devilish fairy he called Will-o'-the-wisp wouldn't carry off the baby in its first hours, he turned my left stocking and the sleeve of my coat inside out. Imagine!"

The women laughed, but Darcey was not convinced Jenna's words reflected a lovely domestic scene.

Pearle sat up. "I'm not superstitious, mind you, but Mrs. Sabel, the midwife, told me to rub my crippled leg with bay leaf and the baby's as well, to be sure it will not be born crippled or have an accident that could leave it with a short leg."

"Oh, for heaven's sake!" Darcey said. "She also told you not to eat blueberries or strawberries and touch your forehead for fear the baby will have a birthmark. What else did she frighten you with?"

"Nothing, only that if the baby is born with a caul, she'd save it for me to dry and eat if I had cramps afterward. Or I could bury it to ensure the child's good luck," she said. Pearle laughed happily and began sewing.

"I wish you'd let me help in the delivery. I'm your mother, after all."

"Mrs. Sabel says it's better to have you near at hand. Mothers upset easily."

"Well, I'm not like other mothers. I've helped birth cats, dogs, hogs, calves, and horses, and I delivered your brother by myself when your father was hunting. I laid in bed for a full two days without help before a neighbor saw I wasn't outside doing chores and checked on me. I'm going to be in that room with you."

"Yes, that's only right, Pearle. You'll want your mother during the labor and birth. I know," Jenna said.

🌢 🌢 🌢

As the days passed, Darcey became increasingly convinced something was not right in Jenna's marriage. Each day, Jenna looked in vain for a letter from Danny. Her disappointment sagged her shoulders, dropping her spirit so visibly, it seemed everyone felt it

Blue and Darcey exchanged side-glances of concern, and Pearle's eyes teared in sympathy.

"He'll send for me, I'm certain. But you know how remote the Colorado Territory is. Almost anything could have happened to a letter or a rider. Indians are becoming more hostile and frightening emigrants and Pony Express riders all the time. He's written, I know. He promised he'd let us know he'd arrived safely and when I'm to meet him. I'm certain to hear this week."

But as the time passed, deeper lines of sadness formed around Jenna's eyes and mouth.

Jenna's bouts of unhappiness never lasted long. How could they when she was surrounded with so much joy and contentment? She found herself sharing Pearle's delight in the coming baby and warming to the tenderness radiating between the parents-to-be.

Harke spent two or three nights each week at home on his routine schedule and made his run to Sacramento and San Francisco the rest of the time. Now, with Pearle closer to delivery, he planned to drive only to Sacramento to be on hand when the baby came. Beaming with pride at Pearle's extended stomach, he kissed her affectionately on each return or parting. Jenna saw his happiness, his love for Pearle, and it delighted her.

Everyone kept a close eye on Pearle as the estimated time of delivery approached. The signs were apparent—the pressure on her small frame and the swelling ankles, the baby's drop and its stillness, as if resting before an arduous journey. Eventually, Pearle was only comfortable lying in bed.

At last, on a late afternoon, while the world outside seemed slow and sleepy, a storm of activity pushed against a bone barrier, the baby raging to be free. Pearle was well into labor when a young neighbor boy ran to Darcey's with the message that Mrs. Polley was going to have her baby, and Mr. Polley said to come at once.

By the time Darcey, Blue, and Jenna arrived at Pearle's bedside, a doctor had been called. "It's a breech birth," he told them. "With her small structure, I'm afraid it's going to be a hard delivery." He sighed. "I think it's best for the family to wait outside. The midwife, Mrs. Sabel, and I will handle everything and call you when we can. We'll keep you informed on her progress."

The hours seemed endless as Pearle's body contorted with contractions. All night and the next day, unbearable pain gripped her abdomen, tightening her insides into a fighting fist, and still the baby, lodged in its small opening, seemed unable to move farther.

The doctor gently tried to pull the baby down, but to no avail. Pearle lay in wet sheets, exhausted, rarely complaining. She tried to detach herself from the racking sensation and pressure forcing her pelvis to widen.

Come unto me those who labor and are heavy burdened . . . and I will give thee rest . . . rest. Oh, my dearest God . . . Fear not, for I am with thee . . . I shall give the angels charge over thee . . . yes . . . fear not.

When Pearle's body seemed to give up its involuntary undulations, the doctor, without further delay, forcefully pulled out the baby. The small form was curled like an unopened bud. It had already strangled and lay dead and bloody in his hands. He held the tiny lifeless body, which had been only a heart beat away from life, and gently placed it in the care of the midwife waiting with a sheet. He shook his head.

Weak and exhausted, Pearle floated in and out of sleep, barely conscious of the birth or the unstaunchable blood flowing like a small spring.

Outside in the parlor, no one heard a sound from behind the closed door. Jenna and Darcey held each other, pale with fear.

Blue looked up to see the doctor open the door, his face telling the story. "It was a stillbirth. I'm sorry, Mr. Polley."

"Pearle? Is she all right?" Harke asked, jumping up from his chair.

"She's hemorrhaging. It's been a terrible ordeal for her. If we can stop the bleeding, she'll recover. If not—well, I'm sorry. It was not a normal birth—happens sometimes. We'll do our best, and say our prayers. The Almighty knows more about these things than I do." He patted Harke's shoulder sympathetically. "You can see her one at a time. If she sleeps, let her be."

Just then, the nurse walked out of the birth room carrying a small bundle. She nodded to the grieving group and quickly moved down the hall to the kitchen.

"It's so tiny," Blue said, "even wrapped up like that . . . such a little life."

"It shouldn't have happened to Pearle," Darcey said, wiping her eyes. "She's meant to be a mother, a better one than I ever was. Loving little things is second nature to her. She mothers everything—dogs, squirrels, flowers, seeds, pinecones, everyone's child, her schoolchildren—even *me*."

"There will be more little ones," Blue said sorrowfully, remembering his first wife's death at childbirth and the tiny bundle tucked inside the casket close to the breast of his beloved young wife.

Harke came out of the room, his face dark with grief. "She wants a moment with you first, Jenna. She doesn't know yet about the baby—too weak. The news can wait. There's hardly a heartbeat left in her. I couldn't find it with my head on her chest. I listened . . . hardly a heartbeat there," he said.

Jenna looked at Darcey, whose expression showed her feelings were hurt, but Darcey nodded and said, "Go on, Jenna. It's all right. You've been a mother to her, too."

Pearle lay against the pillow as pale and transparent as paraffin. Jenna instantly recognized the signs of death behind the protruding dark eyes, the dilated pupils trying to hold the light as long as possible.

"Jenna, listen to me. I know I'm dying."

"No, no, Pearle. You're only weak."

"Hush, Jenna. Don't fret. I want you to take care of my baby. The nurse said a little boy, a son. You'll do that?"

Jenna was like everyone who promises the dying to take care of their worldly concerns. "Of course, dear Pearle," Jenna said, holding the frail woman's feather-light hand to her cheek.

"And call him Matthew—Matthew Polley, like the Matthew in the Gospels. It's a nice name."

"Yes, yes, of course, anything, Pearle, only don't die. You can't—not now. Hang on, *please*. Don't die," Jenna said, blinking away the tears.

Pearle closed her eyes. Jenna took the locket from around her neck, the only symbol of motherhood she remembered from Martha Jane, and fastened it around Pearle's neck.

"And love Harke for me. He loves you so. Call Mother and Blue."

Four hours later, Pearle passed from this earth, leaving a hole in an already lacy world.

"Oh, God!" Harke wailed. "Why do You take the purest, most beautiful away from the world that needs to know goodness and sweetness? She was Your light. We knew You, Lord through her."

He turned to Jenna with bewilderment in his eyes. Jenna held him while he caught the sobs in his throat. Once, long ago, he had held her while she sobbed for Israel. Now it was her turn to comfort him with some idea of Heaven, make some sense of it all.

Jenna gently took Harke's hand. "Maybe, Pearle passed over into another place, somewhere else, to follow your baby. Somewhere . . . to be its mother and care for it—somewhere else. I don't know about these things, Harke," Jenna said softly.

They buried Pearle and the baby a mile out of town in a hillside cemetery among the trees. The dust danced in the shafts of sun slanting through the forest, lighting up a silent stone inscribed, *"She and her babe, too soon, were called away."*

🌱 🌱 🌱

A pall pervaded Higgins House as the holidays approached. While people everywhere prepared for joyful Christmas feasts and family gatherings, Darcey and Jenna wearily hung pine boughs around the front door and the archway of the dining room and parlor. They baked minced pies in polite silence, neither having the heart of celebration.

But a week before Christmas, Harke brought Jenna her long-awaited letter from Danny. The news raised everyone's spirits.

"He's in Colorado Territory—safe—at a place west of Denver, the Gregory Diggings. He wants us to come. He's sent for me and Sage, Darcey! We're going to Colorado!" Jenna smiled, radiating her joy and relief as she held the letter to her chest. For the first time, she heard the church bells chiming out a glorious season not only for the faithful, but the faithless as well.

The letter did not quite say what Jenna conveyed to Darcey and Blue. Rather, it said that he was safe in Colorado and needed a bit more money for his venture in the canyon above the diggings, that he was certain a few more feet would reach the paying vein.

He and his partners had started the Irish Boy Mine Company and had experienced some success in Cherry Creek, enough to hire a crew of discouraged miners to work for a daily wage. He would send for her only if things went well. He reported that barely a handful of sturdy women had dared the savage area, and "those women look like men, some even with heavy facial hair—mustaches on their upper lips!" He'd seen no women where he was mining, only uncivilized men and every kind of threat to the safety of a family.

The letter said nothing about her going to Colorado. But Jenna's mind was set. Her stubbornness was something Danny had not fully experienced.

When Jenna said goodbye to her friends, she knew it might be years, if ever, before they would meet again. Pearle's untimely death had proved how tenuous life could be. Though no one said as much, they all felt that some invisible cord was unraveling, loosening the bond that called itself "family." Jenna had a family of her own, and it was time for her to move on, to go where life's surprising turns would take her.

SEVENTEEN

J ENNA SOLD HER HOME AND POSSESSIONS, packed a trunk to be sent later on the Colorado Overland Express, and with only light baggage for herself and Sage, bought three seats on the Pioneer Stage—one for her, one for Sage, and one for Sheba. She turned her back on the Pacific coast and faced east toward the Sierras, the desert, the Great Salt Lake, and the Rocky Mountains of Colorado.

She would retrace the route she'd taken in 1848, only this time, she would *meet* the steady stream of wagons not winding in single file, but stretching across the land fifteen miles abreast. These wagonloads of hopefuls still spilled into California daily, if not looking for gold, then for land and opportunity.

As Jenna passed the wagons, she saw the dog-tired women, parched and peeling, courageous and silent, just like the women of her remembered wagon train, all of them dropping their seeds of new beginnings throughout the West, clear to the coast. When Jenna met their eyes, an unspoken understanding passed between them.

Jenna was also accompanied by a stream of emigrants leaving California for Colorado gold, riding in careening covered wagons with "Pikes Peak or Bust" written on the canvas. They would travel one hundred miles each twenty-four hours for about twelve days, stopping every ten miles at way stations and inns for fresh horses.

Everything had changed along the route except the piles of stones marking countless graves and dry scattered bones undigested by the prairie.

Jenna's excitement grew with each passing mile. Soon she would reach the plains on the other side of the Continental Divide at a place where the Platte River and Cherry Creek converged, where two competing towns had grown up on either side of Cherry Creek, and a tumble of structures were tossed onto the flat land like the roll of dice; where a few hundred souls scratched at the earth and their gaunt-eyed partners starched their aprons and waited for another female to share a cup of tea; where folks greeted a stranger with this same spirit that had burst open California.

🌱 🌱 🌱

Jenna had left California on a sunny spring day; but it was still winter when she reached the high, snowy Sierras. Blustery winds and freakish, wet snows followed her across the desert, and deep muddy ruts made travel nearly impossible as her party reached Fort Bridger.

She was glad to have a day of rest at the fort before the final drive to Denver. Here, she would say goodbye to the Pioneer Express and be transported by the Pikes Peak Stage Company south to the struggling town.

Fort Bridger was an active military unit, far more populated with soldiers and weaponry than the forts along the Oregon Trail Jenna remembered as a child. Hostilities between Indians and white men had increased as the numbers of emigrants and their livestock crossed the plains, occupying Indian territory, grasslands, and hunting grounds.

As tension mounted and more and more isolated incidents of massacre were reported among travelers and settlers, white men demanded protection and an answer to the Indian problem. In response, military forts had sprung up along travel routes throughout the west.

Meanwhile, the numbers and behavior of white men entering the territories and California overwhelmed the Indians' ability to comprehend the magnitude of the changes surrounding them. Still, they grappled with ways to coexist. Realizing they could never live as one nation with the white man, the Indians agreed to the establishment of reservations on which they would live—a defined tract of land including vast hunting grounds. What the Indians did not know immediately, was that those grounds would be repeatedly diminished until there would be little food, forcing them to scrounge for scraps, and consume tree bark and their own skinny horses to survive.

As treaties and promises were repeatedly made and broken, eventually neither Indian nor white man trusted one another. Revenge and hatred lay just below the surface. Whether it was expressed in war paint or military garb, the two nations clashed.

For a short time, tolerance, even cooperation, seemed to be working, especially after twelve thousand Indians from different tribes, some at war with each other, met at Fort Laramie to work out differences between the two worlds. But again, one broken act of faith set off a string of violence.

As Jenna neared the end of her trip, she was assured that her destination was relatively safe for whites. The tribes living in the area—the Arapaho and Cheyenne—focused on a war against their ancient enemy, the Ute, whom they hated even more than they did the white man. The two tribes had set up an encampment on their land in the heart of Denver, and in the foothills and surrounding plains.

"You're lucky it's so quiet around here, lady," the driver said to Jenna as he loaded her trunk into the top of the Pikes Peak Stage Company coach. "Last year, the Sioux murdered every white soul up north—slaughtered man, woman, and child, all of them hollerin' like wild dogs. I seen things I'd scarce tell a lady—arms and legs dismembered, torsos and heads scattered here and there, farms burned out, wagons torched with the folks inside. And they think *we're* savages for hangin' a man. Something they can't abide is seein' a man swingin' on the end of a rope.

"One thing for sure is you can't let 'em get a hold of Taos Lightning— whiskey to you, Ma'am. They go crazy. Of course, there are plenty of white men makin' a tidy sum of money in the whiskey trade. Sometimes, I think at the bottom of the whole mess is greed. White men want it all—gold, silver, buffalo, land, hides, ranches, even squaws. We got the numbers and the power.

"No sir, a couple of years back, the Indian figured it all out and a man's life wasn't worth a bag of silt on these wagon roads. Up ahead, you'll see the charred remains of a farm and two graves. Somebody wrote, 'Murdered by Red Devils.' Yep, Red Devils is what they turned into. I can't see as how we'll ever be anything but enemies. They'll just turn their hate inside out."

When at last the stage turned directly south toward Denver, the sun felt warm, the trees blew gracefully in feather-green leaves just opening, new and timid like a young girl in her first party dress. The range of white-peaked mountains bordered Jenna's journey, their lofty beauty thrilling her moment by moment; and when a meadowlark sang, her heart sang with it. Never had she seen and felt such glorious scenery, never had she felt so excited.

Denver boasted a hotel, school, all kinds of churches, the *Rocky Mountain News* and other newspapers, saloons that served ice water in summer, Stewarts Department Store, where a man could buy patent leather gaiters and women, a dainty bonnet. Jenna had overheard a salesman remark to another passenger, "I hear Denver has Hurdy Gurdy girls who show their legs above their knees for fifty cents. My friend, I'm saving my money and staying over in Denver an extra day."

But Jenna had never seen an uglier town, nor one that smelled as bad. A fire had destroyed many buildings in the center of the town only a few weeks before, and piles of charred lumber, fallen burned buildings, stores and houses, still lay in mounds of rubble. Pigs and dogs roamed freely, eating refuse tossed casually behind the buildings; soot and smoke from coal-oil lamps coated anything left in the open and smudged the windowpanes; useless mining equipment, not suitable to the Rocky Mountains, lay rusting and abandoned.

On the edge of town, an Indian encampment, with its white conical tepees poking up toward the blue sky, looked strange and out of place. Everywhere, dogs, horses, wagons, and scruffy miners crisscrossed the streets; men hammered, rebuilding the town; a few women, carrying the day's supply of butchered meat, picked their way around piles of manure and avoided the stares of near-naked Indian boys.

It seemed to Jenna that around the side of every building a drunken Indian sat in a stupor. For the time being, the Indians and white men were avoiding each other's eyes. It was a lull of tolerance while Arapahoes and whites exchanged captives at Fort Lyon and tried to imagine living side by side. Still, the Indians paraded around in feathered war bonnets, some down to their ankles, while the brass-buttoned cavalry trotted down the street in pairs.

Jenna checked into the Apollo Hotel with Sage in her arms. Sheba trailed her every move, the temptation to dart across the street to encounter a hooligan mutt quelled by Jenna's sharp commands.

There was no need to stay in Denver—only long enough to deposit money in a bank. Certainly, there would be no such institution where she was going. The next day, she hired Billy, driver of a supply wagon, to give her and her family a ride up to the mining camps in Clear Creek Canyon.

"At your service," Billy said, removing his soiled hat and bowing low so Jenna could see the wide hairless swath slashed over the top of his head.

"I guess ye see my bald head. I was scalped in '53." He bent down and smiled at Sage. "Ye want to touch my head, little lady? Most youngsters do and ye can, too, if ye like. An Indian scalped me right there and left me for dead. Go on, touch it. Most all the children have at one time or another. They say it brings 'em good luck."

Sage withdrew behind Jenna's skirt.

"She's a shy one, ain't she?" Billy plopped his hat back on his head and looked at Jenna. She noticed the whites of his eyes were jaundiced.

"Now, ye say you're goin' up Clear Creek, which is fine by me, but I have a delivery to make on the way. I'm leaving first thing in the morning. The small fry can sleep on the flour sacks in the wagon if she's a mind to."

"Thank you, Billy. We'll be ready," Jenna said.

He agreed to take her to Golden City west of Denver, then up Clear Creek into the mountains where, at last, she would find Danny and the Irish Boy Mine. After buying a pair of heavy boots, she would be ready to start a new life in Colorado Territory.

❦ ❦ ❦

The Colorado May morning had a snap and tingle to it, an exuberance and anticipation in the crisp air, like the first bite of a juicy apple with sweetness to follow. Perhaps it was only spring bursting forth from the bud and summer about to grow into lofty lengths of leaves, but Jenna felt something new—or was it familiar?

She suddenly thought of Israel and herself together, standing on the windy Continental Divide and feeling such heights that at any moment they believed they could fly. Now, as then, her spirit reached high as the snowy peaks and tall lodgepole pines climbing into the bluest sky she'd ever seen.

The supply wagon creaked to the horses' slow pull up the narrow canyon road. In the deep shadow of Clear Creek, the water rushed in white ribbons of melted ice water, slipped over boulders, and splintered into sprays of amber jewels. The river was young and wild, fast and ambitious, reckless, unstoppable—*like Danny*, Jenna thought.

Feeling the excitement and power of the roaring water, Sage squealed with delighted laughter and Sheba barked, his breath steaming puffs in the cold air.

"Did I mention that I was scalped in '53?" Billy asked.

"Yes, it must have been a terrible experience."

"I played dead as a possum when the Redskin come up. He was quick and had a sharp knife blade and didn't go deep or I wouldn't be alive today.

"I was lucky. In them days, I was an American soldier stationed at Fort Laramie to keep things under control with them Cheyenne Dog Soldiers, Kiowas, Utes, Arapahoes, Blackfoot, Sioux—you name it. They all was fightin' each other, and then in '51, all of them nations met up north at Horse Creek to make peace with each other—nearly twelve thousand of 'em.

"Ye never seen such a sight. All painted up, they was, with eagle feathers and lynx skin headdresses and buffalo hats and war bonnets down to their heels, carrying sabers and quivers covered with otter skins. Ye never seen such a rainbow of men, all boastin' and struttin'. They was all proud and handsome."

"It must have been impressive. I hope we can have peace with them. I hear frightening stories about their brutality."

"In the treaty, they agreed to be more considerate of emigrants and we said we'd help protect them from hotheads who like to pick 'em off from time to time—you know, take target practice with them Plains Indians caught hidin' under sagebrush."

"Who could do such a thing?"

"I don't know, young bucks showin' off, I guess. I liked the Indians, then. They were reasonable folks for the most part."

"What happened? Why did they scalp you?"

"Some snake-eyed Sioux with no sense of humor done it. He was with some discontents who wanted revenge for another Sioux. Seems the Indian got fined for skinnin' a farmer's stray cow. That Indian wasn't about to pay no fine, and when he got belligerent, the soldier shot him."

Jenna didn't respond.

"I don't like the Indians much now. But before I left the army, I got me a scalp or two. I figured my scalp was hangin' on some squaw's belt as a war trophy, so I got me a female's skin."

He opened his coat and showed Jenna a long swatch of blue-black hair hanging on his belt. Next to it was a small, scruffy patch of hair laced in leather strips. Jenna turned away and didn't comment.

"I didn't kill them Indians. They was already dead and I figured they wouldn't miss their scalps none. Hell, they had mine."

"One was a child," Jenna said, disgusted.

"Well, like they say, nits grow into lice."

Jenna did not want to talk further with Billy. They rode in silence for a long time.

As they pulled higher, the mining camps began to appear lining the stream, and high on the steep slopes, the open wounds of the mountain spilled out its ocher slag like oozing sores. Many mines were abandoned, leaving their signs of defeat: scars of cone-shaped mine dumps, broken sluices, and wooden structures tumbling down the mountain.

🌱 🌱 🌱

"A lot of miners busted, Ma'am," Billy said, re-opening up the conversation. "Hit water or poisoned air, or just didn't have enough capital or the right equipment to get to the color. Ye seen all them stamp mills and refineries in Mill City a half mile back? The gold is in these here mountains, all right, but it ain't easy to get it. Mother nature is goin' to hang onto what she's taken millions of years to form. If ye ask me, gold miners is damn fools . . . excuse me, Madam."

"'Have you heard of the Irish Boy Mine?" Jenna asked.

"Let me think—maybe so. They come and go so fast. It seems there was an operation about eight miles up above Gregory Diggings where some Irish fellas started a mine. Can't say for sure. I run some whiskey up there once. Ye ain't goin' up there unexpected are ye? And with a youngin'? This ain't a place for ye. We'll ask at the store. They know everybody up here," Billy said, and shook his head in some private afterthought.

The storekeeper frowned and nodded. "Yep, I know about the Irish Boy Mine. It closed up—dead. Never paid enough to keep the mules in feed. It was a good-sized operation for awhile, paid day wages to some Welshmen, but like others, it went belly up. Most miners go lookin' elsewhere. The smart ones are workin' silver, if you ask me. I ain't seen them boys in weeks. They've probably gone over the mountain to the Jackson Diggings. There was a healthy strike up that way."

Jenna's heart sank. Where could Danny be in this untamed, uncivilized land where mountains stacked one behind the other for miles and miles, and deep canyons hid among them? Oh, where could he be?

The storekeeper seemed to grasp her dilemma. "You best stay the night at the hotel here while we ask around and see if anyone knows anything. You can return to Denver with Billy here, in the morning."

From the doorway, a gruff female voice said, "There's no room. I got the last one."

Jenna turned. Framed in the back light, leaning against the doorjamb, was a heavy woman with knobby, black boots made for walking through snow and rocks. Her thick wool skirt and shapeless coat were probably made from strips of old military uniforms, but her knitted cap of many colors, though peculiar, looked new. Her face was still winter-blasted with dry patches, chapped skin, and split, cracked lips that allowed her to smile on only one side of her mouth. Her light gray eyes crinkled with friendliness and good humor.

"You can stay with me if you don't mind two to a bed. It's me or no one. The tyke and dog can sleep on the floor next to you. They got extra blankets. It's no trouble."

"Thank you," Jenna said.

"I think your Irish boys headed up Russell Gulch, or maybe down Virginia Canyon and into Jackson Bar on the other fork of Clear Creek. I'm travelin' to both of them digs tomorrow morning to check on my fiancés. I'll take you as far as a friend of mine who lives at the foot of this here mountain in South Clear Creek Valley. We'll find out where these fellas are. They'll know. It's only a few miles."

"Straight down!" the storekeeper chuckled. "You got a stomach for heights, lady? There are places where the canyon don't have a bottom. Some miners fell off that durn road in '60 and they only found 'em in '62 where there was a specially warm day. The snow melted down enough to find the fellas froze—lookin' every bit alive, even pink in the flesh and rosy cheeked."

"I'll take my chances as long as this kind woman is driving."

"Ha!" She whooped. "You got spunk." She turned to the storekeeper. "Give me a couple of plugs of chew," she said, dropping a coin on the counter. "Tobacco, lady?"

"No thank you," Jenna said. The woman's black teeth were no longer a mystery.

The storekeeper grinned. "You made up your mind yet, Annie, which feller you're goin' to marry?"

"Nope, not yet. Keep 'em guessin'," she said, tearing off a bit of tobacco and tucking it behind her lower lip. "Come on, lady, I'll show you the hotel. It's not fancy but has good eats. Call your dog to jump in the wagon. My name is Annie—Annie Bryggman from Finland."

"I'm Jenna McDaniels; pleased to meet you. This is Sage and Sheba," she said, climbing into a rickety wagon.

As they wobbled toward the hotel, Jenna wondered how secure the wheels were. She grew worried when she noticed there was no braking system at all.

Jenna did not sleep especially well with Annie's snoring and the odor of her oily hair on the pillow next to her. She had met people like Annie all along the Oregon Trail, in the mining camps, and in unexpected cabins tucked away from civilization, and she admired them. She was a breed of woman who grabbed the toughest of life by the horns, threw it to the ground and went on her way. No task was impossible, no vanities, no frills, no dainties or doilies cluttered her life. She was as equipped to live and roam in the wildest of the West as a shaggy buffalo.

Annie seemed to sleep soundly in her rancid stocking feet, red flannel underwear, and her summer gingham skirt. Jenna assumed the woman never took off the skirt all winter. It served as an extra petticoat and became her outer skirt when the days turned hot.

The next morning, the wagon started its descent on a road the miners called the Oh My God Road. Jenna clutched Sage and Sheba and shut her eyes on the switchbacks while Annie told the story of her life.

"Folks don't believe it, of course, but it's true I come from royalty back a ways. You might say I'm a Finnish princess. My papa was in the Russian navy and was appointed to some high office when we was a Grand Duchy. Don't ask me nothin' about that. Then he migrated to America around 1820, married my mama, and I was born in '23.

"Papa became a sea captain, takin' people around the tip of South America from Boston. He died from a poisoned tooth and mama married a man from Missouri. I came out here by myself for the excitement of it all.

"No one ever thinks a woman would like a little adventure once in awhile. Besides, I looked around at the sorry lot of men in the neighborhood and decided I could do better in the West. So here I am, and now I got two gents to decide on."

"And how will you choose which one?" Jenna asked, smiling and more relaxed as the steep road neared the bottom of the canyon.

"Whichever one makes the biggest strike—pulls out the most gold or silver. I can wait. I just keep checkin' on them. One is workin' at Jackson Bar and the other's way up on the bald mountain overlooking North Clear Creek Canyon. If I'm goin' to cook and scrub and mend the seat of a man's breeches while he's wearin' them, then bite off the thread, you can bet I'm goin' to have a few niceties."

Jenna stopped holding her breath, for at last they had reached the bottom of the narrow canyon where shanties, log huts, tents, and equipment looked small and fragile beneath the granite walls. Placer miners dipped and swirled their pans and strained to see the take, while some rewashed the mine tailings taken from the belly of the mountain. The murky streams ran with minerals, and mustard yellow rivulets flowed in shallow places.

Jenna felt she had descended into the bowels of the earth, sunless and poisonous, where no creatures drank from the streams and men had mutated into something less than human.

From high on the steep walls, waterfalls of spring melt cascaded in thin streams down the rocky outcroppings; anthills of yellow slag hung on the mountainsides.

As they traveled alongside the stream, Annie stopped several times and shouted to the men, "Know of any Irishmen in these parts? They had the Irish Boy Mine in Gregory Gulch."

Most shook their heads, but one gentleman with educated speech said, "I knew those four men, and if I'm not mistaken, they worked awhile around here and then headed to the foot of Leavenworth Canyon. There were rumors that the Griffin boys had found something . . . at least they have a homestead there in South Clear Creek Valley. The Irishmen spoke of sinking some shafts up in that area."

"We'll head out that way after lunch if you like," Annie said. She pulled the horse to a stop in front of a neat log cabin. "There are only four cabins up there, kind of tucked away in a box canyon, and a few tents and some dugouts, but a woman lives in one of those places. She calls herself Willa. I can drive you up there, about twelve miles is all. We've got nothing here but me and some grizzlies you can't tell apart from the miners. You can stay with me or with that woman up there. She'll be glad for some company, I expect. This is my place. Come on in for some food. I could eat a skunk."

"Oh, Annie, I feel so close to the end of my journey. I'm certain my Danny is there."

"Well, if he ain't, you can do as I'm doing. I tacked up advertisements around saying I was willing to work as a wife for the right man. I got two interested parties, but I'm not as flimsy as you. You might only get one."

Jenna was surprised at the neatness of Annie's log cabin. Two walls were covered with canvas, the floor was planked, swept clean, and had a braided rug. A wooden work table was nailed in the corner, and above it neat rows of pans and utensils and an apron hung on nails.

In the center of the small hut sat a hand-hewn pinewood table covered with a clean cloth and graced with a bouquet of blue larkspur. A bed, neatly spread with an elaborate quilt and a pillow beautifully embroidered graced one corner.

"Your place is *very* nice, Annie!"

"Thanks. I made it myself—all of it, everything here, the house and all the furnishings. I'm good with my hands," she said, holding them up proudly. "And look here," she said, opening a trunk. "My hope chest." She lifted out neatly folded linens with lace edging and intricate embroidery.

Awed at their elaborate workmanship, Jenna held them with respect.

"I told you I was royalty," she said, laughing. "I got it in my blood."

Jenna watched Annie carefully fold her precious possessions with her large man's hands. How could such fat, stubby fingers create the daintiest works of art?

"They're beautiful, Annie—ingenious work. They take my breath away!" Jenna exclaimed.

"I can do anything I set my mind to," Annie said, closing the trunk. "How about some cold mutton, hot coffee, and brown bread with chili sauce? And I got some buttermilk and chokecherry jelly for your baby and scraps for your hound."

After washing the dishes, Annie shook the reins with her strong hands and drove Jenna higher into the deep canyons of the Rocky Mountains. The late sun caught the tops of the mountains while they drove along the rushing water, now in shadow.

Above them on a sunlit ledge, Jenna saw four Indians watching them. "Annie . . ."

"I seen them. Don't pay no mind—they're Utes. They're probably just curious, but you take the reins while I load my rifle just in case they have a mind to cause us trouble. I'm surprised they're showing themselves this close to the plains. This used to be their rendezvous point to trade with traders and trappers and other Indian tribes, even the Cheyenne and Arapaho. They don't like us being here and can be pretty ornery, but usually they don't bother us in the camps and they are superstitious about this narrow valley.

"A few months back, no traveler or isolated hunter was safe. Now everyone is waiting to see how the peace talks go with them at Fort Lyon. There will be new treaties to break. They don't like the idea of going to them reservations—land of their own where nobody can bother them.

"Problem is, we outnumber them, unless they band together—and they got too many tribal hatreds for that. I get the feeling bloody times are around the corner."

Jenna shook the reins to keep the horse moving up the canyon. She felt uneasy about these particular Indians. They were dressed differently from the Indians around Denver; in spite of the promise of a warm, spring day, they wore winter fur skins and appeared as scruffy as bighorn sheep.

Annie loaded her rifle as the wagon passed below the red-skinned observers, letting them know she was armed. "Call Sheba up front to sit under our feet. I don't want no unpleasant encounter."

"Are these Utes dangerous?" Jenna asked.

"They look to me like a loose band of southern Utes. They ain't on horses. I figure their winter caches are empty and they're looking for food. They've probably been on a rabbit run or been tryin' to fish in the high runoff with no luck. There ain't a lot to eat until things warm up and start growin'. Maybe they've been poking around for roots and looking for rose hips the bears overlooked. They're hungry, all right, and gettin' hungrier all the time."

They thought they had driven past the band and began to relax their guard when three Indian women stepped out from behind a boulder and stood in the middle of the road, holding up their hands for the wagon to stop. Annie placed her rifle on her knees.

"Good afternoon, ladies," she said, then under her breath said to Jenna, "We're being studied like bugs under glass. There's Redskins up above us on the rocks."

An Indian pointed to Sheba.

"She wants your dog for the soup pot."

Jenna stood up. "No! Absolutely not!"

"Sit down, Jenna. Keep calm. We're bargaining here." Annie turned back to the Indians saying in a firm voice, "No dog." She shook the reins to move forward.

More Indian women and a child stepped onto the road to block their way. One woman removed the child's rabbit fur robe and pointed to Sage, then conveyed she wanted the dog for the cape.

"No!" Jenna said in a loud voice.

"I got something they'll take. We're sittin' on it." Annie lifted the wagon-seat lid and brought out a bottle of whiskey that had been neatly tucked in sawdust. "My emergency store in case I get caught in a snowdrift sometime."

The Indians agreed. The deal had been struck. They handed Annie the rabbit-fur cape. Before Annie could move forward, three of the women scrambled into the wagon, chatting and smiling. They wanted a ride.

"It's all right by me. We'll be safe with them in the wagon. I think."

After a short time, the women hopped off, taking Annie's shovel with them.

Higher mountains loomed ahead and began to close around the canyon on all sides. Just before it appeared there was nowhere else to go, two rivers met on the beaver flats of South Clear Creek Valley. Jenna saw a small settlement of houses scattered like a child's toys, toppled wooden blocks resting at the foot of the steep mountains.

It was a majestic place, somewhere out of a fairy tale or a traveler's wild imagination. The smell of pine and wood smoke seemed stronger in this hidden valley, where surely the sun only shone a few hours a day, maybe never in winter. Campfire lights already dotted the darkening canyon and welcomed strangers like Jenna.

She prayed Danny would be in this place, for she felt embraced in its beauty and safety, its enchantment, even holiness. Jenna was moved to tears. This was, indeed, a sacred place for animals and birds, Indians, traders, trappers, white men—maybe even fairies—and it felt like home.

Jenna's excitement mounted as they approached a small log cabin tucked close to the sheer mountain walls.

"Willa's husband hurt his back last summer and hasn't done much mining since. They struggle hand to mouth. I don't know how they survived the winter," Annie explained, and spit an arc of tobacco juice out of the wagon.

Willa Teasdale, a sturdy girl with a round face and kindly gray eyes, came out to greet her unexpected company. "Welcome!" she shouted.

When Annie explained the reason for their visit, Willa was so overjoyed to have the company of another woman she threw her arms around Jenna and rushed to put the kettle on for tea. Like Jenna, she was a young married woman whose love for an adventurous husband led her to this wild land and an uncertain life in the gold camps. Life could now be bearable with someone to share long, lonely days. Jenna liked her immediately and felt certain they would be good friends.

"Not a lot of miners are here," Willa said. "The Griffin family is homesteading down valley, and the boys are working the stream all along the canyon and up the sides of the mountains, 'watching the float' to see where to sink a shaft. My husband hired on with them. Maybe your husband did, too. But come to think of it, there were four Irishmen or Welshmen working up on the Argentine, farther up the canyon toward those two peaks yonder. I'll ask my husband when he comes home next week. He got hurt last summer, but he's gone back to mining. He'll know something. You stay with me until we get more information and send word along the stream that you're here."

"Do you have a horse, Mrs. Teasdale?"

"Yes. You're welcome to use her. I'll take care of your little girl. I understand how anxious you are, but you should wait for my husband to inquire for you."

FIREWEED

"I want to start my search as soon as possible—tomorrow. I'll ride just far enough to find someone either going up toward the Argentine, or coming down. I'll know soon whether Danny McDaniels is here. And if he isn't, well, I'll think about that later."

The following morning after a stiff night's sleep on the floor in front of the cold fireplace, Jenna awakened to the smell of cinnamon. Annie and Willa were outside the house working in a primitive kitchen—a makeshift room of canvas walls tacked to two poles and to the cabin. The floor was hard-packed earth, and the roof and front door were canvas curtains loose enough for the smoke to escape.

Jenna was surprised to see an open fire pit and breathed in a delicious aroma coming from a large dutch oven. Willa had made two handsome apple pies and boiled milk for breakfast.

She explained that her husband hurt his back before he could enclose a kitchen for her. Cooking throughout the winter had been cold. She hoped one day, soon, she'd have a real kitchen and a real stove, but so far her husband had done poorly in mining and they couldn't afford the lumber and supplies to finish its construction.

Annie, smacked her lips over "the most succulent pie she ever et." She added, "It's a crying shame you don't have no kitchen to bake 'em in. I bet we three ladies can build that kitchen in no time flat. I'll show you how to chink and daub better than a man. Come winter, you'll have yourself a dandy place and a stove to go with it.

"Meanwhile, Willa, you start baking them pies and sellin' to folks. A miner can eat a pie apiece. You charge a dollar a pie and in a month's time, you'll have more certain money than any miner. How many pies can you make in a day?"

"I don't know, maybe ten," Willa said.

"Ten! Hell, woman, you can bake a hundred if you set your mind to it! You made two for breakfast while the dog was out peein'. And you only used a portion of one pot. You could bake eight pies at a time. Even if you baked only thirty pies a day, that's, let's see now. You got to rest on the Lord's day—a hundred and eighty pies a week. You'd make seven hundred and twenty dollars in a month!"

Willa laughed. "Oh, Annie, that's down right absurd." Then, suddenly, she looked serious. "Wait a minute! This isn't funny. I could do it. I could!"

"Of course. I'll tell everybody up and down Clear Creek where to get the best pie a man ever et."

"Then I'll start baking right away. I've got flour, sugar and lard, and lots of apples, spices and some canned peaches. Jenna can help me pick berries this fall. I can do this! I really can!"

"Then get busy. Idle hands get you into trouble. I'll be back soon to build that kitchen," Annie said, and drove away in her rattling wagon.

Later that morning, Jenna kissed Sage goodbye, assuring her she would be back by late afternoon; she mounted the horse, called to Sheba and started up the canyon along Leavenworth Creek toward Argentine Mountain.

She had only ridden about four miles when she met a miner on a mule coming downstream. Jenna pulled the horses' reins and asked if the man knew of four Irishmen working upstream.

"Yes, Ma'am, I do," the man said, tipping his hat. "Those men are sinking small shafts up the mountain, tracking the float not far from here, just a ways beyond where the Leavenworth forks. You can see them working up there. The last I heard they was ready to tunnel and start drifting along a pretty promising vein. I asked for a wage a while back and they told me they didn't need anyone yet. Now I'm working for somebody else on up higher.

They might have already had some luck. You go on up about another mile where they are camping. You'll see them up pretty high, maybe halfway—unless they haven't had their coffee. Then they'll still be by the water, right after the string of falls squirting out of the rocks. You'll find them."

Jenna thanked the man. Her excitement was so great, the horse felt it and began a fast trot. Sheba ran alongside, barking for no apparent reason. When the camp was in sight, Sheba stopped, then suddenly bolted. Jenna didn't recognize the black-bearded man that Sheba was leaping in the air to kiss, running circles around, and barking joyfully about. Sheba had been the first to find Danny. When he turned around, he was not smiling.

She stopped her horse a few yards away, almost afraid to move closer. The stranger she called Danny stood before her, whiskered, subdued, dirty, no different than the grizzled miners all along the stream. Only his eyes were familiar, clear blue, intense . . . angry. He said nothing, nor did he walk toward her. All of Jenna's visions of seeing him again, of running to hold him, vanished in an instant and left her paralyzed to speak or move. She should never, never have come! For a fleeting moment, she felt he hated her.

"My God, woman," he said in a low, controlled voice. "What are you doing here?"

Jenna fumbled for her words. "Danny, I see now I shouldn't have come, but I thought your letter—well, I thought you sent for me. At least, I interpreted it so. I wanted so much to . . . I brought Sage with me."

"You're going back. This is no place for you, let alone a child. Jesus Christ, Jenna! I didn't send for you!"

"Would you have, Danny? Would summer turn into fall, then winter bring snow too deep for traveling? Would you wait until it was too late for me to join you? We *are* a family."

"And whose fault is *that*?" he shouted.

His words struck hard. Jenna suddenly had nothing left in her to say, nothing in the heart, mind, or spirit. She turned the horse around and headed down the mountain with Sheba running along beside her. The silence behind her felt like a force pushing her away. The rushing water roared in her ears, and her body felt weak and light, detached. She shut her eyes, shut out all senses, and let the horse plod toward home.

Before reaching Willa's, Danny, trotting on the back of an unhappy mule, caught up with her.

"Jenna!" he shouted.

She stopped but did not turn around. Danny dismounted and walked over to her. She could not look at him.

"Let's start again, girl. You gave me a shock, you know. You're here and that's the fact we have to deal with now. We've got to be sensible. What money did you use to make this trip?"

Once again, the word "money" softened his attitude toward her. "I sold the house," she said flatly.

"You got quite a bit, then? Answer me, Jenna. How much!" Jenna could tell he was trying to smother his irritation.

"It doesn't matter, Danny. I need it for Sage and me. I'd hoped to keep our family alive."

"Jenna, come down off the horse. We need to talk about this, as friends. We can work out an arrangement. Listen, the boys and I are on to a vein, a lode, a rich one—I know it! I was going to send for you as a proud man, a success. I swear, Jenna, you were in my thoughts, girl. A man gets crazy up here—no family, no women, no wives. Maybe you're my angel, my good-luck piece. Come down, Jenna, and let me put my arms around you. I don't smell very good, but I want to let you know I'm sorry. I was so cruel."

Only then did Jenna's tears begin to fill her eyes. She leaned down into Danny's arms and let him lift her from the horse. He put his arms around her and held her close.

"You feel real good, girl—real good.," he said, kissing her softly in the hollow of her neck.

🍃 🍃 🍃

Danny returned to Willa's with Jenna and spent a couple of days with her and Sage, time enough to bathe and wash his clothes—from his long underwear down to his socks. Jenna knew exactly how to boil the clothes, scrub, and pound them. She had helped Darcey with such tasks at Sutter's Fort many times.

Still, he looked like a woolly mountain goat, not the crisp San Francisco businessman, and as he sat in Willa's husband's clothes drinking a glass of brandy, Jenna wondered who the real Danny was. He was a man able to wear many hats, play contrasting roles, live high or low, dine with a king or a pauper—it made no difference to him. He wanted to gather all of life's experiences into his own.

Jenna understood that initially Danny agreed to the marriage knowing it was backed with money, her money; but part of him had tried hard to be a family man and to live the conventional life as provider. It was one of his roles at that time. Why then, Jenna wondered, could he not experience marriage with the same zeal as all his other challenges?

She noted Danny's indifferent reaction to Sage with pain and disappointment, the same sinking feeling she experienced meeting him in the canyon. Could he have changed so much in only a few months?

Jenna had to admit he was different. He held a darkness behind his eyes that she hadn't seen before, a darkness like a forest where no light could enter, where a confused tangle of underbrush snagged and hurt anyone trying to find a pathway. She could not see the flicker of the dancing wild men that had always beckoned her to join in his passion. It was as if the little men had died.

Her move to Colorado Territory was a foolish one. Her fatal flaw was loving him, believing that he loved her and Sage enough to want them with him. She felt as if she'd captured a wild animal and now was trying to teach it to drink milk from a saucer. Clearly, she had interrupted a role he loved, and had robbed him of his joy.

She needed time to decide what to do.

Danny sipped Willa's homemade blackberry brandy and watched Jenna lift the steaming, soapy clothes on a paddle and place them in the rinse tub.

She still cuts a fine figure, even working like a dirt farmer. But, damn it all, she doesn't belong here. Why the hell did she come? I never asked her to. I never intended for her to come here! This is a man's world, not a place for a family. Miners and potato farmers alike go hungry. I don't care a damn if I starve by myself, but damn it all, I'm not going to watch a wife and child starve . . . and I'll never, never lie down on a wife's grave and die because I let her starve, because I couldn't find a lousy potato. I'm not cut out for marriage. That's all there is to it. The boys will think she's got me strung up in her corset laces. Damn it all, don't they have anything but this sickly black berry brandy in the house?

Danny grew silent, brooding about his situation. His eyes followed Jenna back and forth to the clothesline.

She's good for a poke, and that's all.

He poured himself more brandy. Jenna smiled at him as she wrung out a pair of long underwear. Danny winced.

This is no life for her. She belongs in Paris, not in a mining camp. Damn it all! If I had money, I'd take her to Paris.

Gradually, he started feeling great pity for himself. He was not sure about the Irish Boy Mine. It was undercapitalized, he knew that. So did the boys. Unless they hit in the next few yards they'd have no money to keep the mine operating. But, what the hell if they failed? He and the boys were brothers. They'd simply move on together without a woman to shackle any of them—always a new adventure and steamy whores wherever they went. Damn it all, the boys must be making jokes about him getting his clothes washed and beard trimmed. He'd have to do some clever talking back at camp. He'd think up a good story to explain her arrival, one that would make the boys laugh.

Danny swirled the sticky black brandy in the mug, trying to create a story for the boys. What if he didn't send her home? What if he told the boys she came to invest in the mine? He smiled as he thought of a plan. *Danny, old man, you don't need the Blarney Stone; the angels, themselves, have blessed you with the sweetest tongue . . . in more ways than one.*

"Jenna, me love, if you want to stay the summer, I'll hire some down-and-out miners to build us a log cabin—very simple, you understand—where the valley widens on the beaver flats and the sun shines longer each day. I'll buy us some furniture and items to run a household—a stove, washtubs, pots, a bed.

"It won't be like San Francisco, me love. Can you handle the change? Can you spend a summer running a crude household . . . be a miner's wife?

"I promise to ride home a couple of times a week to be with you and Sage. Course I'll still be working the claim. We're starting tunneling and already have gone in about twenty-five yards, timbering the hole. We could hit anytime."

Jenna thought of Annie. "I can do anything I set my mind to," she said, tilting her chin in the air.

"That's my lassie," he said, smiling.

Jenna wondered if Danny was actually building himself and his "boys" winter quarters, but for the moment, she was happy and would dismiss that idea.

Danny's eyes began to shine. "I'll go to Denver and hire some laborers. A lot of them have busted and gone to Denver to join the army or find work there rebuilding the burned-down buildings. I'll even buy a pair of horses to pull a wagon full of necessities up here. What do you think, Jenna?"

"I think it's a wonderful plan. Oh, Danny, I'd be so happy!"

"Jenna, I need money to buy a stamp mill. We've got to crush that ore. We're so close now. I'll make it up to you, darlin'—I will. This time, by God, *this* time, I'm going to hit!" He gulped the last of the brandy in one swallow. "Is your money in Denver?"

"Yes," Jenna said, cautiously. "It's all we have, except for our stocks, which are doing well."

Danny's face split into a broad smile. "I see it workin' this way, lassie. You'll be livin' in the cabin all summer, enjoying the sunshine, but at the first snowfall, if you decide to stay in Colorado Territory, you must return to Denver. Do you understand?"

"Yes, Danny, oh, yes. Sage, Sheba and I will have a glorious summer and fall."

"The men and I will work through the winter months as many days as we can, and use the cabin. I'll be bunking with my boys. I won't be with you in Denver at all, not until the next spring. Is this picture clear enough?

The arrangement seemed fair. By winter, anything could happen. "Yes, Danny, I understand. It will be a wonderful summer!"

"Then it's settled."

🌸 🌸 🌸

The plans went well. Jenna lived with Willa, helping her bake pies, while the log cabin grew from its crude outline drawn in the dirt to a sturdy structure with three cozy bedrooms, a kitchen, and one main room with a rock fireplace at one end. The luxury of glass windows, planked floors and a covered porch was an elegant surprise. She had a fine log house, indeed.

By mid-July, Jenna could set up housekeeping. Like her mother and so many frontier women, she would be in charge of making soap and butter, baking, sewing, washing, and transplanting wildflowers that did not like to be disturbed. Jenna's life, now, already so totally different, gave her more satisfaction than she could have ever imagined.

With Willa's help, she learned how to bake in the high altitude and other homemaking tricks. She did not know how long her life in the uncertain frontier would last, but for now, it was fun, challenging, and each evening she fell asleep quickly and happily.

Each morning, she awakened to crackling mountain air, the scream of a soaring hawk riding the valley's thermals, and fragrance that pinched her senses, quickened her heart—a cold splash of morning that kept a perpetual smile on her face all day.

Sometimes, Willa, Jenna, and Sage, along with Sheba and a parade of jolly dogs—and Annie, when she came to visit—took a picnic to the falls, the Poley Springs, or to the lakes above the valley—a series of icy emerald tarns that stair-stepped down the canyon from the glacial mother.

On one such visit, Annie announced that she had made her choice of a husband—"the one working up in Russell Gulch," she said. "He's doin' right well refining silver out of the ore up there. Besides, he bought me a bathtub and a purple velvet hat. That's treating a lady as she should be treated. He's small, but you can wring out his shirts like they're hankies. He won't be no bother."

In the high plateaus, where the sweetest berries were found, Jenna often hiked to look out at the Continental Divide stretching across the top of the world in majestic peaks. She remembered Israel saying the day before he died, "See, Jenn, we're looking at the other side of the world! Think of it!"

Then, without warning, the tinkling, green aspens began to turn into yellow gold, like suns that burst and blew away in a flutter, and blasts of white snow waited behind the solemn season of quiet change. When the snow flurries began in earnest, Jenna packed her things, embraced a tearful Willa, and said goodbye to her beloved log cabin. She rented a house in Denver and waited for spring.

Danny spent Christmas with Jenna and Sage and visited when the snows were too deep to get up to the mine. Though the winter days were bright and pleasant, Jenna thought winter would never end.

With Denver's growing population, Jenna found friendship with women whose independence and energy she admired. Some women owned businesses. One lady owned a millinery shop; another made vests and gloves; another worked for the telegraph company. Women ranchers and homesteaders came to Denver on business. Some women, like Jenna, had come to Denver for the winter months and were finding ways to supplement their husbands' income, others to support themselves as widows.

Schoolteachers, shopkeepers, boardinghouse proprietors, merchants, seamstresses, entrepreneurs, and investors had become a part of the economic community. There were women who worked as photographers, journalists, actresses, artists, and sculptors.

Women were busy. There was not time to be docile or petted with small vanities.

Jenna became interested in mining. She had already invested with Danny in the Irish Boy Mine and had begun listening carefully to the miners' talk of equipment, new methods, strikes in Cripple Creek and Leadville. The more she learned, the more she thought she had the brains to run a mining operation. Why not? Another woman up Clear Creek was operating a small mine.

Finally, the sun began to warm the earth and winter gave way to spring, overflowing the banks of Cherry Creek and leaving Denver in a sea of mud. Jenna could hardly wait to return to the mountains.

But Danny appeared unexpectedly in mid-April as Jenna was preparing to move back into the canyon.

"A terrible accident, Jenna . . . terrible," he said, slumping into a chair. "Two of the lads are dead. The mine collapsed, timbers snapped—crushed them . . . my oldest friends. We were like four brothers. The third lad got drunk for a week, sobered up, packed his things, and rode out of the camp saying he was finished with mining forever. My God, the luck of the Irish is a joke! I'm washed up." He put his head in his hands and pressed his fists into his eye sockets to stop the tears. "I failed the lads. I've failed you."

"No, Danny—we'll start over," she said, trying to hold him.

"With what? I'm tired, Jenna. There's no money to start again. I've spent it all on foolishness, gambling with a damn mountain! I'm a fool," he said, pounding his temples.

"We'll sell our stocks, start again."

Danny looked up, his face twisted in anguish. "I already sold them— last fall. Everything. We haven't anything left. I'm beaten. This time, I'm beaten."

"You've spent *everything?*" Jenna asked, incredulous. She could not believe what she was hearing. How could Danny deceive her so? That money was her safety, her means to take care of Sage. She looked at Danny slumped in the chair and felt a sudden chill. He cut a pathetic figure, scarcely the handsome, curly-haired Irishman she'd carried in her heart for so long.

"Well, others have lost everything. We'll make it somehow," Jenna said, trying to disguise the panic in her voice. "We'll think of something."

"No . . . no more. I've spent your entire fortune on disastrous moves. You're better off without me dragging you down. You're smart. You'll find a man who's not so dumb. I'm ashamed, woman. Oh God, I can't bear to look at you and Sage. I'm leaving, Jenna."

"You're running away," she said coolly. She understood his grief, but in spite of her compassion for him, she felt something else struggling to free itself within her.

Suddenly, all panic left her. She could not explain the sensation of lifting like an eagle, moving with power and purpose, breaking out from the narrow canyon walls to fly high above the jagged cliffs.

"It's no use, girl. I'm not a family man. I'm scarcely a man. I've got to go, pick up the pieces somehow. With a little luck, I can take an arrow in the chest, or join the Union Army and take a well-deserved bullet in the head." He looked at Jenna, waiting for her to respond, perhaps to try to stop him or reveal another source of money that might get him started again.

Instead she said calmly. "Will you go back to California . . . to Lilly Jordan? At least answer that truthfully, Danny."

"No, my girl, Lilly's loyalty is only as long as a man's pockets are full. She sold her house and left for Virginia City."

Jenna smiled to herself. How ironic are life's twists and turns. She looked up at Danny with her eyes wide and clear. "Sage and I will survive."

"Yes, you'll survive, Jenna. You're better at that than I am." Danny stood up, leaned over, tipped Jenna's face up to his, and kissed her gently. "Be the brave girl you've always been. I don't know how you do it Jenn— some strength you've got—somewhere. May all the saints in Heaven look out for you, and Sage, and Sheba. Goodbye, Lass," he said, with a final, sad smile.

🌿 🌿 🌿

Jenna returned to South Cherry Creek Canyon, to the narrow valley surrounded by high, pine-covered mountains, where day moved along by the march of sun up the sheer slope to the tip of the high peaks.

Had Danny waited only a few more weeks, he'd have been part of the biggest silver bonanza in Colorado Territory. It was part of the stampede from the gold camps to the Silver Queen of the Rockies, later named George's Town from George Griffin's discovery of the silver-rich quartz known as the Mother Lode.

He'd have seen miners and families and rows of cabins neatly poised along the two streams on the beaver flat, and he'd have seen proof of Jenna's indefatigable spirit: Jenna's Place, a boardinghouse like Hattie's and Darcey's. He would have smiled at the irony of Jenna's reopening of the Irish Boy Mine, revealing its rich vein of silver.

Perhaps he would have overheard Jenna say to Sage on a late afternoon, as the sun reddened the tips of the mountain, "Look, Sage, can you see the Maid of the Mountain in the niche of that stony peak? She stands there gazing forever over the valley, her arms outstretched—a beautiful Indian maiden burned alive by her tribe's enemies. On moonlit nights, she glows scarlet, still holding the flames within her . . . like the fireweed . . . strong, unbeatable, unharmed."